THE WAR
AGAINST
THE ASSHOLES

ALSO BY SAM MUNSON
The November Criminals

SAM MUNSON

THE WAR AGAINST THE ASSHOLES

SAGA  PRESS

LONDON SYDNEY **NEW YORK** TORONTO NEW DELHI

FOR REBECCA AND FELIX

SAGA PRESS
AN IMPRINT OF SIMON & SCHUSTER, INC.

1230 AVENUE OF THE AMERICAS, NEW YORK, NEW YORK 10020

This book is a work of fiction. Any references to historical events, real people, or real places are used fictitiously. Other names, characters, places, and events are products of the author's imagination, and any resemblance to actual events or places or persons, living or dead, is entirely coincidental. • Text copyright © 2015 by Sam Munson • All rights reserved, including the right to reproduce this book or portions thereof in any form whatsoever. For information address Saga Press Subsidiary Rights Department, 1230 Avenue of the Americas, New York, NY 10020 • First SAGA PRESS hardcover edition June 2015 • SAGA PRESS and colophon are trademarks of Simon & Schuster, Inc. • For information about special discounts for bulk purchases, please contact Simon & Schuster Special Sales at 1-866-506-1949 or business@simonandschuster.com. • The Simon & Schuster Speakers Bureau can bring authors to your live event. For more information or to book an event, contact the Simon & Schuster Speakers Bureau at 1-866-248-3049 or visit our website at www.simonspeakers.com. • The text for this book is set in Dante MT. • Manufactured in the United States of America • 10 9 8 7 6 5 4 3 2 1 • Library of Congress Cataloging-in-Publication Data • Munson, Sam. • The war against the assholes / Sam Munson. — First edition. • pages ; cm • Summary: "Contemporary fantasy meets true crime when schools of ancient sorcery go up against the art of the long con in this stunningly entertaining debut fantasy novel. Mike Wood is satisfied just being a guy with broad shoulders at a decidedly unprestigious Catholic school in Manhattan. But on the dirty streets of New York City he's an everyman with a moral code who is unafraid of violence. And when Mike is unwittingly recruited into a secret cell of magicians by a fellow student, Mike's role as a steadfast soldier begins. These magicians don't use ritualized rote to work their magic, they use willpower in their clandestine war with the establishment: The Assholes"—Provided by publisher. • ISBN 978-1-4814-2774-6 (hardcover) • ISBN 978-1-4814-2776-0 (eBook) • 1. Magicians—Fiction. I. Title. • PS3613.U6936W37 2015 • 813'.6—dc23 • 2015012624

"SOLDIERS ARE NOT ALLOWED
TO HAVE A RELIGION."
—JACOB FRANK

Nothing ever turns out the way you imagine it will. You think there's going to be someone telling you the great and painful secrets of this world. Or opening a golden, final doorway. Beyond which would lie what, exactly? That's not what happens. What happens is: you meet Hob. All you get. Then again, if you need a more instructive and obvious guide, you've already lost the whole game. Certain schools consider that a radical notion.

You wouldn't have thought there was anything unusual about Hob, other than his being a weak-looking kid in a school full of much bigger, stronger kids (of which I was one, I admit). Saint Cyprian's, where I went to elementary, middle, and high school, under the supervision of Carmelite nuns. I knew Hob that whole time. We didn't formally encounter each other until senior year. His full name is Hobart Callahan. Everyone only ever called him Hob, that I heard. My name is Michael Wood, for which people mocked me. Kids at Cyprian's—a boys' Catholic school, in case you couldn't tell from the name—talked about dicks and gayness a lot. I never dealt well with the consequent teasing I suffered. Because of my last name. In fact I beat up Greg Gilder for giving me shit about it.

That's how I first got to know Hob. Not a lot of friends in the school. He didn't act lonely. He didn't see people. He would walk right past you. Never bat an eye. He always had this book with him during lunch and gym. Coach Madigan had basically given up on him and let him read during class. A small green book. Gold letters on the spine. He put it away whenever anyone got close. I assumed it was either poetry or pornography. Either one would land you in trouble. If Greg Gilder caught Hob reading poetry, he would have knocked him unconscious on principle. At least that's how the operating theory ran. The day Hob actually entered my life was not extraordinary. I had overslept, which happened two or three times a week. The sky was cement colored. Or something. My imagistic vocabulary was limited. No one's fault but my own. I had to wait eight minutes for a train. Pacing the platform edge, staring down my fellow laggards. The main hall of Cyprian's had just been washed when I arrived, and the dead-fruit smell of floor cleaner filled my nostrils as I raced across it. In the center a mosaic of the saint himself: his white-haired head backed with a flat, orange, Russian halo. Our motto carved into the ribbon of stone beneath his thin hands: *Melior Audere*. Sister Immaculata reamed me out for missing the first ten minutes of world history. The Treaty of Versailles. I didn't follow. Wars and treaties: they go on existing whether you know about them or not.

Greg Gilder muttered, "Morning, Wood," as I passed him, and the two kids sitting next to him, Simon Canary and Frank Santone, both laughed behind their hands. I think I may have had a premonition that I was going to kick Gilder's ass at that point. This was more than ten years ago. Risky to rely on memory. Though it's all we have. Hob sat in the back of the class not talking. As usual. He read his green book during gym, as he had for the past three years. Things just got weirder and weirder with Gilder. He kept saying, "Morning, Wood"—like

THE WAR AGAINST

morningwood, like the hard-on you have in the mornings just from consciousness—all day. Gym, lunch, Greek class (I never managed to learn much more than the alphabet), right through math. At least I was well rested. Hob was there too. He might have been watching me, or that just might be my mind weaving another strand of historical narrative. Makes no difference. What happens, happens. My school day ended. It took forever. It always did. When the last bell rang, I caught Hob giving me an up-and-down. I shrugged and he grinned, and then I went down the hot, gray stairs that led to the locker rooms. You could hear the permanent whine of a machine there, behind the deep walls, loud and shrill. We called the hall Old Egypt. As the rest of the team came bounding down the stairs, I changed and started hammering out push-ups. I did this, every day, to get started. After everyone arrived, I calmed down. We muttered our hellos and a few profanities. Gilder didn't speak to me. He grunted as he bench-pressed. "Don't strain yourself," said Coach Madigan. We all cackled at that. Gilder racked the weights and sat up, face pale. We all had to go up with Coach Madigan every month or so, to Yonkers, and help his mother: raking leaves, lifting boxes. Even Gilder went. The Catholic Church knows how to extract free labor from its members. I enjoyed it. Seeing the house and yard of another human being. Call it native curiosity.

"Gentlemen," Coach Madigan said, "start your engines." It was cold enough on the field that Coach Madigan's head—squarish, red haired, it must have weighed about thirty pounds by itself—steamed when he took off his hat. It's absurd to me, even now, that Saint Cyprian's possessed enough real estate to have its own football field in Manhattan. Then again, that's another specialty of the Church: acquiring valuable land. We got into position for warm-ups. Gilder did his jumping jacks and push-ups and screamed. His normal display. Embarrassing the rest of us. When we started scrimmaging, the trouble began. Coach Madigan assigned Gilder to block me and Gilder kept making these late, late hits and muttering, "Morning, Wood," every time. I could have retaliated, then. Coach Madigan wouldn't have said anything, even if one of my teachers had asked him about it. He believed, as he once expressed it, in a wall of separation between church and state. I knew it would be safe. Which explains maybe why I didn't do anything.

Hob was up on the one set of bleachers. Watching me. This time for sure. "Callahan," said the coach, "I see you've decided to honor us with your presence." Hob went back to reading his book. When my side took possession, I concentrated on taking Gilder down. Clean. Every time I hit him, the world slowed down: I could see where he was going and get there first, one second ahead of him, two seconds. Call it poetry, maybe. I'd felt that way before—time slipping—during my best games. I ran the table on him, as we used to say. Tackled him every time. The weird slowdown stopped. My vision cleared up. Hob was just sitting there with his green book.

I kept taking Gilder down. He called me a bitch and a faggot, at first. Then he just transitioned into more grunting. Success leads to success and confidence leads to confidence. So I followed him after practice. I didn't have any other intentions at that point. Then again, you never do. It was starting to get darker. Colder. The sun had already gone down, lurid orange. The faint clouds still carried its tint. My brown cap pulled down to my eyebrows, my brown scarf wound up to my philtrum. Amateurism. I had no other choice. Simon Canary bumped into Gilder on the front stairs and Gilder shoved him. Simon stumbled to the sidewalk. Came up with bloody palms. Gilder told him that's what he got for being a faggot. Simon rapid-walked off. He passed me. Didn't see me. I kept far back. Crows gliding above. Keels of cloud. It was easy to trail Gilder in the crush of kids leaving the school. Then the crowd thinned. I didn't mind. Even if he spotted me I knew I could catch him. I could outrun him. Greatness equals endurance. The air had that blue-black color it gets during winter twilight. Makes you certain of yourself. The crows kept circling. A good omen, I thought.

THE WAR AGAINST

Gilder walked west, into the last fires of the sunset. He had turned into the green, dimming park and was crouched over his shoes, fumbling the laces, when I ran at him and slammed my knee into his lower back. A curt, garbled cry. Then his face hit the path. He stopped shouting. This just made me more furious. I scanned the street: uninterested drivers, uninterested pedestrians. You can get away with a lot of violence when you're a kid. Moral law and human law make exceptions for it. I grabbed Gilder's arm. I frog-marched him. He blubbered. Kept asking me what I was doing. He tried and tried to get a look at my face. I gripped his arm tighter. Locked the elbow. Twisted upward. He shrieked. He said he didn't have any money on him. We reached the deeper shadow of a forked, mottled sycamore. I shoved him against the trunk. He thrashed and gasped. Called me a cocksucker through his tears. Or it sounded like *cocksucker*. The back of his neck was grimy and pale, divided by a smiling crease. I waited for him to calm down. I'm not a coward. I wouldn't have ambushed him ordinarily. But my ribs still ached from his bullshit late hits. So I wanted to make sure we stood on even metaphysical ground. He had these watery greenish eyes that suggested he couldn't see anything. Crowded, crooked teeth: at Cyprian's you never knew if substandard teeth meant the kid was on a parish scholarship or if his parents simply did not give a shit. I never found out. Can't say I cared. A cab whizzed to a halt near where we were. Its roof light came on above the lip of the stone wall. Seven seven one seven. That I remember. Two women got out. I could just see the tops of their blond heads, both uncovered. Their clear, high voices echoed in the cold, empty air. Gilder was struggling again. Throwing his free elbow at my face. Still weeping. Choking it back. One attempt landed. My inner cheek tore on a molar. He asked me, voice snot-thick, if I wanted any more. Platitudes he used all the time. "Who wants some?" "If I ever see that faggot again, I'll kill him." He was no weakling. I'll give him that. He just had a weakness for dialogue.

Most people go through life, I imagine, without ever injuring another member of their species physically. Not me. Not me with blood on my tongue. I didn't care about his tears. I grabbed Gilder's fake-lamb's-wool coat collar and punched him in his temple, as hard as I could, and then I spun him to face me and hit him—mouth, neck, cheekbones, nose, eyes—until I felt a slashing pain in my fist and heard Gilder whimper. Not cry. Not speak. Whimper. His head lolled on his wide throat. I hit him eight or nine more times, ignoring the pain in my fist. It helped, even: your brain releases pain-fighting chemicals when you get injured, Coach Madigan liked to remind us. "And that, gentlemen, that is the only high you'll ever need." Gilder's left eye had swollen closed. Both his lips were split and bleeding, and blood, too, was dripping from his nostrils. Though the sidewalk hitting his face might have done that. He mumbled. Probably asking me to stop. Another piece of dialogue. He'd miscalculated. My hand was aching. Blood warmed the skin over my tendons. I dropped him to the hard park path. He moved his arms and legs. A slow swimmer. I kicked him in the ribs, twice, three times, five times, seven. He cried out at the first blow. He stopped crying out at the second blow. After number eight, I paused to breathe. To consider. I heard someone say: "Nice work, Michael. Efficient."

2

I t was Hob. Leaning against a light pole. The flyer for a lost, black, button-eyed dog above his head. Its fringe of phone-number tabs still intact. Ultimately people don't care about dogs, despite all our sentimentality toward them. Hob was wearing only a sweater, no coat, no hat. He didn't look cold. He looked calm. "I have to say you're pretty stealthy," I said. As I watched, he lit one of his weird-smelling cigarettes with the still-glowing butt of another. "I thought it might be interesting to observe," he said. "And," I said. I was shivering, despite my warm wrappings. "It was interesting, but not for like moral reasons," he said. "For moral reasons," I said. "He'll be in school like telling everyone how four guys jumped him and he beat up three of them. You know how it is. You know how he is." As Hob spoke I could just *hear* Gilder saying that, tossing his sweaty forehead around. "I know how it is, but that doesn't explain why you followed me," I said. "Michael, relax," he said, "I wasn't exactly following you. More like going to the same place you were." "You sound like a faggot," I said, "no offense if you're gay." He said, "So what if I am?" And there I had it.

Gilder moaned a quiet moan. I thought about kicking him again. Hob and I stood there, wreathed by that viscous, sweet smoke. In the harsh light I saw how badly I'd banged up my right hand. The ring finger's first knuckle was sliced open. A chunk of tooth glistened in the black wool of my coat cuff. I pincered it up and held it to the light. Hob went apeshit laughing when I finger-flicked it out over the dead grass. "Oh my god," he said, cackling out his weird high laugh, "oh man, was that part of his tooth." The fragment rustled against the lawn. A rat trotted out from one hole to vanish down another. "You seem to love messing up the natural order of life," said Hob. I said, "This is the natural order of life." He looked at me sidelong. Went quiet. I wondered if he was planning on robbing me. I was pretty sure I could take him in a fight. I didn't know what was what back then. He looked fast, and I was already tired, so I assumed I would have to knock him down and then go to work on him. No one's a brilliant tactician as an adolescent. I don't judge myself for it.

I asked him what he wanted. Shifted my weight. "How do you know I want anything," he said, "maybe I just came out here to watch." I waited. Hob smiled. "I have a gift for you," he said. As he reached into his coat pocket I tensed up, ready to go for him. I assumed his hand would come out around the handle of a knife. Maybe he wanted to make an example of me. Maybe he was an errant murderer. That's a mystery of city life. It wasn't a knife he removed from his pocket. It was the green book he read instead of running sprints. "I want you to have this," he said, "and I want you to read it." "I don't want to read your poetry. No offense," I said. "Just give it a chance," said Hob, "you might like it. It's not even poetry." Green cover. Gold letters on the spine. In the half-light of the lamp. A stage prop. That's how I remember it. "Don't you need it," I said, "or what will you do during gym class." "I'll figure something out," he said. No title: the writing on the spine said HERMANN CORVUS ~ LONDON. "Is that who wrote the book," I asked as I lifted the stiff cover. "That's one of its publishers,"

THE WAR AGAINST

said Hob, "and don't do that." He pushed the book closed in my hands. "Don't read it out in the open. At least at first," he said. "You read it out in the open all the time," I said. "That's because I know what's in it," Hob said.

"And if I don't take it," I said. "I'd have to tell the authorities," he said, "about you and Gilder. My conscience wouldn't let me do anything else." He was grinning now. I have to admit I was too. I could see he was telling the truth. This I admired. He would let Sister Ursula know what I'd done. That much was clear. Sister Ursula ran Saint Cyprian's. Silver hair and dead-black, dead-looking eyes. Drifting around, wearing her brown-and-white habit. "When he wakes up he might do that anyway," I said. "You know he won't," said Hob, "and anyway you snuck up on him." "A moral arbiter," I said. "I'm not judging you for it. That guy's a total fascist," said Hob. He had a point. Gilder was, spiritually speaking, a Nazi. I had no problem imagining him at a rally brandishing a torch. I didn't say anything, though. I couldn't believe Hob Callahan had the upper hand. You never want to believe that. Especially when it's a guy you think you can beat up. Again, that's the nature of morality in adolescence. In adulthood too.

"Just take it," he said, "seriously. It'll change your life." He was sincere, I saw. Which almost made me laugh. *It'll change your life*: that's another piece of dialogue. Nobody's life ever changes. "So I read this book and that's it," I said, "then you drop the issue." Hob nodded and blew out two slow streams of smoke through his large, well-formed nostrils. He stifled a cough. "What are you smoking, anyway," I asked. "Old family recipe. Does a body good," he said. Gilder moaned at my feet once more, and I gave him another kick. No matter how much instruction you provide them, people never learn anything. Not even the most basic cause-and-effect relations. "How do I know you won't ask for more," I said. Hob grinned. The brown cigarette traveled to one corner of his mouth. "I saw what you did to Gilder," he said, "and I'm not stupid." He had a point. It must be a leaf, I thought, that this cigarette was wrapped in. Veins glinted on the surface in the lamplight. "Tell you what," said Hob, "I'll give you a fair chance. You have a quarter?" I handed him one. He danced it across the backs of his fingers, hand to hand; clapped his palms around the coin; and showed me two fists. "Which one," he said. "Jesus, are you kidding me," I said. "It's that or the book," he said. I picked left. He opened it. Nothing. Then he opened his right. More nothing.

That's how we ended it. Hob waving at me. Protected by the yellow lamplight and the fact that a cop car was now driving east along the edge of the park. The smoke from his cigarette hanging. Charcoal and spice. I passed out on the train. From exhaustion, from I don't even know what. I woke up with my mouth dry and the green book in my hands. Still cold, though the train car was hot. Otherwise refreshed. I was only one stop past mine. I figured I would read a few chapters, bluff Hob, maybe threaten him, and he'd forget about everything. I was still sure he was going to work his way around to asking me out. Cold and moonlight. Our doorman, Henry, was sleeping at his desk. He kept an artificial poinsettia near him, no matter the season. Its leaves rustled and trembled in his breath. You make divisions. They're arbitrary. This I know now. I did not know it as a boy. Henry slept on. My healthy blood continued to pound stupidly through my veins. You'll never recapture that headlong speed. That I also know now. My parents were watching a show about apes when I got home. Or monkeys. They climbed up into trees to drop rocks on coconuts. I kept my hand in my pocket so they wouldn't see the cut and said good night. "Late practice," my mother called. "There's lamb, if you want to eat," my father said. I told them I was too tired, but thank you anyway.

No time like the present to embark on servitude, if servitude is your fate. Hob said the book would change my life. Possibly it was the bible of a cult. Or maybe one of the many tenth-rate books adolescents claim have changed their lives. The cover was about the color of a professional card table, that deep, flat green. Though there was no author and no title on the spine, I found both on the first page inside. THE CALENDAR OF SLEIGHTS, BY F. R. ERZMUND. "Are you fucking kidding me," I said. To no one. The amber glow of light from my reading lamp kept on shining, and the beams of my building creaked in the wind. "You have got to be kidding me," I said. I started to read the preface. *This work requires, in the opinion of its author, no justification— all justification being an exercise in casuistry.*

The way it was written annoyed me. It also made me chuckle. *Piety has no place in its atmosphere; neither ready-made and repellent ideas of reform nor the whining of our muddled meliorists will obstruct the knowledge offered here.* Sentence number two. I could see this Erzmund lunatic standing there behind a green table (same color as the book) in a top hat and cape, waggling a silky mustache and gesturing with a cane as he preached about the moral amazements of his trade. Which turned out to be, to my mild disgust, card tricks and prestidigitation, all the techniques you need to master so-called games of chance. I read on. The first ten pages were just that: a long speech written in this annoying-hilarious way. My parents came in to say good night. Not that they came in. They stuck their heads past my doorjamb. I sensed them do it. I couldn't look away from the page, though. "Well, that's encouraging," I heard my mother say when she thought she was out of my earshot. I didn't blame them. Modern parents want to see their children reading. I think mine believed me to be a dolt. My radiator buzzed. I read and read. Erzmund went on in his self-assured vein: *Where we began, the world can judge: in trust, wholehearted; in unshakable assurance; in the overmastering faith we pledged to our own powers.* I read and read. I couldn't even remember the last time I had voluntarily opened a book. Now here was Erzmund, standing right next to me and telling me how to cheat at cards, in order to get what I wanted.

He didn't talk about his life, or his looks, or anything that writers usually talk about. All he talked about was cards. He sounded like

Coach Madigan, who only ever talked about football, no matter what else he was talking about. I read on, not understanding anything of what Erzmund said. Borne along by the nasal, loud (so I imagined it) voice issuing from beneath his mustache. An old-time announcer in a newsreel. When I next looked at my clock radio, it was three. I hurled the book at my wall. It took out a divot near the light-switch cover. The primary and secondary thuds—book hits wall, book hits floor— didn't wake up my parents. They were sound sleepers. I was too.

3

"Y   our nose is bleeding, Mr. Wood," said Sister Michael. In addition to teaching us biology, she supervised study hall. She wrote me a pink pass so that I could go see the nurse. Ice pack and advice. Head back. Head forward. Does not matter. The nurse told me I needed rest. I asked her when exactly I was supposed to rest. "You think school is hard, you don't know anything," she said. Couldn't argue. *No certainty exists as to the author of these traditions, relics of an age more daring than our own. We suffer now constraint on our every attempt to find room. And room is essential to the expert's art.* That's what I'd been reading right before my nosebleed came. A drop spattered the word *relics*. I went back to study hall with two plugs of toilet paper in my nose and kept reading.

I'd never reread anything before, for pleasure. Flipping back to follow his descriptions of shuffling methods, which I had trouble with because they were complicated and because he even wrote about shuffling cards in the manner of a second-rate actor, in that brazen, arrogant prose. (*Brazen* is a word I saw for the first time in the *Calendar*.)

Our eyes were opened and our education commenced; we proceeded along its difficult path through ceaseless study and tireless inner effort, wrote Erzmund. Close application and constant study. They advocated this sort of thing at Saint Cyprian's. It was not possible for me to take them seriously. The pages smelled rich and fragile. They didn't flake or tear. A few had faded brown stains on them: commas, periods. The book had one of those fake-silk tassels, as green as its cover, to mark your place. Not much bigger, as a whole, than a deck of cards. I carried it in my pocket during school hours, the gray hours of a private-school December. I like winter. Then again I like every season. Except spring. Blame my general love of life. I even enjoyed school. Though I was semi-hopeless at it. My grades had never risen out of their initial mediocrity. For which my parents had to pay. Twenty-nine thousand four hundred dollars, that year. I looked up how much Saint Cyprian's charged after getting another C in Greek. They wanted me to go to school in an elevated environment.

Greg Gilder returned the day of my nosebleed. He would not look me in the eye. He did stop calling me Morning Wood. The slice across the back of my hand healed. Gilder's nose was now crooked, and one of his teeth, an incisor, shone out, much whiter than its neighbors. A cap or a replacement for the one I'd broken. Hob noticed this and did pantomimes of me flicking away the tooth fragment whenever he and I were in a room together. Which was all day except for biology. He had physics. Gilder stayed quiet. Frank Santone and Simon Canary stopped huddling around him. Coach Madigan let up on him. The worst of it was I could not relax and enjoy my triumph. That's what it was. I make no apology. Gilder insulted me. I beat him, as he deserved. Nothing complex there. People get offended if you speak so openly about morality. His new tooth and crooked nose proved I was unsafe. Hob could have turned me in at any time. Coach Madigan still paired me with Gilder during gym. Which created unorthodox moral situations. I still took him down as cleanly as I could. He didn't fight it anymore; he seized up as soon as he saw me coming. When I hit him he was totally rigid. He stayed rigid as he fell. Coach Madigan said nothing about it. He ordinarily would have, seeing a player lame out. But he was a man not lacking in compassion. Hence the trips to Yonkers. I liked his mother. She was tiny, pure-white haired, bent into a hook. She served us at the end of every help session baked goods (last time it had been brownies) and lemonade, no matter the season. Too sweet, both. We devoured them. You lack real discernment at that age. *Youth*, says Erzmund, *is the greatest period of stupidity and suffering known to afflict humankind, and therefore when we left it we gave great thanks.*

"Greg Gilder's back in town," Hob told me. We were standing in a sheltered corner of Saint Cyprian's inner courtyard. Beyond us the football field gleamed greenly. We stood next to a gray metal box. Heating or AC, I assumed. No real idea. "I noticed," I said. "You ready for round two," he said. "I don't want to be a dick about it," I said, "but that's life." "Have you not been reading? Aren't you sick yet of thinking about life like that? Like it's just a bunch of shit that occurs. Happens to strangers. To anyone. To you. Aren't you sick of that?" "I have been reading," I said, "but I don't see what that has to do with your metaphysics." "That's a big word," said Hob. He took out a deck of cards. "Are you ready for this," he said. "I'm not not ready," I said. I'd gotten in an hour of practice the night before, and two the night before that. Hob made a go-ahead gesture. I showed him THE MAN WHO WOULD BE KING. This was the first trick in the green book. Erzmund described it with perfect simplicity: you pick up two cards from the top of the deck at the same time, show the bottom card to your target, replace the two-card packet, slide the top card into the middle of the deck, tap once on the new top card, and then lift it to show your astonished target that it's the card you first revealed to him, the one you so ostentatiously slid back into middle of the deck, that it's floated by secret means up through the solid plaque of cards to the first spot. *Thus you shall demonstrate the unconquerable desire of the low to rise*, as Erzmund put it.

It's just a simple motion. The way you have to put a spiral on a football. That in my experience proved more difficult, which is why I ended up playing on the offensive line. Hand to deck, the quick reveal, "replace" the card (except it wasn't replacing the card at all), and then the big show. You just had to let your fingers feel how much pressure to exert. Nothing to it. As long as you didn't worry overmuch. That's how it is with most things in this unpredictable life. Hob told me to do it again, faster. So I did. "Faster, again," he said. So I showed him. "Faster as in faster, meaning do it faster," he said. So I speeded it up. I recognized his psych technique. Coach Madigan did it constantly. I went as fast as I could: show, replace, reveal. Show, replace, reveal. Hob stared at my right hand. The metal box hummed and vibrated. My heartbeat slowed. That weird calm descended. Show. Replace. Reveal. The cards slid against one another like stone slabs. Light and heavy at the same time. I couldn't hear anything except my own blood. My hand was moving with incredible speed and fluidity. I watched it move as though it belonged to a stranger and felt a vacant smile starting to stretch my cheeks. Hob's lips kept moving, too, and I made the mistake of focusing on them, which distracted me. His words started to come through the thump and buzz of my own blood. "That was pretty sterling, but you could still do it faster." First thing I heard as I zoned back in.

Coaches talk that way to make you mad. Make you try harder. There's diminishing returns on it. After a point your anger doesn't do much for your skill. So instead of trying again, I left the deck on the metal box and asked Hob to show me a trick, since he was such an expert. "You don't actually want me to do that," he said, "you'll just get frustrated." "You can only sell me out once, you know," I said, "you only have one bullet. Remember that." "A metaphor," he said, "I didn't know you had it in you." That was all right. I don't mind being insulted.

Except when I do mind. Erratic human nature. "Are you going to show me," I said, "because I have to say you're taking your time." "That is correct, Michael," said Hob. He took the deck. He looked at the sky. I didn't see anything. Just cold sunlight. "Keep in mind I've been doing this a lot longer," he said. "How much longer," I said. "Like ten years," he said, "like since I could pick up cards." "Holy shit," I said, "I haven't been doing anything for ten years." "Well, you should try it," said Hob, "it makes the time go." What an old man would say. He was riffle-shuffling the deck. Five times. Seven times. "Enough," I said. "That's fair," said Hob. He pushed back his coat sleeves. His forearms pale and knobby. A scar crossed the left inner wrist. A black tattoo decorated his inner right forearm. An eye. Schematic, but an eye. He saw me staring. He lifted the shuffled deck in the palm of his left hand. "What happened to your wrist," I said. "Observe, good sir, this ordinary deck of cards," he said. His voice cheery. Booming. "Would you do the honors?"

"What do you mean," I said. "A card, sir, say the name of any card," said Hob. A wing-beat made him look skyward. "Four of diamonds," I said. He stopped scanning the sky. Turned over the top card and showed me: the four of diamonds. "You had nearly a two percent chance of doing that anyway," I said. He let the card tumble. Bright against the air. "Again, sir," said Hob. "I get it," I said, "okay?" "Once more, please," he said, his voice steady, dead-even, hard. "No need for hysterics," I said. I was ready to break his nose if necessary. "All this is done at your behest, sir," he said. Waited. "Ace of hearts," I said. He lifted the top card. "No, hang on. The queen of spades," I said. When it was in midair. I wanted to fuck with him. He showed me: queen of spades. "Okay then," I said. He let it go. The card tumbled and fluttered. "Once more, sir," said Hob. A crow screamed. I said nothing. He showed me the seven of spades. "Once more, sir," he repeated. The crow screamed again. "You're belaboring this," I said. "Again," he whispered. "I understand," I said. "You do not understand a thing," he said. His scarf rippling with wind. The crow screaming and hopping on the cold cement of the lunch court. Hob kicked a discarded apple core at it. Went wide. The crow clattered skyward. I would have hit it. That much I knew. I picked up the cards he'd let fall. I had the queen of spades halfway to my pocket before I saw her slight, sly smile.

4

"Eight of diamonds," I said, and turned the card over. Three of hearts. "King of clubs," I said, and turned the card over. Two of spades. "Nine of hearts," I said. Turned the card over. It was, in fact, the nine of hearts. I flipped two more and guessed them both wrong. One of diamonds, two of diamonds, three of diamonds. All the way up to the top of the suit. I got another, the ten, correct. My luck was improving. My father knocked on the door and asked who I was talking to. "It's Shakespeare, we have to memorize Shakespeare," I said. "It doesn't sound like Shakespeare, but who am I to judge," he said, and thumped away. Four of hearts, five of hearts, six, seven: nothing.

At that point I started to laugh at myself. I mean that literally. I was standing in front of my bedroom mirror, wearing my gym shorts and nothing else, shaking and covered with sweat from concentrating. Because Hob was trying to blackmail me. I didn't know why: the hilarious part. I had gotten through almost all the suits now, in the order of precedence Erzmund describes, hearts as the least and spades as the worthiest. I was quaking, holding back guffaws. If my parents heard these they'd assume I was high. I didn't want that. I just wanted to finish. When I got to the jack of spades, I had to grab the footboard of my bed. These silent laughs convulsing my torso. Painful, my memory suggests. I wanted to stop. I nearly set the deck down. I thought: *Just one more.* I said, in a loud, even voice: "Queen of spades."

Even before I turned it I knew what it was. I just knew. In the mirror I saw her black hair and her hard smile. And then I blared out a brief and meaningless monosyllable. There was a line of human writing scrawled on the card. I dropped it. It fell facedown among the others at my feet. I located it and stared. I must have missed it earlier. This was, at that time, the sole possible explanation. Hob's handwriting. Spiky and neat. Next to the queen's mouth. I read it: *9th and C. 8 PM.* I checked the clock. I had enough time. So I dressed. I slow-walked, holding my shoes, out into the hall. My mother was watching a show about dragonflies and my father was using his exercise machine. Its wheels whirred and its cords whipped and whispered. "I'm going out," I said. "It's a school night," said my father. Breathing hard. Above the high-pitched noises of the machine. "It's not, actually, babe," said my mother, above the British voice droning away about the diets of dragonflies. "You could knock me over with a feather," said my father, "but don't be too late." "I won't," I said. Henry the doorman was asleep when I reached the lobby. His pasty cheek glued to his lectern and his cotton-colored hair leaking out from beneath his brown livery cap. The air outside was brick-cold. As soon as my foot touched the sidewalk a black sedan cruising Park honked. I froze. The car moved on, flashing its brights at no one I could see. I didn't have a car. My parents had one they kept in our building garage. This was true of almost everyone I knew. No one drove anywhere. Yet traffic and parked cars jam the city. A mystery of city life. City life contains a lot of mysteries. Part of why you stay there.

I was out of breath when I got there. I'd had to run as fast as I could, shoes slapping the frigid cement, from the subway to make it on time. Hob slouched against a facade. Smoking his brown cigarette. Near his feet, a quintet of stone-blue young rats had their sharp faces aimed at the asphalt. Gathered around the carcass of a bird. "Well, well," said Hob. "Give me two seconds," I said. "I thought you were supposed to be a top-notch athlete," said Hob. "You have an archaic way of leaving messages," I said. I stopped gasping. The rats chittered and lapped. "They're doing good work," he said, "I hate crows. And don't worry about the blood. It's not a thing." "Nosebleeds, scourge of the common folk," I said. More silence. More rat noise. "They could be siblings," I said, "look at their fur." "As long as they finish it off," Hob said. It looked finished to me.

I saw, after I'd lost interest in watching the rats eat the glossy bird, which did in fact appear to be a small crow, its ribs now naked and gummy with blood, the place Hob was taking me. One of those dim, inexplicable stores, its window full of objects I couldn't really discern until Hob flicked his cigarette against the glass. I saw: a headless, old-fashioned mannequin, with a wooden androgynous body and a wire cage for a head, to which were affixed two huge antlers. Across from it an old globe, ivory colored. Then the cigarette's coal shattered and I couldn't see any more. I saw the store's name, though, or noticed it: Karasarkissian's. "What is this place," I asked, "and it's closed anyway." "It's kind of what it looks like," said Hob, "and *closed* is a relative term. There we go."

He'd opened the door of the shop. "You didn't say anything about suborning burglary," I said. Hob showed me the key. "I have a right to be here, and so do you," he said, "or at least I think you do." He lit up again as we walked in. I followed him. Stepped over a low black table in front of my feet. On its surface the blind-looking moon floated. The store was full of the same kind of crap—which is how I thought of it then—as the antlered mannequin in the window. Couldn't see much. A green statue of a fat woman, I saw, and a number of what appeared to be stuffed bats, hanging from a conduit on wires that glinted in the light cast by Hob's new cigarette. I asked him for one. "You don't even smoke," said Hob. "Maybe I want a new hobby," I said. "You asked me to show you something, and I did, and now I'm showing you something else," he said, "from which you might actually profit." Then we hit carpet. Hob's shoes stopped scraping. He knelt down and rolled back the edge of the rug. I stared at his bulb-tipped nose. A white smudge in the dark of the store. "I have to say, Michael," he said, "it took you a lot less time than I would have guessed," said Hob. "What do you mean," I said. "The first sleight, the first one in the book," he said, "you have to be able to do it at a certain level to get in here." "Who decides," I said. "In this case me," said Hob.

Cut and run. That's what I wanted to do. I mean, here we were with this hatch. Nobody wants to look at a closed hatch. A square steel hatch set in the floor of Karasarkissian's weird-crap store. The hatch swung open, and the sweet stink of booze and cigarettes wafted out, along with a wash of yellow warm light and the sound of violin music. Whoever opened the hatch clattered back down what sounded like a ladder, and Hob crept down into the square opening. "Are you coming, Michael," he said. I climbed down. A hollow space about the size of our math classroom. Strings of warm, yellow Christmas-tree lights snaked across every wall that I could see, so that the place was well lit without there being a glare. In the back of the room was a red-brown table. A rank of unmatched glassware gleaming on it. Huge carboys full of golden fluid. I thought I saw snakes or eels swimming in them. A second later I thought: I hadn't seen anything of the kind. Hob was already at this bar, pouring the golden liquid, about the color of whiskey, into two glasses. The violin music came from a girl with ultra-black hair playing the violin. This weird song that I later found out was by a guy called Janacek. Leos Janacek. Hob was carrying the whiskey glasses back to us, and I was reaching for one when I felt a cold, subtle tap on my shoulder.

I whirled to see who'd done it. A towering and spindly guy, wearing a black suit and a poinsettia-red tie, like it was the middle of the day. Or like he worked in a mortuary. "Can I help you," I said. "I don't know, can you," said the tie wearer. Not harshly. I recognized him. Or thought I did. "You're Vincent," I said. I knew him from Saint Cyprian's. In the murky, awed way I knew kids who had graduated. Simon Canary's older sister Rosie, for example. She didn't go to Saint Cyprian's, though. She had gone to Holy Agony. "You're Vincent Callahan," I said, "right? Your name's Vincent?" "You have good recall," he said. "Why are you dressed like a mortician," I said. You see a man dressed like a mortician and you call him on it.

The violin player lifted her bow and cackled. A bruise-blue spot under her chin. Staring out. A single eye. "This is what I get for trying to raise the tone here," said Vincent. "Vincent," said Hob. He started trotting. Whiskey slapped over the glass rims. These two goblets. "Hob and his strays," said Vincent, "it's like the ultimate in distributed democracy." "I believe in democracy," I said. The violin player laughed, again, from her corner, her green, grubby sofa. There were other people present in the room. A cavern. Or basement. There was a black guy there, too, who looked older than all of us—he had gray in his square beard. He came forward now. Limped up to where Vincent, Hob, and I were standing. His gait loud and arrhythmic. A strong footstep, the thud of his cane, a weak footstep. A dactyl. That's the only other thing I remember from Greek. His cane: black with a silver head in the shape of a badger. Yellow gems or yellow glass for its eyes. A silver tip on the floor-striking end. That part is called a ferrule. A word I learned from Hob.

"Hob," said the cane wielder, "I see you've brought us a guest." His voice was higher and lighter than I thought it would be. He was broad across the shoulders and deep in the chest. Big eyes. A short neck. "And we always treat guests with respect," said the cane wielder. He stuck his hand out. It took me a second to catch on: he wanted to shake. "It's an ancient custom," he went on as we shook. His palm dry and warm, seamed. A knobby scar I hadn't seen scraped the hollow of my hand. "Dates to classical times. When gods traveled in disguise throughout the world, testing their worshippers. Or so the thinking runs. I never saw much in that myself." I could think of nothing to say. So I gave my name. "Charthouse," the cane wielder said, "it's John Charthouse, but people seem inclined to call me Charthouse. You ever notice that? Certain people get called by their last names." Vincent stood next to Hob. Touching his tie.

I couldn't believe this was happening but I could. This same contradiction occurred the time Mary Agnes Ravapinto gave me a blow job and swallowed. A crude analogy. I don't have a better one. The air bluish with drifting smoke. "Truth is," said Charthouse, "we've heard a lot about you, Mike." "Is that necessarily a good thing," I said. "Not necessarily but you have to be a friend to make friends. My father told me that," said Charthouse, "then again, I always thought it was bullshit." "Generational differences, that's what my parents say," I said. Charthouse laughed. His filled molars glinting. "Hob knows how to pick them," said Charthouse, "and he thinks you're a good candidate." I wanted to ask *Candidate for what*. Vincent called out: "He also believes in democracy." Charthouse tapped the red knot of Vincent's necktie with the badger head. A practiced gesture. I wondered how much of a talker Vincent was. "Let's not lose focus here," said Charthouse. "I think he's ready," said Hob, "I think he should take the salto."

No idea what the words meant. A drug, I thought. That's what you take: drugs. I wanted to be a good guest. So I said: "I'm happy to." Neither Hob nor Charthouse listened. Vincent seemed to brighten up. He and Charthouse both smoking those brown cigarettes. Hob's brand. Their sweetish smell in my nose and throat. Enough to make me giddy. "Can I bum one," I asked when Hob had finished talking. Vincent cackled. "You're too young," he said. "Vincent," said Charthouse. Vincent shut off his laugh. "I know you don't understand necessarily what all this is," Charthouse said to me, "but that's no matter. Hob's told us about you. And we value, you might say, his opinion." Hob handed me one goblet. He gave Charthouse the other. Charthouse stared at me over the rim, and we toasted. I had no choice. You can't turn down a toast. "Drink up," he said. Downed his goblet. I downed mine too. I didn't want to look foolish. No immediate ill effects. The whiskey: it tasted strange. Ripe apricot. Ammonia. The jagged strains of the violin rose again. I figured Charthouse would introduce me to the other people there. The violin player, I mean. She looked to be my age, Hob's age, her long head bobbing and her short hair gleaming. She had black eyes, actually black. Black hair. I wanted to go over and talk to her. You can't interrupt a violinist. Or any musician. She saw me looking. She closed her eyes. She smiled. She lifted bow from strings. She said, "Is there a problem." "No problem," I called.

We're raised, in America, to be polite to strangers. Your host offers you a drink, you drink it. Your interrogator questions you, you answer. The root of our sufferings, I'd say. When Hob refilled our goblets, Charthouse and I drank again. I was owed. For the nosebleed and Hob's trickery. The whiskey, or whatever it was, served as payment. When Charthouse asked me questions, I answered. As I said, that's how we're raised. How old are you. Do you like school. Where do you live. "In the city," I said. "We all live in the city, or try to," he said, "and even if you're only trying it serves as enough of a passport." "What the fuck are you talking about," I said. "You curse," he said, "that can be a sign of low creativity. Not many know that." Then he asked me what the capital of New Zealand was. "I know this one," I said, "I really do."

"That's all right," he said. Hob poured me another drink. Vincent stroked his tie. For the length of an eye-blink I saw a sapphire-colored snake or eel twisting through the tawny liquid in the bottle Hob was lifting. Charthouse kept questioning me. As they did in catechism, when I was a kid, except it was not harsh: Had I ever considered the

THE ASSHOLES

possibility of ontological perfection? "St. Anselm, they made us learn that," I said. Which daisies were better, he wanted to know, yellow or white? We're raised to answer. I couldn't stop now. I'd already answered. It's easier to go to war than quit smoking. Whoever said that knew humans. Tell me about the tree with the ten branches. I guessed sycamore. Hob said you got a nosebleed. Correct. If you had to choose your own name, what would it be. Didn't answer that one. Charthouse didn't press me. Vincent bobbed up and down on the balls of his feet. His smile white and wavering. How long have you known Hob. My whole life. So it went. He kept asking and I kept answering. Hob filled the goblets and we drank. I was proud, too, that I handled the liquor. *Three glasses of whiskey*, I thought, *and nothing. I must be a king.* A jerking shadow climbed the wall. The violinist. Her eyes shut and her smile still present, still quiet. "It's so loud," I said. "Here we go," said Charthouse. He offered me a brown cigarette. "House blend," he said. "Oh man, what a good idea," I said. He offered me a lit match. "Wellington," I said around the cigarette. "There you go, Mike," said Charthouse.

The Christmas lights strung up all over the place began to pulse, brighten and dim. "Are you guys getting power surges," I said. "Yes, exactly," said Vincent. Charthouse ignored this exchange. The violin music broke off. "Now it's so quiet," I said. "You have a lot of obser-vations to offer," said Charthouse, "about the obvious. Not that I object. The obvious is where you have to begin." The sound of his voice almost knocked me to my knees. Vincent asked Hob whether he thought this would end well. I had to cover one ear. I had my whiskey in my other hand. Bone-bred guest behavior. Can't just drop a glass. "It's all right, Mike, we're getting there," said Charthouse. "Did you poison me," I said, "strychnine makes you hypersensitive to stimuli." The words boomed in my own head. "We don't have any strychnine," said Charthouse. "I saw that in a movie," I said.

The violin player strutted over to us, swinging her instrument by

THE WAR AGAINST

its neck. I took another swig and found that my cup was empty. Hob refilled it. I didn't actually want any more, but I couldn't think of a polite way to say no, and Charthouse kept asking me questions. He wanted to know how much I knew about theurgists, and I told him I had no idea at all. Did I know what they were. No. Had I heard the term before. No. Was I in their service. No. "You make it sound," I said, and my voice was slow and slurred, "as though it's a bad thing, and if I were, I don't think I'd necessarily admit it, you know?" The violin player snorted at this. She had a vine tattooed on her neck. It disappeared beneath her yellow shirt. "Astute," said Vincent. Pain lanced through my head. Charthouse didn't pay any attention. He stared at me and beat his palm with the silver head of the cane. Even that was amplified: pounding on a wall. I heard another plink. Rain hitting a lake. I looked. Another drop of blood fell from my nose, into my goblet of whiskey. It spread. The first one was mostly dissipated. "I think," I said. Gave up.

"You ever read Flannery O'Connor," said Charthouse. I managed to tell him I hadn't. "You go to a Catholic school and she was a Catholic writer. You'd think they'd make the connection." More blood warmed my upper lip. I told him I had no idea why they failed to. "Well, thing is, she had a story. Called 'A Good Man Is Hard to Find'? And at the end, not to give it away, but at the end one of the characters says about this old lady, 'She would of been a good woman if it had been somebody there to shoot her every minute of her life.' You understand what I'm getting at?" I told him I didn't. "Well, maybe you will, yet," he said. I was about to ask him what the hell he meant. Metal scraped my temple. Cold and hard. A thin, warm, hard forearm crossed my throat. I knew it was the violinist before she even said, "Don't bleed on my arm."

She had a napkin in the hand at the end of the arm across my neck. I took it, pressed it to my nostrils. "You're set now," she said, "just don't do anything ridiculous." No one had ever pulled a gun on me before. They say it can happen to anybody. I'd known kids who'd gotten mugged, for example. Part of city life. Or there was a woman, a few years ago, who tried to make a smart remark when a young sociopath pulled a gun on her. "What are you going to do, shoot me," she asked. He obliged. They called it a tragedy but I never saw it that way myself. You ask for punishment and the universe obliges. Standing there in that sweet-smelling cavern, breathing hard, I blamed myself. You would have too if you'd been there and had any sense. "I don't have any money," I said. "I mean I don't and my parents don't. I mean they have plenty but you can ransom me and it won't do you any good. You won't end up with anything worth your trouble." That's what I tried to say. I figured I might as well let them know, in case they had a fancy plan cooked up. My tongue kept slipping and floundering, adhering to my palate. I kept having to start over. The appeal got less sharp each time. An argument for keeping your mouth shut. So I gave up talking. If these people were going to kill me, there wasn't anything I could do about it, and I relaxed against the violin player. Her skin gave off heat through her tee shirt. I couldn't remember what color it was. Yellow, I thought. I could feel her breasts against my back and the barrel of her gun against my temple. *At least it isn't drowning*, I thought, *nothing could be worse than drowning.* Charthouse grinned at me, right then. He whipped around and started to whistle. A brief song. It repeated. I believed I knew the words. I couldn't summon them up. He reached out and placed the hot, dry palm of his hand, the scarred palm, against my forehead. As his hand approached my head, a blue thread of light leaped from his palm. A strong, curt sting on my skin. A pop of static electricity. No other way to say it: pure darkness, rushing in.

5

I've never liked sleeping. This was worse. No dreams, no relief. Just darkness. Anesthesia. Lost time, nothing more. When I woke up, I was ascending. Cold air. A single car horn. Near my head a motor unspooled a grinding whine. Yellow light flooded my eyes. I could see the back of Charthouse's gray-sprinkled hair. He was still whistling. Flute-toned and clear. Vincent leaned against metal bars. Shadows striping his lean face. "Good morning," he said. We were in a cage. Going up. Hob stood next to me. The white bulb of his nose moved in and out of my peripheral vision. I hoped he felt guilty. I hardly knew him and here he was accompanying me to my death. Truth is, it was funny. That might have been the whiskey, though, improving my sense of humor. "Hob," I said.

Speaking hurt my throat. My voice came out sandpapered. I touched my upper lip. The bleeding had stopped. Drying blood made the skin tacky. The violin player was even-tempered. She didn't pull the trigger. She tapped my temple with the barrel. That's all. "Breathe," she said, "just take a deep breath." Her lips almost brushed my ear. Her skin or her soap smelled like grass, new grass in spring. "What did he do," I said, "to knock me out." "I don't think you're allowed to know yet," said Vincent. Charthouse said: "Don't be coy. We have to attend to our affairs." The violinist laughed. So I laughed again. I kept my footing. "That's better," said the violinist. Up we rose. Outside and inside at the same time. Wind biting and the sky as usual empty of stars. They say the light from the city obscures them. I wouldn't know. Floor after floor of nothing: bare I-beams, drywall, windows without glass. Junk and clutter. You have to expect them when you build. Accidents, too. Deaths, missing limbs. No way around it. A construction site. We were going up in one of those cage elevators. Charthouse whistled his tune. "What's that song," I said. "I like the air tonight," he said, "and I like the odds, too." I preferred the whistling. The light from the lamps, also caged, on each floor we passed poured in. Charthouse's whistling got louder and harder. Nobody else made a sound. Except me. "Where did you learn how to drive one of these," I said, "I mean operate." "It's not a fighter jet precisely," said Charthouse, "but I'm glad to see your natural curiosity's still aflame."

We went up and up. *Had always been ascending and would always be,* I thought. I started saying Ave Marias. Quiet but still out loud. Hob turned to stare. "*Gratia plena,*" I said. "It's not *that* bad," he said. The girl behind me. I didn't know whether to think girl or woman. Couldn't tell her age. I was still half-blind. I was weak voiced and addled. Yet I pondered how to impress her. You can't escape your urges. Charthouse kept whistling his song. I guessed at words between prayers. He tapped time on the bars of the elevator cage. The badger's eyes caught lamplight. The wind was blowing through our cage, making it dance. I caught a whiff of ozone. A high-voiced dog in one of the buildings near us howled. "Natives are restless," said Charthouse. "We're the natives," said the violinist. "You have," said Charthouse, "the majority opinion against you on that question." We came to a halt, the winch above us whining and going dead quiet. The cage swung and creaked.

I prayed more. "Gentlemen's apparel," said Vincent. He opened the cage door. Charthouse's cane boomed against whatever thin surface we were walking on. Wood, I thought. *That's my name*, I thought. He kept whistling. My head half-clear. My body shaking from the cold or the drink. "His heart's pounding," announced the violinist. "Where are we going," I asked. Didn't work any better. "Now, what kind of second-rate question is that," said Charthouse. We passed between two sheaves of rebar. "Crow," said Hob. The clatter of wings. A black flash. He was right: one crow. "Keep moving," said the violinist, "you're obsessed." I didn't disagree. "Shouldn't be up here, though, this late. Should be asleep. Birds sleep at night. That's a fact," said Charthouse. "Look, are we going to suffer or act," said the violinist. "As I said, the natives are restless," said Charthouse. He stopped his strong hobble. He smelled like an overheated engine. Not bad but not what you expect from a human. My captors spread out. Vincent scratched his left ear. His cuticle torn. I was sure I was going to die. Thus the detail. When your life seems poised to end, you remember things. This I know from experience. The violin player chivvied me forward.

Cold air filled my mouth and dried out my eyes. Yellow glare and vertigo. I couldn't accept the view. Or wouldn't. "The valley of bones," said Charthouse. All I could dredge up in response was: "It's not the valley of bones." My throat stung. "An expert," said Vincent. "If it isn't the valley of bones," said Charthouse, "then what is it?" Everyone stood behind me. I had to keep craning my head to see. The violinist held the gun steady. In every glimpse. "Don't do anything stupid. I already told you," she said. "It's the new building they're building on Mercer Street," I said, "with the thing they haven't put in yet. The spire. Glass spire." Which it was. I recognized the orange crane creaking away, near us. From news reports. Concerns over its stability. Then again, what doesn't suffer from such concerns? "Don't be so literal," said Charthouse. The violin player gave me a shove. I objected to this.

I couldn't say anything. At least the gun wasn't scraping my skin anymore. At least my nose wasn't bleeding. I turned to face them. I didn't want to get shot in the back. "I don't know what it is that you think you can get out of doing this," I said. "It's not we who are going to get anything out of it," said Charthouse. "I can tell you this," said Vincent, "you should try to stay calm but you're not going to like what comes next." "You're interfering," said the violin player, "there's no rule I can't shoot you."

"Technically," said Charthouse, "you are correct." The violinist kept the gun pointed at me, though. Not Vincent. I was standing on a platform. Wooden planks, weather-stained. They bowed and bounced under my weight and the weight of my captors. Bright bulbs in their orange cages hanging from rubber cords tied around the exposed girders of the building. Source of that yellow glow. In the middle, a huge square shaft. Three hundred feet deep, I estimated. Four, possibly. The platform edged this. For the spire. For its internal supports. I had no idea. I stared down. More vertigo. I didn't even fear heights. The wind whipped my ears. The plank floor creaked and swayed. All the drowsiness and uncertainty the whiskey brought on drained away. I heard the wind whistle and I heard Charthouse chuckle. Double voice of nature. That phrase is my own. "Let's get to it, Alabama," said Charthouse. Alabama: the violin player. I turned to watch. She shuffled back till her shoulders met a girder, covering me with the pistol. "Your name's Alabama," I said. "You're a real wit," she said, "the girls must love you."

"Charming," said Charthouse. "This is going to be good, I predict," said Vincent. The barrel hole black and enormous, when I twisted to look. "How did you knock me out," I asked Charthouse. "Better and better," said Vincent. "He wasn't talking to you," said Charthouse. The barrel hole steady. A dark eye. It echoed the bruise under the tip of her pale chin. "Just be calm, Michael," said Hob. The crane moaned. "We're getting close," said Charthouse. I tried to crouch, to get stable.

"Stand up," said Alabama. I was still thinking about what she would look like naked. "Where did you get that bruise," I said. "Listen to Charthouse," she said. I was more concerned with the gun. "Did you come to us of your own free will," he asked me. "Are you joking," I said. "Don't be disingenuous," said Charthouse, "Alabama will shoot you." "Yes," I said. It was for the most part true. "With no promises or inducements," he asked. I looked at Hob. "You gave me all that whiskey or whatever it was, does that count," I asked. "'Whatever it was,'" said Charthouse. "That's eloquent," said Alabama. "Does not count, by the way," said Vincent. The wind moved the loose cloth of Charthouse's dark windbreaker. Purple, eggplant purple. White stripes down the sleeves. A robe. I thought, *His windbreaker looks like a robe*. I am literal minded. Secret of my success. Such as it is. "And what do you mean it's the valley of bones," I said. A stupid question. "It's a metaphor," said Alabama, "now get moving." "But what do you mean, though," I said. Another stupid question. "Son, you know what she means," said Charthouse. Alabama twitched the gun toward the outer edge of the platform. "Turn and get walking," she said, "or you know the deal." I didn't move. She widened her stance. My bladder ached. I thought about pissing myself. I didn't. I walked up to the platform edge and stared down. More levels like the one we stood on, more blaring lights in cages. I heard a clicking sound. I knew it was Alabama chambering a round. Drawing back the hammer. Had to be. "All right, you ready," said Charthouse. "For what, ready for what," I said. "You should feel lucky," said Charthouse, "few get the chance." "He doesn't look ready," said Vincent. "Shut up," said Hob, and then to me: "Don't listen, it's totally fine, trust me." This I had trouble with. "I don't know what the salto is," I said, "and I don't know how to take it." "I trust you can figure it out," said Alabama. "She's right," said Charthouse, "it's not genius-level perception we're talking about here."

At the bottom of the shaft, two-by-fours, cement sacks, eleven wheelbarrows. I counted them twice. A yellow hard-hat topping a pile of white dust. "Valley of bones," crowed Charthouse. "I don't see any bones," I said. I knew I was going to die. These cocksuckers were going to kill me for no reason. "You lack a sense for poetry," said Charthouse. True. I'm no poet. I'm no philosopher, either. I wasn't then. I was a kid suffering an already-coming-on hangover, standing on top of a building with a hot girl pointing a gun at him and ordering him to take the salto. "I don't know what that means," I said, "I don't." "Just jump," said Hob. "Or she'll shoot you," said Vincent, "and I've seen her do it before." You could tell by their reedy voices they were brothers. In the shaft, wind-carried fragments of paper circled. On the streets below, the amber and red lights of cars. The air smelled like snow. "Nothing hard to understand about it," said Alabama. "He's not going to do it," said Vincent. "I didn't say that," I called. "You have a point," said Charthouse, "but you need to decide." I pushed my toes over the wooden lip. "Can I just ask you one thing real quick," I said. "Last question," said Charthouse. "How does the rug get back down flat if you close the hatch behind you when you come down. In the store, I mean." Charthouse hooted a long laugh. The cold wind whistled. "You're an observant guy," he said, "and you might even find out. But right now you need to decide." So I decided. I didn't want to get shot in the back. I took three breaths. I clenched my teeth. I leaped into the empty air.

6

My mother didn't wait for an answer. She slipped her head past the jamb to ask if I was sick. "I feel great," I said. I don't like lying. She wanted to know if I wanted any pancakes. She made them for my father every Saturday morning. Blueberry pancakes, summer and winter. I said I was all right. Which hurt. "Well, you look," said my mother, "like you're getting sick. But that's just this correspondent's opinion." I promised I wasn't getting sick. "I should go deal with the pancakes," she said. I tried to get back to sleep. Could not. Even the muscles controlling my eyes burned and sang. To say nothing of the healing wound on my hand. That had started hurting again, like a motherfucker. As Gilder might have put it. Every time I flexed my palm—and I couldn't stop flexing it—it stung and ached. I listened to my mother clattering around in the kitchen and my father singing. He was a morning singer. "There's no business like show business," he sang. Or: "The sadder but wiser girl's the girl for me."

That made me think of Alabama and the tattoo twisting down her neck, beneath the yellow edge of her shirt. I was too sore even to get a hard-on. So I lay in my bed, smelling the detergent on my sheets and hearing my parents' soft conversation. "Is he hungover," my father said. "He says he feels fine," my mother said. "I don't know, he looks a lot worse for the wear," said my father, "and he smells like he's been drinking." They weren't criticizing me, just observing. I drifted along for a while, an hour, two hours. Listening and wincing. When my house phone rang, I knew it was Hob. He'd been calling my cell. I'd been not answering. Listening to the apian buzz. *Apian* means "of or pertaining to bees." I learned that from my parents' nature-TV habit. My father answered and I rasped that if it was for me, hold on, I was on my way. I rolled out of bed and grunted when I hit the floor, and had managed to raise myself to my knees when my father appeared in the doorway, holding his tennis racket in one hand and a phone in the other. "You're wanted on the telephone," he said, and winked and walked away, singing that song about the sadder but wiser girl. "Good morning, sunshine," Hob said.

Then he explained about meeting up. I listened. At times you have to keep your mouth shut. I heard my father leave. He was a tennis fiend. He said it kept him young. Maybe so. Nobody's parents stay young. After I got off the phone, I staggered to the brown-tiled dim half bath off the front hall. I turned on the fluorescents. They hummed, flickered, blazed. My skin looked transparent and green. I could see veins at my temples. I swabbed sweat from my eyebrows. I vomited in the sink. My mother, through the door, asked me if I needed help. I puked up another jet of yellowish bile and told her I was fine. My voice croaking, from the acid. "You don't sound fine," said my mother. "Did you go out drinking last night? Where were you out so late?" I told her I'd been doing wind sprints with Greg Gilder—his name slipped out—and had lost track of the time. "I thought exercise was supposed to be good for you," said my mother. Hovering outside the door. I could just see her: palm spread on the wood, ear cocked near the jamb. "All right, I'm off," she said. I told her good-bye. I waited until the front door creaked shut before spewing a third stream of bile into the white sink. I grinned at myself in the mirror and said, "This isn't so bad, Mikey."

Nobody had ever called me Mikey. Not my parents and not my friends, not any girls. The statue of Simón Bolívar just outside the park: that's where Hob wanted to meet. Why Hob chose it, I don't know. I slipped the green book into my pocket as I left. Seemed like the natural thing to do. He was already waiting when I got there, smoking. I walked up, slow. Again, I had no real idea of what to say. We kind of stood there, watching each other. Hob was smiling a smile that made me want to punch him in the teeth. The wound across my knuckles still stung. He asked me how I felt. "Like I'm the one who got my ass kicked," I said. "And what about your vision," he said. "What are you, an ophthalmologist," I said. "Just tell me right now if you've had any blurry vision or numbness," he said. He sounded old. "Like I caught a beating. That's all," I told him. "I'd rate your health situation normal," he said. A rickshaw rolled by, the driver needlessly and joyfully dinging the handlebar bell. Two fuchsia-clad fatasses in the back snapping pictures of me and Hob and Simón Bolívar. A raven landed on the statue's iron hair, and Hob watched it hop as he spoke to me. "Normal," I said. The raven took off with a raucous caw. "I hate those birds," said Hob. "Hating birds is pointless," I said. He exhaled a cloud of sweet blue smoke. "What's in those anyway," I asked. "All kinds of stuff," he said, "my brother makes the blend."

I took one. I was not much of a smoker. My second in twenty-four hours. No better reason to smoke than the fact that you don't smoke. It hurt to take a drag. The smoke wasn't harsh or hot the way it was from the few other cigarettes I'd smoked, and as soon as it eased into my lungs my bodily pain started to dissipate. "Not bad, right," said Hob. "I didn't say anything," I said. "I know you don't necessarily understand what happened last night," he said. This was true. I did not understand what had happened and I did not understand why it left me feeling as though my bones had shattered. As though I'd lost a lot of blood. "Then why don't you give me the executive summary," I said. Bike hawkers sidled up to pedestrians, holding their rate cards and mumbling, and the stink of roasting chestnuts blew into my nose. "Well," said Hob. "It was a test, right," I said. "It was the salto," said Hob. "Why the salto," I said, "why don't you call it facing certain death or something more accurate?" I drew in another lungful of that sweet smoke. My pain ebbed more. My blood stopped buzzing in my ear canals. "I don't know. It's just what it's called." "And I passed," I said. "You're standing here, aren't you," said Hob. "When does my certificate arrive," I asked. Hob held up his two closed fists. "Pick one," he said. I chose left. He opened up. A key lay there, silver and unscratched, its wards undented.

I knew what it was for. Or guessed. I took it. The raven came back. "Put it in your pocket," said Hob. "What is this thing you have with birds, man," I said. "They like shiny objects," said Hob. "So do a lot of humans," I said. "I'll explain it, soon," he said. I pocketed the key. "And you do," he said, "really feel all right? No blurry vision? No apha-sia?" I told him no blurry vision. I told him I didn't know what *aphasia* meant. "It's like if you can't remember the word for 'door' or 'coffee cup,'" said Hob. "I puked. That's it," I said. "Pretty much par for the course," he said. The rickshaw fatasses: rolling by again, still snapping away. "Hob, man, seriously," I said. "Look, don't think about it too much. Okay? Don't dwell on it," he said. The rickshaw driver stopped. The fatasses got out. He started to berate them about the price. They objected at first. He'd said fifteen dollars. Et cetera. In the end they complied. Hob and I didn't speak as we watched the argument. After the male fatass paid the rickshaw driver, taking a grass-green plastic wallet out of his sea-blue backpack, after he and his fat wife or fat girl-friend had waddled off, I figured it was time. To ask Hob, I mean, the

THE WAR AGAINST

question that had really been on my mind since I'd woken up: "How old is Alabama?"

He grinned and didn't answer. "No, seriously, is she in high school or what, I couldn't tell is why I'm asking." "Yeah, you and every other loser," said Hob, "but you're in luck. Her phone number's on a piece of paper in your copy of the *Calendar*. Along with Vincent's. Use, don't abuse. Memorize and destroy." He was already leaving. He just tipped me a salute and left me there holding the green book. Which seemed too heavy for what it was. Then again, what did I know about the relative weight of books? I opened it: as promised, a slip of paper held Alabama's phone number and Vincent's. Hob had never touched the book, that I'd seen. The raven came back and watched me smoke from the top of Bolívar's head. Or maybe it was a different bird. Couldn't tell the difference then. "Check it out," I said, and held up the book and the key. "Look at this, bird." The raven cocked its head and looked and looked. Book to key. Key to book. It stared at my face. Those black, reflective eyes.

As for wonder, the sense of wonder or what we commonly call that: it's almost if you think about it a way of stopping you from ever working any miracles yourself. Truth is, miracle-working's no big deal. For example, we put boot prints on the moon. No other animal can say that. And when I launched myself into the air above that resonant shaft, it was also no big deal. I didn't think about it. I just didn't have a choice. Hob and his gang, or whatever they were, stood in a rough semicircle behind me. Charthouse staring at me, arms crossed. His windbreaker sleeves pushed high up on his bulky forearms, the skin covered in black writing. Right down to his wrists. Hob shouted, again, that everything was going to be fine. "I have no faith in that prediction," I said, "not to be a dick." Alabama adjusted her stance again. I realized she was going to shoot me. *I jump, wait a while, then land.* A Russian expert said that. A dancer. I think. Jump. Wait a while. Land. Sounds simple. Within anyone's reach. Anyone who can stomach the risk. All you need is the correct impetus. A beautiful woman (or girl) whose age you can't tell, for example, pointing a gun at you. I jumped. I tried to aim for the concrete sacks at the bottom of the shaft. I thought they'd be better to fall on. I started to pray my tenth or eleventh Ave Maria. Waiting for the ground to rush up to meet me.

It failed to do so. I was turning slowly in the blowing, frigid wind. The black soles of my sneakers about level with the plank I'd launched myself from. I didn't feel wonder. I didn't feel anything. No: I sort of felt like an idiot. Or the fraction of my self or soul doing my thinking at that precarious moment suffered the pangs of being an exposed, flailing fool. Mostly nothing. That's what it's like.

"Not bad," said Charthouse. Alabama lowered her huge gun. Vincent said, "Too close for comfort." Hob was applauding. "Sterling," he yelled out, "totally sterling." "Question is, can you get back," said Charthouse. Another gust moved me. I tried to walk. That wasn't happening. So I flapped my arms. Trying to swim. It half-worked. I tumbled and floated out over the middle of the shaft, my pulse vibrating. Another two, three minutes of backbreaking effort and I managed to scrape my fingers on the edge of the wooden platform. I dragged myself forward. The last three feet: not so graceful. I hit the plywood with a bang you could hear echoing and echoing. My clothes heavy with sweat. My captors were now approaching. Alabama still had her gun lowered, so I assumed I was safe. "What the fuck," I said, "what the fuck. What the fuck." She'd already reached me and was helping me up. Yanking me, I should say. "That's just how it works," she said. "How what works," I said. Could not catch my breath. Charthouse limped up. "Hob knows how to pick them. That is the trick to getting by," he said, and jabbed me lightly with his cane. I stumbled. He grabbed one arm and Alabama grabbed the other. My jaw quivered, my teeth knocked against one another, my knees bowed. One of my arms lay across Charthouse's wide shoulders and one across Alabama's narrow shoulders. Her scapular bones dug into my skin. What she looked like naked: still on my mind. Blame my age. She pressed two fingers to the hollow of my throat. "His pulse is high," she said. "I'm cold," I gasped. "You are so eloquent it's amazing," said Alabama. "You watch too much TV, anyway," said Charthouse, "he's fine. Look at those shoulders. Like a young ox."

7

I like winter. I like the cold. I like the monochrome sky. I like the festive secrecy that attends the season. Holiday parties, for example. I like nothing better. Supervised or anarchic. "I didn't end up winning. I think of it as a learning experience." So said Mary Agnes Ravapinto. Everyone called her Maggie. A contraction. "A learning experience," I said. "That actually sounded pretty lame," said Maggie, "I just meant that losing isn't this catastrophe everybody's always making it out to be." She was talking about her failure in a third-grade spelling bee. Wearing a yellow dress and a white kerchief in her hair. We were standing in the kitchen of Simon Canary's parents' apartment. I was doing that thing where you lean against a wall on one arm while you're talking to a girl. I'd seen it in a movie. I was glad Maggie was talking about spelling bees. Helped distract me. She'd taken off her green blouse and black bra the first time I hooked up with her. Olive skin. Dark, small, slightly cockeyed nipples. Areolae crumpled with the cold. In a spare bedroom in this apartment. I couldn't stop thinking about it as I listened to her.

"So what's new in the world of Michael Wood," she said. That stumped me. *I learned to fly. I met a group of weirdos who hang out in a secret basement and tried to kill me. Hob Callahan is one of them, actually, so he's got that going for him*: kind of a conversation stopper. Yet I didn't want to lie. So I said, "I had to go pay tribute to Coach Madigan's mother last week. She made cookies." "Oh, cookies," said Maggie. "Last time it was brownies, right? I hear they're not fit for human consumption." "She's just an old lady," I said, "she actually has snow-white hair." Maggie went to Holy Agony. Which is a sister school to Saint Cyprian's. So she knew about Coach Madigan and his helpless mother. When I was little, a boy, I thought "sister school" meant where your sisters went, since so many of my classmates had sisters at Holy Agony. This I also told Maggie. "Man, little kids are so literal," she said, "it's crazy that you grow up and figure out metaphors." She had a red cup. I had a blue one. We clashed them together and drank. She had wine. It stained her tongue and lips. I was drinking tequila and pretending to enjoy it. That's what Simon had managed to obtain. He was not a genius host. His parents both traveled a lot for their jobs—they were architects, he explained once, "but not for people"—and he lived in this massive apartment on Fifth and Ninety-Seventh. Top floor. Walls of windows. He had parties before major school vacations. He was not an indiscriminate weekend rager. Before Christmas, Easter, and the advent of summer we all at Saint Cyprian's relied on him. You could see the great darkness of the park from his living room. Streetlamps. Bundled-up joggers beside the wall. Cop cars flashing their red-and-blue lights on the transverse.

"Hey, you think there's a deck of cards," I said. This part I could tell her. "People," she said, "usually have one in their junk drawer." Turned out to be true in the case of the Canaries, fancy architects though they were. We found loose batteries, twine, twenty or thirty blank keys, an orange rubber fingertip puppet of a grinning monster, and a deck of cards. "Okay, watch this," I said. I shot the cards from my left hand to my right. Then back again. I fanned them open and closed. Theatrics, Erzmund called this. I riffle-shuffled them seven times. I'd had to practice this less than I'd guessed I would have to. Even making the cards arc hand to hand I mastered with relative ease. I showed her THE MAN WHO WOULD BE KING. With all the patter Erzmund advises. "In this way," I said, "I demonstrate the unconquerable desire of the low to rise." "Spooky," said Maggie. Then I showed her CALLING MR. ASQUITH. A more serious sleight than THE MAN WHO WOULD BE KING. You need a handkerchief. Maggie took my request in stride and unbound her hair. "You sound like a guy at a carnival," she said. CALLING MR. ASQUITH involves extensive narration. You have to tell, says Erzmund, a brief story about England on the eve of the First World War. You then ask an audience member to pick a card. Maggie chose. She was about to speak, say its name. Before she could, I instructed her to slip it back into the deck. After that, you shift it to the top (there's a two-handed move for that) and palm it, wrap the deck up in the kerchief while going on with your story—"It was a time of great need for England," I said, "the right man for the top job was nowhere to be found"—and leave an extra fold to hold the palmed card. It's much harder than it sounds. If it fails, it looks atrocious. It worked, now: I said, "Calling Mr. Asquith," and gave the kerchief a series of light shakes. When you do it right, the card the audience member picked seems to force its way up from the deck through the cloth of the handkerchief. I did it right. Sweat lined my brow but I did it right.

"Do you," said Maggie, "like mind if I have that back." I didn't know what she meant at first. "I just don't want to get any blood on it," she said. Warmth on my upper lip. "Cool trick, though," she said. Walked out of the kitchen, binding the cloth once more around her shining, tawny hair. Not what I'd expected. I grabbed a paper towel and cleaned my lip. I slipped the deck into my jacket pocket. The Canaries did not need it. I finished my tequila. Poured another. Drink and be merry, as the saying goes.

THE WAR AGAINST

The party in full swing. "Wood," called Simon Canary as I crossed his living room. "Great job on this one, man," I said. A girl I didn't know, tubby and blond, was dancing by herself in a corner. "Yo, check out Miss Piggy," said Simon. He wasn't wrong. The girl was wearing pink: sweater and skirt. It wasn't even late enough to be dancing. "Did you hear about Gilder," said Simon, "apparently he fended off these four guys. They tried to mug him. He kicked their asses." I could tell from the way Simon said *guys* that Gilder had made the assailants black in his fake story. "Well, there you go," I said. Simon pushed his long hair back behind his ears. He reeked, already, of weed. "You wanna smoke," he said. He said this ten minutes into any conversation outside school. "I'm good," I said. Over his shoulder, through the glass doors to his enormous terrace, I saw Maggie's white kerchief shining. "Rock on," said Simon. I told him I would.

Outside, bitter gusts. They moved the corners of Maggie's kerchief. She'd put on her coat: bright blue. She was smoking. A regular cigarette. I had a bundle of Hob's brand. I wasn't sure about smoking them in front of strangers. She heard me approach. I was not at that time a master of stealth. "Listen," she said, before I had said anything. She had her hands raised. As though in self-defense. "Okay," I said. "It's generally my experience," she said, "that coked-up football players call you a slut behind your back." "It's not from coke," I said. "Come on," she said, "you still have a blood mustache and you're going to stand there and lie to my face?" "It really isn't, I don't even smoke weed," I said. Technically true. Vincent never mentioned anything about weed in the cigarettes he made. "Pipe tobacco, eyebright, rose petal. Other things. I learned it from my mother," he'd told me. Maggie stopped talking. I waited to see if she would buy this. With the truth, you never know how it's going to be received.

"Well," said Maggie, "you're still a huge nerd for trying that magic trick." The truth wins out. Though not often. "I never pretended to be anything other than a nerd," I said, "even though I play football.

So it's more like spiritual nerddom." "You're just digging your grave deeper," said Maggie. She was starting to grin. She'd opened up her stance. Both good signs. "Card tricks. What am I, seven? You pedophile," she said. I laughed. She was nakedly grinning. "At least I have a hobby," I said. "That's disgusting," she said, and now she was laughing too. "Seriously though, how does it work," she said. "Everybody asks me that," I said. Nobody had ever asked me that. She was the third person I'd ever shown a sleight to. "I see I'm just an entry on your list," she said. "More like I'm on your list," I said. I had moved close enough to her to feel the warmth of her exposed neck. Flushed. From drinking. I think I was too. If two people have big, beaky noses, which both Maggie and I did, it makes it awkward to figure out how to start kissing. Her lips and tongue tasted like wine and ash. I worried that mine tasted like blood. She didn't say anything.

My phone vibrated. I didn't answer. "Maybe we should go inside," I said. She nodded. She'd gotten quiet the last time, too. I didn't mind. I like silence. She led me through the Canaries' apartment. Simon was standing with Frank Santone and Peter Neal, and this kid from Nigeria called Wilton Opuwei. They were all taking hits from Simon's famous bong, which was made of rose-pink glass. He called it the Optimist's Bong. Coughing and howling with laughter. "Oh my god that is quite fine," said Wilton. Maggie tightened her grip on my fingers. Down a hall. Dark and quiet. We leaned against the wall, our faces pressed into each other's neck. I was drunk off the shitty tequila. Drink of innocence. Not in a bad way. Just the first celestial tinges of intoxication. "Hey," she said, "we're wasting time here." At the end of the hall a dim, square room with one window, in which the moon shone. An eye, clear and stern. It was cold. Our breath even fogged. "Why is it so cold," she said. "Man, rich people hate paying their bills," I said, "I guess." "Everyone forgets to pay what they owe," she said, "it's convenient like that."

Her coat zipper stuck. I had to force it. "This cost me three months of saving up," she said. "I won't tear it," I said, "my zippers get stuck all the time. I'm an expert." I was. The door even had a lock button. A daybed stood against the wall with the window, its gray cushion and bolster whitened by moonlight. "Take it off," she said. I did. My jacket. My shirt. She was unbuttoning her dress and thumbing down her tights. The moonlight whitened her skin. I covered my smile. "Don't stare," she said. My phone vibrated. I didn't answer. "A man with an active social life, I see," she said, and sat on the daybed. Arms spread along its bolster. "You look like you're about to interview me for a job," I said. "Maybe I am," she said. She wore nothing now except grass-green underwear. I knelt at her feet to slide them off. I brushed my lips against her knee. She parted her thighs and pressed on the crown of my head. Four warm fingertips. "You owe me," she said. "That's true," I said. Her handkerchief a white, white flag. I had never gone down on a girl before. I did not want her to know. "You've never gone down on anyone before, have you," she said. "Nope," I said. "Well, it's not a mystery," she said. That's when the pounding began. On the door. Maggie grabbed a tasseled taupe blanket and wrapped her torso. Her shins and shoulders bare, her hair brushing her clavicles. More moon-light. I couldn't stop looking. "See who it is," she said. The knob shook. I dragged my shirt on. I said, "No one home."

"More wit," said the pounder. It was Alabama. I could tell by the dark-toned voice. "Can we reschedule this," I said. "Nuh-uh," said Alabama, "we need to talk." "Would it be at all possible," I said, "I mean, can you just come back later." "An acquaintance," said Maggie. "Who's in there with you," grated Alabama, "how could you do this to me." Maggie had already redonned her dress. "Wait wait wait," I said. "Fuck you, wait wait wait," she said. "Is it that blond hussy," Alabama said, "or the tennis player with the shapely thighs?" "Get out of my way," said Maggie. I had to let go of the cold knob to let her pass. Alabama barged in. The door edge caught Maggie's supraorbital ridge. "You shameless harlot," said Alabama. "You really are disgusting," said

Maggie. Covering one eye. I'd expected a more visible show of pain. Even winced in sympathy. Although that science says you can't help. Her stoicism impressed me. "He totally is," said Alabama, "he's a pervert of the first order." "I had a really excellent time," I told Maggie. I meant it. Way too late. Long gone. She turned at the hall's end. Into the light and noise of the main party. Binding up her hair. Certain gestures you'll always recall. "How did you get in here," I said. "How do you think," she said, "she's hot, by the way. I would never have guessed."

8

now. That's the first thing I saw in the street. It had started to
snow. "We're going to that store," I said. "Incorrect," said Hob.
He didn't explain further. Neither did Alabama. "I didn't even
know you were coming to this party," I told Hob. "I thought I should
make my presence felt, for a few minutes at least," he said. "Wood was
just about to get laid, if you can believe it," said Alabama.

She could make me blush. No one wants to blush. You feel weak.
She had on a leather jacket and leather boots. Both about the color
of her hair. When she moved, the hem of her jacket rode up and I
saw the gun butt above the waistband of her jeans. Snow scraped my
cheeks. "You're armed," I said. "Do they teach you anything else at
that school other than mastering the obvious," said Alabama. "No,
actually," said Hob. "She's going to have a shiner, too," said Alabama,
"you better hope she doesn't tell anyone you hit her." "That would be
sort of in keeping with the way things went back there generally," I
said, "you have to admit." I explained about the door. "She's never
done anything ridiculous," said Hob, "that I've seen. And her school is

even worse than ours where the ridiculous is concerned." "Oh, so now she's some noble character," said Alabama. Two crows took off from a snow-dusted mailbox. "It's getting bad," said Hob, "I'm glad we're doing this tonight." "I like you guys so I hope you won't be offended if I say I had other plans," I said. Hob released his odd, high laugh. He was hammered. "They only count as plans if they have a shot at working," said Alabama. She was dead sober.

She made us stop to buy tangerines at the fruit store near the subway at Ninety-Sixth. Full of white light and the blazing colors of leaves and rinds. The guys who owned it were Turkish. A father and son. My mother bought fruit there. The blueberries for her pancakes. "Do you want," Alabama said. I took one. "I don't dig citrus fruits," said Hob. "Who doesn't dig citrus fruits," I said. "This guy," he said, and indicated himself with his thumbs. Even Alabama laughed. I ate my tangerine on the platform. The juice stung my cuticles. Cold air poured over my cheeks. A crack in the infrastructure. A snowflake or two. "Look at that," said Hob, "they survived." The train thundered in. As it slowed, Alabama tipped a salute to the conductor. *Don't hassle him*: I was about to speak. But he responded, jerking his head backward. "Last car," said Hob. When we reached the doors, I saw Charthouse waiting inside. "Logistical perfection," he said, "we all strive for it." He carried a black canvas bag in his left hand and the badger-head cane in his right. I could still smell Maggie's perfume. Vincent sat behind him, legs extended, fanning open and closed a fresh deck of blue-back cards. "Ladies and gentlemen," he said when he saw me, "the daring young man on the flying trapeze." "What is that supposed to mean," I said. "You're losing focus," Charthouse said. And thus we got under way.

Between Spring and Canal, the car lights went out and the ventilation stopped roaring. Hob and Vincent stood by the rear door. The inset door window showed an endless vista of rails and glaring lights. They were throwing cards. "That can of seltzer," said Vincent, and whipped his arm floorward with a grunt. The card whistled as it cut air. The discarded can of seltzer sang when the card struck. "An overhand motion makes you look unprofessional," said Hob. Vincent gave him the deck. "Nature of things," said Vincent. "You have to cave to your elders and betters." "Dr. W.," said Hob. He meant the ad for Dr. Waldengarten, dermatologist, near the opposite end of the car. He threw. He hit the doctor's greasy, bland grin. Still whitely visible in the dimness. "So we're tied," said Vincent. The brakes shrilled. I lurched in my seat. Vincent fell on his hands. The cards splashed. "Due to a signal malfunction at Brooklyn Bridge–City Hall, we are currently experiencing delays on the four, five, and six lines," the conductor droned over the speakers. "Come on, really," I said. "Calm down," said Hob. "Signs and wonders," said Charthouse, rising from his seat. Alabama said, "Wood here's just got blue balls, captain." "Don't we all, one way and another," said Charthouse. He trotted to the rear door, stepping on cards. "I just bought that deck," said Vincent. "It's two fifty," said Charthouse as he opened the rear door. "Or it used to be." A steel rod glinted in his hand.

"You don't know what inflation is these days," said Vincent. "Questions of monetary policy do not concern me," said Charthouse. He handed Vincent a flashlight from the black bag. He gave us all flashlights. "Get moving," said Charthouse. I did. I stumbled when I reached the track bed. My flashlight beam danced across the ties. One palm spattered a puddle of runoff. Scuttering and quiet cries. Rats or mice. "We appreciate your patience": the conductor, again. You could hear the announcement outside the car as the light flickered back on and the train started to move. "Is this safe," I said. "As long as we don't dick around here too long, no question," said Charthouse. The tunnel air didn't stink. I assumed it would. Charthouse and Alabama light-scanned the walls. "Bingo," said Alabama. Her cone of light showed an even deeper darkness. A black doorway. "Up and at 'em," said Charthouse. We had to climb again, onto the access path. This time I didn't stumble. Only enough room to stand single file. The door opened inward. More darkness. The air pouring out colder. "No need to be afraid," said Vincent, "I'm right here." Through a tight smile. I thought about punching him. Cracking him across the mouth with the barrel of the flashlight I'd retrieved. Industrial. Or a cop flashlight, maybe. I assumed Alabama would shoot me if I did. Instead I said: "That's okay with me." "Positive thinking," said Charthouse, "is what I and others like to see."

Tunnels: They wash out your voice. Make it ghostly and thunderous. Like literature. "That round doesn't count," said Vincent. "It does, in fact," Hob said. Their argument close and racketing. The walls of the corridor pristine. White tile. Water dripped. "Let's stay focused, gentlemen," said Alabama. She was bringing up the rear. She had her gun out. I could tell by the way she sounded. I didn't want to check visually. "It amazes me how clean these walls remain," said Charthouse. His cane scraped and chimed. A rat banged my shoe and leaped over. I didn't mind. I like rats. Given the choice of coinhabitants city life offers, rats I prefer to roaches. They're mammals. You can understand their motivations. Charthouse's heavy, uneven gait broke our rhythm. I hoped they weren't going to make me take another suicide jump. A phone trilled. "Are you kidding me," said Charthouse. Vincent held up his phone. "The wonders of the modern age," he said. He was still dressed in a black suit. This time with a purple tie. He'd done that at school, too, I remembered. Even though you had to wear a uniform: blue blazer, gray pants, white shirt, and a blue-and-white tie. If you violate the law's letter while upholding its spirit, I think you can escape punishment. "Who is it," said Hob. "It's Mom," said Vincent. "That is touching," said Charthouse. The tunnel ended. I saw a white, high wall in the flashlight cones. We stopped moving. Bunched up. A beam flashed across a green-painted metal door. A gold, eye-shaped scrawl graffitied near the upper lintel. "Hob, would you do the honors," said Charthouse. Hob slid a key into the door's lock. The key glittered. "What was that thing on the door," I said, "that symbol." "What do you think," answered Alabama. "Easy now," said Charthouse. "I think this might actually be more difficult for you," said Vincent. To me. My hands curled into fists. I thought about Alabama's gun and calmed down. Hob opened the door. Warm yellow light leafed the tunnel floor. Three rats jumped the threshold. We followed them in.

I don't know why I was surprised to see a living room. Well lit and warm. The air smelling of oranges. Some herb. Bookshelves lined the walls. English titles, German titles, French. Other tongues. I was, as I said, no scholar. Leather chairs, their wooden legs gnawed on and scarred. A black, hexagonal wooden table in the room's center. Near which stood an old man in a pigeon-gray fedora. "Mr. Stone," said Charthouse. "Mr. Charthouse," said Mr. Stone, "and the lovely Ms. Sturdivant, I see. Standing there against the darkness. It is always a delight, an encounter with you." Alabama grinned and dipped her head. The door groaned closed behind her. "That's how you can tell you're dealing with a man of high quality," said Charthouse, "is he's polite."

Mr. Stone looked almost seven feet tall. His eyes ocean blue. He wore a gray suit and a silver-gray tie the exact color of his hair. A tiepin, too, set with a green stone. He leaned on the creaking back of his enormous black armchair. A large, tawny rat perched on the leather top edge, grooming its face near Mr. Stone's elbow. "This is the offensive lineman you mentioned," said Mr. Stone. He had an accent. German, I thought. "Come here," he said, "and let us see what we can see." Vincent had no more smart remarks to make. I stumbled up to the tall man with my flashlight still on. We shook hands. His enveloped mine. I have large hands. "Menachem Stone," he said. "Michael Wood," I said. "I imagine you have questions," he said. "Yes, sir, I do," I said. "Sir! That is excellent," said Charthouse, "that is exactly right." "Have a seat, Mr. Wood," said Mr. Stone. "Mr. Wood and Mr. Stone," said Charthouse, "it's the meeting of the natural nouns." Mr. Stone sat. Another rat, gray, leaped onto the back of his chair. I sat too. A black table between us. Charthouse and Alabama grabbed the remaining leather chairs. Hob and Vincent dragged up wooden stools. A third rat, black and beady eyed, scampered onto Mr. Stone's armchair.

"You are wondering," he said, cracking his protuberant knuckles, "why young Mr. Charthouse brought you here." I was. "It is not as simple to explain as it looks," he said. "I have to admit that it doesn't look simple to me," I said. "That is encouraging," said Mr. Stone, "you lack preconceptions." The three rats crouched. The black rat scampered toward his hand, and he stroked its pointy head. "Are you familiar with the works of Wolfgang Amadeus Mozart," said Mr. Stone. *Vulfgong*: his accent. "Not really, sir," I said. "Happily, that is a matter of complete irrelevance," said Mr. Stone. "The point I wish to impress upon you is that not anyone can be Mozart. But we all have a modicum at least of musical ability. This young Mr. Charthouse here understands." I began to wonder if this guy was an escaped Nazi. Lived in a secret tunnel. German accent. Fancy suit. It made sense to me. "Not that," said Mr. Stone, "very much the other thing, I am afraid." "Are you talking to me, sir," I said. "You know very well that I was," said Mr. Stone. "We all have ability. That's a beautiful sentiment," said Charthouse.

Everyone was looking at us. Alabama, Hob, and Vincent. "Mr. Wood," said Mr. Stone, "we are in the middle of a war." I laughed at that. I could not help myself. No one else laughed. So I stopped. When you're that age it's frightening to laugh on your own. "I assure you it is not funny, Mr. Wood," said Mr. Stone. "I've never served," I said. "There is no reason a man cannot don multiple hats," said Mr. Stone. He had a point. He palmed his long chin. "You do understand," he said, "if you say no all this is forbidden to you." I nodded. "And you understand this is quite real," he said. "That's the part I sort of have difficulty with," I said. "Do you have a cigarette," said Mr. Stone. I offered him the bundle of brown ones I had with me. "I'd like you to smoke one," said Mr. Stone. I set one in my mouth. Slapped my pockets. "I can't find my lighter," I said. Vincent snorted. I looked. Hob was holding it up: clear

THE WAR AGAINST

red plastic. "This is not a problem," said Mr. Stone, "put the cigarette in your mouth and light it, that is all. I am not asking you to perform an impossible feat. I am not asking you to *fly*." He grinned as he said *fly*. His teeth huge and white. The rats on his chair chittered in glee.

"What do you mean, 'a war,'" I said. "We're in a war against the assholes," said Hob. He had not spoken much to me so far. I think he was worried I'd make a fool of myself in front of Mr. Stone. "Makes sense," I said, "nobody likes assholes." "Mr. Callahan is correct, I am afraid," said Mr. Stone, "and I know an excessive amount about, as he puts it, assholes. Light the cigarette, please." The black rat danced. The gray rat chattered to the brown one. "And who are these assholes," I said. "They run the world," said Charthouse, "although you've never met any of them, I doubt." "Will Alabama shoot me if I don't," I said, "light it I mean." "You never know," said Alabama. The gray rat ran down from its perch. It crossed the black table and sat at my elbow. I admire rats. I still had to struggle not to flinch. "Wittgenstein likes you," said Mr. Stone, "I take that as a testament to your good character. And no. She will not. I have never permitted violence in my home. Light the cigarette, please."

The deck of cards was in my hands. I found myself shuffling it. The way you might find yourself biting your nails. The cigarette dangled from my mouth. It was still not lit. "Against the assholes," I said. I admired the phrase. I was not fond of assholes at that point in my life. Wittgenstein sat there eying me. As did my human companions. "It is a question of precision, Mr. Wood," said Mr. Stone, "Hob tells me you are an athlete. So you understand precision. Light the cigarette, please." His voice resonant and his eyes clear. He had not blinked once. So I sat there, pondering what to do, the cigarette hanging from my lips. *Well*, I thought, *if I can fly there's no reason that can't happen.* It's easy to let go of your prejudices when you're young. I tapped the deck to even it out. I shot the cards from hand to hand. My parents at home. With their shows about apes and dragonflies and their tennis rackets. The nuns at Saint Cyprian's adrift in their brown habits. My heartbeat slowed. Mr. Stone's voice smeared. I compressed the deck again. It felt alive against my palm. The cards arced out. Slow enough for me to count. They arced in a clean curve from my left hand to my right. *Professional*, I thought. I could see the fine lines of Alabama's ribs expanding and contracting beneath her white shirt, which said the words BIKINI KILL across her breasts. The light in the room changed color. I swear. Amber to bloody orange. Reminded me of a forgotten phenomenon. From physics class. Couldn't say what, precisely. I heard: the flutter of the cards. I smelled: sweet smoke. The cigarette blazed. For a second. It died almost at once.

Sufficient, though. "There," said Mr. Stone. Alabama clapped. Charthouse clapped, too. My whole body ached. My nose was bleeding. Mr. Stone took the deck of cards from me. "You must use higher-quality equipment," he said. "I stole this one," I said. "Praise the lord and pass the ammunition," said Vincent. Loud. Harsh. "Please lower your voice," said Mr. Stone. "A war," I said. "Yes," said Mr. Stone. "Assholes," I said. "Yes, Mr. Wood. Assholes," said Mr. Stone. "Are you an asshole?" "I am not," I said. When you have to choose, you have to choose. You'll have no time to decide. Yet you still have to choose. The inability to choose: that's what afflicts and crushes my generation. "I am glad to hear you say that," said Mr. Stone, "it is important to know where we all stand." I blotted my lip. I asked about the book. "Everybody asks about the book," said Mr. Stone, "I myself asked about it, when I was a younger man." "That's not an answer, though," I said. "It is not, I admit, but that is precisely the problem, Mr. Wood. We do not know. Who or what. No one does. There are theories. There are rumors." "Rumors," I said. Sweet smoke in my lungs. "The author was either a man of total obscurity or so expert at covering his tracks that even I have been unable to discover them, and I have been looking for fifty years." Wittgenstein danced and slapped at his whiskers. "Fifty years," I said. "It is a sad truth that the theurgists

THE WAR AGAINST

have done their best to ensure they remain nothing more than rumors. Nothing more than empty guesses," said Mr. Stone. *Theurgists*: no idea what it meant. The word Charthouse had used the night I met him. To ask if I served other masters. I assumed they were identical to the assholes Charthouse had mentioned. "And why can I light cigarettes now," I said, "it seems like a comic book thing." "First of all, I would not say that you can light cigarettes now," said Mr. Stone. "Point to you, sir," I said. "And you do not ask yourself, do you, why you can play football," said Mr. Stone, "or why you can sleep. The answer is simple: because you can. The book is anamnestic, to speak Platonically. Anyone, as I said, can whistle. Perhaps you remember certain moments on the playing field. Certain sun-flooded moments. Perhaps I, a salamander of fate, to quote one of my most beloved authors, escaped from the clutches of Hitler's minions. Anyone can whistle. And everyone does. Do you understand what I mean, Mr. Wood?"

Anamnestic and *Platonically*: also bafflers. I caught the general gist. I didn't say a word but I had already sided with him and with Hob, with Charthouse and Alabama, with Vincent, even. Against the assholes. Certain pledges you don't have to make out loud. Certain pledges it's better you keep silent. "By and large we live in ignorance of our abilities," said Mr. Stone, "which our antagonists prefer." "Is it magic you're talking about," I said. "Call it what you like," said Mr. Stone. He was up now, his hat scraping the ceiling. He swayed. As if in pain. Seemed to be part of his regular stance. "Look," he said. Pointing at a blank wall on the other side of the audience room. Eighteen feet of space. Rough, marked concrete. I got out of my chair to examine it. "I think this is about your reading level," said Vincent. "Please save your witticisms," said Mr. Stone.

The concrete warm against my fingertips. I saw what made it rough: hatch marks, cut into it. Four, then a slash through them. Another four, another slash. What you see in old prison movies. Where they're marking the days of their suffering and confinement. The marks covered the whole wall. Floor to ceiling, nearly. A blank patch near the upper left corner. Waiting to be filled in. "Is this how long you've been down here," I said. "Even I am not that old, Mr. Wood," said Mr. Stone. "These represent casualties I have seen. That I am responsible for. In the sense that a commanding officer is responsible for the deaths of his men and women." Hundreds. Thousands. I counted a few sets. Then gave up. "Casualties," I said. "Casualties, Mr. Wood," said Mr. Stone. "Of the assholes," I said. "Yes, Mr. Wood. Of the assholes," said Mr. Stone. "And do these assholes have names," I said. "Their names are legion," said Vincent. "If there's one thing I will not abide it's misquotation and misappropriation," said Charthouse.

9

He talked a lot about Hitler, the old man. The failed artist, he called him, the true spirit of the bourgeois. His motivations differed from no other second-rater of his era or ours. To be Hitler takes imagination, said Mr. Stone, though not too much; it takes will; it takes a certain inordinate love of reality. I tried to look serious and sensitive. That's what I do when Jews start talking about Hitler. Not that I've been around a lot of Jewish discussions. I remember only one Jewish student during my tenure at Saint Cyprian's, Reed Aschenfarb. He didn't last long. He didn't talk much about Hitler, either. I appreciated the way Mr. Stone had explained my situation to me. No nonsense about my unique nature and important fate. I liked the concept of a war. All adolescents do. He filled me in on the Erzmund problem, too: the best candidate, he said, was Alfons Froch, a professional Viennese gambler and fortune-teller whose checkered and obscure career came to an end when he died of syphilis in the midst of the Russian arrival in Berlin. His corpse, said Mr. Stone, was interred in a pauper's grave, in the shadow of a limeworks. In war, he said, no time is permitted to weep over such matters. Especially when you are the hunted, the quarry. He asked me if I knew what the word *Freiwild* meant. I told him no.

Mr. Stone's front door let us out in a building's garbage alley on Eleventh Avenue. I'd been expecting to return to the tunnel. I didn't show my surprise. I forced my mouth shut. You can't look like an innocent all the time. We had to hop a fence to reach the street. The raw scent of the water washed over us. Charthouse waved good night with his cane head and staggered off. Vincent went with him. He matched Charthouse's gait. My parents were asleep when I got home. They stayed that way. It turned out that *theurgists* meant "practitioners of ritual magic." *Anamnestic* meant "that which enables our recollections." The name he'd mentioned, Alfons Froch, appeared in my dream, otherwise unremarkable. I was alone in a meadow. At night. Great sky above. The dizzying health of the stars. I recognized no constellations. And the shapes of the distant trees at the meadow edge seemed alien too. Even the smell of the grass, strong and strange. A tall woman with pale hair was walking among the trees, her face turned half-away. Crows croaked. Water glinted in a stone basin. At the edge of which, along the lip, ran the simple, incomprehensible words ALFONS FROCH. In large yellow letters. Like a NO PARKING announcement on a curb. I woke up at dawn. I remembered fragments of my dream: a pale female face. A black bird. I did not feel tired. I'd slept four hours at most. My throat raw from the cigarettes. That's all. I wanted to laugh aloud.

Theurgists went to special schools, said Mr. Stone, a network of primary and secondary schools spanning the world. Most of them came from theurgist families, whole families, Mr. Stone said, of the obsequious and mighty. They spent their childhoods studying for the Certamen, also known as Damnation Day. A test, said Mr. Stone, a tragedy. I asked him if it was like the salto. Theurgists frown on our more immediate methods, he said. There was one such school in

THE WAR AGAINST

Manhattan, called Mountjoy House. I'd never heard of it. The chief patron of Mountjoy House was a man named Verner Potash, who also served as the de facto head of the theurgical community on the East Coast. The legend of Mountjoy is known far and wide, said Mr. Stone, and you would find echoes of it in all manner of mendacious and saccharine books. The school had existed more or less since the Dutch first arrived on these shores, originally under the supervision of a man called Godfried Brink. When the colony had fallen to English control the institution changed hands and changed names. William Mountjoy served in the Cabal Ministry of King Charles II, said Mr. Stone. An eminent scholar, he said, among the greatest of his age.

Hob rustled and groaned. Dawn, blue-gray dawn, in the windows. Alabama asleep in my desk chair, snoring. A higher register than my mother. Arms loose, feet on the floor. Her pistol on my desk, next to the biology textbook. The book's yellow cover displaying an enormous photo of a grasshopper's face and mandibles. The gun's huge barrel pointed at the door. Hob lay on my rag rug, underneath his coat, a ball of dust kicking around in his exhalations. He and Alabama both looked pale and weak in the morning light. They'd come home with me. I'd invited them. I didn't want to be inhospitable.

De facto: I had to dredge that one up. As in not de jure. Not by right. Simply by brute fact. Potash is the informal name for potassium salts. That I knew from my mother. The rest of Mr. Stone's lecture gripped me because it was absolutely strange to me. Nothing exerts the same hold on you as the completely unknown does. Like: theurgy's success depended on incantation, formulae, alchemical techniques, wands. In other words, theurgy's success depended on fear and weakness, said Mr. Stone, as the cigarette smoke thickened around us. It seemed to me a white spotlight had isolated us from Hob, Alabama, Charthouse, and Vincent. Like we sat alone, in deep, slow discussion, on a stage. Theurgy has its roots in the early priesthoods of man, the Sumerian, the Greek, the Judaean, the Zoroastrian, said Mr. Stone.

THE ASSHOLES

I listened. Theurgy is not in fact different from religion, in the sense that it requires supplication and nothing more. Humans, he said, are constantly hunting, forever seeking and finding an idol to abase themselves before. For centuries, theurgy had been the dominant form of magic practiced in the West and the East. While most theurgists never attained public, historical prominence, Mr. Stone said, notable exceptions existed. Adolf Hitler, he said, had been a minor theurgist and had enjoyed the aid of one of the greatest theurgists of the twentieth century, Rudolf von Sebottendorf. The art Mr. Stone practiced had no name. Call it what you like, he said again and again, it would be an act of presumption to give it a name. Like all slaves, he said, theurgists were full of irony, anger, and presumption to authority.

From my bed, my dream of the concrete pool draining away, I watched Alabama. I admit it. Her skin looked fragile. Bruise-blue hollows under her eyes. I watched Hob. He grinned in his sleep. I thought about how to explain her presence to my parents. Hob they would not object to. I'd never brought a girl home before to spend the night. What the theurgists tell us requires study and paraphernalia requires only courage and will, said Mr. Stone. I hefted Alabama's gun. Rubber bands corrugated its butt. I quick-drew three times, into my mirror. "You talking to me," I said. Dark circles under my eyes. Inexplicable bruises along my ribs.

The nature of war, said Mr. Stone, was simply the tyrannical nature of the majority making itself known. He bore no grudge against the theurgists, he called them slaves only because they were. Slaves of what? Call their masters what you like. His pet rats kept stone-still as he spoke. Since the Treaty of Constantinople, he said, when, perhaps, the theurgists realized for the first time what an advantage they had in numbers, this war against their freer compatriots had been unceasing. Mass exiles. Mass killings. The crushing under the heel of the most innocent and helpless. Those who wished merely to save their families. To grow crops. To protect their wives and children. Those who wished

THE WAR AGAINST

to fly unaided. Without rods or staves. Without incantations. In the smoke I saw images. A long, gray line of oxcarts snaking across a far horizon, between the green grass and the blue sky. A man dressed in red robes, carrying a crosier in one hand and a dagger in the other, limping toward the naked throat of a young woman chained to an oak board. Her head shaved, her legs spread, her arms bound, her irises slate blue, her mouth clenched in anger or pride.

My head still ached. I crept into the hall. My mother still snored. My father was already awake. Not a catastrophe. He had no reason to be suspicious of anything. "Morning, professor," he said, "more wind sprints last night?" I told him yes. "Well, it's not so much me but your mother gets worried," he said. "She's still asleep," I said. "She fell asleep pretty early, too, not even one," he said. My mother's deep sleeping had served as a joke of long standing between us. "Sawing logs," I said.

Mr. Stone himself was a victim. Before the Second World War he had been a mathematician in Berlin. In the field of harmonic analysis. He told me when I asked what it was that he could not explain concisely. I told him that was all right: I never pretended to be a genius at math. He was no genius either, he said, just a humble observer. As such he could not explain the events of that war, he said, other than as Hitler's search for Froch, or rather von Sebottendorf's search for Froch, who managed to elude him, who managed to escape, said Mr. Stone, into the arms of an obscure and sordid death. This search had claimed as incidental casualties Mr. Stone's wife and child, his promising career. His life. Mr. Stone's wife and child had been named Helen and Gerhard. He'd wanted the boy to have a German name, to avoid the kicks and insults he had suffered due to the alien nature, he said, of his own name. At that time he had not even known who Froch was, he was innocent of any expertise, he had only discovered Froch's work in the Mauthausen concentration camp, when a fellow prisoner named Weisbrod introduced him to it. This fellow prisoner was soon executed for being unable to work. He died in a ditch, shot at the base of his skull, his face submerged in a shallow, muddy pool. Mr. Stone had taken his book, and thus taken the first step on the unpredictable path that led him to this redoubt, he said, beneath the streets. At Mauthausen he'd seen one of Sebottendorf's minions saw a woman in half. Not as an illusion. In order, he said, to provide enough blood and agony to appease the powers he believed he served. Mountjoy House, he said, was not of course Mauthausen. Yet the fundamental nature of man does not change, and a murderous slave is still a slave. Verner Potash was a Jew. He was not suggesting anything to the contrary. Nonetheless you might see in the events of the Second World War a logical end to the activities of the theurgists. The great trample the little and the strong trample the weak. That, said Mr. Stone, was the method of the human world.

"Got any big plans for break," said my father. "Nothing special," I said, "there's really not a lot going on. I mean other than Christmas." "Your grandmother is coming," said my father, "so we'll have to hide the liquor." As long as Hob and Alabama stayed in my room, I'd be fine, I calculated. I didn't trust either of them to do so, was the problem. I could just see Alabama waltzing out into the living room to thank my parents for their hospitality. Gun and all. Hob they wouldn't mind, although I'd heard them express the opinion, once, that both he and Vincent were weirdos, as were their parents, Padraig ("He changed the spelling of his name, for Christ's sake," as my father put it) and Laura. My father wore his tennis clothes: a crimson tracksuit and white shoes, which he cleaned every Sunday with a toothbrush, and a yellow sweatband across his forehead. He was gulping water. He advocated early-in-the-day hydration as a cure-all. He seemed to be correct. I can't remember him ever being sick. I removed a glass from the prongs of the dishwasher, to fill it. "What's that on your arm," he said, "is that a tattoo?" I looked. I saw. I crowed out a laugh. I'd managed to forget it happened. Compared to the rest of the night it was a minor event.

Hob was already mostly unconscious when I got inked. "Good night, sweetheart, weeeeeel, it's time to go, ba-da-dum-da-duuum," he crooned. Seconds later: deep breaths. As a result I had to sit stiffly on the edge of my bed, avoiding staring at Alabama, who was leafing through my biology textbook. Each page made a loud, precise crack as she turned it. We had my desk lamp for light. Nothing else. Alabama kept yawning, and she spun my chair around—the mechanism squealed—and lurched over toward me, grinning, her eyelids half-down. My pulse started to race. I started to reach for her. She grabbed my right arm. Her fingers dug in hard under the bracelet of fortune. She pushed up my sleeve and placed her index finger against my forearm. "Ready," she said. I nodded. I was. For anything. She made a few quick, firm, curving strokes against my skin. Tongue extruded in concentration. She didn't speak while she was tracing these lines and she didn't look at me, she looked at my inner forearm. She passed out in my desk chair right afterward and I hadn't bothered to examine her work. I saw now: It was the symbol. From Mr. Stone's green door. The schematic outline of an open eye. Neatly, blackly inked into my skin halfway between elbow and wrist. I scrubbed at it. No pain. Nothing.

"It's a team thing," I said to my father, "it's just for football." "You better hope it's temporary," said my father.

10

The eel was staring at me. Looking at me with an intent you can't find among animals. Its eyes vibrant. "I think you'll agree that my presence would be creepy," said Vincent, "especially if the kids are your age." "I concur," said Alabama. "We're still going," said Hob.

I didn't object. As I said, I like parties. This one, said Hob, wouldn't really get going for a while. I didn't object. I like the aimless hours before parties. For me they meant, once: drinking and bullshitting with Simon Canary or one of the other social actors in my life. What it meant now, I had no idea. An eel looking at me. One element, at least, of the new preparty regime. "I can't come anyway," said Vincent. "What do you have like a date," said Hob. "Just an appointment," said Vincent. "Play another round at least," said Hob, "we got interrupted in the subway."

Hob's warm-up: muted compared to his brother's. Vincent yelped, swung his arms. Snapped the fresh deck open in a fan. Snapped it shut. He unknotted his tie. Knotted it back up. I knew the maneuvers. You see similar rituals in locker rooms. All Hob did was crack his knuckles,

THE WAR AGAINST

twice. "You ready," said Vincent. A card-throwing contest. The latest installment of what I gathered was an eternal fight between Hob and Vincent. In which they fared about the same. That's fraternal life. Or so I'm told. I have no siblings. Only children have to wonder if their status is an implied insult. Their targeting rule was simpler, this time. You had to hit this one lighter brick up high on the wall. I failed and failed to do so as Hob and Vincent racked up points. "Jank," said Vincent. Alabama didn't join. "Hey, sub in for me," I called over to her. "Nope," she said. "Playing against her is boring," said Vincent. "What do you mean," I said. "You want to show him," said Hob. "I always knew you were a voyeur, Wood," she said, "look at your eyes hanging out of your head." Went back to her violin. "What's the kid's name again," I said. I meant who was throwing the party. "I don't know the host's name but there's this guy there I need to talk to," said Hob. "There's this guy there you need to talk to. What are you, like a professional of some kind, now? Who is it," said Vincent, over the violin. Alabama was playing as we threw cards. Sad, strict music. "This kid named Quinn. Quinn Klayman. You don't know him. You never met him," said Hob. When I asked Alabama what the music was she did not speak. Her closed eyelids fluttered. Alabama's bow arm moved, rapid and certain. I saw the mark on the inner forearm, same as mine. I wondered who had done hers. "It's the chaconne," she said when she finished and opened her eyes, "from J. S. Bach's violin partita in D minor. Don't stare at me." I was staring. She had that effect on me. "I thought that was pretty sensational," said Hob. Vincent applauded with just his fingertips. We all drank. The music unspooled and unspooled in my head. One of the perils of being illiterate about the arts is that you can't just shrug a piece of music or a painting off as X or Y classification. You have no framework to imprison them in. You have to confront them as is.

A holiday mood. No other way to describe it. Charthouse was gone. "Ladies and gentlemen, you'll have to excuse me," he had said as left, "but I must go see a man about a dog." He had a suitcase with him in Karasarkissian's basement. Brown leather, seamed with age. He wore a black suit and a white shirt, glowing against the pointed high lapels. Instead of a necktie an aquamarine scarf, folded into a fist-sized knot. "Later, captain," said Alabama. That's just what she called him. He held no official rank. "Where you going," said Vincent. "Why do you even ask that question," said Charthouse. We all lifted our glass goblets, our plastic cups, the fake skull Vincent preferred to drink out of. ET IN ARCADIA EGO carved into its truncated brow. "Alabama, you know how to get in touch. Merry Christmas and happy Hanukkah to our Jewish friends," he said. We all echoed his double farewell. He climbed up the ladder and closed the hatch. His cane-aided, three-beat steps echoed. And then we were, basically, alone. Hob brought everyone refills. He wanted all of us to be welcome. Or be at the same level of intoxication.

It didn't affect Hob's play. Didn't affect his brother's. Mine: possibly. When the card-throwing ended, the score stood at eleven to Vincent, twelve to Hob, and precisely zero to me. "Well," said Vincent, "I believe etiquette says you are in the catbird seat now." "You don't have to order me around," said Hob. The sleight Hob showed us is called THE FOUR WINDS. He cut the deck and fanned it open, two halves, and spread the cards on the table at the feet of the bottles, to show us it was complete and intact. "Everybody take an ace," he said, "and, Alabama, as a woman, I insist you take the extra." "Insist shit," she said. She took two, though. The brilliant-blue eels in the whiskey blinked their golden eyes. "What are they," I blurted out. "They belong to Charthouse," said Vincent, "he says they brighten up the place." He refilled the skull cup. "Mark the cards," said Hob, "don't lose focus." I made an X. Vincent drew a pentagram. Alabama wrote EAT ME on one and HOB on the other. "Hand them over," said Hob. He shuffled the deck, made the cards jet between his hands in a bending arc. Then he said, "Check your wallets." My ace, the club, I found between two one-dollar bills. Alabama found her two: spade and heart. The writing had been changed. *IN YOUR DREAMS*, said the spade. *SUCKER*, said the heart. Vincent pulled his out and said, "I admit that's well-done, Hob." Instead of an ace, he had a joker. Instead of the regular joker, he had a double-headed drawing of a stick-waving fool in blue and red motley: his own face and a gaping skull. The eels, or legless salamanders, or sea serpents, circled and circled in the carboys. "Quinn," said Vincent, "definitely a van rapist." Hob said, "It's not a date. I just need to see him. It's not even a thing." "Well, don't get van raped," said Vincent. "Rape jokes aren't funny," said Alabama. She was hooting with laughter as she spoke.

"Since you opened your mouth, the burden falls to you. You know the rules," said Vincent. He handed her the deck. "I'm not your trained monkey," she said. "It's for Wood. It's educative. Besides, he's been staring at you since he got here," said Vincent. Alabama sighed. She shut her eyes. She took the top card between the index and middle fingers of her shooting hand. Flung it. No warm-up. No knuckle-cracking. Blind. The card, the eight of clubs, hit the lighter brick Hob and Vincent had aimed at. She took two cards. Handed me the deck. Repeated the maneuver, two-handed. They both hit the brick. "Ninth rung of the ladder," she said. Turned her back. Threw the card over her shoulder, still blind. It hit the ninth rung. "You didn't say from the top or bottom," said Vincent. "The third doorknob, then," said Alabama, "from the right. Okay?" Eyes shut, back turned. She used her left hand. It hit the doorknob. Hard enough to make the metal ring. I never knew cards could do that. "Hob," she said. "And this is the thanks I get for being the perfect gentleman," said Hob. She took two cards in each hand. "It's payment for those aces," she said as she hurled them. They all hit him, at the same time, in the face. He leaped back. "That hurt, seriously," he said. "It never fails to annoy me," said Vincent, "that you can do that." "I think that satisfies your bullshit requirement," she said to Vincent.

He already had a book in his hands. ELEMENTARY BOTANY, said the spine. He flipped it to a page and showed us: a plate illustration of a sunflower. "Nothing up my sleeves," he said, "nothing in my hands. Well, other than this book." He shut his eyes. He balanced the book on his palms and then flipped it upside down. A torrent of sunflower petals poured out of it. Bright yellow. Golden yellow. Vincent was gritting his teeth. When the torrent stopped his shoes were covered, his cuffs. A yellow carpet spread around him. Reached almost to our feet. I lifted a petal. "No counterfeits here," he said, "right, my athletic friend? And don't miss part two." It was real. Warm as though it had just arrived from a spring night. I cupped it in my fist. Vincent closed the book, hurled it onto the green couch, and spread his hands above the petals. Long white fingers trembling. "He overdoes the gestures," whispered Hob as his brother raised his spread hands ceilingward. The air hummed. Or not hummed. Thrummed. Your hand on the hood of a running car. With a grassy, murmuring rustle, the sunflower petals rushed together, green spots appeared, spread, stretched, the rushing rustle grew and grew, and sunflowers rose up from the high yellow carpet of petals, or the petals became sunflowers, forcing themselves higher, their green stalks lengthening and thickening and the centers darkening, shoots curling down into the cracks of the floor. Leaves springing erect. Until Vincent was obscured by the growing grove. He cried out. In triumph and pain. He stumbled back into view. His forehead sheeted with sweat and his face empty of blood. "Sterling," said Hob, "one hundred percent." His brother swayed. "I'm okay, thanks for asking," he said. He clutched at his stomach. The sunflowers waved on their green stalks. Above us the streets. On the streets filthy snow.

My heart pounded. In gratitude. My hands and fingertips hummed. Then I saw everyone looking at me. The way you look at a guy who's waiting too long. "Uh, I think it's your turn," panted Vincent. "What do you mean," I said. "Do I really have to explain," he said. "You've already done the hard stuff," said Hob. Alabama was fiddling with the pegs at the end of her violin. "You mean just," I said. "We mean

THE WAR AGAINST

just," said Vincent. He had a cigarette screwed in now. Ribbons of blue smoke curdled and floated. I had no plan. With pickup games or a gym, instrumental purposes leap out at you. The objects here lacked that family resemblance. On one shelf: four plastic army men, a small metal model of the solar system, a jagged thumb of amethyst, a postcard with Mao Tse-tung's face surrounded by a sunburst. The silence stretched. Alabama tested the tone of a string on her violin. Above her, an age-dimmed mirror set in a frame of blue metal. Openwork. In the mirror, I saw Hob grinning. Right at me. And that's when I had my idea. Nothing to it. A simple reaction. I took the mirror from its rusted hook. I looked into it. "Ladies and gentlemen," said Hob, "allow me to introduce the Master of Enigmas, Michael Wood." He gestured at me. Doffed a top hat he wasn't wearing. Swept a cloak that didn't exist through the air. He hadn't given anyone else an introduction. *I lucked out*, I thought. I brought the mirror to eye level. I kept breaking into a grin. I had no idea what to say or do. I felt Hob's bright eyes on the back of my neck. So I said the first words that bubbled into my empty head. "Maggie Ravapinto." I spoke to the faded glass. Nothing happened. My heartbeat was slowing. That's all. "Maggie Ravapinto," I said. Voice low and strained. The mirror's surface flickered. Reminded me of a television screen, an old cathode-powered one, warming up. The metal thrummed. A single high note. "Maggie Ravapinto," I whispered. I'm not a pervert. It was just the first thing that occurred to me. The screen flickered again, the metal hummed higher, and the glass flared into life. A white, circular blaze. It hit my face like sun.

When the light cleared, I saw: A blue-walled, neat room, containing a large bed. On one wall a poster for the Museum of Natural History; on another a black-and-white enlarged movie poster, a woman's face painted in outline with a mustache scrawled on. JULES ET JIM, said the title. A white curtain waved in a draft. Everyone was gathering around me to watch. Maggie entered the frame. Her hair was wet. She wore a lilac towel. Nothing else. "Damn," said Vincent. "I told you she was hot," said Alabama. Maggie tugged at the flap of her towel and pulled it free. I saw again her breasts, her hip bones, her thighs, her tawny pubic hair. All beaded still with water. *What you're doing is not wrong*: a whisper. My arms started to shake. A drop of blood slid from my nose and struck the floor. "There he goes," said Vincent, "displaying his sensitive side." The mirror slipped from my grip. It threw pale streaks of light as it fell, the beam hitting wall, floors, ceiling. Left these briefly phosphorescent patches wherever the beam struck. When it hit the ground, as the physical laws of the universe dictate, it shattered. Glass shards flew. I figured I was done. The Christmas lights on the wall flickered. A dry, sewer-scented wind rose up. "Jank," said Vincent.

In the dimming room, images of Maggie flickered into life all over. Above every shard of glass, I guessed. I was still shaking. The images wrapped their towels around their hair. "What is this," said Vincent. The images paused. They turned. "I think they heard you," said Alabama. The images stared off. Distracted or frightened. They adjusted their eyes so that they were looking at us. Each of us. My blood thudded in my ears. More drops hit the floor. Hob said, "Okay, enough." The images grinned a slow unitary grin. Their faces stretched. Their eyes, even the whites, were getting paler. Their hair losing its color. Their pointed teeth gleamed. The air temperature dropped. The images opened their black mouths. I was not afraid. I was cold. I could not look away from those open mouths, those black mouths, which seemed to be forming the words of my name. "Mike," said Alabama. The images of Maggie: I could see inside their throats. Black and red. "Mike," said Alabama. The images raised their pale arms. They opened them. Scars, I saw, began to blossom across their white throats. I counted twelve. The apostles: that's what I kept thinking. "Mike, what are you doing," said Alabama. "I don't know," I said. My voice driven up an octave. Terror and incomprehension.

"You don't know," she screamed, "what do you mean you don't know." "Can you just," I said, "don't you have a gun." "A gun?" she said.

Voice raw and high. The images of Maggie now moved off the mirror fragments and advanced, their hands raised, the fingertips flexed into white hooks, their mouths open in soundless cries of hunger. They all turned to face Hob. Who had his back to a corner. Vincent made the first move. He ground the broken glass beneath his heels. This did nothing. The images encircled Hob, who was gasping and saying, "What do I do. What do I do. Nothing's working, guys. Mike, what did you do." The air was iron-cold. The sewer stink deeper and ranker. The light almost gone except for a pale, nauseating glow. The images. Their skin. Leaking from them. Vincent's sunflower grove black, wasted, the flowers crumpled, the stalks split and dry. It tumbled into ash as I watched. "Come toward us, just come toward us," Alabama shouted at Hob. "I can't move, they're like stopping me from moving," he yowled. A subtle keening sound rose from everywhere. The noise of a distant wind. Or a siren. I ran without thinking. Rushed toward the images. That same weird wave of slowness hit, the reddening of light I'd seen in Mr. Stone's home. I had no idea what I was going to do. Only that I was going to do it. Trouble was, I tripped. Like a fucking idiot. Over a three-legged stool I missed in the near-dark. Knocked the breath out of me and left me on the cold cement. I was back on my feet soon. Not soon enough. "Get up, get up and help him, it's your fault," Alabama yelped. Vincent just sobbed his brother's name over and over again. The images had closed on Hob, the two in the lead, and one was restraining his arms while the other tore red wounds open in his torso, his face, his throat.

He screamed. He screamed himself into silence. His mouth working. His shirt bloody. Pink foam covered his lips. The images bent to finish their tearing. Hob went down. Fell in on himself. I heard his head strike the cement. The images, as one, wheeled. To face me. I saw blood on their talons. On their teeth. I screamed too. Deep and raw. The last light failed. I closed my eyes. Waited to feel the cold blades of their nails and fangs.

What I heard first: Vincent's laugh. Dry and sure. Then a slow, steady clap. I opened my eyes. The lights were back on. Alabama was applauding. Hob, who still lay in his corner, whose shirt and skin were still covered with bloodstains, rose to his feet. The wounds lipping shut and the continental red patches on his shirt fading as I watched. He crowed out laughs even as he apologized. "Sorry, Michael. I'm so sorry, Michael. It's like a tradition, okay? Kind of a good-sportsmanship litmus situation." I looked around. No images. No pale, dead light. Just the warm, oddly furnished basement. The eels calmly turning in the whiskey carboys. The doors sitting in their frames. Vincent was crouched down over the mirror shards with a whisk broom and a dust-pan. "What," I mumbled, "what." "Someone has to keep this place clean, Kreskin," said Vincent. "What's Kreskin," I said. My numb lips and tongue loosened. My pulse slowed. The sweat on my brow dried. "So I," I said. "Flying colors, you passed with," said Alabama. "He made me think I was already dead," she went on, "walking the halls of the dead. I literally pissed myself." She admitted this without any visible shame. "Oh yeah," said Vincent, "I remember that. With those sconces of blue fire." "Let's go to this motherfucking party," said Hob. Out of breath. But only slightly. "I am like totally wired."

11

Three bulky crows. At rest on a huge windowsill, into which a series of leaves and curling vines was carved. You could hear music leaking down into the street, from very high up. Total crap. Singing, indifferent plucks at an acoustic guitar.

"Why are there crows here, Hob," said Alabama. I hadn't spotted them until she spoke. He said, "Don't worry. It's not even a thing." "Are these kids from Mountjoy," she said. Hob said, "Maaaaybe." "Maybe," said Alabama. "Look, they're not like dangerous," said Hob. "Nonetheless, I'm going home." And she was off the curb. Arm up in a cab salute. "No, wait, please," said Hob, "I'm sorry. I'm sorry. I didn't say because I thought you wouldn't come. I promise it's not weird. I'm not like trying to do anything." He looked forlorn. His eyes wet in the streetlight. He even had a hand on her arm. Small and pale. The fingers hard looking and slender. The nails blunt. That amazed me. "I just don't want to go in there alone and I need to see Quinn, okay? He took something from me, okay?" The crows twitched their heads. In unison. So that they all had their eyes, dark points, turned toward Hob and Alabama. "What did he take," said Alabama. "It's stupid," said Hob. "If it's stupid then why are we here," said Alabama. "Okay, look. Okay. It was a gift. What Quinn took. From a friend. Okay? From this guy I used to know. Okay? Said he wanted me to have it. Okay? And it like *meant* a lot to me. I know you think that's gay or whatever"—and as he said *gay* he curled his fingers into quote marks—"but that's what it is. If you want me to go in there myself, then I will. Or just with Michael." Alabama looked up at the crows. One of them shat. A brilliant streak on the concrete sill. "You and Wood," said Alabama. "If you leave that's what'll happen, though," said Hob, "I mean not that we'd kill anyone or burn anything down or anything." His eyes still wet. Still liquid. He looked young and frail. His lever worked. Alabama was already leaping up the short staircase to the building door. Her boots scraped the cold pavement. "What number," she said. "Penthouse," said Hob. "Of course," said Alabama. Rhythmic and precise. Behind us the naked elms of Gramercy Park rattled. A sadist's park. My father said that. Because you can slip in behind a key holder. And not slip out again until a key holder releases you. He knew from experience.

Alabama's mood had improved very modestly by the time we got to the apartment door. She was explaining about the crows. "They're like drones, sort of," said Alabama. "Way worse than that. They have eyes. They have actual brains. Drones just have cameras or infrared sensors or whatever," said Hob. "Actual brains. I like that. Who's the actual host," Alabama said. "Eleanor. Something. Eleanor something," said Hob. "That's helpful," she said. I think it was the surprise that upset her. People hate surprises. Rightly so. The Mountjoy factor was less irksome. She even started talking shit as we waited for the door to open. "Oh, I go to Mountjoy, my pussy hurts," she said, "oh, I go to Mountjoy, I got sand in my vagina." I was cracking up. We'd killed two pints of whiskey in the cab. The driver telling us, again and again, "You are too young to drink, mister and miss." Alabama lifted the third pint and pulled. The liquor chuckled. The door swung. Hob said, "Hey!" His voice calm and bright. He slid past the elongated, hollow-eyed girl standing and watching us. Alabama just stared at her, pint in hand, until she quailed. I came last. I could already tell the party, considered as a party, was a failure. Knots of kids stood stiffly. Twos and threes. Talking in quiet, serious voices. Or loud, serious voices: arguments had broken out among the knots. In the grating, pleased tone used to deliver correct answers. The lights: too bright. The liquor laid out on the kitchen counter: too meager. I smelled no weed. No cigarette smoke. The music rattled and whined onward. Hob was asking everyone where Quinn was. Alabama and I just drifted in his wake. "Hey," said a towering kid with floppy brown hair. Two long wings against either side of his face. He wasn't talking to me. He wore a blazer. Navy. A corn-colored crest on the breast pocket: an owl with a sheaf of wheat in its talons. The Mountjoy school jacket, I assumed. Most of the kids had them on. Alabama didn't speak. "I said hey," said the floppy-haired kid. A reader of long books. I could tell. To impress girls. And then, when they aren't impressed, tries to make them feel stupid. So that they'll fuck him. Suck his cock. Been known to work. Peter Neal used that method. Seemed dishonest to me. Alabama didn't answer. She took another pull and belched in the kid's face. He stepped back and flapped open his mouth to speak. He flapped it closed. "That's right," said Alabama.

Hob wanting company made sense. This thin hostility poured off all the party elements, off the kids in their stiff-looking jackets, the shitty music, the harsh light. Didn't get any quieter when we strode in. It was quiet in the first place. But the pitches of the arguing voices fell. Though whomever Hob asked answered back. Physical cowardice: it distorts your behavior. The elongated girl from the door watched us. I waved. Hob was standing, now, at the mouth of a dark hallway. He jerked his head. "He's apparently like tripping really hard," he said as we walked away from the minimal noise of the too-bright party. "Even better," said Alabama. The hallway long. Photos of a family on the walls. I couldn't make out their faces. Certificates. The lettering blurred when I leaned in to read it. "Don't worry about that," said Hob, "it's just part of their general BS." A darkened, wide room spread out before us. The floor slabbed with moonlight. The walls mostly glass. An empty, lightless terrace beyond. "He's out there," said Alabama. "I wouldn't want to be around these dicks if I was tripping. Were," I said. My mother had a habit of correcting me on subjunctives.

Two of the kids in jackets were peering at us from the bright end of the hallway. "Can I help you," I called out to them. They looked at me. Their faces blank and still. "What are you doing," said the guy. One had his hair buzzed almost down to the scalp and round, red-tinted cheeks. The other wore a modest fake diamond in a stud in her nose. It caught the light. "We're contemplating the absolute," said Alabama. They backed off. The limping, muddy noise of the party continued. Hob had slipped out onto the terrace. I followed with my fists cocked. Alabama had pushed her jacket aside. Her hand hovering over the gun butt.

The air brick-cold. You couldn't see much: the terrace was big but had an impoverished view. The backs of other buildings. A concrete courtyard with a black, endless-looking drain in it. There were some green wooden chairs and a green table, a green-and-white folded umbrella. All looking deadened. The way patio furniture does in the winter. Even though it was clear someone had been using the table. A bottle of vodka, half-drunk, stood near the umbrella pole. A woolen hat. A pair of gloves. Some slender black object I couldn't make out. Hob grabbed it. Alabama closed the glass door. I couldn't see the drinker. "Really genius idea, Hob," said Alabama, "can we leave now."

Then we heard it: the unmistakable sound of male urination. Rattling, ringing. And a tuneless whistle that rose and fell, rose into a stream of mumbled, muttered words and fell back into wordlessness. The terrace had a panhandle-shaped area screened off by two juniper hedges in green wooden planters. The pissing and singing noise came from there. It was flush against a blind brick wall. No windows. A bunch of decorative crap hung on it: tiles with green glazing, fisherman's nets, wooden masks with big mouths, a mirror in a round green frame. At the end of the narrow oblong, a kid stood by the terrace railing, pissing over the edge. His back to us. Between his spread legs I saw the pale, lit stream of urine falling as it arched beyond the railing, falling into whatever access alley the courtyard looked over. The void, I thought. His whistling had a whining, self-infatuated quality. He stopped pissing. A soft, quiet flapping sound: he was shaking his dick. The tight, short buzz of his zipper. Alabama's shoes squeaked. Setting up her stance for shooting. The kid turned around.

A little older than us, I guessed. Short, like Hob. Thin, like Hob. The moon blanked his glasses. Shone on his wet, pudgy lips. "Hello hello hello," he said. We didn't answer. The famous Quinn. The thief. "Who are yoooooooou guuuuys," Quinn drawled. His voice uncertain, a little hoarse. Loose. He sounded the way all the kids I'd spoken to while they were tripping sounded. I could see his pupils, too, dilating and contracting in the dead yellowed light. "Give it back," Alabama said. "What are you talking about," said Quinn. "Give it back," said Alabama. Her voice dead still. Dead cold. "You're not from enforcement. I know what enforcement looks like," said Quinn. When he spoke, I saw his teeth: more pointed than they should have been. Ivory yellow. Vincent's van-rapist remark seemed prescient. He kept glancing over our shoulders. I figured it was a trick. To get us to take our eyes off him. He was clearly a pussy, anyway, so I wasn't too worried. "Are you thieves," he said, "there's nothing here for you to steal." He was smiling now. A real shit-eater's grin. "Give it back," said Alabama. She had her gun on him. He looked into the barrel.

"I'm here to claim my destiny," he said. I had to hold back a laugh. You can't take anyone who talks about their destiny seriously. The whole concept is a joke. "Your destiny," said Alabama. "I'm here to claim it," he said. He went into his pocket. Alabama said, "Do not move." Quinn stopped. "I just want to show you the map." And giggled. Dead echoes. That uncertain, there-gone-there smile and those chaotically active pupils. "What map," said Alabama. "It's a map, it shows you things. You just have to ask it the right questions," said Quinn, "it's a maaaaaaagic map. Surely you know what a map is. The map is not the territory." He had gone into radio-announcer voice. I figured we were in the clear. Three of us, one carrying a gun, against a drug-addled nerd spouting incomprehensible nonsense about a map. Quinn was moving. Slow. Still moving. "You're not from enforcement. The map told me to come here. It's mine by right," he said, "but fuck my uncle, though, okay? But I love him. I love him. Listen, let me past, okay?" "You don't get to make the decisions here," said Alabama.

And also: "Hob, what is he talking about." "I have no idea," said Hob. "This is a test," said Quinn, "but the problem with tests is that they can't get all the way in, you know? I have a soul!" He was yodeling. "I have a soul, fuck yeah!" Then he grabbed his ears and held them like he was trying to keep his head from flying away. "Calm down," said Alabama, "you have something that belongs to us. Return it. Then we leave. Then you can leave." "My choices are none of your business," Quinn growled. He let go of his ears. "Give us what you stole and this will all be over," Alabama said. "If you leave now I won't hurt you," said Quinn. Another dialogue addict. My life was full of them. Alabama said, "You shouldn't use language like that." "Get out of here, come on," moaned Quinn. Sweat shone on his forehead, behind his glasses lenses. "You're just stupid and envious. You don't even know what this is. It's fucking destiny! Can't you see that," he shrilled. No one responded. An asshole. An archetypical asshole. I don't say that as an insult. Merely as a description. It occurred to me that he probably had excellent grades. Or marks. Or whatever you got in his school. "We're going to take back what you stole," Alabama said, "and that's the end of it." "You insect," said Quinn. "I already told you you can't have it." "Don't make this any harder than it is," said Alabama. "You're not going to shoot me," said Quinn. "That is a matter of contention," said Alabama.

Quinn fingered his weird teeth. He cleaned his glasses with his white shirt edge. "I left a thing on the whatever. On the outdoor table. Back there. Do you mind if I get it? I won't like make any sudden moves," he said. He was already walking. I didn't like this. Alabama was getting set to fire. Feet planted and neck tense. "You worthless failure." Not Quinn. It was Hob. "What did you just say," said Quinn. Maybe he hadn't actually understood him. In the end, if you're a big enough asshole you can't understand anything. "It's mine," said Hob. "Who are you to dictate terms," said Quinn. He finger-combed his hair and made a yelping, rubbery noise. I have never understood why people love hallucinogens so much. Hob was holding up the thing he had snatched from the table, whatever Quinn had left there. A long black pencil. "You insect. I'll kill you and your friends. I'll kill your family," Quinn said. Panted. "Oh Jesus," said Alabama, "really?" "Give me what you stole," said Hob, "you orphan."

"Hob," said Alabama, "back away." She'd lowered her gun and was tracking Quinn's movements. I'd never seen anyone get shot before. I wasn't looking forward to it. Quinn didn't deserve it. Shooting's too stiff a penalty for being an asshole. Or so maturity counsels me. I would have been philosophically gratified to see Alabama shoot. She didn't. Quinn was on Hob, grappling with him, pummeling him. Hob pummeled back. Neither of them had the faintest idea how to throw a punch. They landed blows almost at random. I was rooting for Hob. He needed technical help. Alabama kept her gun up. I hoped she was planning on wounding Quinn. He annoyed me but I didn't know him well enough to want him dead. "You insect," Quinn shrilled over and over, "you insect." He was practically weeping. I didn't feel sorry for him. Whining over this pencil-like object. You know what it is: so said my conscience. I didn't want to admit it, maybe. I was asking myself who stays alone outside in the cold at a party, in the half-dark, tripping their balls off. Then again, I had no right to judge. That's what makes adolescence so difficult. You judge and thus you fear judgment.

The long pencil they'd been fighting over: Hob hurled it out of Quinn's reach and clinched with him. Quinn battered the back of Hob's head. Alabama ran past them and grabbed the fallen object. "Don't touch that, you stupid cunt," whined Quinn. "Okay then," said Alabama. She took a bead. She chewed her lip. *Please aim for the leg*, I thought, *we can't drag a corpse out of here*. Hob punched Quinn in the throat. "Hob, you got this?" asked Alabama. Quinn yowled in rage. He didn't crumple, as I'd thought he would. Instead he opened his mouth and sank his yellow, pointed teeth into Hob's ear and tore a triangle of flesh out of it. Hob kept silent. He sucked in air and locked his hands around Quinn's throat. Squeezed until Quinn let go of his ear. Blood striped the side of his face. Smeared his lips. His chin. "Do you even know who my family is," Quinn said as he spat out the ear chunk. His voice wet and raucous. "Do you even know who they are? I hate them but do you even know who they are? They represent everything in the world!" Nerd brawls are entertaining. Nerd dialogue, too. Though what Hob did next surprised me. He slipped his hands down to Quinn's white collar. Took a solid hold. Smashed Quinn's face into the brick wall. Quinn gulped, gagged. Fell. He whined. He writhed. His nose spread out. He sprayed blood on the terrace bricks. "Nice work," I said. Couldn't help myself. Hob didn't answer. He was drawing rapid, high breaths. "Well played," said Alabama. Slipping her gun back into her waistband.

All the crying and writhing: hard to watch. Our inner lives are all sordid. Or so I've come to believe. When I saw it happen it weirded me out. Hob was not finished, however. He kicked Quinn in the ribs and chest. "My uncle," Quinn wailed, "my uncle." He was making me curious. Family members have to be pretty stellar before you invoke them during moments of great personal crisis. "Who's his uncle," I said to Alabama. "I'm no genealogist," said Alabama. Hob said, "You can scream all you like, you little bitch." He kicked Quinn between each phrase. He kicked him over and over again. He grunted and gasped as he kicked. The kicks thudded. Quinn cried out wordlessly. His glasses shattered. He started to cough. More blood sprayed. "Hob," I said. He didn't listen. He kicked Quinn in the face. He kicked Quinn in the balls. Quinn stopped crying out. He just flopped around with every blow. "Hob," I said. Hob didn't listen. One hand clamping his handkerchief—drawn from nowhere—over his bleeding ear. "You little overachieving asshole, I hope you spend the rest of your life in a coma, you effete useless mediocre cunty thief," he said. "Hob, maybe you should stop that now," I said. Hob didn't listen. He bent down. Got in close and started punching Quinn. In the face. Over and over. Blood dotted Hob's chin. Looked black in the grim light. He grunted "where is it" between each blow. High and hard. Eventually Quinn stopped moving. Only his chest rose and fell. Hob said, "There you go, you scrotum," and started frisking him. He stopped at the inside blazer pocket. "Bingo," Hob said, straightening. He was covered with blood. His own and Quinn's. He was holding a slim silver oblong. Also covered with blood. A black stone plaque on one face. "Real obsidian," said Hob. Cool workmanship. I had to admit. "Oh, that definitely looks like it was worth it," said Alabama.

12

It seemed, initially, like a brilliant plan. Then again, we were hammered. Quinn was lying at Hob's feet. "We should go," I said. "And leave him like this," said Alabama. "We don't have to leave him," said Hob. "You make it sound like you have another totally brilliant solution," said Alabama, "but maybe you should spare us." Hob told us to lift Quinn up. "What is this shit," said Alabama. "We don't have a lot of time," said Hob. "You little fuck," she grunted as she heaved Quinn's right arm up. I had his left.

Quinn was not awake. He wasn't out either. He moaned and bubbled blood. Hob was already holding the mirror. The nail against the brick wall a period. End of a sentence. Hob inverted the mirror. Stood behind Quinn. "For this next effect, I ask my brave assistants to release our volunteer at my command. Should they fail, the consequences will be severe." "Just get it done already," said Alabama, "okay." Her voice strained. She wasn't looking at Quinn. Or at Hob. Or at me. Hob raised the mirror as high as he could. The reflective side aimed toward the terrace floor. He held it above Quinn's weakly tossing head.

"This is going to be a tight fit," said Alabama. Before my suspicion could take shape, Hob grunted, again, and brought the mirror downward. He said, "Release." And I let go of Quinn's left arm. Not because of the instruction. In terror. The mirror did not break when it hit Quinn's scalp. He passed into it. As easily as a good diver passes through the surface of the water. Hob completed the action and flipped the mirror. "I had my doubts about that one," he said. I saw Quinn. Lying on the floor of the reflected terrace. Trying to lift himself up on his elbows. I looked to the herringbone bricks on our side. Nothing. I looked to the herringbone bricks on the other side. Quinn. New bloodstains. "And what if it hadn't worked," said Alabama. "Broken glass and what have you," said Hob, "not as bad as the original sin, here." He caught me gaping. "That, Michael," he said, "is how you do it with mirrors."

The elongated girl was waiting for us. Started giving us shit as soon as we walked back into the living room. "Excuse me, but you need to leave," she said. "We just got here, Eleanor," said Hob. He had his handkerchief tied around his head, and his hat on above that. It hid the wound. Sort of. I was glad the cloth was red. We'd used the last of the whiskey to clean him off, and to sterilize—Alabama's idea— the tear in his ear. It didn't faze him. He just asked if he was clean enough to pass inspection. He was. I thought. I was holding his bag. It shook. "Excuse me, but if you think you can just come in here and," she said. Stopped. "And what," said Alabama. "We'll call the police," said Eleanor the Elongated. "I doubt that," said Alabama. The way Eleanor's curd-white, set face softened announced that Alabama was, in fact, correct. "Just get out," said the floppy-haired kid who'd tried to hit on Alabama. "Fucking ow," said Hob. The music still terrible. Now it was the Dead, I was pretty sure. No band I hated as much as a kid. No band I hated as much later on. Or it might have been a version of the Dead. An iteration. Not even the real thing. The kids still standing, with the stunned look of people who don't know what to do with their hands. I was holding Hob's bag. The mirror quivering at unpredictable intervals. Even through the scarf we had wrapped it in. Even through the green canvas. You could mistake it for a phone set to vibrate. For that I was glad. None of the Mountjoy kids seemed to notice. "Just get out, you insects," said the floppy-haired kid. *Insects*: a standard term of opprobrium with them. Not hard to see that. A failure of imagination when you have a communal term to abuse people. Your imagined inferiors. "Keep talking shit," said Alabama. The floppy-haired kid, again, went silent. And we were on our way.

"It's shaking," I said as I handed the bag over. "Yeah, well," said Hob, "nobody's perfect." The crows on the stone sill were eyeing us. "Are they going to attack us," I said. "No sweat if they do," said Alabama, "there's like only three." "That's one for each of us," I said, "by my count." She snorted. "Don't worry so much, Michael," said Hob. "Now, it's precisely that kind of attitude," said Alabama, "that gets us into trouble like this in the first place." The crows dispersed when we reached the end of the block. Winged off into the dark. Their periodic calls went on and on. We walked. We couldn't think of what else to do. I can easily say that this was the worst event I had ever participated in. Up to that point. We flanked Hob. Like his bodyguards. He kept one hand on the bag, until Alabama said, "If you keep doing that a cop is going to notice. And then we'll all be screwed." Alabama took a flask out of her jacket. "You been holding out on us," I said. Trying to raise a laugh. Dead silence. She handed it to Hob, who drank and handed it back to her. She handed it to me. I recognized the taste. The liquid in the carboys. The neck of the flask still warm from Alabama's lips. We were walking vaguely. Alabama took the lead. I asked if she lived around here. "Why do you give a shit," she said. "Just making conversation," I said. "You're really skilled at it, anyone ever tell you that," she said. I drank. "Don't bogart that joint, my friend," said Hob. And I saw it again, without warning: the smooth, inevitable, swift swallowing of Quinn Klayman.

I expected to feel more guilt. I won't lie. I was faintly uncomfortable.

THE WAR AGAINST

That was because of the vibrations from the bag. Not for moral reasons. Also, it was unclear what we were guilty of, so far. Assault: absolutely, for Hob. Aiding and abetting: maybe, for me and Alabama. Beyond that: kidnapping, unlawful imprisonment. I didn't know what the law said about mirror confinement. I wasn't that worried about Klayman. Physically, I mean. He had taken a beating. Not the kind that will kill you. Hob, I was confident, could release him. What bothered me was: where. Yes, we could in theory have avoided this question. We failed to. A pure example of human psychology. And now we were fucked for options. We couldn't leave the mirror on the street. We couldn't let him out in my house. Not in Hob's. Not in Alabama's. Not in the base- ment. I thought: the park. The vibrating mirror suggested Quinn was up and about. Staggering and bloody, as I saw it. If he started yowling there it would draw cops. I thought: *The subway*. In the subway, they had cameras and even more cop access. "And seriously, what was he talking about, a map," said Alabama. "I do not know," said Hob, "but people like to expound on their personal theories when they take acid. That I do know."

I stayed with Hob, smoking in a doorway, while Alabama ran into a drugstore. She came out with a loud, white plastic bag. Bandages, per- oxide. She seemed to know what was necessary. She led us to a diner, called the Gravesend. I don't know why: nowhere near Gravesend. Maybe the owners came from there. Maybe they were immigrants and thought it sounded cool. The fake wood inside was dark and warm looking. The air smelled like frying fat. A guy with a shoe-black toupee was sitting in the booth next to us. Staring into a plate with six slices of wheat toast. Nothing else. We ordered Cokes, to earn bathroom access. I was hungry. But ordering food seemed against the tone of the evening so far. "You need help, you have to get it from Wood," Alabama said when Hob rose. "I have this under control," he said. "Sure you do," said Alabama. The waitress came. "I am going to check in there when he gets done," she said, "and if I find what

I expect to find, I am going to call the cops. You kids think we're so out of it." I didn't know if she meant, by "we," waitresses or adults in general. Alabama gave her the finger when her back was turned. The bag sat between us on the red banquette. Jumping whenever the mirror vibrated. "Do you think he's pounding on the mirror," I said. "I can't believe you can't smoke in here anymore," said Alabama. I did the math. She would have been at most seven when the ban passed. Nostalgia's powerful. Even if appropriated. When Hob came out of the bathroom, the waitress ran in. "I hope you were thorough," said Alabama, "the waitress is going in for a search." "I had another really good idea while I was in there," said Hob, "but I feel like my credibility with you two is strained." "I'm listening," said Alabama. The waitress trudged back out of the bathroom. Her face slack in disappointment. You'd be surprised what a loss it can be when you miss out on a chance to call the police.

Alabama thought Hob's idea was stupid. She wasn't wrong. Even I saw that. But an idea's being stupid isn't a real argument against it. We'd be nowhere without stupidity. It also, like all stupid ideas, contained a powerful logical argument. We couldn't keep the mirror. We couldn't abandon it. We couldn't destroy it. We couldn't return it to its owners. So we had to leave it in the custody, Hob said, of a certain type of organization. An organization with the requisite knowledge and skills to release the prisoner within it. One with the savvy to understand, he said, that just by leaving it there we had made an act of contrition. "No, no, no. No, no, no. And no. No way," said Alabama, "no fucking way." "Do you have anything else," Hob said. She kept arguing until we got off the bus. The 15. Her argument was basic. Just the word *no*, in various forms. I could see she was hoping to win through attrition. Because, as noted, Hob had a point. To which she had no real refutation. We were fucked for other options. And if the last option you have is also the stupidest, you need to make your peace with it.

Mountjoy looked like a school for the failed. "Jesus H. Particular Christ," said Alabama, "the roofline." Against the yellow-brown-blue of the moonlit sky, three or four dozen crows. Two hopped into the air and breezed down toward the shuttered and garbage-green news kiosk we were crouching behind. "Well," said Hob, "they are one hundred percent looking at us." They were. He was not projecting. They weren't freaking out. Maybe they had higher objectives, I thought. The place needed surveillance. No guard. No slumbering rent-a-cop. I'd imagined a knight. A polished suit of armor. Nothing. Not even a doorman, that I could see. Just a narrow, rain-grayed town house sandwiched between two much newer buildings, one red brick and one faced in glass. The brick one alight and the glass one dark. "I used to go to the dentist in the one on the corner," said Hob, "I think." On the bowed gutter of the shingled roof, shining in the moonlight, the rank of crows. On the eaves. On the windowsills. The door heavy looking. Made of normal brown door wood. A brass knob. A brass mail slot. Lamp glow within. "Are they on vacation," said Hob. This hadn't occurred to me. "Makes this easier, if true," said Alabama. Light leaked from the brick building next to the gray house. Light leaked from the streetlamps. City streets look like set stages at certain hours. Ten feet of iron fence fronted the gray house: black palings, ending in the usual spikes that guard town homes. Crows perched on those too, one per spike. A curlicued handle on the gate. Two patches of lawn and two large maple trees. Both red and full leaved. "That's weird," said Hob. "Must be how they know it's there," I said, "I bet not everyone can see them." "You're more astute than you look, Wood," said Alabama, "but that doesn't do anything about the crows."

I admit: the view of Mountjoy House from the south was much more impressive. In that it was identical to the view from the north. Same fence. Same fancy handle. Same lawn patches, steps, door with its gleaming brass knob. Same maples and same crows. The best place to hide the strange and inexplicable is in plain sight. The glamour—that

THE ASSHOLES

was another term Mr. Stone used, he told me it meant a kind of stand-ing spell—we were seeing probably kept most people away. Welcomed the right ones in. And taunted the aware but excluded. "I could kill a few crows," said Alabama, "this thing has better accuracy than you'd think at a distance. It's why I use this model." "I'm all in favor of that," said Hob, "but it wouldn't really get us anywhere." The weather was winter-perfect. Cold but not too cold, and the air still. Moon enormous. I didn't mind just standing and looking at that doorknob. "We can go in from next door, I bet," I said. "Now, that's what I'm talking about," said Hob, "that's real innovation." "Look at you, Mr. Logistics," said Alabama. She had begun to believe in the plan. I could tell. Her tone had thawed. I already believed in it more. And besides, I wanted to see how the assholes lived. You want to understand your enemy, you have to know his habits.

The crow guards didn't seem interested in the fact that we were within the property line of the building next to Mountjoy. They didn't have a lot of attention to spread around. Their brains being the size of a chickpea. No guard at a desk. No lights on. "Observe, ladies and gentlemen," Hob said, "I will now consume this key and suffer no bodily harm." He took a yellow-brass key from his key ring and placed it in his mouth. Made a theatrical gulp. Showed us his tongue. Nothing there. He knelt and placed his lips against the street door's keyhole. Blew through it. Pushed. The door swung inward. Runoff light from the street filled the bland room. Lit up an ocean-vista paint-ing. Seaweed and sails. Lit up the beige chairs. The rattling of a motor. Distant or well hidden. "I bet there's an access tunnel in the basement," I said. "Please," said Hob. He was pacing back and forth, eyeing the wall. His ear bandage catching the light. "Consider this ordinary paint-ing, ladies and gentlemen," said Hob. Alabama drew her gun.

Hob pulled his handkerchief out of nowhere. Again. "With similar ease, I will transform this creation of canvas and oils into a very portal," he said. Red with white spots, clean and creased. His bloodstains gone

THE WAR AGAINST

from the cloth. He dusted the wall and whipped the handkerchief through the air. Then: nothing. Erzmund calls this a vanish. You can do it with cards, too. "You should actually watch this, you want to learn precision, Wood," she said. I was already watching, however. Hob produced (the technical term) the handkerchief again. Placing his palms together and whipping them apart. The cloth held between his pincered indexes and thumbs. Spread to its full extent. Kept on spreading. I stared. It grew in width. Three times its initial size. Four times. Hob kept pulling. No visible effort. Smiling lightly. When the cloth had exceeded the width of the ocean painting, Hob gave it a violent shake, and it unfurled. About the area of the canvas, I estimated. He stretched his arms, held the cloth before the painting. Frowned, swallowed, let the cloth flutter to the earth. "Holy fuck," I said.

Instead of the ocean painting, the frame now held an interior. Not a painting. Or if it was it was executed with such perfection as to be indistinguishable from reality. We were looking into a hall, its floor covered by a slab of lamplight. About the color of a ripe pear. "All right, let's do it," Hob said. "Conquering hero," said Alabama. She was holding her gun with the barrel pointed straight up. They say it's safer. And then she stepped through. Hob followed. I waited. I couldn't muster the will. My feet: leaden. Like the beige floor was exerting beige gravity. "Come on, Wood," said Alabama. She didn't have to look. "Michael, don't worry," said Hob. I lifted my shoe. I brought it to the surface of the painting. Or where the surface had been. It passed through. Empty air. Nothing else. I could smell the corridor. It smelled like a library. I didn't see any books. It smelled like old paper and ink. Walls paneled in rich red wood. The carpet silent and soft under my soles. When I looked behind me, I saw: a blank wall. No painting. No portal. Identical black sideboards spaced every two feet. The lamps stood on these. Darkened cubic lamps swung on chains from the vaulted ceiling, too, covered in wood a shade darker than the walls. Hob was breathing deeply. Calmly. The painting maneuver hadn't taken that much out of

THE ASSHOLES

him. "I mean, not to be distracting, but you guys could rob banks with that," I said. "We're not a gang of criminals," said Alabama. "It didn't," said Hob, "look this big on the outside." He was right. The room we were in was two or three times the area of anything that the gray house could have contained. To say nothing of the ceilings. Twenty feet at least. The room, or corridor, or foyer, or antechamber, or whatever it was went on and on. Black sideboard supporting lamp, blue-painted door, paneling, black sideboard, blue door, paneling. "Now, this makes it looks like where they send fuckups," said Alabama, "my brother went to Choate and it looks like Choate. Sort of. It's fancier. But he's a fuckup for sure." She slipped her gun back into her waistband and swigged from her flask. "He lives in Austin now," she said, "which is like fuckup paradise."

A hotel hall. Silent, carpet-baffled night. The near-silent hum of machines. That was the whole gestalt of Mountjoy House. *Gestalt* is an expression I learned from my father. I admit it confused me. I took the concept of the war Mr. Stone had mentioned literally. We crept along. Alive to every sigh and crack from the building. "This doesn't look like enemy headquarters," I said. "What's your point," said Alabama, "I bet the inside of the Gestapo was a regular office building. Cabinets and pens." Could not argue. We seemed to have entered a basement-level corridor. A short stairway at one end terminated in a white, stone-looking door. The long one at the other end seemed more promising. I ran up it first, before Alabama. To show my bravery. Hob was still panting, just lightly, in third place. They had crimson runners of carpeting on the stairs. The indoor air was freezing. The banisters too. That no one had yet interfered with us filled me with literal delight. At the top of the stairs, another long hallway. Identical to the first, in that it seemed far too large to be contained within the gray town house.

We tried the blue doors. All open. The first room Hob opened was biggish and moonlit. A reddish rug, one corner curled up. A made bed.

Light stink of sweat. Wheeling dust motes in the pale light. It looked clean. It looked empty. It looked packed up. "Just a dorm room," said Hob. "You don't even want to look," I said. "Would you keep anything valuable in your room over break, if you had a room?" said Alabama. She had a point. One of the doors I'd failed to open had four copies of the *Times* in front of it. "I think we're alone," I said, "and I also think they get more vacation than we do." "What a world," said Hob. "Big readers," said Alabama. At that age I found my contemporaries who read newspapers pretentious. So the presence of the *Times* made sense. I kicked the short pile. Broadsheets scattered. "There ya go," said Alabama.

At the end of the hall a bigger, bluer door. "Promising," said Hob. "Easy," said Alabama. The door swung. We were staring into an enormous room, about the length of a football field. Nonathletes use that as a vague large measurement. I use the phrase with knowledge of what it means in concrete terms. "You could play sports in here," said Alabama, "it makes you want to run drills." She was literally correct. Close to four hundred feet long, almost two hundred wide. The ceilings thirty, forty feet high. Walls clad in that rich, reddish paneling. From the strip of wall immediately beneath the ceiling dozens of metal shields hung, each covered with different symbols. Six golden beehives. A green serpent eating its own tail. A fox and a hawk perched on a black battlement. A blue key on a silver field. Bound yellow sheaves of wheat. Three orange circles interlocked in a dizzying way. "That's called a Borromean knot," said Alabama, gesturing with her gun barrel. "Mr. Stone didn't say anything about coats of arms," I said. "It's probably just scenery," said Hob. The smell of paper and of ink I'd smelled before was almost choking here. Hob and Alabama inhaled it gustily. Huge windows, divided into small panels of glass. Through them came moonlight. From niches set into the walls between the bookcases, what appeared to be fireflies flickered in jars. Five or six amber points to each vessel, dodging and looping.

THE ASSHOLES

Hob took the wrapped bag out of his mirror and smiled into it. "Hey, asshole," he crooned. I heard it vibrate. Alabama was scanning book spines. I had to bite my tongue about the whole size issue. I mean its obvious impossibility. It bothered me. In a way that the snakes in the whiskey didn't. Or the crows. Or the fireflies, or whatever they were, enslaved in their jars. It was just so obviously a violation. I said nothing. I didn't want to make myself into even more of a bungler. The fireflies, or whatever they were, provided a rich, warm, and inconstant glow. Ladders on wheels. Study tables: I counted thirty. Also empty. Also clean. No rustlings from the building, no singing of pipes. We walked on, into the flickering light. Our shoes scraped the bare floor. I took down a book. I could not read it. It was written in Greek. I recognized the characters. I put the book back. I didn't want to pretend it was meaningful. I looked through one window and then the next. All framed the icy moon and constellations. None of which I recognized. The earth below the stars: not the city. A lap of green grass. A tangled-looking forest. The trees strangely shaped. A night-colored river bisected the lawn. Where it flowed into the woods, a cairn squatted. "Where are we," I said. That I could not keep silent about. "Come on, Michael, it's just trees," said Hob.

The main point of the mission—which is how I thought of it; no shame—we'd forgotten. Surrounded by all this grandeur. All the power of the throne. That's what it was. The mirror in which Quinn Klayman was trapped lay on its plywood back on a table carved from ebony. We wandered the length and breadth of the great library. In the alien starlight. All our concerns forgotten. No worry. No hurry. We owned the place. "Damn," said Alabama. "They have a sixteenth-century edition of the *Amphitheatrum*." "Taking that," said Hob, shoving a ladder, "would make what I did look smart." "Yeah, but still," she said. And then: "I don't even know anyone I could actually sell it to anyway. Personally. Mr. Stone does." "Is there a market for antiquities," I said. "Are you kidding," said Hob. "You could get a million

THE WAR AGAINST

for this, easy, or like eight, nine hundred thousand. You just have to know the right people. It's how Mr. Stone makes his living. I think. Trading. Selling." I pondered this. You don't necessarily think about how impressive old men with underground lairs earn their living. Or that they need to. "Can't he just," I said, and waved my hands. "Just what," said Alabama. The ladder Hob had shoved rolled and squeaked until it hit the opposite wall. Past the moon-filled windows. "Is that bothering anyone else," I said, "the whole forest thing." "Perpetual motion, look at that," said Hob. "Doesn't bother me," said Alabama, "I think it's a nice aesthetic touch." That's when I saw it. As she said the word *aesthetic*. I knew: *We have to take that.* "Look," I said. "Holy moly," said Hob. "Really? Are we really," said Alabama, "at the golly-jeepers stage of language still?" She stopped scoffing when she noticed what I was looking at, though. Just looming there. Between two bookcases. Glowing a bit with the copious moonlight.

We were not going to steal anything major. No books. No furniture. None of the shields hanging from the walls between windows. But we had to take something. To diminish their magnificence. Even just by a fragment. And owls are impressive. Stuffed owls doubly so. Find one in a moon-flooded, vast library and you're bound to be bowled over. It was perched on a dead, leafless, shellacked-looking tree standing in a metal bucket. Glass eyes. The color of honey. Or lightning. "Insects, huh," said Alabama. "No one likes to be called an insect," said Hob, "not even insects, probably." "Is it their mascot," I said. "Yes," breathed Hob. "And all we have are those lousy copperheads," I said, "plus you'd think that they'd stay away from snakes given the whole Garden of Eden thing and everything." The owl gray-feathered. Tones of purple and blue. Crimson talons. "She's named Irmgard," said Hob, "or so I've heard." He stroked the bird's feathers. "Guys, try it," he said. We did. Subtle electricity. "Do you think it's alive," I said. No nails. No pins. Hob pulled at a bluish breast feather. It came loose. "Amateur hour," he said, "look at this janky workmanship." "No wanton defacement," said Alabama. The bird's crimson feet gripped the crooked branch. I grabbed the tree and lifted: not as hard as I'd thought. Though the bucket was full of cement. The owl heavy and light at the same time. Birds have hollow bones. I learned that from watching nature shows with my parents. "My vote is," I said, "that I think we should take this." "Sterling," said Alabama. "Sterling," said Hob, "it's unanimous." Alabama stroked its staring, yellow eyes. "You can't just touch eyes," I said. "They're glass," said Alabama. "I'm confident we can get her out of here in one piece," said Hob.

13

T he owl proved a major contributor in terms of interior décor. It made me understand the whole mount-your-kill's-head-on-a-wall-plaque theory of design. Antlers and the like.

Hardest part: finding a cab that would take us downtown. A bus seemed too exposed. The train out of the question. A lumbering slow learner, a small kid with a freshly bandaged ear and bloodstain remnants on his face, a huge stuffed bird, and Alabama, who defied categorization. Four cabs sailed past us down Second, their roof lights arrogantly lit. "They're not even pretending to be off duty," said Hob, "that is blatant racism." "Against the race of jackasses," said Alabama. One stopped. The driver leaned out and asked, "Where you go?" He talked the whole ride about his brother in Tbilisi, whom he said was the most famous bass guitarist in Georgia. We carried the owl across our laps. The bucket holding the base of tree branch stuck out one window. We set her up in the back of the basement, near the couch where Alabama sat to play the violin.

Vincent was gone when we returned. We yelled and yelled for him.

Sunflower dust still adrift. No answer. Hob's ear: fascinatingly gross, under the bandage. Which we of course undid. Using the pretext of changing it. His blood going black as it dried. He had a bruise on his cheek. Could have been a smudge of coal. I couldn't stop staring and neither could Alabama. We caught each other looking and she grinned over Hob's brown hair. A real grin. Hadn't seen her actual smile before. "Please don't," said Hob in a phlegmy, constrained voice, "please don't look." "Sorry, man," said Alabama, "but you look like such an urchin. Like a chimney sweep." "Of course Vincent isn't here. He could fix this," said Hob, "or maybe I should just go to a doctor." "You'd have to come up with a really good lie," I said. Hob sucked down the rest of his goblet of whiskey. "I'm happy to try," I said, "I mean with your ear." "No offense, but I'll take my chances," said Hob. I didn't blame him. His voice wasted. Droplets of sweat sliding from his forehead to the floor. Like all the pain and fear were hitting him now. After the adrenaline had dissipated. I sympathized. Alabama said, "Easy. You need help just say so."

At times it's simpler to keep your mouth shut. I can say, now, that the teachings of experience are largely identical with the wisdom to know when to keep your mouth shut. I had to ask him. I didn't want to. I had to. "Hey, Hob," I said. "What can I do for you," he said. "How did you know that guy was an orphan." "What do you mean," he said. He was still shut-eyed and sweating. Voice hollow and sententious: that's a lie. Confused and modest: that's the truth. "You called him an orphan," I said, "you didn't suggest you knew him all that well before. You kind of made it seem as though he was a rando interloper who took your cigarette case. So how did you know." "That's actually a good point, Wood," said Alabama, "painful as it is to admit."

Hob didn't say anything. "How well do you know that guy, Hob," said Alabama. Her voice dead-even. She was starting to get pissed again. "Is there history there or was it just he stole your cigarette case," she said. Hob was rocking back and forth, back and forth, his

THE WAR AGAINST

forehead muscles working and his lips white with pressure. "Well," said Alabama. "Look, he could have killed us all," said Hob, "seriously. If he'd had that thing." "That wand, you mean," I said. Hob nodded. He looked miserable. Carsick. "Jesus Christ, Hob." This was Alabama, waving her arms. She was on her feet. I hoped she would be too angry to remember her gun. Then again, she was probably just as dangerous without. My tattoo twinged. "Do you think he's dead," whispered Hob. "I'm not an emergency physician," said Alabama, "so I don't know." "He took my spot," said Hob. His voice breaking. He sounded as though he was about to burst into tears. I didn't blame him. When you're not used to defending yourself, you feel guilt about hurting people. This has never been a problem for me. "Your spot," said Alabama. "Quinn Klayman," said Hob, "took my spot." "What spot," I said. "I didn't get in," said Hob, "and I met him during the test. Damnation Day. What the fuck ever. That's why. That's why. Okay?"

"So you did," I said, "that whole certification thing Mr. Stone was talking about." "Certamen," said Hob. Pronouncing the c like ch, as in the second syllable of concerto. "You have to perform for a board of auditors. They decide." "Does Charthouse know about this," said Alabama. "I never told him," said Hob. "He told me all about his life, sort of. Quinn, I mean. About his parents being dead. He's like two years older. Three years older. It was his last year of eligibility. I remember that. And who tells a total stranger about his orphanhood. I think he was high." Taking tests while high or drunk was a custom, I admit. I never engaged in it myself. I was a weak enough student without impediments. "He just kept talking on and on. The proctors overheard. The auditors. You weren't supposed to talk. Like any test. They pretended to ignore him." Hob still looking carsick. The eels writhed in their jars. "Isn't the school going to be pissed," I said, "or their board of directors. Or whatever." "I'm sorry," Hob blurted out, "but Quinn is just such a little bitch. No offense, Alabama." "You have offended me already to the point of no return," said Alabama. (Also, side note:

there's no point in living, at all, if you have to kowtow to orphans.) "And I kicked ass at the Certamen," said Hob. This I believed.

Hob opened up after that. He just needed to get over the hurdle of the first question. That's how interrogation goes: everyone wants to confess; you just have to give them a reason to. He told us about his application to Mountjoy. You only got one shot, you had to be under eighteen, and you had to be able, first of all, to read instructions that to most people appear to be ad flyers for a laundromat. These lay out the guidelines for your test, different for every applicant. They explain the goals and standards of the public performance required to get in. "I did this thing with owls. Because I knew about Irmgard. It was great. Swooping and scaring them. I made them out of paper and cloth. Dust and light. Stuff that was around in the room already. I made them fly. I wish you could have seen it. The audience wore these robes," he said, "like actual robes, purple trimmed with gold. Behind a wooden table, drinking water and making notes." Verner Potash himself had been in the audience at Hob's test. Hob described him as resembling this actor who's in everything but you never can remember his name. Pudgy and brown bearded. "I still see his fat face, just all stony," said Hob. After he got the news of his rejection, which came to him via a postcard from Cairo, Egypt (or so it had seemed to his parents, who asked him why he was getting correspondence from the Middle East), he tried and failed to kill himself. Vincent had stopped the bleeding, closed the wound in his wrist. "My parents still don't know," he said, "and Vincent told me I hadn't even done it the right way. You have to go up and down the vein, not across."

Everyone wants to confess. Everyone secretly believes it will do him good. It doesn't. Hob still looked ill after speaking: bloodless, eyes wild and glistening. "It was pretty funny though," I said, "the whole scene back there. I'm here to claim my destiny and all that. You actually didn't do so badly, man. You have unexpected fighting skills." "Don't touch that, you insect," said Alabama, "comedy gold."

Our words did not have the intended effect on Hob. To cheer him up. Show him the lighter side of physical violence. He went paler. Greener-grayer. We had no vomit bucket. I didn't want to have to mop up. So I quieted down. "Rest up," said Alabama, "we'll talk about this when Charthouse gets back. He can ask the man downstairs. He'll know what to do." Hob was already yawning. Didn't puke. His color returned. He fell asleep in, literally, thirty seconds. On the couch. His head wrapped up in that kerchief. "That guy ordinarily can't keep his mouth shut," murmured Alabama.

Still furious. Albeit less so. She lit up. Blue smoke. She slipped her gun out of her waistband and put it on a metal library shelf screwed into the back wall, next to her violin case. Hob snored. "Are you going to tell Charthouse," I said. "I haven't decided," said Alabama. "So how bad is this," I said. "We're going to find out, I wager," said Alabama. "There was something I wanted to ask him," I said. "Well, A, he's asleep, and B, if you think about it you'll never remember," said Alabama, "so just let it go." "Man, everybody's got secrets," I said, "everybody's ashamed of their lives." As though I'd just realized. Even when you're complete-seeming as Hob. She snorted. "If you're going to be ashamed, don't do whatever it is, and if you've done it, don't be ashamed of it," said Alabama. "That's kind of amazing," I said. I knew it would cause only problems. I said it anyway. Another example of when you have to speak up. "Are you trying to flatter me," said Alabama. She took down her violin case. She clicked open its silver locks. "I was trying to compliment you," I said, "or not even you but your philosophy." "You're very bad at it," said Alabama. "I am bad at many things," I said. Alabama went silent. Thinking, maybe, about how to phrase what she planned to say without offending me. Or how to achieve the sole purpose of offending me. "It's not a universal," she said. "What do you mean," I said, "it's not you just decide and that's it. You don't even get to decide. You have to find what you're good at. It's not up to you."

Like Hob, she said: concealment and deception, illusion and theatrics. Like Vincent, she said: a knack for living things, plants, animals. "He's good with dogs. Cats. He won't touch the crows, though. They freak him out way more than they do even Hob." Alabama stroked her bow with a cake of amber rosin. "And what am I good at," I said. "I don't know, but even if I did I wouldn't tell you. You have to determine," she said. "That's okay with me," I said. "Why do you keep *saying* that," said Alabama. The dark spot under her pale chin flashed at me as she swept the violin into place. "It's from a movie, I think," I said. *Never doubt*, writes Erzmund. *Doubt is the sign of the amateur. It vouchsafes his eternal secondary standing. We have nothing to do with doubt, as we have nothing to do with pride—or any other moral affectation.* "And what about Charthouse," I asked. "He can do precise stuff," said Alabama, "but the big stuff is thunder and lightning. You wouldn't believe it." Bow to strings. The music started. "And what about you," I said. "Take a guess," she said.

14

The rest of break: less remarkable. Christmas came and went. As did my grandmother. My father's mother. My mother's parents died the year I was born. My father did not hide the liquor. My grandmother got slurring drunk and started to denounce at the end of the meal blacks and Hispanics. A tradition, with her. We all sat in frozen silence around the goose. Its skin rich looking, almost red. "I'm not saying anything that isn't backed up by the facts of the matter," said my grandmother. "Spirit of the season," said my father. "Tommy, you can debate all you like but just look what happened to the street you grew up on," she said. "I think you're exaggerating, Ma," said my father. "I never once in my life have exaggerated," said my grandmother. Not true. We all exaggerate and we all lie. It's human nature. You can't argue with your elders. No matter how incisive or brilliant your attack. They win by default. Simply by having survived longer than you. End of story. Her denunciations didn't last long. "They're all good people, just confused," she said. She said this every year. She gave me a savings bond: fifty dollars. To mature when

I was thirty-three. I kissed her slack cheek. My parents gave me a set of weights and told me I no longer had a curfew. I was stunned and touched. I assumed all my recent late nights would have made them assert their authority. People surprise you. They grant you more freedom than you'd expect. "Don't make me regret this," said my mother. "You know what your responsibilities are," said my father, "so no buffoonery, please."

I did a lot of reading. By which I mean read and reread sections of the *Calendar*. I imagined Alfons Froch as Mr. Stone had described him, fleeing Hitler and Sebottendorf, sick with syphilis and poor, cold in the Berlin winter and ultimately victorious. If you die a free man, you win. No matter how sordid your death. I also learned THE FOUR WINDS, although I discovered Hob had cheated to perform one of the flourishes. I checked in with him every day, to see how he was carrying it. He sounded sick. I told him over and over Quinn was probably not dead. I had at that point inflicted serious physical harm on five people: Greg Gilder; the Barry brothers from Cardinal Corrigan, who jumped me after a football game; a kid at one of Simon Canary's parties in ninth grade, whose name I to this day have never managed to learn; and Robert Gmielko. Gmielko groped me—he grabbed my cock in the showers when I was a freshman and he was a senior. I punched him in the throat, and then, when he'd collapsed, kicked him in the balls. He cried in front of me, from the pain. I nurture a dim hope that he in his post–high school years managed to avoid a criminal sexual conviction. The kid at Simon Canary's party I cold-cocked for looking at me funny. The Barry brothers: Desmond suffered a dislocated right shoulder and James a dislocated left. Gilder I've explained. You have to have gone through it. Otherwise it seems wrong. When in fact it's merely another form of human expression. Or so I've decided. At the time I did not think about it at all. Merely acted. I did a lot of running, too, when I wasn't talking to Hob. Coach Madigan recommended it when we didn't have practice. To stay lean and mean: his words. I would have done it anyway. I love running. I like walking but I love running. Point A to point B. As fast as possible. With no reason.

Crows followed me. At first I didn't want to admit it. They'd glide from tree to tree in the park. They'd be hopping around ahead of me on the path and would only take flight when I got near them, ignoring the other runners. They perched on the points of the iron fence around the reservoir. Croaking their glad, hoarse croaks. If they were going to watch me, there was nothing I could do about it. An obnoxious one I tried and failed to kill. It was early in the morning, six or seven. I'd been running since dawn, when having to urinate woke me. I was gasping and footsore. This crow followed me for the duration of my run, treetop to treetop, bench to dry water fountain. Now, as I caught my breath, it perched on a branch and looked at me and laughed. Dry and raucous. "Too far, pal," I said as I checked the path: no one. No other joggers, no park service employees in their leaf-emblemed golf carts, no cops, nothing. So I cleared my mind and stared at the crow. It stared back. "Turn to stone," I said. My teeth locked. The words came out choked and sibilant. The crow did not turn to stone. Its feathers turned ash gray. From the talons up. Meager haunches, breast, wings, and glossy head and eyes: all went gray. When the transformation reached the top of its head, it leaped from the branch and winged off. Harder to spot than before, in fact, against the stony winter sky. Laughing its raucous laugh. My nose bled, a dense trickle. I wiped it away with my wrist. "Can't fight city hall," I murmured.

Failure. Failure at minor things. I got the cigarette-lighting man-euver down. Modern technology had rendered the exercise obsolete. Or hyper-refined Stone Age technology. Depending on how you look at it. No card impossibilities. No mirrors. I didn't want to risk another fiasco. Even the niggling, useless things I did caused pain. Cigarettes. Making a pencil change from yellow to bright green. I got more nosebleeds. My lungs and spine ached. Once I suffered a crippling bout of diarrhea. From trying to fly, as I had done at the construction site. The valley of bones. Nothing dramatic. Just straining to levitate from the floor of my room. Two inches. Three. A foot at my peak. Then total collapse. A run to the bathroom. My father knocked, I was in there so long. If you desire struggle, you'll struggle. If you worry, you will suffer. If you act, you conquer. The motto of an adolescent. Football inflicted worse pain. Football had no benefits I could discern, other than raising my various physical thresholds. Hob, short and frail: I wondered what it cost him. He masked it. My ache had gone underground: bones, the nerves behind my eyes. I was not sick. I was not tired. I needed less sleep. I had vivid dreams I could not recall on waking. I half-remembered having them before. Unknown stars and trees, unknown scent of unknown grasses. A woman's face. A scar. A crow. I ate with twice as much vigor as usual. I consumed in one sitting five or six leftover pounds of Christmas goose. My mother asked where it had gone. "I wish sometimes we'd had a girl," she said when I told her, stroking her forehead and arranging her hair, and pushing her glasses back onto the bridge of her nose. *The expert's art requires silence, concentration—and gratitude.* That's Erzmund also, from the prefatory remarks to his explanation of bottom dealing.

So I won't call it suffering. Yet the pain never left me. I woke early every day of Christmas break. Open-eyed and ready. Mornings I ran, late mornings I read, in the afternoons I practiced with cards and after that with no instrument other than my will. I would go for long walks at night. Terminating at Karasarkissian's. Or east to the frigid esplanade. Hob joined me. Vincent once, Alabama more than once. We avoided talking about Quinn Klayman. Crows followed us. We let them live. None displayed the same presumption the crow in the park had. When I told Alabama and Hob about this, they both applauded the idea. Even though I'd failed. "Seriously, they need to like have a bird Holocaust," said Hob. His ear had healed. A faint, thumb-shaped scar decorated the formerly torn flesh. You would never imagine that a future van rapist had torn a sail-shaped chunk from the cartilage and skin with his teeth. Alabama, however, did not joke about it. So I also refrained. The scar Vincent refused to eradicate. "You need a reminder," he said, according to Hob, who had finessed him. Kept the important events of the night to himself. Told him he'd gotten into a fight. Told him Quinn had bitten him in a drug-induced frenzy. The words he used: *drug-induced frenzy*. A newscaster phrase.

Alabama kept the wand. We studied it thoroughly one night, in the basement. When Vincent was out at another appointment. Hob couldn't clarify what these were. The wand smooth and black. Carved from a single piece of wood: no seams, and you could detect the grain. "I've never seen one this close before," said Hob. "It looks kind of shitty, to be honest," I said. "Typically useful analysis," said Alabama. She pointed it at the wall and closed her eyes. "Anything," she said after several seconds. "Nothing," said Hob. "Maybe it's keyed to the owner," I said. "Now, that actually sounds possible," said Alabama. Cold and heavy. The wand, I mean. "So they all get issued these," I asked. "I have no idea," said Hob, "maybe. I'm not exactly an expert, remember?" "We could show it to Charthouse. I bet he knows," I said. I realized how stupid this idea was before I'd finished forming the last word of my sentence. Alabama didn't respond. Hob aimed the wand at one of the whiskey carboys. The eels went apeshit. Shooting around in the amber liquid. Spiraling, writhing. Alabama took the wand and examined it again. "No point in being delicate," she said. Broke it between her slim, hard-looking hands.

I was expecting green sparks. Pyrotechnics. Nothing. Just a dull snap. Just a dead dowel of black-brown wood. The eels calmed down. "I know you think it's wrong," I said, "to use it to get by." "She's a purist, though. It's not wrong," said Hob, "*wrong*'s the wrong word." "If you want to lie about everything that matters," said Alabama, "to yourself above all, that's on you." She was still holding Quinn's broken wand.

One half in either hand. "Would you," she said, "do the honors?" Hob took the halves. Said: "Abracadabra, bitches." Each jagged end lit up. Blazing white jets. Summer sparklers. The heat bent the air around his face. "Sterling," I said. And I saw it in his eyes: the bone-deep, persistent, dizzying pain.

15

"A re you awake, Mr. Wood," said Sister Immaculata, "or are you dreaming?" I'd half-heard her question. She was asking the class about the origins of German nationalism. *They're assholes*, I almost said, *that's the origin of their nationalism.* I'd been toying with the pictures in my textbook: making the stiff generals and adjutants in the overdone paintings dance and wave their swords. They smiled louchely up at me. One of them waggled a gray mustache and winked. My head ached. My nostrils hurt. I did not mind. "Sorry, sister," I said instead. I meant it.

And then I shouted a single, stupid syllable. No form or meaning. When I lifted my eyes to apologize, when I raised them from the slowing images in my textbook, I saw sitting on the windowsill a woman dressed in a black business suit and a white shirt. She placed her right index finger athwart her purplish lips: the gesture for silence. A broad, forking, pork-hued scar crossed her white throat. Her hair snow colored. Her eyebrows snow colored. Her irises crimson. On her shoulder a massive raven. Settling its wings and clacking its beak.

"Mr. Wood, please control yourself," said Sister Immaculata. Hob glanced at me and wagged his head at the white woman. At least it was not an episode of insanity. The white woman grinned and slid fluently down to the floor. The knife points of her heels made two discrete clicks.

"Since Mr. Wood has proven so incapable of answering what seems to me a very simple question," said Sister Immaculata, "perhaps someone else would like to hazard a guess about the origins of German nationalism. Mr. Canary." The raven shifted its wings. Obsidian: shanks, talons, beak, eyes. Two broad and irregular bracelets surrounded the white woman's wrists. "Mr. Gilder." Extruded, cancerous rings of iron. They rustled against her sleeves as she walked between the columns of desks. Pressing her palms together and parting her lips. "Mr. Malinowski." She was strutting. No other word for it. This dead-white woman clad in black. A hip-shot stride. Past Simon Canary, who was digging in his left ear with his pinky, past Gilder and Wilton Opuwei and Matt Malinowski, who had a glass eye he used to remove and drop in girls' drinks at parties. None of them noticed this woman. She was still grinning as she reached me. Her black heels clicking against the broad, lacquered planks of the floor. I wanted to leap backward. I wanted to run. But I did not want to look any more insane. So I locked my molars and tensed my thighs. Posture of courage, no? Hob stared. His mouth half-gaping. The white woman bent toward me. Lips parted. Half-smiling. Her teeth flawless and her tongue vibrant pink. She was going to kiss me. I didn't flinch. I closed my eyes. The raven shifted again. Whicker of its feathers. Her hair grazed mine. Her breath brushed my cheek and ear. Frigid. Wet slate. One finger stroked the line of my jawbone and lifted my chin. When I opened my eyes the white woman was no longer standing there. Sister Immaculata continued to drone.

"That was unexpected," Hob said during lunch. We were sitting on the steps of Old Egypt. Smell of sweat and ozone. "Yes," I said. "Do

THE WAR AGAINST

you think it's like retribution," Hob said. "I literally have no idea how the rules work on this," I said. "Well," said Hob, "if they're going to get back at us, at least they sent someone you think is hot, right? Being an older lady and all." "Fuck you," I said. "It's not a crime to like someone who doesn't reciprocate, Michael," Hob said. "Except it basically is," I said, "not that I grant your first point." "You have a unique moral system," said Hob. The white woman's cold, firm fingers against my chin. The odd scent of her breath. I kept recalling them. I had a massive hard-on. Fear can do that, they say. Or shock. Or the presence of death. Luckily, I was seated. I don't think Hob noticed. "And she even had that crow," he said.

"It was a raven," I said, "yes it's a corvid, it's the same family, but the big ones are ravens, the medium ones are crows, and the little ones are daws." More expertise I garnered from my parents' nature-show addiction. "Did she kiss you," Hob said. "Came close," I said, "sort of presumptuous." "I didn't know you were such an expert, anyway," said Hob, "in bird taxonomy." He scrambled up. I waved good-bye. My cock was still stone-hard and I did not want to stand up. I had a fetish for menacing, raven-owning women. Psychological news to me. She wasn't bad-looking. Just odd. That white hair and that scar across her larynx. "I hope you'll agree," said Hob, "no matter what comes next, that Quinn deserved it." "Should we run," I said. "Not much point," said Hob, "seems like." I had to agree. The white woman had just waltzed in. He caressed his healed ear. "It was hurting this morning," he said, "I wonder if it's now like a bum knee before it rains." "You're not an old geezer," I said, "don't worry so much about your bodily ills."

He ran off. Late for chemistry. I had a study hall to kill. I ambled there. Through the pious winter light. Whoever designed Saint Cyprian's knew what he was doing. The church is big on that: reverence through architecture. High, vaulted ceilings; stone floors; and silence. Like being hit with a baseball bat made of nothing. If they came for us here, I could stand and fight. I knew the terrain. I was calm.

THE ASSHOLES

I was surprised at how calm I was. Then again, it's easy in school to be at peace. You know where you are supposed to be and what you are supposed to be doing. A luxury not afforded you when you leave. And if a dark bird flashed past the window I sat under in study hall, what of it? Sister Michael didn't care. I didn't care. I was reading Erzmund on mechanical methods for the concealment and production of cards. He called these devices *hold-outs*. He spoke of them not with scorn. With fondness. As you might remember the follies and weakness of your youth. In English, Sister Faith Hope announced that we would begin studying the poetry of John Keats. "One of the greatest, one of the very greatest," she said, "English poets." I had never heard of him. I do not come from a poetic family. "Pages four fifty-five to four fifty-nine in the anthology," she said. I flipped through the assignment. A line leaped up: *And no birds sing*. Coach Madigan complimented my ferocity during gym. He had set up a crude boxing ring, blue tape outlining a square on the gym floor, and had paired us up according to "weight class," as he called it. Proof of his essential fair-mindedness. A lesser coach and gym teacher would have made his biggest students fight his smallest ones, on the principle that the weak and frail deserve only humiliation. This is the principle governing the actual world. As even a brief glance at it will show you. I commend those who resist it without giving in to their sentimentality.

I had been assigned to box Gilder. Boring and dispiriting. He didn't try. He didn't say anything to Coach Madigan. He didn't say anything to me. He stood in the center of the blue-tape ring with his arms limp. So I shuffled around and landed a shot to his temple, his jaw. Padded in red neoprene. The mouth guard distorted his lips and made him resemble an ape. "Get those dukes up, Gilder," said Coach Madigan. He tore gently at his own red hair. Gilder did not listen. I punched him anyway. Hob whistled when I struck him. Two fingers in his mouth. The kind of whistle you envy because you can never imitate it. "If you want to editorialize, Callahan, I'm afraid you'll have to participate." I hit Gilder in the ribs, thumped his sternum, dodged back, landed two more blows on his curdled, neutral face. Hob's hands looked empty without his book. He looked naked. Exposed. I punched Gilder again and he didn't react. His eyes bulging out and his arms limp. "You all right, Gilder," said Coach Madigan. No reply. He wasn't paying attention. Listening to a distant voice: his face was that slack. "Gilder," I said under my breath, getting up close, "Gilder, listen." An apology at the ready: possibly. I'll never know. He lurched to life. Punched me. A solid shot. A left hook to my jaw. I stumble-stepped back, two looping hops, and regained my footing. Kids booed. Hob catcalled: "For shame." I did not lose my temper. Coach Madigan had missed Gilder's shot. Too bad for Gilder. He'd timed it well.

Then again, there's never an audience for your best acts. Your most precise blows. I was getting back into my stance and taking aim at his slow, bluish right eye when the gym doors banged open. The hair on my nape rose. The way it had when the white woman appeared in world history class. Whoever was walking in now did not pass unnoticed. Coach Madigan ran past me and said, "We're in the middle of a bout here. What can I do for you." He stopped. So abruptly his soles squeaked. Hob was already on his feet, darting his eyes: wall, window, wall. For an escape route, I realized. I turned to examine the door banger. It was not, as I'd feared or hoped, the white woman. It was a man, middle-aged. Short. Hob's height.

"A moment of your time, good sir," he said. To whom, it was unclear. Big-bellied, slope-shouldered, an oval, sly, balding head and a neatly pointed brown beard. The dark eyes sleepy, the flesh around them fat or inflamed. He spoke with an eroded Brooklyn accent. I recognized it from my father's voice. "You can't come in here," said Coach Madigan, "I don't know who let you in but you need an escort. This is a school. Private property. Once you check in I can help you." The fat man chuckled: soft clucks. "The peanut gallery," he said. "What did you say your name was," said Coach Madigan." The other kids had gone dead silent. Gilder's heavy breathing echoed. I think his nose had healed badly. "The grief I'm getting over what you've done," said the fat man, "has put me off my feed." "If you think," said Hob, "if you think this is a showdown." "You have something of mine," said the fat man. Not to Coach Madigan. To Hob. "The fuck I do," said Hob. "Callahan, you're dangerously close to detention here," said Coach Madigan. The fat man gestured with one pudgy arm: he was now holding a wand. Like Quinn's. Lighter in color, blonder, inlaid with threads of gold and tipped with a golden point, a golden claw. He spoke a phrase, a scrap of what I thought was Greek. I caught the word *dunatos*, which means strong. He traced a tight, convoluted pattern in the air with the wand's golden tip. Now blazing. Not alight or aflame. Inwardly blazing. A warm, gentle, invisible blow struck my forehead. Coach Madigan, Gilder, and all the rest of our class (except Hob) stopped speaking and moving.

I just lost a breath or two, and my balance. Less of a blow than the one Gilder landed. "We already broke the wand," I said after I'd recovered, "the black one." "He speaks," said the fat man. I spat out my mouth guard. A rope of saliva stretched and broke. I pulled off my gloves. My knuckles cracked. I removed my head protector and looked and looked. The fat man's effort with the wooden wand had not exhausted him at all. No nosebleeds, no sweat sheening his brow, no glaze of pain in his eyes. "The black wand," I said, "it's done." "You're tougher than you look, Mr. Wood," said the fat man, "and you've already met my associate. She liked you very much. Very much indeed. But she's impolite when called upon to be so, as I'm sure your instincts informed you. Don't interfere." My instincts had other ideas regarding the white woman than fear. I didn't tell the fat man that. It seemed wrong.

"You heard him," yelled Hob, "it's broken, it's destroyed. No need for repetition." He had nowhere to go: stranded on the top seat of the bleachers. "I don't give a good goddamn about the wand, Mr.

Callahan. Or about the owl. Or my nephew. Don't play coy. You know what you took. And you need, laddy buck, like many young people, to learn the difference between yours and mine." I surveyed my fellow student-statues. Simon Canary: caught drawing on a boxing glove. Errol Coward: cupping his balls through his blue shorts. Errol was a veteran fondler of his balls. Coach Madigan had one justice-seeking finger extended toward the fat man. Who had now moved out of its line. I pulled off my gloves and touched Coach Madigan's arm: warm and totally immobile. "You fat coward," said Hob. "We've proceeded to the stage of tender endearments already, I see," said the fat man. He wore a purple suit. Rich, soft-looking cloth, shining in the warm light of the gym. His shirt glare-white, his cuffs cleanly enormous, closed with gold-and-onyx links. His necktie pollen colored. His fringe of brown hair cropped and combed. A thick ring set with a hunk of agate—cat's-eye, my mother called it—gleamed on his left ring finger. A silver chain encircled his fleshy neck, and from it hung a brilliant chip of bone. He looked like a fucking magician. I went for him anyway.

I never got close. Two steps. Three. The fat man turned and smiled. One gold incisor. As opulent as his ring and wand. The white woman reappeared: from nowhere. A shadow moved, boiled up in the bright light of the gym; a breeze kicked my hair; and there she stood. Before I could think, I launched a punch. Aiming for her chin. To snap her head back. That's the quickest way to knock your opponent out. My heartbeat slowed. The world seemed to slow with it. Light thickened. The white woman's hair fluttered as if moving underwater. My fist struck her skin. It was like punching a marble carving. My hand sang. But her head did rock on her long neck, and she staggered back. *At least she's real*, I thought, *though now you're a shitbag who hits women*. I stepped up to hit her again. She was already smiling. Already moving. Her raven took wing with a knowing shriek. Her fist struck my chest. In the hollow under the sternum. Pure white filled my eyes. Blind and blinding pain. Rushing ocean noise in my ears. My limbs and torso:

THE ASSHOLES

stony cold. As though I were submerged in icy water. The center of the pain my solar plexus. My vision cleared. Gym ceiling and light fixtures swinging on their blackened chains. I was on my back. I could feel the waxy floor against my nape. I tried to focus. My vision blurred. Cleared. Blurred. Her pale, sharp face above me. Her cruel scar, her kind smile, and her crimson eyes. Saliva ran from my slack mouth. "Hob," I tried to say. A dry groan all I could manage. The white woman put her finger to her lips.

A scream: totally human. Not mine. Hob's. He leaped—flew— from the top of the bleachers, roaring, his arms spread out. He moved so quickly I barely saw it. An undersized sparrow flickering away. Headed for a window. Pure panic. Not fast enough. The fat man lifted his ringed hand and cried out another foreign phrase while Hob was still midair. The agate glowed yellow, red, sick umber, sicker black. I comprehended nothing of what he said. Hob plummeted and hit the gym floor with a brutal, soft thud. At the top of his arc his dark head had been among the upper chains of the light fixtures. His meager shadow had crossed my face. He must have fallen twenty feet. The fat man smiled. No sweat stood out on his brow or lip. No blood dripped from his nose.

"That's how it works, though," I said. Or tried to say. "That's how it works." "Out of the mouths of babes," said the fat man, "so goes the proverb. Though you might consider keeping your wisdom to yourself, laddy buck." He showed me his wand. Floating horizontally between two upraised palms. He clapped them together. The wand vanished. "Presto fucking change-o," he said. He strode over to Hob and prodded him with his shining shoe tip. Hob mewled. Tears flowing down his face. "You people and your romanticism," the fat man said, "it's fatal." All around us my unmoving classmates. Frank Santone's hands tangled with his shoelace. Wilton Opuwei's cavernous yawn. The human face and human body can be ridiculous propositions. They also can inspire love. He grabbed Hob by the collar of his school jacket and hoisted

THE WAR AGAINST

him off the floor as if he were hoisting a suitcase. Hob groaned. His tears hit the wood. I tried to reach for him. I could not move. Fat men often possess a mysterious strength. So do bald men and ugly men. Hob's fingernails scraped the oiled wood as the fat man carried him out. His head hung down. His hair. "And may I compliment your performance," the fat man said as the door mewed shut behind him. I had no idea if he meant me or the white woman who had knocked me unconscious. He could have meant both. Or Hob. He seemed like an expansive complimenter.

The stony scent of the white woman filled my nose. She was straddling me. The small, still-clear segment of my mind was shocked at her presumption. Her right hand gently encircled my throat. Her raven was clicking and hopping next to my head. A sudden terror that the bird would jab its beak into my eyes gripped me. I lifted a hand to shield them. Or attempted to. Nothing. No movement. The white woman smiled. Her iron bracelet burning against the skin over my clavicle. She bent her face to mine and pressed her lips against mine. Her eyes closing. Her breath frigid as before. When her tongue entered my mouth I almost came. My pulse drummed against her fingers. Her breathing grew heavier, quicker. Her hand never left my throat. When she broke the kiss, the white woman licked her lips and grinned at me. She stood and her raven took wing and landed on her extended arm. Blood rushed at once into my brain and my cock. Stupidity and clarity at the same time. I closed my eyes and opened my mouth and sucked in ragged lungfuls of air.

16

Our school had a mascot bodega. Hello Garden 72. They would sell you cigarettes and beer. They would even let you use their bathroom, if they knew you. The main guy was called Osmondo. He wore a name tag pinned to his sweater, even though he was the only employee.

There was an etiquette to dealing with Osmondo: You couldn't be obvious or loud. If you wanted beer you brought it up front only when there was no one else in the store. If you wanted cigarettes you made sure you were alone before you asked. That went for the bathroom too. Using the bathroom cost a dollar. You paid up without question. I never understood why more bodegas didn't adopt this business model.

People also believe, before crises arrive, that they'll know what to do. Universally. I didn't. I wanted to tear at my own skin. Sky. That's what I remember. I was shaking. My hands spasming. Running down Fifth Avenue. Our chapel bells rang the time: quarter till the hour. Did not know which hour. Sky harbor-gray. Or the color of cement. Crows on the branches of the bare trees and crows on parked cars. Hers. I knew it. They had to be. Surveillance drones, Hob had said. I was relieved she didn't use pigeons. Then again, pigeons are stupid. Then again, theatrics are important. Erzmund said it and I believe to this day that it's true. You can go through your youth and young manhood breaking noses and blacking eyes, as I did, or systematically deranging your senses with drugs or alcohol, as others did. Reality will intrude. Hob, for example. His disappearance made me ill with fear. Worse than cops marching him off. I considered my options. I could try to chase the fat man and the white woman down. Stupid: they were long gone. A wave of nausea. I fought it back. The muscles in my torso were still heaving. "That sucker-punching bitch," I said. She had not sucker punched me, to be fair. I still wanted to fuck her. Just in a limbic-system sort of way. Nothing moral. Nothing aesthetic.

Potash. The fat man. Had to be. He matched Hob's description. I had no idea what Hob had taken. When I had struggled to my feet in the gym, the white woman was gone. In the hall, no trace of her, Hob, the fat man. Other than blood drops. Hob must have left these. Warm silence, the hall air smelling like dead fruit, as usual. Whatever fluid they used to clean the floors stank sweetly. My classmates and Coach Madigan statue-still in the crosswired windows of the gym doors. I assumed Potash's handiwork was not permanent. Verner Potash. It's always a fat man in the end. Mr. Stone had called him the de facto head of his community. Sounded archaic. Quinn Klayman. That perfectly toolish name. Potash had called him his nephew. At which point I stopped walking and muttered, "Goddamn it." Another fact Hob had failed to inform us of. A woman pushing a stroller, in which slept a gaunt dark-haired child, stared and veered to the other lane of foot traffic. I called Alabama. It went right to voice mail. "You know the drill," said Alabama. Then the shrill tone. "Just call me," I said, "like now." I fished a brown cigarette out of my bag. I had two left. I figured it would help with the pain. "And of course I don't have a lighter," I muttered. Before I remembered. I just cupped the tip in my hands so passersby wouldn't see. They probably wouldn't have noticed anyway. The smoke helped. My head cleared a bit. The cold didn't bother me as much. I was still wearing my blue-and-white gym clothes, under my parka. Army surplus. Forest green. With paler patches indicating where insignia of rank once had been sewn. Nothing is worse than waiting for your phone to ring. Not even the smoke from the cigarette could calm me down.

That's when I saw. Or noticed. Or observed. Or lucked out. A rat. Grayish white. Waiting by the curb. Darting its head up to look at the sky. For crows. It froze when it saw me. When I got close, it moved. Slow. Careful. It stopped. Looked at me. I followed it another step, another two, another three. It led me. I let it. We kept up our weird pace. At moments I had to visually seek it out again: it got lost among the legs. "Good Christ, the size of that thing," squeaked an old woman, leaning on a cane. She'd seen it. I rushed past her. When the rat turned on Seventy-Second, it sped up and darted under an access alley fence. I looked up. The HELLO GARDEN sign shone, gold and green.

Osmondo nodded at me when I came in. There was no one else in the store except for an old man. As usual. Osmondo's father, the rumor went, who slept in a chair all day and all night, a newspaper tenting his lap. I wandered the aisles. I took down a can of onion soup and blew dust from the metal top. A crow perched in the naked sidewalk tree across from the bodega doorway. "How long has that crow been there," I asked Osmondo. He shrugged. His father, or whoever the old man was, cried out in his sleep: a high whine. "Bathroom," I said. Osmondo held out his huge, pink palm. I laid a damp dollar in it. The lore said he used to let junkies shoot up in there, during the heyday of junkies. A brown scrawl crossed the ceiling. The lore said it was blood. Whatever it was, they never cleaned it off the tiles. The bathroom, otherwise: nothing special. A mirror. A toilet. A poster of a green valley cradling a white house. A narrow door in the rear wall, inset with a brass lock, a cramped figure in yellow paint in the upper

THE WAR AGAINST

right corner. The same alien, faint smell I'd detected on every previous visit.

My piss sang against the porcelain. I pissed for a long time. Groaning with relief. The bell by the bodega door rang. The old man rustled his paper. Osmondo said *la puerta*. The door. I kept pissing. My balls ached. As the toilet flushed, Osmondo mumbled more. I couldn't even catch one word. I propped myself on the rear wall. The metal of the door cooled my forehead. I wanted to sleep. I find sleeping uncanny, as I said. To sleep and wake, and return to the simple, violent routine of my life: school, football, fights, failures with girls enlivened by the odd success. I didn't mean the white woman. I wasn't thinking of her. I was thinking of Maggie. How chance had intervened. I caught another draft of the Osmondo-bathroom scent. Not disgusting at all. Fragrant and dry. No one had knocked. I had time. I wanted to sleep. My eyelids slipped. The scent lulled me. The patch of door cooling my head got warm. So I shifted. The yellow mark flicked through my peripheral vision.

Not new. An old element of visual clutter. I'd never paid any attention to it. That day I examined it. I had to squint. But when I saw it, I saw it. An open eye. The symbol from Mr. Stone's tunnel doors. The symbol Alabama had decorated my arm with. The symbol, I supposed, of our war. Such as it was. "Hob's an asshole," I said, "an asshole in the hands of other assholes." I cracked myself up. Osmondo murmured again, to his father. *La puerta*. I knew what to do. I hooked the bathroom door latch. I unhooked it. If my idea worked, I didn't want anyone to be prevented from taking a piss. I slipped the silver key Hob had given me the day after the salto into the lock on this yellow-marked door.

Melior Audere: it's better to dare. The silver key fit. To my surprise, I would say. Except I was not surprised. I knew it would work. A small shock traveled up my arm. I turned the key. I turned the handle. Warm, sweet-smelling air blew into the bathroom. Grass and citrus. I pushed open the door. Orange light greeted me. More of the same scent. Richer and purer. I stepped over the toilet brush in its white holder. I stepped across the threshold. Into a short corridor lined with bookshelves. It ended in a long, low-ceilinged room. Leather armchairs. A hexagonal black table. I'd guessed right. I looked behind me. The door was closing on the brown-tiled bathroom at Hello Garden. You never know about people. Osmondo the silent. Rats chittered. Wittgenstein scampered up to my white tennis shoe and lifted his front paws. At least I thought it was him.

17

L et me put it like so," said Charthouse. "This is an absolute fucking catastrophe." He'd never said *fucking* before in my presence. He lifted the badger-head cane. He tapped his chin with it. That made me nervous. "I would say that *catastrophe* is putting it mildly, Mr. Wood," said Mr. Stone. I had spilled it all. The party. Quinn and the mirror. The owl theft. Mr. Stone balanced his silver-gray hat in his hands. That frightened me more than Charthouse's business with the cane. Charthouse kept quiet as I explained everything. I assumed he'd be furious. He sat, not speaking. Getting more silent. If that makes sense. Then he started in with the cane business. Bad enough. But when a figure like Mr. Stone begins fingering his hat, you can't help assuming the trouble you're in is serious. A rule of life. Charthouse had gotten a haircut over the holidays: trimmed almost down to the scalp. His beard gone, too. He looked younger, despite the streaks of gray. "I admit," I said, "I'm culpable." "Culpability, that's just narcissism by another name," said Charthouse. "He came in with a woman," said Mr. Stone. I explained again: the woman had appeared before Potash arrived; they did not come in together. Tall, white skin, white hair, a scar on her throat. Wearing a business suit and heels. A pet raven. I left out the part about wanting to fuck her. Didn't seem right to repeat. "And did you recognize her," Charthouse asked. "No," I said. "You can do better than that, Mr. Wood," said Mr. Stone. "I didn't, okay," I said. No reason for me to be protesting. "Come on, Mike, let's commune with the ancients before we make any rash decisions," said Charthouse. His breath smelled like spearmint gum. Mr. Stone was scanning his bookshelves as he talked to me. "Here we are," he said. He held a book at my eye level, in one palm. It had an iron-looking latch. "Is this mug shots," I said. "Not exactly," said Charthouse.

Smell of old paper. No title on the cover. A metal emblem inset: the open eye. The book was written in German. It took me a long time to realize that, because the writing was spiky and hard to decipher. Even then I could only tell from the umlauts. Long, blearing passages of text. Diagrams: I saw a tree, rooted in the earth and reaching to the sky. Concentric spheres. A symbol that looked, to me, like a stick figure with horns and a unibrow jumping up in the air, its arms spread. There were actual illustrations. Images. A long-haired young man standing in an empty amphitheater. His left hand resting on a globe and a rose clutched in his right. A donkey and a lion yoked to a cart, in which rode what appeared to be the sun, wreathed in fire. "What is this," I asked. "It's a book by Erchaana of Dachaaua," said Charthouse, "which clearly makes no difference to you. Keep flipping." I did. I saw a woman, tall and slender, naked, with long colorless hair covering her nipples. At her feet a raven. A skeleton astride a mountain, lifting up a sword. I turned back to the naked woman. "Yes," I said, "it's her." "Well, that's just marvelous," said Charthouse, "I leave you alone for a week and it's the end of the world." "The crows work for her," I said. "You are a master of the astutely irrelevant," said Mr. Stone. "I dreamed about her, I think," I said, before I even realized it was true.

I could not recall anything other than fragments: a stone basin, stars, a throat. "I'll wager you did," said Charthouse, "she feels at home in the dreams of young men. Me? No longer troubled." "Nor am I," said Mr. Stone.

Messaline. That was the name—once I'd deciphered the thorny script of the title plate—under the naked woman's feet. "And you hit her," said Charthouse, "as in your fist made contact." I nodded. The ancillary pain of her blow had faded. Where she'd landed the punch still ached every time I breathed. "She must be slipping, in her dotage," said Mr. Stone. "You have hidden talents," said Charthouse, "not to mention the fact that you're walking around. Lift up your shirt." I did. "Holy mother of god," he said. "What," I said. I assumed he'd be delivering a death announcement. "It's just a bruise," said Charthouse, "you got off easy." "So she's a sorceress, or whatever," I said. "We've seen indications that she was present in the city," said Mr. Stone. "She was one of von Sebottendorf's consorts. Although it would perhaps be more accurate to describe him as one of her many consorts." "The crows," I said. "It's better," said Charthouse, "not to talk about them. There's a large crow community in the tristate area. They're diligent." Charthouse was pacing and hammering his palm with the cane. Mr. Stone sat in his chair, spinning his hat on a finger. I looked at the image of Messaline again. "Aren't you guys going to do anything," I said. Wittgenstein and his brothers and sisters took note. My voice echoed: Mr. Stone's house had strong acoustics.

"'You guys,'" said Charthouse, "misses the facts of the case. There's no you guys here. There's only us." "Well, then maybe we should hit back," I said. "How would that go," said Charthouse, "you don't know where he is. You don't know what he took. I assume he's hidden it somewhere. They want us to hunt it up for them, I'd say. But there's a real knowledge deficit here, no, Mr. Stone?" Mr. Stone stopped spinning his hat. "'A knowledge deficit,'" said Mr. Stone, "does not begin to capture the situation." This is what I mean. You find the secret key.

You stumble on the secret door. And no revelation awaits you. Mr. Stone's hat spun on his finger and rats leaped over Charthouse's shoes. For the first time I wished I'd let Hob sell me out. Just to be done with this. Then my head wouldn't hurt all the time, my lungs and muscles wouldn't burn. "Sheer sentimentality," said Mr. Stone. "Look, I understand you're a wizard or whatever," I said, "but could you not do that. I can't do it to you." "Mr. Wood," said Mr. Stone, "you go right now to Mountjoy and sign their contract. You have to, before they admit you, you know. In blood. With an iron pen. You would have an excellent chance of admission. Their standards are, despite their pretenses, low. They seek the obedient, nothing more. They themselves are obedient. Like all cowards they dress up their cowardice as bravery. I can alter your face," said Mr. Stone, "if you are so inclined." "Fuck you," I said. "That is the spirit, Mr. Wood," said Mr. Stone, "we all are in pain. And I am considerably older than you. So please do not complain until you better know what it is of which you speak." His accent increased. Just for his last exhortation. Accent shifts happened to my grandmother and father too, when they got excited. Except they sounded like they were from Canarsie. Mr. Stone sounded like a movie Nazi. "I told you that anyone can whistle. That everyone does. That this does not mean we are all Mozarts. You understood." I nodded. "Hob Callahan could be described as Mozart. A talent of such depth and breadth," he said. Stopped. "In fact, to describe his abilities would only demean them. Language being, as you will discover if you attain your maturity, eternally insufficient. He is a potential champion of this cause, in which we serve as mere soldiers. You understand, I trust, our concern. So, Mr. Wood, let me ask once more: are you an asshole?" said Mr. Stone.

I almost said yes. Charthouse was watching. Wittgenstein was watching. "I am not an asshole," I said. "Then you must decide whether you're in or you're out," said Mr. Stone, "equivocation, my boy, will not do." Wittgenstein quirked his whiskers and his pink nose.

THE WAR AGAINST

I thought of the white woman. Of Potash. Of Hob. Of my mother and father, inexplicably. I didn't know what they wanted. I didn't know what would be asked of me. Only that it would be. That, when you're a child, is sufficient. "I'm in," I said. "We don't work with contracts, you understand," said Charthouse. I nodded. "You are a man of your word, Mr. Wood, I can see that. A rare thing in this unpredictable life," said Mr. Stone.

Image of the lithe, naked woman. Or girl. It was her. A raven at her feet, a fountain next to her. Above her head the crescent moon. *Messaline, die Verräterin.* "She was a witch," said Mr. Stone. "That's an archaic term," I said. Mr. Stone shook his head. "It is a term of perverse respect. It means merely a user of the art who refuses the yoke they offer. I cannot blame her for accepting it. Most of her colleagues died, if this text is accurate, at the Massacre of Amiens in 1172." "They never taught us that," I said, "in world history. No massacre." "It has nothing to do with the teaching of history," said Mr. Stone, "it is a fact." "Thou shalt not suffer a witch to live," said Charthouse, "unless you give her a job. And you really hit her," he said. "She works at Mountjoy House," I said. "We believe so," said Mr. Stone. "Head of enforcement, is our best guess," said Charthouse, "as to what her business card says." This made sense. "And she's immortal," I said. "All men are mortal, and Socrates is a man, therefore Socrates is mortal," said Charthouse. "She seems to have grasped the essentials of longevity, however," said Mr. Stone. "What does verraterin mean," I said. "*Verräterin,*" said Mr. Stone. His Nazi accent alive again. "It means 'traitress.'"

A silverfish crawled peacefully over the naked woman's long body. I watched its pointless progress. Mr. Stone reset the fold in his silver-gray hat. He could have been any quiet and irascible old man of the Upper West Side. Except we were in what could only be called his lair. "And the wands," I said. "They make the pain stop. If you use them. I'm right, aren't I," I said, "instead of just doing it." "Insofar as pain on this earth has an end point," said Mr. Stone, "then yes. Congratulations." "And it's just a philosophical difference," I said. "All differences are philosophical, Mr. Wood," said Mr. Stone. "They will absolutely kill you though if you lift your head up too much," said Charthouse, "and that's not metaphysics. It's just a tyranny-of-the-majority thing."

He had a point. That is how the human race functions. The strong crush the weak. No matter what people say. "Can't we just murder him from a distance," I said. "I cannot," said Mr. Stone, "can you? Would you care to attempt this feat? You will find that you have no idea where to begin. It is not an improvisation with a mirror. Say we succeeded. What good would it do Hob?" I didn't argue. He was of course correct. "And Potash said nothing more than that: you have something of mine," said Mr. Stone. I nodded. "So why does she have a scar across her throat," I said. "It is one of their punishments, or it used to be," said Mr. Stone, "for violating their law. Silencing. Some it renders powerless. If they have become dependent on incantations. It comes with the first offense. There are other more serious penalties." "She didn't *seem* powerless," I said. "Some cases," said Charthouse, "and you see what I mean about the tyranny of the majority. I bet they had her in brace-lets, too." Cold, tumorous metal: that I remembered. Her tongue in my mouth: that I remembered. Wittgenstein was running around in lunatic circles. His siblings watched in suspicion.

"Mr. Wood, why do you care what happens to Hob," said Mr. Stone. I did not speak immediately. I knew the wrong answer would be fatal here. Not only to me. To the whole endeavor. Or maybe this was just another test. I was sick of tests. Of guessing. "Professional courtesy," I said. It was a phrase my father used to describe the obligation binding him to other lawyers. Even those who outpaced him in his craft, who were always running ahead. Charthouse started guffawing. "I appreciate that answer more than you know," said Mr. Stone. "Professional courtesy," repeated Charthouse. He took down a decanter and three glasses from a high cabinet. The decanter tall and graceful. Filled with liquor. In which swam a single delicate aquamarine eel. "And what about those," I said as he poured. "Do you actually want to know," he said. "Not really," I said. "Few do," said Mr. Stone. "Happy new year," said Charthouse. "You're late," I said. "Spirit of the season," said Charthouse.

18

No matter what philosophers argue, you can't take the long view. Not in your own case. You can't say that nothing matters because we all die anyway. You can, however, draw a knife. A black-handled one. From the breast pocket of your black suit. If you were Vincent Callahan, this might have been your course of action.

And I watched. Could do nothing else. He flicked the knife open: the blade short and curved. A trickle of water, constant and fluting, ran down the wall. A vivid green moss grew on the bricks in its path. With the opened blade he scraped a long strip of the moss into his cupped hand and crumbled it. The fragments floated slowly down, glimmering, and came to rest on a large pile of other fragments: pipe tobacco, rose petal, eyebright. He stirred the crumbled moss into the mixture with a finger. His knife still open. He wasn't looking at me. "You know," he said, "if you'd told me." Left it at that. Tapped the blade against my chest. I didn't flinch. We breathed in the smells of his herbarium. A small room behind one of the many doors in

THE WAR AGAINST

Karasarkissian's basement. I'd never spent so much time in basements. I hoped it would not adversely affect my health. They say you need sunshine. Then again I still spend a lot of time underground. I'm healthy as an ox. "This is at least thirty-three and a third percent your fault," said Vincent. I didn't deny it. "Speak," said Vincent. "I'm sorry," I said. "Fuck you and fuck your apologies," said Vincent. He was shaking, mildly. A sign he might hit me. I would have to overact if he did. To spare his feelings. He had thin arms and thin shoulders. So did his brother.

He left me there. Alabama was waiting in the main room. He didn't say anything to her. He sat on the green couch and covered his face for a minute. Two minutes. A scene in a domestic drama. Inflated and real at once. Odd the turns your life takes, in your youth. "I have no idea what I'm going to tell my parents," he said, "and I don't want to lie. But I can't." He stopped speaking. "Charthouse will do it," said Alabama. Vincent nodded. "Nothing else for it," said Vincent. "So what did you take," he said. "I took the owl, and Hob took the wand," I said, "but that's not what he was talking about." "What was he talking about, then," said Vincent. "I do not know," I said. "Well, that's just delightful," said Vincent. He closed his eyes. He locked his hands. Irmgard's concrete bucket rattled against the floor. Cords stood out in Vincent's neck. Irmgard's wings, with audible, pinpoint percussions, opened. "Okay," said Alabama. I went to examine. The owl snapped her beak at me. Spun her head. I pressed a finger against her breast. Not warm. She took off. "At least she won't shit everywhere," I said. "Owl, speak," said Vincent, "tell us the secret wisdom we lack, o great and mighty owl." Irmgard clacked her beak. Vincent's eyes lustered. Tears. His chin shook. Irmgard floated in a slow circle. "Does she need mice," I said. "Why do you assume it's a she," said Alabama. "Her name's Irmgard," I said. "That is a fallacy," said Alabama. "What else did Quinn say," said Vincent. "What did he say," I said, "let's see. He talked a lot about his destiny." "He called us insects," said Alabama.

Irmgard swooped down when Alabama said *insects*. "Great, sentience," said Vincent. "He said he would kill us. That his family was important," I said, "that the map is not the territory."

"Thanks, genius," said Vincent, "that's a really useful contribution." He was already climbing the ladder. "One of you grab that owl," he said. Irmgard was perched on the green couch. I snagged her. She hooted and struggled. "What do we do with her," I said. "What do you think," said Vincent. "Hold her by her talons, maybe," said Alabama. This worked. Though I had to climb the ladder one-handed. A clear night. We could see it through the plate glass, beyond the black inverses of the word KARASARKISSIAN'S. "I've been coming here for six years and I still have no idea who the guy is," said Vincent. Irmgard was fluttering and thrashing. Not too hard. Then again, she wasn't too alive. The air cold. The sky full of stars. Unusual for New York. We walked. It wasn't that late. Pedestrians saw us. No one really cared. It's a forgiving city. Despite what people say. "Could you do that to a person," I said. "Could I do this to a person," said Vincent, "do you think I'd be hanging out underground with jack-offs like you if I could do this to a person." Irmgard snapped her beak on empty air.

One bum in Stuyvesant Square. Bundled up to his eyes. We walked along the curving path. Empty benches, yellow windows, and stars. When we reached the rough middle, where the paths open up, Vincent told me to get ready. Irmgard was struggling harder now. A memory of night-flying in her dead, hollowed body. Life's tenacious. You can't escape what you've done. "Do I just throw her," I said. "Try," said Alabama. I did. Irmgard took wing and hooted. A hollow hoot. The kind you'd expect from a stuffed owl. The bum said, in a modulated appraiser's voice, "That's a hell of an owl." She was winging away. Their wings don't make noise. I'd forgotten that fact. We stood there in the park, watching her flight. Listening to the bum chuckle and huff. Alabama's arm grazed mine. We both jerked back. "I am so tired," said Vincent. He walked away without saying anything else. His tie gleamed in the lamplight. "Two kids in love," said the bum, "damn right."

"Listen," said Alabama, "don't take this the wrong way but do you want to come back to my house." I nodded. I didn't want to be alone. A rain-and-hail combo started as we walked. "It's not far," she said. I didn't mind the weather. It was clearing my head. We walked west. Rain glittered in her hair. Hail fragments glittered in her eyelashes, in the yellow street light. She lived in an actual house on Perry Street: Old brick, three stories. Ivy and tall windows. Her parents had inherited it from her great-uncle Avery, who died without children. When we got there, her parents ambushed us in the living room. Mark and Lena Sturdivant. I asked them what they did for a living. That was my single conversational opener with adults. They both claimed to be artists. Alabama rolled her eyes as they spoke. "We're going upstairs," she said. "Do you need tea," said her father. "No, I think we're okay," said Alabama.

I'd never been in a house in the city before. Floor-to-floor stairs: new. At their top, a long, dim hallway. Black-and-white photographs on the walls. A wagon wheel in a tangle of grass. The evil, cronish face of a hen, in close-up. "They're just rich people," Alabama said, "on both sides. I don't know why they tell everyone they're artists. My father painted when he was in college. My mother used to perform these weird plays. It's not art." She hurled herself onto her bed. Huge and white. I rocked in a rocking chair, cutting a deck of cards one-handed. To relax. There wasn't much to say. Hail beat the windows. Alabama wore a gray sweater that reached her knees. It made her look younger and bonier. Her parents' laughter drifted up: explosive, hollow. Her mother was far less beautiful than I'd expected, her tear-shaped, lightly prognathous face framed by dull, dull hair. I'd been reasoning from Alabama's appearance. She looked exactly like her father: same jaw, same long eyes. She was taking a year between high school and college. "They were totally for it," she said, "for my

THE ASSHOLES

exploring. It was really disgusting." She told me she'd met Charthouse during her last year at Brock Hall. He'd come to their college fair, as an alumnus of Columbia. "He's an electrical engineer," she said, "I mean I had no idea what he was talking about but he showed us this generator. We all held hands. Our hair stood up. He said that's what Columbia would be like. It was so absurd. Then we got to talking. He asked me all these questions. He gave me a copy of the *Calendar*." I kept rocking and I kept cutting. "You know you get silent at all the wrong times," said Alabama. "They're not going to kill him, right," I said. "They probably would have just done it right there, if they were," she said. "What do you think Irmgard is doing right now," I said. "Getting rained on," she said.

She had books. She kept them in her closet, out of sight of her parents. Books on theurgical history, including an English translation of Erchaana of Dachaaua. She knew much of what I asked without having to look it up. The Treaty of Constantinople, concluded in 901 by Sviatoslav the Mad, a Croatian warlock, and Pope Benedict IV. Or the Massacre of Amiens: shortly before the city of Amiens joined the crown possessions of France, an emissary came to its lords from Louis VII. He demanded that, as a precondition for assimilation, the city fathers gather together the local witches and warlocks, of which there had long been a thriving community, since the days of Chlodio. This emissary was called Perrin de Cissey; he ranked among the greatest theurgists of his day, a master in the art of scapulimancy, the art of divination by the use of shoulder bones. De Cissey offered the assembled warlocks and witches a choice: convert or face execution. All of them, all of the Great Hundred, as they are called, refused. Except one, a woman. De Cissey spoke a phrase; the gathered men and woman cried out in agony, as pain raced through their veins and arteries, as their feet grew into the ground and their arms stretched skyward, as their senses deserted them and their skins hardened into bark: a stand of elm. He meant it as a mark of respect. He offered the traitress a place but with a condition. She accepted. He chained her to an oaken board and cut out her vocal cords with an iron dagger. Had iron bracelets hammered closed around her wrists. She survived, said Alabama. She survived even de Cissey, who died at the hands of Philip Augustus.

A lineman in a rocking chair and a lithe girl, armed. Alone in a room in the cold rain. You could not ask for anything more aesthetic. To this day the memory fills me with vague shame. Youth, youth, and more youth. "Good night," I said, "I enjoyed meeting your parents." "I don't know why," she said, closing her eyes. The lids rosy. She stuck out her hand for a shake. She was lying with the book tented over her abdomen. I walked down the stairs and out into the weather. Her parents told me I was always welcome in their home. I had to bite back a laugh. They stood framed in their open doorway. Stone wolfhounds, navel-high, one on either side of the door. "We love meeting Ally's friends," said her father, "it's *très* cool."

19

The world, says Erzmund, *will invite you to struggle. Gainsay it. The expert has nothing to do with moral struggles or any other of the trumpery decorating this unpredictable life.* No use telling an eighteen-year-old not to struggle. Yet I tried to heed his advice. It was difficult. Nobody noticed at school that Hob was gone. They just stopped calling his name in class. Sister Immaculata never mentioned him, once, during chapel or world history. Coach Madigan said nothing. Gilder made no jokes about his gayness. Potash had done his work well. Whatever charm he'd spoken, whatever incantation—pure art, seamless and whole. It worried me. Against that, what hope do you have? Then again, if it hadn't been for Messaline, I was fairly sure I could have at least punched him in the face. He didn't look tough. A lifetime of getting by, of working your will without pain or cost, without even having to think, you wave your wand and speak a formula and there it is: this would damage you. Such a life could make you weak. Such a life could make you lazy. Such a life could make you stupid. One of the hallmarks of stupidity is the

THE WAR AGAINST

overrating of your own talent. This is universal to the truly stupid.

School buildings on Saturdays: ghost city. Especially a Catholic school. Your steps echo. Your voice falls flat. The high ceilings menace you. The pious, piercing eyes of Saint Cyprian stare up at you from the floor mosaic. Cyprian was martyred in 258 AD in the city of Carthage. Beheading. He knelt and blindfolded himself beforehand and thanked his god. I hate pictures of saints. Even now. But Coach Madigan liked to remind us that we had duties to higher powers than ourselves. Thus the football team had to come in two weekends a month. Coach Madigan would set up early practices and make us do endurance training: sprints, tire courses, weight vests. That morning he made us run suicides in the gym. Errol Coward puked on the red synthetic-clay track that encircled the field. I did not puke. "Gentlemen, this is a disgrace," he said, "a disgrace." I'd asked him about Hob, right at the start. Just to see what would happen. To see how complete Potash's victory was. Coach Madigan looked through me. My words did not register. "You gonna die today," Greg Gilder said to me as we lined up for the tire course. Pointing. Dead grin. Those teeth. "That's the spirit, Gilder," said Coach Madigan. "Yeah, that's the spirit," I said. Low and hollow. "Do you have precious thoughts to share with the team, Wood," said Coach Madigan. I wanted to assert that Hob existed. Despite all their empty heads. I didn't say anything.

Coach Madigan dismissed us at noon. I showered and dressed, my clothes sticking to my damp skin. I went for a wander around the halls. That's what I did after weekend practices. To see what was going on. I once caught Sister Immaculata eating cherries, framed in the doorway of the teacher's lounge, eating them out of a blue paper cone and spitting the pits with demonic accuracy into a metal trash can. It rang. Every hit. Cyprian's seemed empty. I was ready to leave. When I saw Hob's locker. Then I knew. The padlock shining. It made me feel like a moron. I thought: *What if it's in there?* This also seemed moronic. Too obvious. Too easy to access. For Potash, I mean. But I couldn't shake the thought. Maybe it was. I remembered that story by Poe they made us read. I walked over. On tiptoe. Number 318. I fingered the padlock. Heavy and cold. The building creaked. A rat ran out of an open classroom door. "Don't remind me," I said. It paused at my feet. Stared up. I shook my head. It scurried on. Claws clicking. I wondered if all the rats in the city worked for Mr. Stone.

Hob's combination. I knew I couldn't guess it. So I just held the lock in my fist, letting it get warm. I checked the length of the hall. I even ran up to either end and stared down the connecting corridors. No one around. The rat had gone. I shrugged off my equipment bag and kneeled. I took the lock in my two hands. I pictured the wheels inside of it—not that I had the faintest idea of how a lock was set up internally—spinning and aligning. I tried to let go. I tried not to struggle. Nothing. I took a deep breath. I tried again. Clenching my jaw. The dial budged. A tick or two. Again, nothing. "Please, god, please, god," I said. My curt prayer echoed. Useless. I knew. I said it anyway. I concentrated again. A drop of blood slid from my nose. The dial twitched against my palm. Nothing. "Fuck it," I said. I turned to leave. I saw Hob fall again. I saw Potash's opulent head. Then I was breathing through my clenched teeth. Furious. I drew back my fist, to punch the metal door. Yellow. About the color of the sigil of the open eye. Why we had yellow lockers I never knew. And then I realized. Things had slowed down. My heartbeat. My breathing. My blood flow. All the trembling and effort, gone. I just felt calm. Like I was standing within a quiet, clean-aired auditorium, as a spectator to my own actions.

My fist was moving toward the door, a fluid centimeter at a time. A water pipe rumbled. I heard each bubble breaking. My fist continued. I watched it, fascinated. It was going to hit, I saw, the door of Hob's locker high up, near the louvers. *You're going to fuck your hand up,* I thought. No fear or worry. Pure observation. *The lock,* I thought, *would make a more logical target.* So I changed my fist's course. All it took was a simple, subtle bending of my right knee. I watched, from my invisible

THE WAR AGAINST

theater, as my fist traveled at a dignified pace through the light-filled air, in which dust motes slowly swam. My fist gathered speed. All I had to do was think and it happened. My fist was now moving faster than the motes. When my skin struck the lock, my arm thrummed, and then my whole body. The metal of the U-shaped shackle fractured. A clean, elongated chime. The metal gave up heat. Singed my knuckle. The lock fell. Clanged. Spun on the floor, throwing glints.

Time resumed its normal stupid hurry. My pulse and blood sped up. A red spot blooming between my first and second knuckles, blooming and fading. That's the only harm I suffered. I pocketed the broken padlock. When you see the first evidence that you're not a total failure, you want to hang on to it. His locker door mewed as I opened it. A slight gust of slightly stale air. Lucky he had not left a sandwich in there. I assumed Potash's incantation would have concealed that from the numb minds of my schoolmates and teachers as well. I smelled only metal and soap. Deodorant. His school books stacked and squared against one wall. His crimson scarf and coat hanging from the hook on the inner side of the door. I thought of his parents and his brother. My stomach twisted. I almost vomited. More blood dripped from my nose. I didn't want to rifle through his possessions. It seemed obscene, now that I had the locker open. His coat first: checked the pockets, inside and out. No luck. I felt his scarf, and my heart leaped when my fingers detected a pin. It was attached to nothing. I heard Frank Santone blare, "Let's move it, fatass." Probably aimed at Errol Coward, called by most of us Bitchtits. Not his fault. Santone's voice watery and diminished. The golden vibration that had filled me when I broke the lock blackened. I don't know how else to express it. Became throbbing, body-wide pain.

Nothing in Hob's calculus textbook. Except symbols and problems I could not understand. I had not placed into calculus. I took a math class called Advanced Topics. A euphemism. You can't call anything remedial in a school that costs almost thirty grand per year to attend. Nothing in his biology textbook. The same grasshopper stared out from the cover. Nothing in his physics textbook, except for a few shreds of herb and moss from a cigarette. I picked up our English anthology and began to leaf through its tissue-thin pages. I tore on, across a section from Beowulf. The edges of the book were clean and white, no dog-ears, no gray grime. This did not surprise me. When I came to the section on the Romantics, to John Keats's poem "La Belle Dame sans Merci," I saw he'd excised a shallow oblong trough in the pages. A hiding place. Like in a crime novel. Lying in it was the cigarette case he'd taken back from Quinn. A gift from an ex. The stupid, insignificant reason he was suffering now. I opened it. I don't know what I thought I'd find. It was empty. So I pocketed it, along with Hob's spare deck of cards and his wristwatch. Why he had decided to remove it that day, who knows. One of those gestures that gets lost in the tangle of history. His textbooks and coat and scarf I crammed into my equipment bag. I wanted to look them over again to make sure I hadn't missed anything. The voice of a crowd rose and fell, and I heard the hollow boom Cyprian's front door made whenever it shut after being opened. Barring any rats or random school staff, I was now alone. The broken lock and the cards and Hob's watch in my left pocket, the empty case in my right. Such are the tools with which you confront your life. Always insufficient.

20

The Black Dog. That was the name of the bar Vincent worked at. On Amsterdam, near a synagogue with the facade of a shut, fortified armory. I remembered the name because Simon Canary once asked Hob about getting his brother to let him in there. Hob told him that the bar was a shithole, and there were plenty of shitholes in New York happily serving the underage that wouldn't require his owing his brother a favor. Such actions impeded his popularity. That's how life is. Follow your principles and you will suffer. As it turned out Simon wouldn't have needed any help getting into the Black Dog. I walked through the doors in the middle of a Saturday, carrying a school-emblemed gym bag, and nobody asked me for identification. There was in fact nobody there except Vincent. Standing behind the bar in a black suit and golden tie. Drinking from a white mug with the words WORLD'S GREATEST printed on one side and a large, canine-shaped chunk missing from the lip. Flies: also present. They came in for the warmth. "Prove it," sang whoever was singing on the jukebox. A guitar arpeggio followed. "Oh come on," Vincent said when he saw me. I held up my hand. "I have an idea," I said. "Wood, seriously, your ideas are terrible, all right," he said. I let him finish. I explained. He didn't scoff. He didn't say anything at first. "We should at least check, right," I said, "even if I didn't find anything the first time." He took another slurp. "What do you expect me to find that you didn't," said Vincent. "He's your brother," I said. "Don't fucking remind me," he said. The jukebox emitted its underearthly blue-green glow. Vincent clicked his tongue. I said nothing. The singer continued to sing. Half yowl, half pure. The light the exact shade, I realized, of the sea serpents in the whiskey carboys. "We need to be quick about this," he said. Started moving. Shut off the lights.

His apartment: bare. A bed. A lamp. A tall mirror canted against one wall. Four bookcases. Crammed. The shelves bowed under the weight. Four windows looked down onto the street. You could see the sign for the Black Dog. "You have an easy commute," I said. "Do you not understand what quick means," said Vincent. He was already pacing. Foot routes worn into the uncarpeted floor. I dumped the contents of Hob's locker. The bio textbook landed faceup, the grasshopper staring. I wish the world could survive without insects. They make human rapacity seem gentle and moderate. "All right," said Vincent. He lifted his brother's empty coat. His knife flashed. That same short curved knife he'd used to collect the cigarette moss from the water-lapped basement wall. He drew it with frightening speed. He cut out the coat's lining from the torso, using the knife's point. Wrist tense. Shook the coat. Nothing. He removed the sleeves and opened them. The scarf he examined and tossed away. The textbooks he cut up with the same cool-handed, orderly haste: spread them, cut the glue or thread that held the pages in, run the blade under the endpapers, shake out the bundles of pages. "These are called," he said, lifting a bundle, "signatures, by the way, you ignorant ape." I'd never heard the word used in that sense before. "I remember this book with the katydid," he said as he sliced the bio book's binding, "or maybe she didn't. Fucking Katy." The grasshopper stared, hungering, blank.

His cutting drew and held my gaze. He did it in a professional-seeming trance, eyes nearly closed. When he had reduced the books, the coat, and the scarf to neat rags, he said: "Well, that was a total failure. Is there anything else?" I almost didn't give him the case. I almost failed to mention it. Because it had come from Hob's nameless ex-boyfriend. Because it was empty. Which I told Vincent. "Nothing in it," I said. He popped the latch and eyed the metal interior. "Nothing, huh," he said. "I mean just look," I said. "You do not know my brother very well, Wood," said Vincent. He stared at the metal interior again and jabbed his thumbnail at the top inside cover. The plating behind the obsidian plaque. "There we go," he said. A panel had popped open. Inside, I saw a yellow-white square of paper. "What," said Vincent. He had the paper or parchment or vellum open, close to his eyes, nose against its surface. His breathing intensified. He inhaled its—I presume—scent. "What," he said. Low and whispery now. In reverence. "Michael Wood," he said. "What," I said. "No, shut up and look," he said.

The paper was no longer empty. From its outer edges, lines sped toward the center, making precise ninety-degree turns, dividing, ending. It was hypnotic. When the lines had finished moving, I saw a square room. One of its outer walls had a section of dots and dashes. Directly opposite was a solid black line. A window. A door. At the middle point between them a large, ornate letter M. "Vincent Callahan," said Vincent. A V appeared. "Eileen Chao," said Vincent. The view shifted, zoomed out: the paper showed two clean-lined rectangles now, sharing an edge. In the upper right corner of the second, an E. "She's your neighbor, right," I said. "Your deductive skills have improved," said Vincent, "I didn't even know any of these things still existed. Charthouse is going to shit himself." It was a floor plan. The type you see in real estate ads. "Hob said he got this case from a guy he knew," said Vincent, "no way. Not possible. Do you know what this is? This is like a museum piece. Dr. Henry Alfred motherfucking Kissinger."

The paper changed. The lines faded, then raced, straight and steady, across the ivory surface once more. They formed a large, irregular rectangle, subdivided into smaller boxes: an apartment or an office. A black *H*, in elegant, spiky handwriting, appeared in one of the smaller boxes. "He must be taking a shit or jerking off," said Vincent, "he's been in the bathroom forever. At least I assume it's a bathroom." "Who's Henry Kissinger," I said. "I remember the instruction at Cyprian's being poor, but that's ridiculous," said Vincent. The black *H* floated from the small room into a larger room, one that shared a border with the empty space around the diagram, and paused before a dashed-and-dotted section of the line representing the wall. You could tell right away what we were seeing: a human being looking out a window. Around us lay the torn strips of paper and cloth that had once been Hob's possessions. "He loved that scarf," said Vincent.

Mappa mundi. That's what the folded parchment was called. They had first been used during the early Renaissance, when the technique for creating them was mastered by the monk Udo of Brescia, a calligrapher and theurge in the employ of the library at the Abbazia di San Colombo in Bobbio, Italy. So Vincent told me. *Mappae mundi* required, he said, the labor of a hundred days to make, during which the cartographer had to remain awake. Otherwise the map would stay merely an empty sheet of paper. This prolonged insomnia carried with it the risk of insanity or death, so the cartographer also had to be a past master in the use of medical herbs and the spells and formulae governing the body in order to survive it. Cartographers could make a sufficient fortune from creating one *mappa* to live on for the rest of their lives. The initiator of the art, the loyal Udo, had made not one but six, according to Vincent, and made them only for the greater glory of the church and his public god. Not for money. You could observe the location and precise surroundings of anyone or any place whose name you knew. You could ask it even more than that. The true powers of the *mappa*, Vincent said, had never yet been exhausted. Ask and be answered. It required nothing of you. No effort. Just a word, that's all. It struck me as unfair. "This is how they live, all the time," said Vincent as we walked down Amsterdam, grimacing into the wind, "do you understand me?"

The gritty wind drew tears. They careened down my cheeks. "No one's ever been able to explain, to my satisfaction at least," Vincent said, "why they keep trying to stamp out any opposing tradition. Look at what they have. Why do they care if a few jackasses are stubborn enough to work their wills without the aid of stuff like this?" He had a point. I had one too. "Why take him? Couldn't they just have read his mind or used an incantation or something? I mean about the map." "Hob is very good at hiding things," said Vincent, "in case you hadn't noticed." "People who are good at hiding things don't use lockers," I said. "Hidden in plain sight. Obscurity through transparency. And the only reason you were able to find this at all, I'd guess, is that it was his like contingency plan for you or me or someone to do so," said Vincent. "Why did he lie, though," I said, "in the first place." "I assume, and I'm just speculating here," said Vincent, "that he didn't want to tell Alabama because she would have straight-up murdered him." "And that case wasn't his or a gift or whatever," I said. "Exactly, Holmes," said Vincent. "So how did he know that Quinn had it," I said. You never get over catechism. "Hob has light fingers. He has tremendous instincts. People talk to him when they should shut up," said Vincent, "simple as that. It's the weak-little-boy act he does. Put yourself in his place. Can you honestly say you wouldn't have given in to temptation? If you came into possession of that info? Especially given things are the way they are? That's a big no. That's a big fuck no." A crow was tracking us, high overhead. Cawing and circling. "You see," said Vincent, "that's what I'm talking about." "Tyranny of the majority," I said. "It doesn't have to be that way." Vincent's mouth crimped and wryed. Disgust formed his primary visible emotion. That's how it goes with idealists. This I've since learned. I nodded, trying to look wise. "Why are you making that face," said Vincent.

He called people as we walked. A true pro. An apartment broker, I thought. He had an impressive phone voice: he dropped his regular reedy voice about half an octave and injected loud, confident joviality into it. He spoke to a coworker whom he got to cover his shift. He spoke to a woman named Kavitha, crowing her name, out of an appointment with whom he had to wriggle. "Sorry, I know I've been a flake," he said, gnawing a thumbnail, "I know. I know it's ridiculous. I know. But then again that's why you like me so much, is that I'm unpredictable." More gnawing. He pumped a fist in silent celebration when she bought (I assumed) his excuse, which was that he had to go to the dentist. I was impressed. His life possessed a complexity mine innately lacked. When you're not yet twenty you venerate those older than you but under thirty as paragons of autonomy. "The master at work," said Vincent. He made a third call. I realized it was Charthouse as soon as Vincent started speaking: all that fake timbre and depth was gone from his voice and he sounded as he had when he spoke to me the first night we met. He said he'd found it. Found what it was. He explained. Waited. Then he told Charthouse I had helped, for a change. "Yeah, we'll meet you there," said Vincent, "I think bringing some's a good idea, you never know. Okay. Okay. In a bit." He hung up. He exhaled. He said, voice steady and cold, "Hats off to the great masters." We kept walking. Vincent kept smoking. "There's a chance that idiot might survive, assuming they didn't kill him already," said Vincent. "Why would they kill him," I said. "It's true that what he took is a value proposition for them," said Vincent, "but you never can tell when you're dealing with Nazis." "You mean metaphorically, right," I said. I remembered Mr. Stone's tales of Hitler and Sebottendorf. "*Metaphorically*'s a big word," said Vincent.

There. Turned out to be a concrete staircase leading upward and inward from Cathedral Parkway onto a dead hill in the park. Stained steps, no balustrades. Charthouse waited at the bottom. Face stony. He wore a heel-reaching leather coat and a glazed bush hat, and he carried his cane and a white plastic bag. The sky had gone leaden. Snow speckled the steps, their rectilinear, scarred path. "How did Hob end up with it," he said. No preface. No preamble. "He used to rob my mother's purse. He used to rob my father's wallet," said Vincent, "and he wouldn't even spend the money. He would show me. So draw your own conclusions." Dry thunder. "Let's get to it," said Charthouse. We climbed the stairs. His cane clattering. The silver badger's yellow eyes seemed alight. I knew the stairs. I knew the hill. At the top lay the plateau where I had smoked weed for the first time. With Simon Canary. He called it the Magic Mountain. Stone benches. An empty malt liquor bottle, into the neck of which an optimist had inserted a black, dead twig. A view out over the Meer, which is the name of the lake in the park's northeast corner. Islands of gray-white ice drifting. Dead high grass. Dead-glinting foil shards. Charthouse tossed me the grocery bag. It contained, I saw, three shrink-wrapped packages: ground beef, tripe, and deep-hued, gleaming liver. "Only the finest," said Vincent. "Looks tasty," I said. "Dump them out," he said. I did. The maxi-pad-like oblongs of paper and Styrofoam they package meat with clung to my freezing fingers. Watery blood dripped. "Is this a sacrifice," I said. "Only of eleven American dollars," said Charthouse.

The meat sat on the cold stone. It looked human. Vulnerable. The way eyes glisten. You can see their fragility. Charthouse took up a position at the head of the stairs, cane readied. Vincent megaphoned his hands around his mouth and started screaming at the top of his lungs: "Verner Potash is a bearded bitch who blows goats." Other imprecations. Charthouse watched the lead-gray skies. A couple of kids started up the stairs and noticed us. Made for us. I lifted my fists. They looked weak, thin, necky, their ball caps cocked at an angle.

Charthouse stared at them. Swinging his cane. The ferrule struck each of his white sneakers: ticktock. "What you looking at," said one. His colleague spat. Vincent kept shouting. "Damn, man," said the spitter, "why he yelling like that." Charthouse yanked on the badger head. The cane's body divided. A shrill, single note. Metal glinted in the heavy light. "That nigga got a sword cane," said the spitter, who wasn't black, to his colleague, who was. The kids got this glazed look in their eyes. They adjusted their ball caps: both Yankees fans. They headed back down the stairs, their hissing laughter echoing. "Faggots," the observant one called. Charthouse kept the point of his blade aloft till they reached the street. I was impressed. I hadn't figured Charthouse for a swordcane user. That requires a lot of inner fortitude. The wind rose. More snow fell. Vincent kept on with his stream of obscenities. "Alabama's going to meet us later," said Charthouse. "I didn't say anything about Alabama," I said. "Don't insult my intelligence, Wood," said Charthouse. "You fat cunt, we are going to murder you and eat your heart, do you hear me," said Vincent. "Is he just blowing off steam now," I said. "They're like cabs," said Charthouse, "they're everywhere until you need one."

That's when I heard it. Beneath Vincent's uproar. The whicker of wings. "Come and get it, you beady-eyed motherfuckers," said Vincent. Three crows clattered down from the harbor-gray sky and hopped toward the piled meat and offal. Then another two birds, one a hulking raven with a crumpled foot. He (you assume ravens are male) hopped gingerly while earthbound. The five darted their beaks into the meat and came up carrying glossy shreds. Clicking and cooing. Scrape of their beaks against concrete. Smack of the meat as it vanished down gullets. The combined sounds resembled human eating noise. This repulsed me. Then again, we're animals. The crows and the crippled raven ate and ate. They slowed. They stopped. They didn't fly off. "I know one of you has a direct line," said Vincent. The crows chattered to one another. Blood flecks flew. "I know you can hear me, you child-molesting necrophile," said Vincent. Maybe the phrase *child-molesting necrophile* did the job. I don't know. The crippled raven hopped forward. Toward Vincent. Froze in place at his feet, staring up. As if a circuit inside of it had snapped closed. Its eyes locked on him and its beak open. It balanced on its good foot. It cocked its head.

And listened. Obviously listened. Vincent saw. He took out the *mappa*. "Hobart Callahan," he said. I couldn't see what the lines showed. The crow seemed interested. "You want this back, you can have it," said Vincent, "but you're going to have to convince me my brother's alive. Otherwise you get nothing. Do you understand me, you fat prick." His phone began to ring as he said the words *fat prick*. Spoiled the effect. The raven, out of its daze, stumbled toward the stairs, picking up speed, and hurled itself into the air. The other crows remained and went back to jabbing their beaks at the remaining meat. The snowy, chambered tripe now dark with dust. Vincent's phone kept ringing. He lifted it. He looked. Eyes wide and frightened. He answered. "Hello," he said. I heard the insectile whine of a human voice, speaking through a distant phone. Wind. Or nothing, maybe. Vincent didn't speak. His face went white. Then flushed. His nostrils quivered. He grabbed his left ear. A good sign, I assumed. You only really care about the living. "Hob," he said, "I need to ask you a question." Charthouse sheathed his sword. "No, I need to ask you a question. What was the name of your horse, the one you rode when we played outlaw," he said. Hob answered. I could only hear the faint buzz of his voice in the still, cold air. I wanted to know what he'd called the horse. More human rapacity.

Vincent hung up. His hands shook. "Well," said Charthouse. Vincent straddled a stone bench. He picked up the bottle with the twig in it. "What's the news," said Charthouse. Vincent's eyelids fell and a vein bulged into relief on his forehead. Green shoots curled outward from the twig, opening into full leaves. Threadlike roots spread and shattered the glass. Twined around Vincent's bare, reddened hands. The noise of the breaking bottle echoed above the moist, masticatory sound of the plant growing. "He's alive," said Charthouse. "They're willing to make an exchange," said Vincent. His voice dry and hoarse. The twig burst and burst insanely into leaf.

21

Your appetite never ceases to amaze me," said my father. I'd eaten two slabs of steak and three baked potatoes. He fried steaks and baked potatoes when my mother was traveling on business. She had to go to a pharmaceuticals convention in Tempe. So my father had made what he called his swinging bachelor grub. He even gave me a beer, which he never did when my mother was around. "Tough practice," I said. "Got to keep my strength up," I said. I told him I had a date. "With that girl I saw sneaking out of your room the other day," he said. I said yes. Not even a lie. I realized he must have seen Alabama, the morning after she gave me my tattoo. Our parents observe more than we as adolescents credit them with. "Don't get anyone pregnant," he said. I promised I wouldn't. He had nothing to worry about on that front. My phone vibrated. "I gotta go," I said. "Let me not to the marriage of true minds admit impediments," he said. "Now that's Shakespeare."

Hostage exchanges: new to me. I was not afraid. When you are young you do not fear the unknown. You welcome it, in fact. If it so happens that you need to go rescue a fallen fellow soldier, all the better. Your desire for novelty: satisfied. Your desire to be in the right: satisfied. Except such desire is never satisfied. You need to abandon it. That's all. Vincent and Alabama were waiting in a taxi at my building door. "Fancy address," said Vincent. He was holding a canvas sack, which he opened to show me a rosewood cigar box. PERFECTO, it said on a small brass plate. Inside, I assumed, the *mappa*. Alabama shifted in her seat. Her rubber-banded gun butt caught a flash of yellow street light. A Colt Commander. That was the make and model. Vincent was flicking open and flicking closed his horticultural knife with his free hand. That's all we brought with us. Other than our clothes. Vincent in the middle. He had the box in a canvas sack. Alabama leaned out the window, watching the street. I kept cracking my knuckles. The driver didn't speak. A Bible lay open on the housing of the transmission knob. The Old Testament. I prefer it. Did then too. Odd for a Catholic. A pillar of fire by day is much better than Jesus. Who resembles nothing so much as your overpraised, exemplary cousin.

The wind kicked up. Wood smoke. Tea-scent of leaves. Water and stone. The red maples in front of Mountjoy House rustled. The crows sat on the roofline and fence. They rotated, one unitary battalion, to face us. A few clacked their beaks. A few readied their wings. "Do we wait," said Alabama, "it's freezing." "Someone'll come out," said Vincent. The crows hopped and muttered. A dog barked. No moon. No stars. No lights in Mountjoy House. "How long do we wait," said Alabama. "It's not the cable guy," said Vincent, "they didn't give me a window." Alabama sighed. "Sorry, I'm sorry," she said, "that was a retarded question." We foot-danced in the cold. Vincent smoked. He threw away cigarette after cigarette. Taking one drag. Or two. "Come on," muttered Alabama. "They're just trying to psych us out," I said. The wind kicked. The crows took flight. Alabama got ready to draw. Vincent ground out his smoke. The crows circled above us: a ring, their wing beats overlapping. "There's always main force," said Alabama. Sighting down the barrel. A light came on behind the glass-and-wood front door of Mountjoy House. Two indistinct human figures silhouetted against the pane. Soft edged. The glass smoked. The door opened.

"Is this a joke," said Alabama. It was just two kids. About our age. They stood half in, half out of the vestibule. A girl and a guy. The girl short and round, long brownish hair dancing in the breeze. She was wearing a white oxford shirt. Her absolutely huge tits strained against the cloth. Alabama caught me glancing and clucked. "Look who it is, though," she muttered. Then I saw. The guy standing next to Big Tits was Quinn Klayman. His glasses flashing in the indoor light. His brown hair shaggy. He grinned. Showing those pointed, yellow teeth. He waved at me. At Alabama. A brown bruise under his left eye. Otherwise healed up. He looked even more van-rapey sober, I have to admit.

"Are you guys here for us," Big Tits called. "Yes," said Vincent. This was so far way more of an amateur hour than I'd expected. On the other hand, we were going up against a clique of full-time careerist students. "So what happens now," Big Tits said, "my name's Sasha, by the way." "I was told to come in," said Vincent. "All right then," said Sasha. "All right then," said Vincent. We all stood there. Nobody stepped forward. The wind rushed. Compound smell of winter. "This is ridiculous," said Alabama. She walked up to the iron gate and pushed it open. I followed. Vincent followed me. "Don't do anything stupid," she said to Quinn as she passed him, "or I'll shoot you." Quinn tried to laugh it off. Sounded fake. Horsey. Whiny. "You're not going to shoot me," he said. "Wait and see," said Vincent. I grinned at Sasha. She grinned back. No reason to be unfriendly. And the ancient voice that all adolescent males hear, no matter the circumstances, no matter the time or the place or the alleged seriousness-slash-impossibility of the occasion, that voice of sexual hope, said: *Hey, you never know.*

THE ASSHOLES

No reason a simple transaction had to be anything more than that. We hand over the map. They hand over Hob. A priceless relic for one lightly used adolescent warlock. A better deal for Potash and his crew. Considered objectively. Charthouse had not come. Vincent insisted. He said it was too dangerous. I thought he was being dramatic. Alabama had agreed with him. So Charthouse stayed behind. Vincent had the canvas sack slung over his shoulder. "Is it in there," said Quinn. I kept my mouth shut. I wanted more than anything else to hurt him. Worse than Hob had. Just on principle. All this, I reasoned incorrectly, was his fault. "Are you going to go get my brother," said Vincent. "You have to come upstairs," said Sasha, "Verner wants you to come upstairs to see him." This I disliked. Referring to your teachers and superiors by their first name. A gesture of fake equality. "Come upstairs," said Alabama. I didn't like the changing-locations aspect either.

The great entry hall of Mountjoy House: cathedral sized. We'd missed a lot by going in through the tradesman's entrance, during our first visit. They clearly kept the hotel-hallway stuff out of sight of first-time guests. Made sense. Places need to live up to their reputations. Here was nothing but white marble. Or travertine. The ceilings fifty feet high. The white walls inset with white niches, each holding a white bust. One I recognized: Francis Bacon. I'd been forced to write a paper on him when I was in ninth grade. I will never forget his flowing hair or his offensive, well-groomed beard and gaze. Eight white stairways led up in the eight cardinal directions. Owl-headed banisters. More white stone. You could feel the cold coming off the floors and wall. In the center of the hall a fountain plashed. Carved from the same white stone. Four statues guarded the rim: a youth with a feather quill and a cornucopia; a woman with a book and a sword; a scroll-bearded, helmeted man seated on a lion; and a matron with a torch, wearing a shift. The hall was illuminated. No lamps or light fixtures visible. Quinn was wearing slippers, I saw: beaten red leather. Sasha had on only socks. Blue-and-purple striped.

"So what year are yooooou guys," said Vincent. He drawled. I started to worry. "Seniors," said Quinn. He was sweating. "And do you like liiike it here," said Vincent. His voice cramped and falsely sweet. I'd never heard him sound so sincere. "It has its advantages," said Sasha. "I bet," said Vincent. "So I guess we should take you upstairs," said Sasha. *I'd like to take you upstairs*, I thought. "We're not going upstairs," said Alabama. "That's what my uncle said," said Quinn, "Verner, I mean." "I don't give a fuck what your fucking fat faggot uncle told you," said Vincent, "we're not going upstairs." "You shouldn't use that word," said Sasha. It was like being at that terrible party: you don't know the kids at all, really, but you are already almost in a fight with them. This did not surprise me. I've never gotten along with the studious. Did not make it any less difficult for me to avoid looking at Sasha's tits. They shelfed an odd necklace: a bicycle chain, from which hung what appeared to be a jade-colored slice of petrified wood set in a brass rim. I wondered if it served a purpose other than decoration.

Quinn wore his blue blazer with the owl-and-wheat crest. "You guys are big on owls," I said. Trying to ease the tension. "With us it's snakes." "You're the faggot," said Quinn, "if anyone's a faggot here." "Oh, that's clever," said Alabama. I was grateful only Alabama had a gun. I was examining Sasha's ass, which was as impressively massive as her tits. "What did you just say, you cunt," said Quinn. "Come on," said Alabama, "really?" "You heard what I said," cried Quinn. Still a dialogue expert. Maybe he'd come out with a *you want some* next. Hard to tell. Strange strain in his face. Smooth and young. Old looking at the same time. Defeated. By a secret vice. An ineffable shame. His hand dipped toward his waist. This puzzled me. We'd deep-sixed his wand. Maybe they'd given him another. Seemed about right. Reward stupidity. How kids like Quinn end up that way: through rewarded stupidity. His hand slipped farther. Sasha started to mutter. "Vincent," said Alabama, low and hard. She strode up and planted herself behind Sasha, who was standing with her back to us and (it seemed) talking to a blank white wall at the back of the lobby. "All right," I said. I took a breath. I clenched my muscles. *Where we began, the world can judge: in trust, wholehearted; in unshakable assurance.*

The world slowed down. My pain flared up. Brain, eyes, lungs, spine. No longer merely companionable. The lobby's gentle white light had deepened in color. *Redshifting*: the name of that phenomenon. I had time to remember the word. From my physics class. I had all the time I needed. Vincent, Alabama, Sasha, Quinn: slooooooooooooow. Vincent sliding his hand toward his pocket. Going for his knife, I assumed. Alabama reaching toward Sasha with one arm and drawing her gun with the other. Stretched-out, dancerly movements. Sasha's eyebrows winging up, a chevron of light creeping across the surface of her green pendant. Me in the midst of these stone-slow fellow humans, calm, in pain, and alert. More absorbing than anything. Better than any movie. It sounds insane to describe it that way. I watched Vincent's sneer begin. I watched Alabama's thin forearm make contact with Sasha's neck. I watched the divided skirt of Quinn's blue blazer billow with aching lassitude. It revealed his wand—a new one, as I'd suspected; black metal and inset with silver wire—in a fake leather rent-a-cop holster belted to his back. A pearly bead of sweat slipped millimeter by millimeter down his pale, pious forehead. Not from pain. Not from exertion. Just nerves. I could hardly breathe from the pain firing up and down my lats. I did not mind this, I discovered. As though I were at ease inside myself, inside this lumbering body and this pain: Mike Wood watching Mike Wood.

Call it whatever you like. It isn't any different from anything else. Not even less probable. Your body cries out. Your soul cries out. The cries find expression or they die off. Just that simple. Just an extension, as Alabama said, of what you're already good at. I walked up to Quinn and broke his wrist. Incredibly satisfying. Easy, too. At least when your target is one degree more animate than a statue. I took hold of his forearm with my left hand and his hand with my right, and I twisted them as hard as I could in opposite directions. One quick, hard flexion, putting my shoulders into it, my back. My body thrummed. His bones moved. The ulna bent and fractured. A green twig. It pressed the skin. A loud, long thud: the noise of its breakage. Would have been a quick crack, had I been moving at normal speed. Quinn started to yowl. This came out as a deep, smeary rumble. Alabama was still looping her arm around Sasha's neck, moving a centimeter or two at a time. Vincent had just started to open his mouth in surprise. Or so it seemed. He might have been sneezing. I saw all this with great contentment from within the confined and friendly theater of my corporeal form. It occurred to me that if I wanted, I could kill all of these people. Friend and enemy. This thought pure and childish. Mine. Another's. My clothes stuck to me. I'd broken into a fever sweat, armpits, knee backs, feet, and hands. I slid Quinn's wand out of his holster. I was dizzy with pain, nauseated with it. The wand's metal cool-warm. The world was speeding up again.

"What was that, Wood," said Vincent. I tried to break the wand. It bent—a U. I twisted. It snapped. Quinn groaned. In clear pain. Or was already groaning. I loved that. Sasha was breathing, "Okay, okay," and Alabama was saying, "it's okay, just be quiet." She had the Colt to Sasha's temple. Barrel dimpling skin, one arm locked around the girl's soft-looking throat. Now flushed in panic. Quinn on the ground now, cradling his hurt arm. Repeating, "What." A question: why does academic achievement so often breed physical cowardice and even debility? I've never managed to answer this question. And so I remain strong and lumbering. "Do you have reinforcements on the way," said Vincent. Quinn snorted and gasped. "I don't know what you mean," said Sasha. "No wonder they let you in here," said Vincent, "being so quick and all." "Maybe we should get moving," I said. "Open the door you were trying to open or whatever it was," said Vincent, "but if you do anything stupid she will kill you." Sasha swallowed spit. She pointed to a bower of vines carved into the otherwise blank wall.

"It's that middle blossom," she said. "You do it," said Alabama. Sasha did it. Stroked the blossom edge. A morning glory.

Death: what I was expecting when Sasha touched the white stone flower. A mild grating hum: what I got. Upper-middle-class ease and opulence, in other words. A panel of the white wall slid into itself. Behind was what appeared to be a brass-and-wood elevator cabin. Quinn started blubbering. With no acid in his brain and no new wand, a total pussy. No shocker there. "Are you going to kill us," he said. "No, but if you don't shut up I'll break your other wrist," I said. He shut up. Vincent pulled him to his feet. "You're coming up with us," he said, "and seriously she will shoot your friend if she has to." "So now we *are* going upstairs," said Sasha.

The elevator was also larger than it could possibly have been. It had that unmistakable elevator smell. Smell of the mundane. High-test brass polish and lemon oil. Alabama and Sasha went in first, scuttling backward. Sasha seemed to be taking her captivity with detachment. Then again, I hadn't broken her wrist. Quinn was sucking air in through his mouth. Expelling it. Vincent had Quinn's wounded arm twisted up behind his back. Smart play. You get hold of a broken limb and you can make sure its owner stays docile. The elevator moved slowly. Alabama kept her gun at Sasha's temple. Sasha pressing her lips together and staring dead ahead. A look of total shutdown. True, taking hostages is a surefire cockblock. You have to make sacrifices in the name of the greater good. "Frankly," said Alabama, "I didn't think you had it in you." I managed not to puke on my shoes. "What floor," I said. "It's not like that," said Sasha, "it just goes to Verner's office." "Hey, let me ask you," I said, since I figured I really had no shot with her now, "why do you get to call him Verner. He's in charge. In my school it's nuns and I don't even know their actual names." Sasha ignored me. Quinn sobbed. I got a weird vibe: this is your life, Mike Wood, fist-fights and walking around at night and never getting a straight answer.

I started to chuckle. So did Alabama. "Not funny, you guys," said

Vincent. He was already laughing. "I'm sorry, I'm sorry," I said, or tried to say, to Quinn, who was looking at me with fear and glittering hate, "it's just funny, you have to admit." I was whooping now, propped against one wall, my whole body aflame. Vincent guffawed and wiped his eyes with his free hand. "Sociopaths," Sasha whispered. "Hold on, Dr. Freud," said Vincent, through his dying chuckles, "we're not sociopaths." I was—as I would have put it then—fucking dying, gasping for air. Alabama bit her lower lip again and again to stop herself. Her gun never left Sasha's temple. Quinn kept sobbing. We stopped moving. "Okay, okay," said Vincent, "everybody get serious." This set me off again. Alabama too. My jaw ached now. The doors slid back. We all shut up.

Stars. Night sky. A painted dome. A glass dome. No dome, rather. The night sky itself. The blue night and its unrecognizable stars, and the strange, aching scent of its trees. Before us, a long, wide room appointed in leather and blond wood: two huge sofas, an end table supporting a massive, brown-and-beige globe. Bookcases, loaded. The skeleton of a gazelle, I thought, set up on wires. White-painted walls with dark wooden beams and doors set in them. I counted four. The vast night for a ceiling. The air cool and fresh. The air of the out of doors. A comet streaked, hair-thin and bright. Vincent jerked his head to watch and Quinn slipped away. I didn't care. I didn't care if they killed me. To have seen this would have made death worthwhile. This vast alien sky and this lonely, warm platform beneath, across which we were marching. Quinn was yelling, "Uncle Verner, Uncle Verner." Tears throbbing in his voice. I didn't see Potash, at first. Then I noticed him, sitting on the edge of a vast desk, shooting a deck of cards from one hand to the other. "How does it go about the mountain and Muhammad," he called. "Verner, they tried to kill us," said Quinn. Emphasis on *kill*. That whiner. "Quiet," said Potash. His thin nephew, the boy with the animal teeth, stopped speaking. "Come in, come in, *mi casa* and all that," said Potash. He was speaking to Vincent and staring at the canvas sack he carried. No wall behind Potash's desk. Just more night and the branches of an enormous tree, thick as human waists and thighs, knotted and covered in waving, sword-shaped leaves.

The white woman: nowhere. I kept checking behind the sofas. For quick-moving shadows. I sniffed the air for her wet-stone scent. Nothing. Did not mean we were safe. I was glad I detected nothing all the same. If she was going to appear and slaughter us, I'd rather it come as a surprise. Potash was bobbing his head. If he went for his wand, I decided, I'd have another run at him. He had a punchable face. "Mr. Potash," said Alabama, "we don't mean you any harm. We just came to make the exchange. All this is accidental." Sasha gulped. Didn't speak. Alabama's version: not strictly true. True enough, however. "I trusted," said Potash, "my own blood. No one believes as firmly in their right to screw you. And this one has always been more than a bit of a moron. So the blame, I think, lies with me." He stroked his right palm with his left. Like a usurer. No offense to the Jews. Quinn stared at his uncle. Lips quivering. I didn't know how I'd feel if my uncle sold me down the river, morally speaking. Then again, I don't have any uncles. Just aunts. "Where's my brother," said Vincent. "He's in the next room," said Potash. "Get him," said Vincent. "You're being hasty," said Potash. The tree rustled. I stared. "Miraculous, no," said Potash. He was right. No other word for it. "Iron Tom, he's called," said Potash. The name filled me with a yearning ache. Or simply the fact that this great and unknown tree bore a human name at all. "Is it an oak," I said. "No," said Potash, "this is not really the neighborhood for oaks."

"How is it spring," I said. "Go get my brother," Vincent said. Sasha tried to break free. She whined and gasped as Alabama choked her. "Your brother's asleep," said Potash, "he wakes up when what he stole is in my hand." I started praying. Ave Marias. For Vincent not to fuck this up. All he had to do was toss Potash the canvas sack. Vincent was staring at the fat man. Who smiled. A sunny uncle. Alabama's shoes squeaked against the floor. "*Gratia plena*," I muttered. Without

THE WAR AGAINST

meaning to. "A religious man as well as an educated one," said Potash. Vincent tossed him the sack. "Through that door," said Potash, gesturing with his ringed hand: a two-fingered pass. A benediction. The one nearest us. Vincent ran and leaned against the jamb. Said his brother's name. No answer. "Still groggy," said Potash, examining the *mappa*, "Verner Potash." I could see the inverses of the lines forming: the warm lamplight poured through the paper. "Hob," said Vincent. Louder. Again, no answer. He tried the handle. Locked in place.

"You motherfucker," said Vincent. Alabama let go of Sasha and aimed at Potash. "Don't move and don't speak," said Alabama, "and get your hands up, palms facing me." Potash had gone gray. Now I was worried. Vincent started throwing himself into the door. Grunting each time. He got nowhere. Sasha's hand crept toward her green pendant. "I'll fuck you up," I said to her, "if you try anything. Even worse than him. And you're really cute, so it would doubly suck." I don't know if I actually would have gone through with it. The threat worked. I felt like a shitbag but what can you do. Sasha dropped her hand. I kept watch. Vincent placed his palms against the door. Veins stood out in his neck. The living wood cracked, groaned, cried out—a crease, a furrow appeared in the middle and deepened. Sap leaked. Sprayed. The door split. The hinge side swung limply. The handle side fell. Vincent sprinted in, his gasps for breath ragged and high. Calling his brother's name in between them. Dead silence. "Hob," I heard. Not a shout. A whisper. Then: "Fuck, fuck, fuck, motherfucker, fuck." Screams. Each rawer than the last.

"Let's get to it," said Alabama. Before I could do anything, before I could speak, she started firing. Just like she was pointing out a vista with her index finger. Not aiming at her target. Who was already chanting (I caught the French word *feu*) and moving his lifted hands. His ring starting to glow: umber, black, crimson, aquamarine. He'd decided to take his chances. Not quick enough. Alabama shot him in his right palm, then his left. He stopped chanting. The ring stopped glowing. Alabama shot his left knee, then his right. No recoil, no repositioning. Point with the barrel and fire. That's all. Before Potash fell, squealing, Alabama shot Sasha and Quinn. She kept her eyes on Potash the whole time, firing to her left, her arm out and stiff. This huge gun. Quieter than I'd guessed. Then I remembered. No ceiling. The shots half-echoed. Noise lost in the huge night. I could not move. Sasha and Quinn each took a bullet. In the same spot on both their bodies: about three inches from the right clavicle edge. I saw the blood bloom. I saw them stumble and hit the wall. Slide down. Leaving red traces. They were both whining and yowling with pain. Animal pain. Potash hissed: "This isn't." The *mappa* fluttered on his desk edge. "If he starts talking again, finish him off," said Alabama. To me. "Okay," I said. My lips cold with panic. I'd never been given an order to kill before. The fat man curled in front of his desk, gritting his teeth and grinning. I had to give him credit. He took the pain better than his students. "Necessary," he said. His neck and jowls oyster colored. "It's not in my hands," I said, "any longer."

Vincent charged through the side doorway. The still-attached door half banged against his shoulder: a swift blow. He ignored it. He was sobbing. He leaned against the wall, his face wet and his fists clenched. Alabama crossed the carpet. I remember the precise, padding sounds her feet made, left-right-left-right, amid the cries and labored breathing of the three people she'd shot. She looked through the door, one hand on Vincent's chest. She looked a long time. The side room lamp-lit. I could see a bed. Two shoes. A wooden table. The brown edge of a blanket. It looked military. That's all. I was looming over the hard-breathing fat man. His bone-chip necklace clicked as he shook. Shock, I guessed. "Who did this," said Alabama. Still staring into the room. Potash's chin thudded on carpet. Blood from his knee and hand wounds spread. The carpet drank it. He started to move his mouth. Alabama interrupted: "No, no. I'm asking you once. If anything other than a person's name comes out when you answer, that's it." Potash gulped air. He set his teeth. "Go ahead," said Alabama. "You don't," said Potash. As far as he got. Alabama half-turned toward us. Stiffened her arm. Bit her lower lip and fired. She might as well have had her eyes shut. Potash's bulky body leaped. His forehead caved in above his left eye. Blood sprayed my shoes and pant cuffs. The noise still not the thunderous sound I'd been expecting. Flakes of smoldering yellow wood dust fountained into the air. The bullet had struck his desk after passing through his head. Potash kicked. His glossy shoes drummed. Their laces scuttered against the floor. He groaned. Then he was still. "Jesus," I said. "Come here," Alabama said. Vincent was weeping.

What it was, I knew already. A sweet stink in the side room. A leaden, long-brewed silence. I shut my eyes, I admit it, as I stepped across the threshold. I didn't want to look. In the end, you have to look. A simple bed. I'd seen its foot already. Above it the same impossible and starry sky. A wooden table, on which sat a half-drunk glass of water, now bubbling and stale. On the bed lay Hob. Or what had once been Hob. His throat sliced open. I saw: white gristle, blackish inner flesh. Gray tubes. The pinkish root of his tongue. The bedclothes brown with dried blood. His eyes open. His mouth open. I touched his palm. Without meaning to. His small hands locked and flexed as though in terror.

22

He was alive when I talked to him," said Vincent, "he was alive when I talked to him." "You don't know that," said Alabama. She was chivvying Quinn and Sasha upright, their backs against a wall. They left curved smears of fresh blood, charting their movement. "Please don't kill us," said Quinn. Pleading. His face ashen. His animal teeth agleam in the lamplight. Sasha wasn't talking. Her eyelids fluttered. I respected her silence. "Fix them," Alabama said to Vincent. "Not going to happen," he said through his tears. "There's already one person dead here," she said. "Fuck you," Vincent said again, "there's two." "You know what I meant," said Alabama. Vincent took Quinn by the throat and spat into his face as he pressed his palm against the wound. Cords stretched in Vincent's neck. His eyes bulged. Quinn's color returned: ashes and chalk no more. Vincent palmed Sasha's shoulder. "Don't look at me," he said. Chin shaking. Sweat dripping. She kept her face turned. When he removed his hand the red patch on her white shirt stopped growing. He showed Alabama his open palm. Two bullets. Still gory. "Satisfied," he said. He pocketed the rounds. His knees buckled. He steadied himself.

Are you an asshole. So said Mr. Stone. *One true art exists: the art of choice.* So said Erzmund. No comfort to be derived from those words. Even though Potash had killed Hob. Worse: tried to deny it. You only redouble your guilt through equivocation and lying. Still, when you're young, your stupidity, commonly called innocence, enfolds and insulates you. All the same I was cold. Stunned and light-headed. Potash lay at my feet. One arm upraised as though in victory. Even dead, he looked like a fucking magician. Far more so than his protégés. Who seemed to have fallen asleep under Vincent's ministrations. Sasha snored. Mouth open. Her tongue large and pink. Quinn cradled his broken wrist. Even in sleep. "This is bullshit," Vincent said. His voice crumpled and low. "He was alive. It was him. This is not how it's supposed to go," he said. "I know that," said Alabama. "What am I going to do about my parents? They think he's on a trip to Spain," he said. His voice broke.

The elevator entrance we'd stepped through: gone. Replaced by blank white plaster. A reproduction of a painting hung smugly on the wall. Farmhouse, hillside, golden crops, and in the foreground a white-blossomed chestnut tree. "How long are they going to sleep for," said Alabama. "I don't know," said Vincent, "but can we kill them too." "Let's not argue in circles here," I said. Alabama slid her pistol back into the waistband of her jeans. "He's correct," she said. She looked pale. Even for her. Sweat gemmed her hairline and her cheeks looked hollow. We checked the other side rooms: they all had beds. Beds and end tables and starry ceilings. Another comet streaked. Vincent kicked Potash's corpse. His bone chip rattled. Vincent knelt and snapped the chain. Worked the ring off his finger. "Vincent," said Alabama. "Don't try," said Vincent, "to lay any solemnity bullshit on me. He's my brother. Plus Stone will want these."

Cold pressure against the underside of my neck. The flesh on my arms knotted into goose bumps. Horripilation. That's what that's called. Another word I learned from Hob. "We need to leave," I said. No certain knowledge. I had a strong guess. She was on her way. Messaline. My cock got rock-hard. This bothered me more than anything else that had happened so far. Another sign of youth, which is to say stupidity. Mike Wood: standing in a room with two corpses, sporting a hard-on for a nine-hundred-year-old witch. "We have to take him with us," said Vincent. Not a question, or even a proposal. Just a simple statement of fact. "You know that's not possible," said Alabama. Vincent examined the bone chip. Held it up in the air, to catch the sourceless light. The chip glowed, translucent. "It is possible, Alabama, so we're going to take him with us." He pocketed the necklace. Slipped the ring on his own finger. "That fat cocksucker," he said: the fit was too loose. "We can't do it," said Alabama, "I'm sorry." Vincent bent over Sasha, his hands at her throat. He was removing her green pendant. Not hurting her, as I'd first imagined. He did not look at Alabama. His voice: quiet. The voice a teacher uses when talking to a stupid and recalcitrant child. "We can do it, and we are going to do it," he said, "we are going to take him back with us."

"You know how to get back," said Alabama. Vincent didn't answer. The cold draft started to stir the papers on Potash's desk and finger the pages of the phone-book-sized volume that lay open upon it. Angular characters, tiny, covered them. "You even know how to get out of here," she said. Vincent said nothing. Sasha whimpered in her sleep. "We need to leave," I said. The air carried the scent of stone or snow. Her scent. My blood pounded. Rose to my neck, cheeks, hairline. "Vincent, I am so sorry to say this but we can't, we just can't," said Alabama. She barked the last word. I'd never heard her raise her voice before. "We can, we can," Vincent said, "we can and we're going to." His voice broke on the final syllable. Sasha's pendant dangled from his upraised fist. The chain tinkling in the rising cold wind. I think Vincent knew we couldn't. He still had to object. That point comes for everyone.

Keep silent and you won't able to face yourself every morning in the mirror. Hard enough to do that anyway. The air: cooling down. "Do you feel that," I said. Alabama nodded. "No exit," said Vincent, "like that stupid play." "That's not true, though," I said. Alabama followed my glance. The branches. The night. A long, singing sigh ran through the cooling air. As though Mountjoy House itself were sighing with weariness. "Just climb down, you mean," said Vincent. "Why not? I'd rather die on the run," said Alabama. "They're not going to kill us," said Vincent, "they're a bunch of cowards."

Hob. His thin throat open. Bleeding out in that guest bed. Vincent looked at me. I looked at him. Another musical groan filled the air. Growing colder. "Do you really want to wait around," I said, "until whatever it is shows up to deal with us?" Alabama sat astride a branch. "It's stable," she said. "No," said Vincent. "You think he would have wanted you dead, too," said Alabama. Vincent ground his fists into his eyes. I felt even sicker. I'd never seen anyone killed. When you've beaten a guy into unconsciousness, he still breathes. His eyes still quiver. Under his lids. *Never, never, never, never, never.* The words chased themselves, a mocking chant. Vincent was breathing through his teeth and saying, "Fine, fine, fine, fine, fine. Okay? Okay? Okay? Okay? Okay?" He finished by screaming. Alabama didn't respond. Iron Tom, Mr. Potash had called the tree. It. Him. "Smells like lavender," said Alabama, "the leaves I mean." Vincent said, "You useless." Voice clogged with spittle. Didn't supply a noun. I breathed the lavender scent. Not lavender. Similar. It masked the cloying smell of Potash's blood. He put one hand on a wide, warm branch. He lifted his right foot.

And then he lowered it. He seemed to be listening. To a voice he could barely hear. "Don't be an idiot," said Alabama. "Don't tell me what to do," said Vincent. The air got colder. My blood pumped. Heart, lungs, brain, hands, cock. It increased the after-pains. I had to bite my lip. "Do you see what's going on here," said Alabama. "I'm not leaving

THE ASSHOLES

him," said Vincent, "I don't care what happens. Do you understand me? Do you understand me? Do you understand me?" He'd started crying again. So, to my shock, had Alabama. Not weeping. Tears were sliding down her face. I was on an outside branch already. Alabama was still bathed in the warm light of the office. Which is how I saw her tears. "Vincent," she said, "he's dead, all right?" Vincent shrugged and smiled. His brother's crooked, abashed smile. "I'm going," he said, "to be fine." He chewed his lip as he spoke. I thought from tears. Wrong. Laughter. I didn't blame him. Alabama didn't speak. She squirreled out and joined me on my branch and we started to climb down. The air strange. I inhaled. Balmy. Still. Leaf scented. Water scented. Calming and still. It reminded me of the smoke from Vincent's cigarettes.

Vincent: outlined in shadow, poised among the branches. Mountjoy House sighing and the cold wind rising and rising within it. The night-colored river I'd seen from the library windows divided the lawn below us. Not far down: thirty, forty feet. The geometry of the building I could not fathom. From our perch in the tree we could see that the roofs of Mountjoy, angled and canted and looking built up over time with no plan, spread and spread. The roofs of a small city. The roofless projection of the building that housed Potash's office—former office, I should say—was half supported by wood and masonry and half supported by the trunk and branches of Iron Tom. The elevator ride made no sense in this context. Then again, neither had the lobby or library. Or the fact that we were shimmying down a giant tree of no known species under a sky full of stars neither of us recognized. Not that we were nature scouts. Night sounds. Babble of the river.

You don't get a lot of tree-climbing practice in Manhattan. So we struggled. I admit. Though the tree seemed to have been designed for human climbing. Deep hand- and footholds in the bark, honey colored; branches sticking out every five or six feet. I say *we struggled*: I mean I struggled. Alabama never missed a grab or a foot-plant. The large, serrated leaves rustled as we passed through them. They brushed our

THE WAR AGAINST

faces and ears. With curiosity, almost. Nothing malign. "I can't believe we're actually doing this," said Alabama. I did not know if she meant descending to the unfamiliar ground. Or leaving Hob's dead body and Vincent's living one in Potash's office. Or both. Or neither. Out over the lawn fireflies pulsed gently, white, amber, orange, pink. The same insects had been trapped in the jars in the library to give light. I couldn't believe we were doing this either. Descending. That Hob was dead. That we were alive. That Alabama Sturdivant had just murdered the de facto head of the theurgical community on the East Coast, as Mr. Stone would have put it. I could not believe how easy it had been. Mr. Stone had made him sound extremely dangerous. He had taken Hob, the first time, with such little effort. Then again, all I'd had was my fist. He had a bodyguard. Fat guys, I reasoned, get complacent. And if you have to jabber on for two to five seconds before you get down to business, a girl with a gun will defeat you. Especially if you are doing the jabbering on in a foreign language. A simple question of tactics.

The grass of the lawn lapping Mountjoy House reached my ankles. We stood there in the unseasonal warmth in our coats and hats. Alabama pressed her hand against the tree trunk. Then we started off. Walking along the river toward the forest edge. Across the meadow field. Under the alien stars. Cry of night birds. At least I assumed they were birds. "He's going to get killed," I said. "Yes. I think so. The air kind of smells like Connecticut in April," said Alabama.

23

Are you awake, Mr. Wood, or are you dreaming? So Sister Immaculata asked me. No mortal can answer that question. We left the amber penumbral glow of Mountjoy House behind us. I kept checking to see if pursuers had appeared. Flashlights on the lawn. I didn't know what to expect. Maybe they'd let us go to die of exposure. Maybe they would consider it a wash and move on. You can't judge the personality of a whole organization. Especially schools. Schools value only one thing above cruelty and stupidity: caprice. We ran. Alabama taking long, choppy strides, holding her pistol with two hands to keep a grip and be ready to fire, I thought. I wished I had a weapon. Two fists and a hard head don't count.

The grass hit our knees. The soil by the river was spongy but not muddy. The multicolored fireflies blinked on and off as we ran along the water, heading toward the woods. The over-the-shoulder looks stopped. The night was quiet enough that we would have heard any ruckus of pursuit. Nobody came. We still trotted. We hit the edge of the trees. "Okay," said Alabama. Slowed down. "What now," I said. "I have no idea," she said. So we kept going. The air much cooler within the border of the trees. The moonlight and starlight much brighter. We had to march with care. The forest coalesced. From wide-spaced stands of trees to dense bramble. Trees that looked like oak. Like Iron Tom. Trees that looked like sycamore. Almost-birches. I peeled a scrap of bark as I walked by. Papery. Just like at home.

"Did you ever write on them," said Alabama. "Of course," I said. "I used to write messages for people on them," she said. A hollow, plaintive, and melodic cry rose and fell. "That makes sense," I said. "Not people I knew," said Alabama. The lambent moon above us. Its shadows and pockmarks different. No gouty face. Instead I saw a dragon. Rearing. Foreclaws raised. Or just a smear of ashen gray. You never can tell with the moon. "There's a birch outside my house," Alabama said. The wild cry repeated. Closer and clearer. "And you used to tear bark from it," I said. More to hear myself talk than to answer. Your own voice reassures you. A branch swiped my face. Fruit dangled from it, under heart-shaped leaves. Grape-black in the moonlight. "Do you think we could eat these," I said. "I mean, we could," said Alabama. One had burst against my forehead: a cool, sticky juice trickled down. It smelled like smoke and mangoes when I wiped it away. "I used to write on it with black crayon and send the bark down the gutter stream in front of my house," said Alabama, "Mark and Lena loved it. They have like thirty million pictures."

Progress: simple. We followed the river. "It has to end," said Alabama. "In a sea," I said, "or its source, right?" Primitive truth will not fail you. Copious moonlight. Not a crow to be seen. I wondered if they existed here. Wherever we were. I didn't mention that. Neither did Alabama. As far as terrain went it was no worse than walking through the woodsier parts of the park, in the dead of night. Mild hills and dips. Knuckly roots. I tripped over one and stumbled. I soaked my coat sleeve in the river. "Shit," I said. The water teemed with darting, golden fish. Faintly alight. Tiny black eyes. Tiny yellow fins. They didn't flee my sleeve when it broke the surface. They scraped the cloth and the skin of my wrist with their delicate jaws. They knew me. Or had been expecting me. At least that's the first thought that flashed through my head, watching them swim and arrow, point to point. Watching them glow. "Wow," said Alabama. I'd never heard her sound impressed before. She dipped up a double handful of water. The fish circled between her palms. The faint light touched her chin. Lit up her eyelashes and dark eyes. The sweat at her hairline and at her temples.

To my amazement, the flickering points in the water started to rise into the air. Forming a small cloud of golden motes above her cupped hands. The fish leaving their element behind, floating off among the dark branches. Their illumination so delicate I could not see them once they'd drifted beyond Alabama's narrow head. "Wow," she repeated. She got down on her knees. Held up one finger: *wait a second, let me finish talking.* Loudly, violently, wrenchingly, she vomited on the black soil. Her cropped head bobbed. Her shoulders shook. Bile fountained out of her open mouth. She aimed away from the river. "You okay," I said when she'd gotten back up. "Now I am," she said. Her breathing still ragged. I took off my wet-sleeved coat and sweater. So did she. The air warm and sweet. Another brace of that nameless fruit hung over us. She took one down and examined it in the river light. Deep red. She opened her mouth and placed it on her tongue. "There are worse ways to die," she said around the fruit. I took one. I ate it. As soon as the juice touched my tongue I knew we'd be all right. It tasted the way it smelled. Smoke and mangoes. Fall and summer at the same time. No pit. No seeds. Flesh of a cherry. Also of an apple. Alabama crammed two more into her mouth. The juice blackly stained her lips and shining teeth. Trying to erase the taste of bile. "These are delicious," I said. "And nutritious," she said.

Silence. River sound and river light. The loud cries were, I was sure, following us. I wasn't worried. Alabama could take care of animal threats. Especially birds, I figured, which was what these sounded like.

We loaded up my sweater with berries: Alabama tied it into a bag and we stripped three branches. I was starving. She must have been, too, having emptied her stomach. Her hairline still glistened with sweat in the moonlight. She walked with her gun out, pointed at the earth. The river followed a straight course. The dragon-shadowed moon above and its twin in the phosphorescent water. "Do you think it's two parts of the life cycle," I said. "What are you talking about," she said. "The fish in the water and the fireflies," I said. My mouth full of berry. "I'm no zoologist," she said. She sounded anxious. Her shoulders, at least, under their blue shirt, expressed anxiety. Some people have expressive backs.

I shut up. I'd never killed anyone. Even a knockout carries moral consequences. I didn't want to console her. Would have been presumptuous. I didn't want to joke it off. Would have been cruel. So I said nothing. We walked on. The cries followed and followed. Clear and curt. Twigs snapping under our feet. The dragon-marked moon above. The ground dipped further. On either side of us, hills rose. A valley. The noise of the river increased: large stones, which looked pink and orange in the moonlight, complicated its course. It broadened. The banks steeper, serrated. Spike-leafed plants thrust up from the soil, in stands of eight or nine. Waist-high. Chalice-shaped flowers with bulbous green pistils. Alabama stopped to vomit again among these night flowers. I was glad she had short hair. Otherwise I would have been faced with an impossible choice: not holding it back or holding it back.

"I sent the messages to made-up names," she said, "and then when I got older I used the names in the phone book." It got darker. The moon got lower. Until it was a silvery slice above the tree-spined horizon. We sat on a shelf of rock by the river. Spray hit us. The golden fish agitated and shining in the eddies. I took a short branch from the nearest tree. Snapped it off. It smelled resinous. A good sign. I tried the cigarette maneuver on it. The broken end glowed orange and a small, dim flame licked up. Alabama broke a branch and lit it from mine. Our pathetic torches reflected on the rushing, inwardly lit river. "Look," Alabama said, "look at that." In an upper groin of the tree from which we'd taken the branches, the torchlight glinted on eyes. They flashed green. Didn't flee. Just regarded us with calm contemplation. An outline: a squirrel, a cat. Two massive ears protruding from a small, vulpine head. The animal opened its mouth and cried out. The source of the cries we'd been hearing. "It's like," said Alabama above the noise of the river. "I feel as though I should be frightened of it but I'm not," I said. We raised our torches. For an instant we saw: tawny, red-striped fur; white paws and white, lashing, curling tail tip; delicate, quasi-human hands; the narrow, clever face and vast ears, also tipped in white fur. Its golden gaze on us. The tree fox released its melodious, avian cry. Leaped away. A branch creaked as it took the animal's weight.

Joy. Why? I didn't know. Still don't. With true joy you never do. Bodily joy coursing through me. To have seen that unrecognizable beast. Half-familiar. I grinned at the ground. Didn't want Alabama to ask me why I was smiling. The river widened as we followed it. Our torches lit up more green-glass eyes in the branches. My joy only grew. Hob was dead. I'd witnessed a murder. Vincent would not survive. My joy was not legitimate. It had nothing to do with the moral world at all. That tawny fur. Those golden eyes. Those hands. Nothing more than that. I ate another berry. My fingertips, I saw in the torchlight, dyed now the deep red of its skin. "Why," I said. Alabama knew at once what I meant. She dodged a branch and answered me. "To find them. To save them. People I'd never know otherwise. Alone out there in the great world. And they took pictures," she said, "you see what I mean?" Torchlight. Dark berry. Her white hand. Her forehead. River, night, immense air. Our need to remember is repulsive. We'd never survive without it.

24

S un in my eyes. Sun in my open mouth. That's what woke me. And Alabama prodding me with her shoe. "We should keep going," she said, "look how high the sun is." My limbs and torso hurt so much I did not care, for several heartbeats, if I died on the soft dirt of the forest, with my coat thrown over me for a blanket. Alabama could have spent the night in a hotel: her face was scrubbed, her hands clean, eyes bright. Droplets of water glinted on her neck. I struggled up. My lungs burned. My throat burned. "The water's safe to drink," said Alabama, "I drank like ten handfuls an hour ago and I'm fine. There's like no fish in it during the day, I guess." I knelt at the bank and plunged my head in. The water chilled. It tasted of minerals and snow. I drank the way a pig or a dog drinks, on my knees. Alabama gave me the last of the red berries. "I ate my share while you were asleep," she said. "Are you a morning person," I said. "Only after I've killed people," she answered. Stared me dead in the eye. Did not smile.

The trees looked even odder in the sunlight. Seven- and nine-pointed leaves on the fake oaks. The fake birches had white, papery bark. All of their leaves and branches grew near their tops in spearheads. Leaves bright orange. As though it were fall. The trees the red berries came from were squat and many-armed, with lime-colored leaves and symmetrical holes in the bark of their trunks. I saw a tree fox clamber around one and dart its paw into the hole, drawing it away grasping a bright blue, frail-looking object: an insect, wing case shining. The ground continued to slope down and the riverbanks to steepen. The air smelled sharp and sweet. There did not seem to be any birds, at all. No crows. No jays. No sparrows. When we got thirsty, we stopped and drank from the river, which was growing colder and clearer as we followed its course. Deeper, too. The bed lined with pink and orange stone, and long blue fluid flute-shaped weeds. Larger fish glittered in shafts of sun: apple colored, mottled red and gold. When we were hungry, we gathered more of the red berries and wolfed them down. Our lips and fingers stained. As though we'd been gorging on raw flesh, or simply been careless with paints. We caught a glimpse of this in the river's surface as we bent to drink and both burst into loud snorts of laughter. Like in the Mountjoy elevator. But more debilitating. We threw ourselves back against the earthy bank and roared till we were breathless. "I can't believe this, I just can't believe this," I kept gasping. "I know, I know," Alabama gasped back. May seem callous. Given the events of the previous night. Joy is joy and will not be denied.

We lay next to each other, against the sun-heated earth of the bank. Recovering from the fit. Staring into each other's face with childish intent. Five, six inches apart. Both breathing hard. Her breath on my cheek. It was one of those times when you think you should go in for the kiss. Before you realize that doing so would not make any sense. "Fuck it," I said. "Fuck what," said Alabama. "You know what I mean," I said. We lived. Beside this river. Breathing these unknown scents. Under this strange sun. I got to my feet. Nothing, to my surprise, had changed. My joy remained. To judge from her grin, so did hers.

Tree foxes gathered to listen to our laughter. They clung to the branches of the berry trees, staring down at us with their golden eyes, their ears adjusting jerkily. They chirped and chattered to one another. One of them even gestured at us with a forepaw. "Did you see that," said Alabama, brushing earth off her nape. Another one opened its palms and shrugged its shoulders. "That's uncanny," I said, "though of all the things to find uncanny it does seem sort of minor." "Hey, you little bastards," Alabama cooed. The tree foxes all stopped talking. All stared at us. Then scattered, hurling themselves through the branches. "You clearly offended them with your silence," Alabama said. "Clearly," I said. The river sound masked our words. Our path was harder here: more pink stone, less soil. The spray from the river as it hit the banks made the stone slick. Alabama walked as surely as a mountain goat. I was less lucky. I fell. I stumbled. I knocked my knuckles on stone. I tore the new skin over the gash Gilder's teeth had left. In what seemed now to be a previous century.

"You all right," said Alabama. I stiff-armed a rib of stone to steady myself. "Wait," I said. "I'm not going anywhere," she said. "No, that's not what I meant," I said. My palm pressed against a hard surface. I could feel its complexity. I did not want to look. I knew what it would be. I removed my hand anyway. "You need to see this," I said. Leaf-work and vine-work, carved into the pink stone. Dust and leaf litter had filled the intaglio. That's a technical term. They hammered it into our heads in school, when we were learning about sacred sculpture. I found a twig and dug and cleaned. Alabama used her fingertips. "I bet they're all dead, anyway," she said when we had cleared a spot on the stone rib, or tusk, or former pillar, or signpost. Letters I could not read. Though when I looked at them it seemed to me that I knew them. They ran in an arc above a simple image: a naked woman, her hair bound up with a vine, carrying a small two-handled phial. Farther down the sloping path another rib jutted up. The decorative capital on this one still intact. "It's like the Acropolis, or something," said Alabama, "who do you think she is." "I think she's a goddess," I said. "The goddess of this river." "That's surprisingly poetic, Wood," said Alabama. She marched up to the next pillar and started scraping. "Same thing," she called. Two on the opposite bank, swathed in vines, bearing nine-pointed bright yellow leaves. If you stared down the bank, you could sight more of these ribs, broken and unbroken, vine wrapped and naked, rising from the smooth stone at regular intervals. "We're walking on a fucking floor," I said, "a broken floor."

A colonnade. In the middle of a forest, full of tree foxes and mysterious fireflies. The river tumbled alongside us as we walked. Its banks rising higher and higher. Like man-made walls. Which they were. Stone brick set on stone brick. No mortar that I could detect. Pink and orange squares and hexagons. Corroded by water. Their colors still alive. At sunset they seemed to blaze. One of the berry branches thrust through the stone. We both knew it was the last one we'd see. We loaded my shirt sling. Juice dripped as we walked and I swung it. Growing shadow awaited us, blue and cool. Rising from the columns ahead of us: arches. Intact. Their keystones, pink and alabastrine, half-lit-through by the falling sun. Cut with the same symbol as the columns: a blank-eyed, peaceful young woman, nude and holding a two-handled phial. Vines and leaves above and below. The presence magnified the rushing roar of the river. "Mr. Stone," said Alabama, "never mentioned anything like this."

He had not. Either he didn't know about it or he thought we didn't need to. I went with the latter. If your semisuperior is going to withhold information about, say, the existence of what appears to be another world, you have to ask yourself what smaller details they've failed to mention. The sun fell farther. The tree foxes returned in golden masses to the berry trees. Now forty feet above us, their roots breaking the upper edges of the stone walls, growing higher and higher the farther we followed the river's track. Their complex song: louder and more alarmed. "We're kind of big news for them, I guess," I said to Alabama. "That's one possibility," she said. The sun had set. Above, in the rectilinear eave of sky we could still see, the last rich rags of its color: crimson, salmon, pollen. The stone we walked along exuded cold. The spray from the river struck higher and higher. The slabbed floor, built of the same pink and orange stonework as the walls, had widened to the point where we could easily walk abreast. Even if we'd been four people. Still signs that the forest was in charge: branches thrusting through the wall, and weeds growing up through the floor. Small, absurdly orange, many-petaled blossoms. They too seemed to glow on their own. Alabama broke off a branch and handed it to me. "I want to keep my hands free," she said. I didn't blame her. The tree foxes laughed. Slowly, in golden threads, the fish returned from their daytime hiding places to the water, filling it with a wilder light. Here it beat against the sides of its channel, carved and curbed in stonework, between the two halves of this ruined corridor or tunnel or whatever it was. The water's agitation hurled fish skyward. They floated or swam off into the growing darkness ahead of us in great numbers. Trails of stairs. Minor constellations. Whatever you like. "Everything is unbelievable here," I said. "Get that lit, please," said Alabama. I obliged. It burned. Emitted sparks and crackles when flame hit a pocket of sap. Sweet smelling. Little smoke.

I don't know when I noticed we could no longer see the stars. The cool coming off the stone, the noise of the river, and the flicker of my torch mingled. Mesmerized me. The way a long walk will. I looked up and saw flame-glow dancing off a stone vault dripping with water, festooned by red-brown weed strings. The streams of fish would cling to these. I tried to keep my torch as far away from the fish as I could. Seemed delicate. "We are officially back indoors," said Alabama. Her voice echoed. "Yep," I said. My voice echoed. I hate echoes. When the dead talk to us in dreams they speak in echoes. I didn't know that then. I still hated them. "Echo, echo," shouted Alabama. "Echo," the tunnel said. "Please don't," I said. "Don't," the tunnel whispered. "Uncanny," Alabama said. The tunnel didn't reply.

Three hours ago, or four, in an access of delight I had almost kissed her. Here we stood in an empty, echoing human structure. Trouble with joy: not much separates it from terror. I was afraid. Wandering through a forest, with floating fish and tree foxes, anyone can survive. Evidence of human life, however: bad news. The human world being far more of a menace and threat than the natural world. We are almost animals, anyway. Human cleverness, malicious and cold, I have never been able to stand. A wind blew, for example. Not a breeze or a gust. One of the insane winds that human structures produce. Basically, I'd be happier if we could all live in tents, on the grassland. I hate civilization at times. That aspect of my character has not changed. The tunnel vault rose. The walls rose. We walked in silence. A stray vine scraped the wall in the draft. No more laughter of the tree foxes. No more stars. No more moon with its draconian smudge. The weeds hanging from the tunnel ceiling collected more and more of the floating golden fish. The torchlight gradually became unnecessary. I left the burned branch in a wall niche. At the foot of a statue on a hexagonal pediment. A naked young woman. Her hair bound up. Holding a two-handled phial. It annoyed me that I did not know her name. Alabama did not, either. "She's not the goddess of the river, though, I bet," she said, "she looks more like an indoor type of goddess." "Goddess," the echo said. Cold, light, skewed.

And vast. We were out of the tunnel. A ceiling above us. Maybe a hundred feet. Huge fronds hung from it, almost touching the surface of the river, which had widened. Enough fish clung to the hanging plants to provide light. What you get in a movie theater, before the previews start. "It's a temple," I said, "I think it's a temple." Not that I'd ever been in a house of worship other than a Catholic church. "Looks that way," said Alabama. The room circular. Its walls interrupted by tall, smooth columns. Radii of orange stones inlaid among the pink ran from each plinth toward the room's center. It's only thanks to Sister Immaculata that I know the word *plinth*. Or *capital*. The orange paths terminated at the foot of an enormous version of the hexagonal pedestal I'd seen in the wall niche. On which stood an enormous version of the naked woman whose image had pursued us as we made our way between the steepening banks into this shrine. Or temple. Or whatever it was.

The river churned beneath the lip of the pedestal. Seemed to end. Its noise great enough that we had to shout over it. "Has to keep going underground," said Alabama. I nodded. The statue's face: I could not quite make it out. At first just a white-eyed statue. Then Alabama. Vaguely. Sister Immaculata. My mother. My father's mother. A cashier at the Green Mart where I did my parents' shopping twice a week. Messaline. "Shit," I said. "What is it," said Alabama. "Look at the statue," I said, "look at its face." "It's just a face, Mike. Don't get freaked out," she said. The statue's features had settled into their placid, omniscient expression. White eyes. Parted lips. Phial extended. I could see, at that scale, the same sharp writing that surrounded the pillar images. It made my head hurt, my vision blur, to look at it directly. "Are you losing your eyesight," I said to Alabama, yelling over the vibrating thunder of the river, "when you look at the letters?"

The worst part was: an inner voice kept telling me, insisting, I'd been here before. When that was utter nonsense. Not even in dreams had I visited this echoing, stony place. Yet the quiet voice would not stop. I did not know what to do. Alabama was walking along the edge of the room, stroking the walls with one hand and holding her pistol with the other. "Come here," she said. She cupped her free hand around her mouth. The absurdity of the gesture struck me. It doesn't help. Yet all humans do it. I watched her beckon me over. I went. "It's the Treaty of Constantinople," she said. I didn't know what she meant. She gestured at the wall. I saw.

A fresco. That's another term I'm indebted to Sister Immaculata for. Stretching up into the darkness. Its color still present, over the faint colors of the stone. A man in a crude gray robe, leaning on a crutch.

One eye destroyed by a scar curving down from his brow to his chin. A man clad in red robes. A pope: you could tell from the hat. They stood face-to-face, on the foreshortened ground. Knights in gleaming black armor, their visors raised to reveal pale, bearded faces, flanked the pope, as well as a number of men and women in tunics and sashes, holding metal wands tipped in crescent moons, pentagrams, the symbols for man and woman. Other glyphs I did not recognize. Some held astrolabes. From the palms of others, stiff tongues of fire leaped. The man in the gray robe had far fewer followers. A hunchback holding a sickle. A young woman in a green dress, a leash draped over one fist, its other end connected to the collar of an ape. None of the splendid uniformity and power of the pope's followers. Between the pope and the one-eyed man, a table. On the table a document. Its letters rendered in that eye-blurring writing. The river noise rose. The river noise invaded my ears. My sinuses vibrated.

Green dress and sickle. This explained, more or less, everything. Which side I was on. Why. In the end, you have to side with the few, the damaged. With the hunchback farmer and the ape trainer. If for no other reason than simple perversity. If I died now, I would at least die knowing. "There's more," said Alabama. She had to struggle to speak. The river noise kept rising and rising. Beneath it a drilling white hum. A thread of mike feedback. Each arch enclosed another huge image. The Massacre of Amiens: Messaline standing apart from her hundred brethren. Who already had branches in place of arms and kinked roots instead of legs, and Perrin de Cissey smiling slyly (Potash had smiled that same smile) and gesturing at the witches and warlocks with a long silver wand. He had black hair and eyebrows. A heavy chin. A thickened, pugnacious nose. A real motherfucker. Other scenes: I didn't recognize them. Three men in togas standing on a cliff, clustered around a snake encircling the stem of a golden basin. A woman with violet, cloudy hair mounted on a white horse, holding a green-and-red bantam rooster in her left palm and what appeared to be the planet Earth in her right. A family—young father, young mother, and child—crossing a snowfield and leaving no track, no footprint, accompanied by two gazelles. "Pelagea and Ariston," I heard Alabama say. Barely. Pointing at the young couple. Their gazes fixed on each other. Each holding one of their child's hands.

And blood on her upper lip. Alabama's, I mean. I called to her. The river noise blotted it out. It had risen. I was certain of this. I touched my own lip. Drenched in blood. When I grabbed Alabama's shoulder she looked at me with half-lidded eyes. Dazed, glassy. The blood covered her mouth. Her chin. My palm was slick and tacky with my own blood. The noise of the river penetrated my skull. Vibrated in my brain and chest cavity. My kneecaps and fingertips. Eyelids slipping down. Despite my leaking nose and the insane thunder of the river, I was almost at the edge of sleep. A light, heavy sensation. Your limbs relax. You stare down into a black crevasse, warm and healing. And then you're asleep. The noise of the river brought us both to our knees. Facing the statue of the woman with the phial. Her face calm and blank as ever. Despite the pain the river sound inflicted. Her stone hair. Her stone eyelashes. Immobile. We knelt before her. As though we belonged to her sect. I saw a thin thread of blood descending from Alabama's ear. Over the lobe and down her neck. Beside the delicate tattoo of the vine. I was too afraid to check my own ears. The thrumming and throbbing of the river sound grew and grew. It made me nauseated. It altered my vision: the face of the statue began to shift and change. A cruel, capacious smile. Pointed teeth. A horned mask. The frescoes stretched and flowed as well. Their colors pulsating. Alabama was heaving deep breaths. No sound. I watched her rib cage inflate and deflate. I held back vomit. I wanted to fall into unconsciousness. I did not allow myself. I bit the inner skin of my cheek. Where the molar tore it. When Greg Gilder hit me.

Alabama was crawling. Toward the exit, I thought. We'd never make it. The sound would kill us first. Heart attack. Embolism. Simple flickering out of the soul. Then I realized she was crawling toward the statue. Toward the water boiling down below its base. I bellowed to her. Nothing comprehensible. No need to come up with a good line, under the circumstances. No sound. She looked at me. She gestured with her head. I followed. No choice. I followed on my hands and knees. The pain worsened the closer we got to the river. My skull: close to fragmenting. My heartbeat: accelerated to the point of near-asphyxia. At the edge of the stone Alabama stopped. Waited for me. I managed to get near enough for her to whisper. "Underwater," she said. Her lips adhesive with blood against my ear. She levered herself out over the white foam of the river. It would kill her. Smash her against the base of the sneering, openmouthed statue. She steadied herself. Plunged in. Her arm thrashed up. Went under. I said good-bye to her. Inside my about-to-split-apart head. I dragged myself up. I smelled the mineral smell of the water. Anything's better than drowning, I once believed. Not true. My shoes scraped the temple floor. My head and shoulder hit the twisted surface of the water. I was in the river. Hurled left and right. Tossed. Suffocating. I could not see Alabama. The pain had stopped. My blood drifted around me in red threads. Now I was beneath the statue. Carried beneath it. The opening in the stone floor of the temple, a circle of light, diminishing and diminishing. Soon the water was dim. Blue. Night-blue. Black. My air almost gone. I kicked my legs and swam. Upward. Nothing. No cavern ceiling. Just more cool, utterly black water. A faint glimmer of white under my feet. I dragged myself farther upward. My lungs flaming. Vertigo. I wanted to open my mouth and inhale. Drink the black water. Just to end it. To get out from under the weight. I kept swimming. The white glimmer spread. Up from my feet. Up to my head. My eyes and ears. Sound of radio static. Smell of metal. Taste of ozone. This void. Absolute.

25

Nothing ever turns out the way you imagine it will. You think there's going to be someone telling you the great and painful secrets of this world. Or opening a golden, final doorway. Beyond which would lie what, exactly? At least that's what you spend your childhood, boyhood, and youth thinking. But that's not what happens. What happens is: your alarm clock wakes you up, painfully, from a dream, and you can't really remember any of it. I've never liked sleeping. I'd been feeling sick, or half-sick, for weeks. Since before Christmas. My body constantly aching. I never missed practice. I never missed school. Probably just the flu. I hadn't been running a fever. Although I caught myself thinking that I had lost a large swath of my time, the way you do after a fever.

I had to keep shaking my head. To clear the dregs of this complicated dream. A repeat. Ten, eleven times I'd woken with scraps of it still vivid in my memory. A bearded man. A boy in the air. A long, delightful, worrying, inexplicable story. That was the day my father finally stopped giving me shit about my tattoo. I'd gotten it in a fit of drunken inspiration, with Greg Gilder and Frank Santone and Simon Canary. We'd been high and drunk at Simon's house. "Didn't you like try to bone Maggie Ravapinto here," said Simon. This was true. I'd passed out, though, before I could do the deed. I don't think she'd forgiven me. Or ever would. Gilder chuckled. "Limpdick," he said. "Why are you so concerned about my dick," I said. Simon told us he knew a place where they'd give you a tattoo without ID-ing you. So we went. We were completely hammered by the time we got there. The guy giving the tattoos didn't care. He was middle-aged, black, bearded. I chose mine—an eye, an open eye—out of a thin green book of samples. "Now, that is what I call an excellent decision," he said. My father freaked out when he saw it. "It's a team thing," I told him. At times he let me off the hook for acts done in the name of team spirit. "You better hope it's temporary," he said. He and my mother got used to it. You can get used to anything.

My father was in the kitchen. Wearing his tennis outfit. Crimson tracksuit. Yellow sweatband. Critics could say he looked ridiculous. I thought he looked like a pro. "I think I'm finally getting used to it," he said. "To your new racket," I said. He'd bought himself one for Christmas. White and black polymer. The size of a snowshoe. "No, to your portable artwork," he said. Pointing with his cup of coffee. "When I was a kid the only people who had tattoos were in the navy, more or less," he said. In the apartment beneath us, Mrs. Lorbeerbaum started yelling at her husband. "Then again other people have real problems," said my father. "That's true," I said. "Good luck," said my father, "though I doubt you'll need it."

I was playing a weekender that day. Against Cardinal Corrigan. I was looking forward to it. After our last game against them I'd beaten up two guys from the team, two brothers. They'd attacked me as I was walking to the subway. Desmond and James. I'd hurt them both. I hoped I'd have another opportunity to. You win a fistfight, you can't then consider the matter closed. The matter's just beginning. I whistled as I showered. This one repeated phrase. Don't know where I got it. I'd been whistling and humming it also since around Christmas, it seemed to me. It brought to mind the guy who'd given me my tattoo. Didn't know why. Maybe he'd been humming it as he worked. Maybe the vibrating, thrumming noise of the tattoo needle had obscured it. It had been shockingly loud. Then again I'd never gotten a tattoo before, so I had nothing to compare it to. My mother: still asleep when I grabbed my bag and left. I had to get to school to meet the team. Coach Madigan liked to give us a brief talk in the gym before we piled into his van. Painted blue and white, the school colors. I think he did the paint job himself. Looked totally jank.

Gilder's hoots filled the gym air when I arrived: "Who wants some? Who wants some?" Amplified and doubled by the echo. He danced around the school seal painted on the wood floor, punching the air. Gilder was a big precelebrator. Simon Canary: also present. Wearing the utterly terrified look he wore before every game. He was small and thin but he was extremely fast and agile, with huge hands. Coach Madigan had made him a halfback. One of those seemingly nonsensical decisions that proves to be epically right. Simon, running breakneck, gasping with fear and exaltation, between the guys trying to bring him down, was our most reliable scorer. His before-game face made me wonder what face guys who jump out of planes for kicks must make as they stand in the open bay door and try to remember if they folded their parachute correctly. Eyes large, terrified, and exalted. Grinning against his will. I greeted Gilder. I greeted Canary.

"Settle down, gentlemen," said Coach Madigan. Gilder stopped dancing and hooting. Coach Madigan drew a big breath and took off his ball cap. He removed his hat before any speechmaking. Sign of respect, maybe. Today's theme: appearance and reality. We'd all heard this sermon before. He had thirty or forty. On the value of hard work, the nearness of death, the importance of correct diet, the care of our immortal souls. He delivered them in a rough cyclical order. If you

THE ASSHOLES

stuck it out on the team long enough, you heard the cycle repeat. "We live in the world of appearances," began Coach Madigan, "but, gentlemen, the world of appearances is not to be trusted. The guy who you think will be weak"—here he gestured at Simon—"is indispensable to success. The guy who you think will be an idiot"—and here he gestured at me, which provoked everyone to guttural laughter—"turns out to be less of an idiot, and a huge blasted asset out there on the field. You know who we're playing. You've played them before. You've beaten them before. Don't let that fool you, either. The appearance of your enemy remains the same, but his nature always changes. Through wisdom, perseverance, and freedom from fear, you will win. Appearance. Reality. Gentlemen, don't get confused by this unpredictable life. I'm here if you have any questions. Now take a knee." We did. He led us in an Ave Maria. In Latin. *Gratia plena.* It was a tic of his. A superstition.

A boy in the air. A man with a beard. A human cry. That dream. Couldn't shake it. I sat in the back of Coach Madigan's van. We piled in alphabetically by last name, which meant that Dalmacio Zingales would have been the only person who went in after me. But since he lived in the Bronx, Coach Madigan didn't make him come down to Cyprian's before games against Corrigan, which he could walk to. Coach Madigan was not an officious man.

Blue, hard sky. Carved-looking white clouds. The yellow sunlight of winter. No traffic. The bare trees waving in a stiff wind off the Hudson. Gilder did an impression of the headmaster of Cardinal Corrigan, Brother Ignatius, widely regarded to be a pederast. "If that child molester gets anywhere near me," said Frank Santone, "he'll end up in the next world." "The next world, Mr. Santone," said Coach Madigan, "that's an archaic way of putting it." "Well, I'm an archaic guy, coach," said Santone. I was 90 percent sure Santone didn't know what *archaic* meant. We reached the Corrigan campus. We drove past the sleeping guard in his green-roofed guard shack. We had a guy of

THE WAR AGAINST

that species: Officer Houghtailing, but he slept in a small room off our main lobby. RUIZ, read this one's name tag. Why were these men, I wondered, in charge of our protection, always asleep? The thought disturbed me. Anxiety or misery constricted my throat. We had to drive all the way to the ass end of Corrigan's green, hilly campus to find a spot. The Corrigan guys did this on purpose. To make us walk to the field house. To psych us out. We saw their black-and-gold colors and emblem everywhere. Bunting on the fence. Fake plastic crows taped to every tree. The Corrigan Crow stares down at you with sly, human eyes, and he's smoking a stub cigar. Wearing a cocked brown hat with a white card tucked into the brim that says PRO FIDE ET PATRIA. This stupid cartoon.

Black and yellow everywhere in the field house, too. Corrigan's coach, Coach Pizzuta, was five foot one, five foot two. Must have weighed nearly two hundred pounds. All of it, you could tell, muscle. Even the fringe of gray hair around the top of his neck looked strong. He and Coach Madigan shook hands. That's when I saw him. The guy who'd given me my tattoo. Through the window of the field house. Walking along in the brilliant winter sunlight, wearing a black coat and a gray fedora and leaning on a cane with a silver head. "Look at that guy," I whispered to Gilder as Coach Madigan and Coach Pizzuta exchanged in hushed, serious voices tips for deck treatments. "He must live up here." "What guy," said Gilder. "That guy in the coat. He's the one who tattooed us." "What are you talking about, Wood," said Gilder. The fedora guy: gone now from the window's scope of view. "Never mind, it doesn't matter," I said. "You're goddamn right it doesn't," said Gilder, "nothing matters except getting out there and kicking their faggot asses." He had a real gift for dialogue.

Green, green grass. All colors become more intense in winter sunlight. Out on the field, breath rose in weak ribbons from within the helmets of the Crows, gold with a black stripe and an image of their mascot on either side. "*Pro* faggots *et* pedophiles," muttered Frank

Santone. I saw the Berry brothers. They both played in the offensive line. I lined up against James. Gilder hiked the ball. Santone dropped back. James leaped toward me. Desmond, next to him, smiled. The world seemed to slow down. One blink. Two. I hit James low. I hit Desmond high. I planned to do this all afternoon. I knew I'd be able to. If you're easily entertained, as I am, football is by far the best sport. Repetitive. Violent. You don't have much time for calculation. You come out of your starting position. You act. Black and gold dazzling in the steely sunlight. The crammed stands. Men my parents' age cheering. My own parents could not come. My mother had to work. My father had his weekly tennis date. Iron and unbreakable. I didn't blame them. I wouldn't want to waste a day with the fools in the stands.

I hit James low. I hit him high. I hit Desmond low. I hit him high. I hit both of them late. I managed a subtle face-mask of James. I managed a knee to Desmond's balls. The refs did not notice. I decided that if either of the brothers complained, I would hurt them even worse. To my surprise, neither of them did. Desmond went white-faced, then red. That's all. By the half, we were up seven–nothing. Simon Canary had snaked a touchdown. Matt Malinowski, our one-eyed kicker, hit the extra point. He hardly ever missed. Despite lacking depth perception. Call it pure art. "That's right, you homos," Greg Gilder screamed, "that's how we do in the two one two." As I said: a real dialogue expert.

The Crows didn't respond. Shadow covered their quarterback's face. He gave Gilder a silent finger. Cyprian's fans in the stands. Their wet, dark mouths torn open. Their eyes wide. The Crows drove four times and failed. They kicked off to us. The whistle for the half blew. We were filing into the locker room for the break when I noticed him. The guy in the black coat and gray hat, I mean. I would never have seen him if one of the stand dads—couldn't tell if he backed us or the Crows—hadn't fallen over. Loose-eyed drunk. His flailing attracted my attention. Next to him the guy in question. Staring at me. Not with anger or the grin of team support. With a kind of curious pity. I had sworn it was the guy who gave me my tattoo. Now I was less sure. I knew him. Maybe. I hated it when strangers stared at me. I hated it more when my memory failed.

26

The storm came out of the clear sky. In the third minute of the third quarter. Slashing ropes of frigid rain. Hail tapping our helmets and skin. Dry thunder and lightning. I watched it boil up in no time at all. We had just gotten into position. Santone was barking out his commands. The sky went dark. Blue to lead-gray in fifteen seconds.

A wind rose. Rain, gently, started. Within ten minutes we were surrounded by a thunderstorm. The dads in the stands opened their umbrellas. Or stood there in the downpour. We played on. I kept hitting James. I kept hitting Desmond. They fell harder in the churned mud. Santone fired a pass to Canary, who caught it and raced it in. He slowed to a trot right before the goal line. He did his minor celebratory dance on the other side: three shuffle steps and a head nod. I was clambering up from a tackle. That black guy was still watching me. Not the game. I wasn't worried. I was confident I could beat him in a fight. The only metric you really need. I gave him a two-finger V sign. For victory, not peace. He lowered his eyes and massaged his

THE WAR AGAINST

temples. The storm got way worse: thunder doubling and redoubling its grinding boom. Lightning arcing down. To building tops. To trees on the Corrigan campus. It just made the dads in the stands lose what little remained of their restraint. Zoo animals. Apes or boars. Hooting. Howling. Mouths agape. Eyes wide. When the lightning started I got pissed. The rule was that they had to call the game if there was lightning. An insurance thing. Which meant we'd get the win. But a win by called game is no win at all. You have to play to the end. More lightning touched the earth. The sky got darker. The referees dog-trotted onto the field, their shoes kicking up more muck. Their whistles shrilled and they waved their arms. Rule enforcers I've never liked. "That's right, you faggots," said Gilder as we did the handshake line. He had no conviction in his voice. The Crow quarterback, his face illuminated by lightning, his blond shag of hair adhering to his bony forehead, just flipped him off again. ROBERGE, said the gold name across his black jersey. Number 6.

Coach Madigan skipped the postgame speech. He only had two. One for victory. About the impermanence of victory. And one for defeat. About the impermanence of defeat. You might call him a stoic. Words fail even a stoic when no recognizable outcome has occurred. It had not even been a game. We showered and changed in the field house. We trudged out, silently, across the hills of the campus, back to the remote and now empty lot where he'd parked the team van. The rain still slashing down. I wondered why we'd bothered showering. I saw it as soon as we crested the lip of the last hill separating us from our goal: our two front tires deflated. The van looked like it had gone down on its knees. A courtier. A battle victim. I didn't say anything. Coach Madigan saw it next. "Jaysus Mary," he murmured. He never used profanity. He ran up to his van and slammed the side panel with the flat of his hand. Five times. Ten times. There's no reason to punish inanimate objects. Yet we do.

"They really fucked us in the ass on this one, coach," said Simon

Canary. Blinking those big liquid eyes. "Don't use language like that, please," said Coach Madigan, "and pardon my hypocrisy too." "Coach, can I just go home," said Dalmacio Zingales. Coach Madigan waved his hands. "Later, everybody," said Dalmacio. Rain beaded on his scalp. Naked. He was the first guy I'd ever met who voluntarily shaved his head. "Don't you need an umbrella, man," I said. "Umbrellas are for the weak," said Dalmacio, and jogged down to the iron gate at the campus edge. The rest of us stood there. Uncertain. I did not want to wait by Coach Madigan's side in the parking lot until a tow truck arrived. I did not want to cut and run. So I stood there in my windbreaker, listening to the rain hit the nylon and watching the fingers of lightning descend to the rusted-looking, rain-ravaged buildings along the Grand Concourse. Traffic built up. A chain of honks and cries from the street soon filled the quiet between each clap of thunder. Coach Madigan gritted into his phone, "No, you blasted idiot, I need you out here now, it's a blasted deluge." He showed serious discipline in saying *blasted*. You have to respect that.

"Gentlemen," he called out, "you're all adults. I trust you to get home. Should a mishap befall you, please keep it to yourself. I do not want to face any lawsuits from your parents, much as I love them." He had extracted a black, seal-slick umbrella from his van and ratcheted it open. "The subway is thataway," he said, "and a good afternoon to you all." I envied Dalmacio. He was, I guessed, already warm in his living room. I now had a long subway ride to look forward to. Listening to Greg Gilder talk about what a bunch of faggots and homos we had just defeated. It suddenly seemed unbearable. So I took off, at a light run, to get there first, and possibly get on a train by myself. My teammates were just standing around, anyway. "Look at him go," said Coach Madigan, "that's the spirit." Ran past the iron fence at the edge of the Corrigan campus. Game-day banners, also featuring the Crow, eyes slitted and wise, smoke curling from his cigar stub. There had been an outcry one year. Against a smoking mascot, I remembered. Corrigan had prevailed. Ran past a guy seven feet tall, wearing a yellow poncho and standing silently behind a white quilt spread on the sidewalk. A pyramid of purple-black plums near his feet. Bare and ulcerated, I saw. The other street hawkers had not given up in the rain, although their would-be customers lingered in door embrasures. Guys selling incense and soap. Bootleg movies. Books about Pan-African nationalism. Used appliances. "Must be white-boy day," I heard. A chuckle followed. Ran past the chuckler and the other silent hawkers. My bag banging against my kidneys. New sweat coming to my brow. I could have run over to Jerome Avenue but I just wanted to get out of the rain. So I ran to the green posts of the D stop on the Concourse. Ran down the stairs. Ran past the empty attendant's booth. Vaulted the turnstile. I had a card. But a train was there. I heard it downstairs, on the southbound side. No one hindered me. No one said a thing. No one else there. Except for a bug-eyed bum, sitting on a crimson milk crate and lecturing an invisible audience.

The train empty. The conductor announced the stops in a jovial voice. I didn't listen. Rain dripped from the hood of my windbreaker. Rain dripped from my hands. I wanted to sleep. But I didn't want to miss my stop or have my equipment bag lifted. So I forced my eyes open. Slapped my own face. Chewed on a knuckle. A boy, aloft. A pale woman. A whistled phrase rising and falling. Just in my mental auditorium. Great remembered pain I now could detect no trace of. Sleep. I needed to sleep, that's all, I thought. "That's all," I said. Which is when I noticed the sheets of water sliding down the windows of the car. Through one, its upper section propped open, water poured in. Smelling of metal. Smelling of stone and filth. Ropy streams spreading across the car floor toward my feet. *Must be*, I thought, *a breakdown in the rain-venting systems between here and the street. A clogged gutter.* "Ladies and gentlemen, what the fuck," said the conductor over the mike. His voice rising to a panicked shout and then cutting off. The train brakes shrilled. A violent halt. Momentum hurled me to the floor, to the inch of rising water. The car lights went out. "Hello," I said. Nothing. From the conductor, from anyone. The air temperature in the car had dropped. Because all this frigid water was getting in, I thought. Up to my ankles now. I banged on the door. The water kept pouring in. I was in the last car. I could see back down the tunnel. I figured if I could get the rear-facing door open I could just walk to the next station. Don't know why. I had no experience in subway outages.

A scent reached me. Above the smell of the water. The smell of a hot-running machine. I thought: *Engine fire.* Then I thought: *Subways don't have engines.* Then I thought: *I'm actually not sure if they do or not.* Through the square window, blue-white flickers and flashes. An electrical wire had fallen, I thought. In the long linear darkness behind me. A dead static buzz came over the PA. I checked the window. The blue glow was getting closer. I jabbed the red emergency button. Nothing happened. Other than another dull buzz. The glow seemed to be moving at a human pace. Made no sense. Weather phenomena don't move at a human pace. And this, I told myself, was a weather freakout. Nothing more. Ergo it couldn't have a human pace. It couldn't have any human component. So I kept watching. Transfixed. My desire for sleep gone. Through the water pounding the car roof and sheeting the window, blurring my view, I watched and watched. The light jumped and blazed. Shadows leaped and receded. An ecstatic celebration.

Then I saw: all this activity was in fact centered on a human figure. I caught glimpses in the blue light. Male. Walking with a broken, rhythmical gait. Thud of a cane. Weak footstep. Strong footstep. The glow clung to him. Arcs and crawling threads. "No way," I said. My voice scraped out. The glow lit him up: dark skin, a rain-darkened hat, a cane. That's what he was swinging. Its shadow stretching and vanishing. Shadow of a blade. It was my tattooer. I needed to leave. That much I knew. I threw my weight against the rear door. Hurt my shoulder. I yanked at the between-cars door. Jammed shut. I tried to pry the side doors open with my fingertips. Hurt my hands. I could not remember what the procedure was to open them in emergencies. *There should be a window release*, I thought. In the darkness I couldn't locate it. Blue-white flashes. Lighting up the tunnel sides. Steel struts, corroded. A blaze of yellow graffiti.

Another blue flash. Another concussion. I hit my knees. The six side doors opened simultaneously. Before I regained my footing, my tattooer climbed into the subway car. "Let's salute our city's infrastructure," he said. Water ran from his coat and hat. The head and tip of his cane glittered in the half darkness. The blue blaze still clung to his clothes and hair, his skin. The air crackled. He smelled like lightning. "What do you want, man," I said. "Problem is," my tattooer said, "nobody can answer that question, Mr. Wood." "You know my name," I said. "How soon they forget," said my tattooer. Blue light still clung to him: strings of it crawled over his coat, face, hands, beard. They were dimming. Dying out. "Please excuse this disarray," he said, "but I have to admit I lost my temper." "You lost your temper," I said. "Yes, indeed," he said.

His cane whickered upward. I heard it above the rush and patter of the water. He cracked me across the side of my head. My temple. My skull rang. I fell. I floundered. Sucked in a mouthful of the runoff water. It tasted, to my shock, clean. "Naked to the elements," he said. Pain flared in my spine. He had jammed his cane against my vertebrae. Its ferrule. Also: how did I know the word *ferrule*?

Pinned. Beetle on paper. Or human in a cold, filthy three inches of water. Not to use grandiose metaphors. The runoff water tickled my chin. "How did you get stoned," said my tattooer. Quiet. Clipped. "Get stoned," I said. He dug in. My spine pain increased. I almost pissed myself from it. I whined. More runoff on my lips. Dysentery, I thought. If not immediate death. "Don't play the goat with me," my tattooer said. "I smoke weed, you fucking crackhead, how do you think," I said, "and I don't even do it really anymore." The pressure on my spine increased. I whined again. Paralysis would be worse than

THE ASSHOLES

dying. I had no idea how much a spine could take. "What," said my tattooer. "No, what did you say," I said, "and what was that about goats." Rain dripped. I writhed. I gasped. I groaned. Didn't want to. Couldn't help it. "Stone's dead," said my tattooer. "Okay," I said. He was talking in a slow, hollow voice. "It's just me now. So there's no restraints on my behavior," he said. Self-assessment. A trait common to any number of psychos. "I don't," I said, "know who that is. But I'm sorry for your loss." I meant that. When a stranger nakedly tells you about the death of his friend, there's no reason you can't be sympathetic. Even if he blames you for it. Even if he wants to murder you. Professional courtesy, I thought. "Sorry for my loss," said my tattooer. The pressure of his cane tip on my spine vanished. "Stand up," my tattooer said. "Are you going to kill me," I said. "Stand up," he repeated. I stood up. He grunted. A little blue light appeared, a dancing, flickering condensate of light, poised above his finger. A flame. A spasm of lightning. "What is that," I said. "Ars gratia artis," said my tattooer. He had a square beard. Shot with gray. My forearm thrummed. Where the tattoo was.

"Is Hob dead," said my tattooer. "Who's Hob," I said. Though I thought, for a breath or two, that I once knew that name. Can't just admit anything, though. "Is Hob dead, or is he still walking," said my tattooer. "I do not know," I said, "and you can go ahead and murder me if you want but that won't change facts." And what if, I found myself thinking, I knew him? Why wouldn't that be possible? The point of blue-white light wavering above his index finger. There are always other possibilities. A whistled phrase. Dark, cropped hair. Mangoes and smoke. "Mike," said my tattooer, "look in my eyes." I looked in his eyes. The skin around them freckled. The brows heavy. The white pinked with capillaries. You see that in people his age. A sign of their exhaustion. "Do you know my name," he said. "Your name," I said. I had nothing else. My spine ached. My joints and lungs. Vibration built within my skull. The light emitted no warmth. Just a low, hushed roar. Muffled. Leafed. He brought his cane knob to his lips. The way a kid would. A badger head. Silver. With yellow gem eyes. He whistled against it. A quick phrase. I knew it. I did not know how I knew it. But I knew it. "I see I've been mistaken," said my tattooer. "Been mistaken," I said. Maybe this meant he would not murder me. He lowered his cane. "The human condition, though, when you stop to think about it," he said. "Human condition," I said. "Yes indeed," said my tattooer. I watched the leaf of light dance above his index finger. That blue. It spread. It gloved his hand. His molars ground against one another. I heard them. Sweat beads reflected the blue glow. I saw them. Before I could react he grabbed my forehead. The water on my skin hissed. Evaporated. His palm, rough and seamy, grazed my eyebrows. No other way to describe it: pure darkness, rushing in.

27

O r so I remember it. Remembering amnesia: paradoxical. Unavoidable. Dead-real as the black eye of, say, a crow. Perched on the stone head of a wolfhound. Staring at me. "Smug," I said. The bird didn't answer. "We'll see about that," I said. The bird cawed. Clacked its beak. I wondered who was looking through its eyes now that Potash was dead. Messaline, I assumed. No time to think about her. Footsteps shuffling within the house. The crow got agitated. Flapped off when the door opened. "Well, she can be a real cunt," said a rich-voiced pedestrian, behind my back. Mrs. Sturdivant recognized me. Took her three seconds. Her eyes radiated factitious warmth. Then she said, "Michael! A pleasure." I shook her hand. Her bony wrist jutting from the worn-thin sleeve of a purple bathrobe. Slippers made of rope. "Is Alabama at home," I said. "She's in her room," said Mrs. Sturdivant. "As is usually the case these days."

I held my breath as I walked up the stairs. Ambushing a lumberer like me is one thing. Springing yourself on the Alabamas of the world is another. I'd seen her accuracy. But we were in her parents' house.

So I might be safe. Then again, she didn't seem too troubled by filial duty. So I might be at risk. Through the window of the Sturdivants' second-floor corridor—octagonal, lead seamed, and illuminating on a wooden pedestal a thumby fist of metal that I took to be a piece of sculpture—I saw Charthouse, watching from the corner of Bleecker. His breath vapored upward in the cold. He spotted me through the pretentious window. Gave a thumbs-up. I returned the gesture. My stomach churning. I was 85 to 90 percent sure Alabama would not shoot me. Discouraging odds when it comes to life and death. The photos I'd seen before looking worse in the daylight: wagon wheel and hen. Monuments to the moronism of the photographer. A sneeze from the first floor. "I think it'll be good for her to see someone," I heard her father say. Didn't know if me meant me or a psychiatrist. "She's in her own space," said her mother. "I understand that she's in her own space," said her father, "but being in your own space doesn't mean you can't also participate in other spaces."

Rest of this conversation: lost. Her parents moved to an area of the first floor where I couldn't hear them. I stood in front of Alabama's door. Breathing hard. "Okay," I said. Raised my fist to knock. The door rushed inward. So quickly that an audible gust of air followed it. She wasn't holding a gun. I took comfort in that. I saw her recognize me. Which comforted me more. "How did you know I was outside your door," I said. "You have a really distinct way of walking," she said, "kind of like what I imagine a retarded dinosaur would sound like." She had me there. "Do you want to come in," she said, "and I hope Mark and Lena didn't say anything too stupid." Didn't tell her about the conversation I'd overheard. Didn't want to ruin her mood.

"Charthouse came too." The first thing I said. So she would know I wasn't here on merely personal business. She didn't say anything. The scents of soap and steam filled her room. Her skin, I saw, was slightly pink. Water jeweled her hair. Fresh out of the shower. "Did you have a memory thing," I said. She didn't say anything. "Alabama,"

I said. "Look," she said. She reached a book down from her closet shelf. *The True Rites and Rituals of the Archonticks*: the title in spidery gold. "What's that," I said, "archonticks." "A synonym," she said, "but look." She opened it. Between two pages, a leaf. Bright orange. Nine-pointed. Like nothing in this world. Still fresh, still alive. "I couldn't remember, for days. Then I found this in the lining of my coat. There was a hole in the pocket," she said. I remembered. Re-remembered, maybe. The dark berries. The river that had almost killed us. The alien moon.

She closed the leaf back into its book. Sat on her bed. Cross-legged. Her skirt hiding her shins. I sat in the rocking chair. My foot drumming the floor. Nervous habit. The chair squeaked and quacked. "What is it that you want, Mike," she said. Staring at her knees. I didn't speak, at first. I was choosing my words. With care. Hard for a mediocre thinker. "What I want," I said. On the first floor, her mother sang. A scrap in Italian. Her voice full and off-key. "Mr. Stone's dead," I said. Her father sneezed. Coughed. You could tell even from that he thought of himself as an artist. "Vincent's dead," I said. The chair noise got worse. I didn't stop drumming. "Hob's dead," I said. "Did you come here to tell me that," said Alabama. Beads of water slid down her cheeks. From the shower, I kept telling myself, from the shower. "No," I said. "Then why did you come here," said Alabama. Looking into my eyes. The way an optometrist does. With intent to prove how blind you are. I didn't blame her. "What I want is to know what to do next," I said. "Well, I can't," said Alabama. I interrupted her. "So does Charthouse. So would anyone. And I think it's incumbent on you to have some say." The chair sang on. I'd revved up my leg-twitching for the last part. What I'd been most afraid of saying. To tell a shooter with a recent death on her conscience that she still has an owed duty: seemed risky to me. I don't like lying. I avoid it when I can.

"They wanted me to see a psychiatrist," she said. Instead of drawing her gun. Instinct told me she wasn't carrying it. She was wearing a dress, for the first time that I'd ever seen. Dark blue. It looked odd on her. "Don't take this the wrong way," I said, "but I've never met anyone who needed a psychiatrist less than you do. Not that I'm some expert or anything." I don't like lying. I like telling the truth. I do it when I can. "That's what I think, or usually think. But I didn't know," she said. "You were sick. You thought you'd been sick," I said. Right as Alabama said: "It was like I was sick. I thought I'd been sick." Our voices struggling and interweaving. Soap. Steam. Her deodorant. The clean, calm scent of her room. Her space. To use the absurd language of her parents.

"I looked it up," she said. Without her leather jacket her shoulders seemed much frailer. "You looked what up," I said. I wanted to put my arm around her shoulders. Not anything carnal. Just human-to-human contact. "That river, that whole scene," she said. That would have been the height of idiocy, however. So I did not move. "That whole scene," I said. "It doesn't have a name. It flows all over and leads to the temple, no matter where you start following it," she said. No surprise there. Not everything bears the burden of a name. "And did you find out who it was dedicated to," I said. "There's theories on the subject. Mr. Stone," she said. Stared at her hands. Gnawed a thumbnail. Her mother sang another throaty, off-key phrase. "The Weald," she went on. Her voice quiet. "And they say it's Hecate, in the temple. I don't think that's true. And they never saw it." I didn't know who Hecate was. Alabama told me. About her underearthly origins. The sacrifice of black cocks and puppies. The pouring of wine and the burning of grain. Had to agree. No connection with what we'd seen. The Weald. Sounded spacious. Ancient. Free. What you crave at that age. "Those berries," she said, "they say they're deadly poisonous. So that shows how much they know anyway. Rosenkreuz, the Chronicle of Sviatoslav, and even bullshit moderns, even Levi and Crowley: on that point they all agree. 'Eat not the fruit watered by that river.' Like the Bible." I wanted to ask about the tree foxes. I decided to keep quiet. She didn't look to be in an information-please mood.

"Do you know how he died," said Alabama. "I don't," I said. She gnawed her nail again. "Unless what we do next," said Alabama, "is burn their school down, I'm not interested." She was smiling, though. "That's not off the table," I said. I was smiling too. That's the thing about adolescence. For all its miseries, you're resilient. You can endure anything. And endurance equals greatness. "You gonna wait outside while I get changed," said Alabama, "or are you just like going to admit you're a sick voyeur." I waited outside. I heard her dress fall, in the quiet. Her soles dance from point to point. I heard her cough. I heard her stumble. Collide with a trustful object. The rocking chair, I guessed. "Are you all right," shouted her father. "She's not a toddler," shouted her mother. "I never said she was a toddler, Lena," shouted her father. "I never said you did, Mark," shouted her mother. "It's this way basically all the time," said Alabama. She'd come into the hall. No more dress. Wearing her uniform: beaten jeans, a tee shirt (orange; it had an ink stencil of a duck with humanoid arms on it, giving the world the finger), and the leather jacket. Her walk had that mild swagger. Which meant she was armed. "I'm going out for a while," she said as she ran down the stairs. She was through the door before her parents could answer. "Have fun," cried her mother. "Thanks," I said, "we'll make sure to."

28

The Library of Alexandria: I first heard about its destruction from a graduate student whose name I never learned. Never met him before. Or after. Late spring of my twenty-third year. I was drinking and listening to the rain tap the window of the bar, and overhearing this vehement student. The death of antiquity, he called it. When you lose knowledge, you die, said this student, speaking fervently to a woman with long, crimson hair and a ring through her septum. I didn't need anything other than my memory to understand the outrage and fear in this student's voice. I even sympathized. Though there's nothing I hate and despise more than aging students.

Winter sunlight. Air smelling burned. A metal door, set into the frame of a steel security shutter. The yellow eye streaked crudely across both. Perry Street, between Washington and the highway, and farther on the leaden river. The Hudson. Knowing the name makes a difference. "This is where we get on," said Charthouse. His dented key glinted. The lock glinted. Did not turn. A beech tree, naked, rose above the low roof. Reaching upward. Charthouse sighed. It turned into a wet, ragged cough. Which went on for a long time. Bent him over. He finished by spitting. Wiping his mouth. "Losing my touch," he said. "Hey." A chirp from a window in the next building. "Hey." The chirper a lanky guy with huge glasses. Leaning out. "Can I help you," said Alabama. The glasses guy stared. His breath floated up in streams. A fool: thin-lipped, thin-mustached. He drew his meager torso back in through his window. "So are we like in exile now," said Alabama. "We all experience failure," said Charthouse, "it's no reason to despair." He closed the door. "Mike," he said. I took my key. My arm throbbed as its tip bumped against the metal of the lock. The key slid home. The lock turned. The door opened. The dry-citrus smell of Mr. Stone's place wafted out. "Shall we," said Alabama. "I have to warn you," said Charthouse. He didn't explain further. The darkness beckoned. Charthouse gestured Alabama in. The glasses guy thrust himself out of the window again. "What," I heard him say as I crossed the threshold. "Indeed," said Charthouse. Farewell, glasses guy. The sheer number of people who enter your life for a fleet, irrelevant moment or two would crush and destroy you if an accident of nature ever forced you to confront it. Memory is love. I don't know who said that. Wasn't me. Scent of lemon skin, orange skin. Scent of sand. We crossed the threshold. One room to the next. The glasses guy crying his puzzlement and outrage to the hard, azure winter sky.

I was no melodramatist as a younger man. All the same: a ruin. The word forced itself to mind. No other way to describe it. Books thrown from Mr. Stone's shelves. Their pages slashed and defaced with ink, black and red. With brown smears. Dried shit, I could tell. The shelves pulled from the wall and hacked to white, blue-painted kindling. The glass-covered prints hurled to the floor. Bearing boot marks. The sourceless orange glow that filled the place had dimmed, blackened. The light dirtied. Long grooves and runnels had been cut or clawed into the white tiles of the wall: the work of human hands.

Water was trickling in. I heard it. Musical and steady. The sound of wreckage. "Lie there, my art," said Charthouse.

We picked our way. Pages slithered. My sneaker heel landed on an isosceles of glass and broke it further. It made me want to weep. I am no scholar. Maybe that's why. The ignorant either hate books or they revere them, in superstition. Covers tumbled from the piles. Empty. The cases of insects. "They didn't burn them," said Alabama. She lifted a blue-bound book from the floor. I recognized it. Mr. Stone had shown me the picture of Messaline in it. Whole. Unravaged. "Why do you say they," said Charthouse. We walked through the long vestibule. The orange light fluttered. Reasserted itself. "Not long now," said Charthouse. We had to high-step over wood debris. "Where's Wittgenstein," said Alabama. "I assume," said Charthouse, "he's with his maker." We had to plant our feet and avoid the nails that stuck up from the scattered planking. "Where's Mr. Stone," I said. "You'll see," said Charthouse, "just keep walking." Black holes stared from the wall next to my head. Each the size of woman's fist. "This is like escalation bullshit," said Alabama. "Art of war," said Charthouse. I kept expecting to smell the smell of a corpse. The sweetish smell that had filled the room holding Hob's body. Nothing. Just the lemon-rind-and-sand scent of the place. The smell of wisdom. No other way to describe it.

In the room where Mr. Stone had questioned me, razor cuts defaced the armchairs, their seamed hides. Stuffing, yellowed in a repellent way, vomited from every slit. The black table I'd sat at as Mr. Stone ordered me to light a cigarette: reduced to sticks and splinters. This struck me. A pointless gesture. A table can't conceal anything, the way a book or an armchair can. There's no reason at all, in other words, to violate the faithful, trustful slumber of a table. "Were they looking for something," said Alabama. "Don't give undue credit," said Charthouse. More of those shit-colored stains defaced the concrete wall covered in hatch marks. In the end, even the vanquished are trampled on.

"Well," said Charthouse. Standing amid the heaped ruined books and the splintered furniture, amid the gouged, torn walls, was Mr. Stone. Towering and still. Or rather what had once been Mr. Stone. Now no more than what his name suggested. A tall, erect figure. Gray rock. Hands, eyelashes, the triple point of his folded pocket handkerchief. Concrete, I determined when I got nearer. What you'd use to put down fresh sidewalk. His enormous hat in his enormous, scarred hands, modestly hiding his groin. His eyes open to their fullest. As though he were addressing his students, explicating harmonic analysis to them. Except for the fact that his mouth was resolutely closed. Back straight. Head brushing the ceiling. His unmoving hair. Piled at his feet, pressed against his ankles and shins as if in flight, as if seeking comfort, the concrete forms of rats: fifteen, twenty. The water noise grew. A pipe, broken. A rupture. Alabama touched his lapel. "Is it her," she said. "Eliminate the impossible," said Charthouse, "and all that." "That white-haired cunt," said Alabama. Her voice resonant with fury. She was still stroking Mr. Stone's lapel. "So what now," I said. "What do you think," said Alabama. "Don't be hasty," said Charthouse. "This isn't real stone," she said. "Charms of city life," said Charthouse.

The orange light flickered again, returned, fluttered, ceased. Utter darkness. My hands curled into fists. Though even I knew: you can't defeat darkness by punching it. Charthouse grunted. A blue leaf of flame appeared, cradled in his palm. I saw that Alabama had drawn her gun. "No need," said Charthouse. "There is a need," said Alabama. Another deep, atonal groan from the ceiling. "We should do triage on the books," I said. "No," said Charthouse. Alabama kept fingering Mr. Stone's lapel. "Okay then," I said. "It's not even stone," Alabama repeated. She stopped speaking. She holstered her gun. The blue light made her look young and hollow cheeked. I knew what she meant. The concrete. A final indignity. I banged my foot into one of the concrete rats. It fell over. A stony crack. The light from Charthouse's palm had grown enough for me to see: the tail sheared away, the ears

THE WAR AGAINST

fractured, the fine-built paws snapped. "That cunt," repeated Alabama. "It's revenge," I said. "She could have just killed us. So that doesn't make sense," said Alabama, "and if they know enough to know about Mr. Stone, they know enough to go after like our parents instead." Drip, drip, drip. Mournful and precise. Hard to think of any good boded by the sound of a split, leaking pipe. A fundamental, just perceptible shudder running through the foundations, the ceiling.

When you're seventeen, concern for your parents' life does color your character. Your mother and your father still have the half-terrifying immortality you see in them as a child. "This is all prologue," said Charthouse, "if you take my meaning." "I'm sorry," said Alabama, "but we didn't have a choice." As she spoke I saw Potash fall again. His ring and its malevolent colors. His beard. His gray face. His forehead opening above his left eye. I heard him say *you people and your romanticism.* "I never said you had a choice," said Charthouse.

The ceiling groaned. Charthouse raised his hand. Above our heads, a long crevice was opening. Another drip started up. That water hit my scalp. "The integrity won't last," said Charthouse. "Even now it's just an echo of his wishes." "So let's go," I said. "We can't just leave," said Alabama. More water dripped. "We don't exactly have options here," I said. "This isn't," said Alabama. A scutter and a squeak. She whipped out her gun. Holstered it again. A large gray rat was dashing across a heap of torn pages. Leaves for the burning. "Well, now," said Charthouse. I knew it was Wittgenstein as soon as I saw him. Even in the blue half-light. I bent. Extended my palm. He ran up my arm and onto my shoulder. "Most people have a thing with rats," said Charthouse. "I admire them," I said.

The ceiling drip sped up. Hunks of plaster fell and shattered at my feet. "Good-bye, Menachem," said Charthouse. "Good-bye," said Alabama. The blue light flickered against Mr. Stone's hard, composed features. Structural rumbles. From under us, this time. Wittgenstein went tense. Stopped his squeaking. We followed Charthouse and his blue light back to the door. Wittgenstein chirping and chattering into my ear. "Are we like going to have to learn rat now," said Alabama. "If you can manage it," said Charthouse. "No offense, Mike, but I have the impression that your talents lie outside the scholarly realm." He had me there. The big rat's delicate claws I could feel through my coat. This was going to be a lot harder to sell my parents on than a tattoo, I realized. Through difficulties to the stars. Also not a quote by me. That's the state motto of Kansas. I knew we were crossing Mr. Stone's threshold for the last time. I knew his petrified body would be crushed by a ceiling collapse, along with his rats. That the remains of his library would be lost for all time. Yet I was not upset. I was at ease. Mr. Stone's calm face watched us leave. No fear. No pain. Just that clear-eyed look and set mouth. I guess once you've faced down actual Nazis, not metaphorical ones or people whose behavior verges into Nazi-esque territory, you don't have a lot left to fear. Call it what you like: so said Mr. Stone. I still had no name for it. The ranks of people who could provide me with a name had thinned. I didn't mind. You don't need a name. You don't always need to know. In fact you only need to know one thing: if you're an asshole or not. His door creaked. Beyond it a blinding oblong of white light. We inhaled the unplaceable scent. Wisdom, knowledge, whatever. We crossed the threshold. And then we were standing in the sun, a heavy door squealing closed behind us.

Shocking that it did not shock me. To violate the real laws of this world. A small, asphalt-bisected park. Benches, two wedges of grass, and rails. Our exit point a gray and stately building. We'd left through the service entrance. The doorman saw us come out. "Excuse me, excuse me," he was saying, "excuse me." I ignored him. Alabama ignored him. Charthouse said, "At your service." He tipped his fedora. The doorman tipped his livery hat. A Soviet cadet's. Charthouse tips his hat, and you reciprocate. Law of life. "You can't just," the doorman said. Charthouse grinned and slowly replaced his fedora. "Can't just what," he said. His teeth glowing. "Screw it. What am I, the Gestapo," the doorman said. He adjusted his hat. He returned to his post. "And a good day to you to, sir," said Alabama. "Sutton Place," said Charthouse, "still a fancy address."

Blue air. FDR traffic. Beyond, the sun-peaked sullen water. In the clear distance, the thick bridge, the gleaming domes of a facility on Roosevelt Island. Two crows watching us. "See, this is why people get issues about them," said Alabama. "Heckle and Jeckle," said Charthouse, "I enjoyed that cartoon despite its racial overtones." I let the dark birds have it: double-barreled middle fingers. Didn't bother them. "So what happens next," I said. "Do I look like a teller of tales to you," said Charthouse, "I have no idea." He closed his eyes. Lighting our way had taken it out of him. I could tell. "You know what my vote is," said Alabama. "It might have to go that way," said Charthouse. "I can totally live with that," I said. I was expecting Charthouse to tell me I didn't know what I was talking about. I was expecting Alabama to take a jab at me for claiming more experience than I possessed. "Good to know we're all on the same page or whatever," said Alabama. No jab. "I advise you both to spend as much time as you can in public," said Charthouse. No jab from him. Shock and gratitude. Not the kind you can express. Charthouse left us then. Hobbling along. He had another coughing fit that stopped him. Bent him. The crows stared. Those empty, watchful, oil-drop eyes. He started off again. His cane scraping the ground. "He seems young to need it," I said. "We'll need them," said Alabama. "Assuming we live that long." Wittgenstein chattering and chattering on.

29

THE UPPER CRUST. That's the name of one of the most complicated sleights in the *Calendar*. The premise is simple. Four queens are taken from the deck and laid out on a table. Each is then covered with a packet of three cards. The expert leafs through the first three packets to show that the queen has disappeared from each. He takes up the fourth to show that the three queens have migrated there, forming, with the fourth queen, a royal coterie. Erzmund supplies, along with the technical instructions for the sleight, a lengthy chunk of descriptive patter: the predestined failure of the vulgar in their assays to enter aristocratic circles, the wily means of each noblewoman's escape, the fatal vanity that gathers them together at last.

I never mastered this feat. Hob did. He did it not with face cards, not with aces. He used twos. Lowest of the low. He called his version THE HOLE-IN-THE-GROUND GANG. His line of patter inverted Erzmund's. He talked, as he showed us the twos beset with royalty and aces, about the crushing, philistine world, the violence inherent

212

THE WAR AGAINST

in our lives, and the hope and succor flight and privacy alone can offer. First time I heard the word *succor*. His version added another level of functional complexity, since he had to produce not just the twos but the tyrannical, two-faced kings, queens, and jacks as well, and the priestly aces. I've never gone in much for revolutionary sentiments. And there's no need to improve, through adaptation, masterworks. Yet I never minded Hob's version. I admired it. We all did. Charthouse went apeshit the first time he saw it. "You, sir," he said, "are a genius." We applauded. Hob bowed. Whipped his red-and-white handkerchief out of nowhere and swept it over the table. The cards had vanished when he'd completed the pass, and he showed us the deck, neat and squared off, in his left hand.

"Would you like more zucchini," said my mother. My daze ended. "Yes, please," I said. "One thing's for sure," said my father, "whomever you end up marrying is going to know we raised you correctly. You always say please and thank you." He pointed at me with his fork. Absurdly, I saw Hob, making one of his precise, mildly theatrical gestures. "Stop with this insanity about his future wife," said my mother. She was chuckling. "I'm just saying," said my father. Beneath us Mrs. Lorbeerbaum took up her tirade. The same tirade. Broken up by hours and days. "Nathan, this is the last straw," she thundered. The floor dulling her voice. My mother and father both snorted and guffawed. I had to admit it was pretty funny. Even though I was thinking about Hob. Who was dead. You don't know many dead people at seventeen. Hob was, for me, the first. "This is super tasty," said my mother. "Why thank you, my little chickadee," said my father. Other kids, and I knew this for a fact, found their parents embarrassing. I never saw it that way. Longevity is a form of endurance. Endurance equals greatness. Therefore, respect your elders. I think this is why I volunteered to take Wittgenstein. He fell asleep as soon as I'd gotten him home. Hidden in my jacket. I put an old tee shirt and a sock in a shoe box and put him in it and slid it into the back of my closet. Whether he stayed put or got into the walls, I considered it his own affair. In a building like the one I lived in, a rat will thrive. Rat mind and human mind. Call them cousins.

My parents left the dishes for me and then went out. To the movies. They went to the movies on Saturday nights. An unbreakable engagement. "Like Kant and his walks," said my mother. She had to explain who Kant was. I got the point. You can get past your human weakness with a little routine. A little practice, no matter how dull or insane it seems when described or viewed from the outside, will save you. Redeem you, even. If that's possible. I washed. My limbs ached from football. On top of the regular ache. Which had returned with my memories. My head twinged every time I tried to get a focus on the statue's face. Still shifting. The script still hurting my eyes. Charthouse said that was common, in accounts he'd read on the matter. "They call it the high speech," he said, "no known translations exist. Not even any transcriptions." About the temple he had as little that was definitive to say as Alabama. Aside from the speculation about her being Hecate, which he also dismissed. No name. Like the river. Its statue nameless as well. This didn't bother me. The place had almost killed me. I didn't necessarily want to know every last particular. The frescoes were enough to give you the general idea. That's the real paradox. You understand your place in the world only before it's taken away from you. Point out a case where that hasn't happened and I'll hand over my meager accumulations. I said good-bye to my parents when they left for the movies. Shook my father's hand and embraced my mother. "We'll let you know whether it's a renter," my mother said. Her standard premovie valediction. In their opinion nothing was a renter. Even and especially the worst films. "The big screen ennobles them," said my father. For all I knew it would be the last time I saw them. If they could get to Mr. Stone, they could get to me. I was not afraid. Just wanted to see what would happen. To know the ending. The great curse of humanity, a desire to know the ending. I found

THE WAR AGAINST

myself humming Charthouse's little melody. Whose name I also did not know. Stroking the rims of the dishes with a sponge.

And yes, I was waiting. I assumed I had little time left in the world. I was not afraid. Tired. Concerned for my parents. That's all. Hob Callahan could be described as Mozart. So Mr. Stone had said. Mozart died young, too. Maybe, I thought, a prerequisite. Precocious. Able beyond his years. His small hands. His failed flight in the gym. Beyond a few sleights of hand, what had I seen? Not even the shallows of his gift. Assuming Mr. Stone was correct. I racked the dishes. Mrs. Lorbeerbaum was screaming now. Top of her smoked voice. "I tell you every time, Nathan. I tell you every time." Her husband's reply: bass and inaudible. The voice of a moose at bay. A large, pathetically dangerous forest animal. City life can put you on a first-name basis with strangers against your will. One of its less-observed qualities. "And still you do it, just as though I'd never spoken," screamed Mrs. Lorbeerbaum. I'd met her once. In the hall. She'd accosted me and accused me of walking around the apartment too loudly. She wore a pink, cabbage-embroidered robe. Short loose sleeves. Fat swung beneath her upper arms. Her hair pumpkin colored. "I would appreciate it," she said as I walked away. I don't waste time on the insane. "And what do you think you are doing, young man, and what do you think you are doing," she'd shrilled after me. Her husband: another random victim. Some humans can't be distinguished from disease or car accidents. One of the oppressing queens in Hob's sleight. Clinging and vicious. Harridans. That's a word I learned from my mother.

Nothing left to be done. No word from Charthouse or Alabama. No crows. No dishes remained, even. So I went to my room and practiced. THE MAN WHO WOULD BE KING. THE MOUNTAIN AND MUHAMMAD. THE FOUR WINDS. I hurled cards at my own reflection: eyes, mouth, nose. The cards thunked into the mirror. My reflection never flinched. Mrs. Lorbeerbaum was now screaming at the loudest pitch I'd ever heard. The pink back of her throat. Her pink robe. Her husband's mumbled, helpless replying. I shot the cards hand to hand and squared the deck. Made the Joker pop out. Erzmund called that I'LL NO MORE GO A-ROAMING. He suggested using it as an obscure means of compulsion. *The speed itself will unnerve,* he wrote, *and so assert your mastery.* The Lorbeerbaums continued. On and on. I checked in with Wittgenstein. Asleep in his shoe box. He'd been through a lot. I didn't blame him. Even envied him. He didn't have to hear the Lorbeerbaums. I leaned out through my living room window and smoked one of my last cigarettes. With Vincent gone, I'd had to ration them. The sweet smoke slipped down. It palliated the ache. Cleared my head. "Fucking Mozart," I said. To the cold night. The bitter bright stars. "If you're so amazing why did he get you then," I asked no one. No one answered. No echo returned.

Problem with waiting for death: boredom. At least for me. At least at seventeen. So I tried a few stoic poses before the mirror. Flexed my biceps and triceps. Made my pectorals dance. I admired my tattoo. Without thinking I put my shirt back on, rushed to the hall closet, and grabbed my coat. Better to die on the run. Thought about leaving my parents a note. If they got back and found it, and then I failed to die, however, awkwardness would result. I left no note. I turned out the light. Took a deep breath of the apartment air. Your home, the house of your birth, has an irreproducible smell. Even if you never notice it. I charged down the stairs. Could not wait for the elevator. Passed within earshot of the Lorbeerbaums' door. Their screaming increased. Mrs. Lorbeerbaum's voice sawed my eardrums. Mr. Lorbeerbaum's voice thumped and floundered on, beneath it. Nathan. I saluted him. Invisibly. Ran past Henry, our doorman. Still asleep, still disturbing the leaves of the poinsettia with his exhalations. His livery hat on a nail. His hands gently, modestly folded. He woke up as I skidded through the building doors. Gave me a wave. Eyes bleary. I waved back.

Cold air hit my cheeks. All thoughts of death, I won't lie, vanished.

THE WAR AGAINST

The high stars. The moon. Our moon, with its bilious face, not that sleek and terrifying dragon. I slowed down to a walk. Headed east. The foot traffic thin and the air pierced by every car noise. The hissing of tires and the squeaking of brakes. A fruit seller was closing up for the night. Shutting his umbrella. Balancing it on his shoulder. Grapes gleamed in the sourceless yellow light from the street. You only see that in big cities. I had a dollar. I bought a cluster. The cold had almost frozen them. Lacy frost on their skins. Their juice poured onto my tongue. Man and woman in their late twenties. Behind glass. In the stagey light of a restaurant. Their faces still and kind. Their hands laced across the white cloth. An old woman with a dowager's hump, clad in a bed's worth of linen. Dragging a dachshund behind her in a grocery cart. A whole long life would not be enough time to know everything. I was eating the grapes off the stem. Carrying it in front of me. As classical figures do. The images from the temple. Pelagea and Ariston: I'd forgotten to ask Alabama about them. The name of the cigarette moss, which I'd never asked Vincent. Names matter. Details matter. Memory is love. Who said that? Not me. I planned to go on repeating and repeating it until they came for me. Messaline. Her crows. Whoever. When they did, I'd kill and maim as many of them as I could before they overwhelmed me. I knew I could do damage. I'd managed to hit her. Before I even really understood what I was doing. I grinned at the thought. One grape left. The denuded stem resembled a complex of human blood vessels. Or something. I held the grape up, next to the moon. Adjusting till they were the same size. Ate the grape. The moon remained. I was lowering my eyes back to the street when I saw Vincent Callahan scurrying along the east-side pavement, gaze aimed at his shoes, in a black overcoat.

The green flash of his tie. The glint of the streetlamps on his lacquered hair. I couldn't speak, at first. The surprise was too great. The sudden happiness. It's criminal that happiness can reduce you to silence. I regained my voice. He stopped to adjust his tie. "Vincent," I called. Through a hand megaphone. He kept walking. His duck-footed walk. His brother's feet had splayed, too. I wondered if he remembered. Or if his return journey had taken even that knowledge from him. I assumed it had. Which meant that I was a complete stranger. Who knew his name. He finally looked up, however. "I know this might sound strange," I said. I crossed the street. Was six pavement squares behind him. He turned. Saw me. He stumbled to a halt. "Hey, man," I said. He still didn't speak. His eyes wide and white. "Do you know who I am," I said. A bolt of pain lanced through my head. My eyesight blurred. I grappled my temples. I saw, all the same: Vincent started running. Like a fucking madman. Tie afloat in the wind.

30

The pain was just that. Pain. If a man can heal you, he can hurt you. Philosophers, take note. It's a useful fact to remember. If a man can hurt you, he can kill you. That's just logic. So either I was dumb lucky. A strong possibility. Or Vincent was too much a coward to straight-up kill me. Another possibility. Could have been both. Or so I told Alabama. "You're overreacting," she said. Ate one of my last french fries. "You didn't remember either. When you got back." "Then how," I said, "did he know how to hurt me? It can't be one and not the other. That's not logical."

She hid her face in her hands as I said this. I thought I'd scored a big point. Then I saw she was laughing. "Logical? Logical? Are you kidding me?" Everyone else in the diner looked up from their food at her cry. With that sick gaze of expectation people wear when they overhear a fight in public. It was the Gravesend. It had not changed since our first visit. Even the customers seemed to be the same. At least the guy with the shoe-black toupee was sitting in the same booth, eating the same meal: six slices of wheat toast glistening with butter. The best diners don't change. A waitress came over with a pot of coffee and asked if we wanted refills. An emotional intervention technique. Way too late. Alabama was paralyzed with laughter. Slamming her hand on the table and gasping for breath. Her pale skin flushed. I was overcome, too. I hate my own laugh: a donkey's bray. Couldn't help it. I gulped for air in between gouts of laughter. The waitress refilled our cups anyway. She didn't recognize us. She was the one who'd accused Hob of some unclear crime. The night he lost part of his ear.

"It's not logical! It's just not logical," Alabama said, "attention, everybody: Mike Wood has declared it illogical." We slowly recovered. Still a few trembles of pain left over from Vincent's parting shot. "In the tunnel," said Alabama, "you were scared. With Charthouse. You thought he was going to murder you. Racist." I admitted I was. Scared, not racist. "Then that's what it was. Try calling him. See what happens." This had not occurred to me. I dialed Vincent's number. Seventeen rings. No answer. No voice mail. "He doesn't even have his message set up," I said. "And that proves what, exactly," answered Alabama. I had no retort. The waitress brought out my second cheeseburger. "A growing boy," she said. "Yes, ma'am," I answered. "And polite, too," she said, "you should try to hang on to this one, young lady." "It's not like that," I said. Before Alabama could say anything more insulting. "So you say," the waitress said. Her mouth lipsticked pink. Her eyebrows plucked. I could not determine her age. Between forty and sixty. "How can you eat like that," said Alabama. "You're a fry parasite. You're in no position to argue," I said. And ate. And ate. And ate. I was ravenous. I'd eaten with my parents. I'd already eaten, to Alabama's disgusted amazement, a previous cheeseburger. No reason not to eat another one. Alabama's explanation: I bought it. She was calm. She'd been calm when I called her, babbling about having seen Vincent. About what he'd done. She told me to meet her here. That itself had calmed me down. She explained. That calmed me further. I was eating. That calmed me yet more. An instinctive reaction. A quirk or quiver of memory, that's all. The patrons around us chatting or silent, gloomy or exalted. The way it is in diners, in the later part of the night. The old and the young. The defeated and the soon-to-be-defeated. You have to take comfort in that.

"So what do we do now," I said. "Do you want me to call Charthouse," said Alabama. I forked up a fry. "How come you're the only one who has his phone number," I said. "You can't reveal what you don't know," she said, "under torture I mean." "Does he know a victim of torture," I said. "What do you think," said Alabama. Not pissed. "He's been around a long time, Mike. He's our parents' age. And this isn't new, as you may have noticed." She sucked down coffee. With air. To cool it. I ate another fry. Our waitress gabbled to a colleague in a corner. "Don't call him," I said, "there's no need." "See," said Alabama, "it's not even a thing." She ate another fry. "You can have the fries," I said, "to me they're ancillary and you ate most of them already anyway." "Not true," she said. She ate another. "They are extremely tasty, however." I thought she was high. Didn't say so. She smelled like weed when she met me. She seemed a lot more laid-back than she normally did. Smiled a lot. Covered her neck. Touched her hair. She seemed at ease, whereas normally she was on alert. No other way to describe it.

"Who are Pelagea and Ariston," I said. To avoid mentioning weed. The names had not been tugging at my memory. They floated up. "What," she said. "That painting," I said, "that family." The first of the truly great naturals, Alabama explained. They came to their abilities as a young married couple in fifth-century-BC Athens, and they fled the persecutions of the Persian magi. Which were tentative though still fierce. The first historically documented witch and warlock. The gazelles are their traditional symbolic companions, representing the fleetness and lightness of their souls. The snowfield they allegedly fled across can be found in present-day Turkey. The name of their child: lost to history. "That's quite a story," I said. "You asked," said Alabama. "I did," I said, "but I'm still impressed." "Take a look, it's in a book," sang Alabama. "Which one," I said. "It's actually like," she said, "you can piece it together but it's in about eleven books. At least that's how I read it. Charthouse has different theories."

For an ignorant man, there's no greater pleasure than listening to the learned. Maybe why I brought the subject up. I ate my last fry. "Do you want anything," I said. "I ate at home," she said, "it was only curried kale but it fills you up." I caught the waitress's eye. She swooped past and said, "A check for the lovebirds at table six." Alabama looked me dead in the eye. I was tempted to drop my stare. I didn't. It was an excuse to look at her face. Her inky eyes and eyelashes. They were compelling. The way she moved her arms was compelling. The way she laid her hands palm up on the table. Not near mine. Not *not* near them. "Are we in a staring contest," she said. Looked away. "You lose," I said. The waitress came back. "Good night, sweetheart, weeeeeel, it's time to go, ba-da-dum-da-duuum," she crooned as she deposited the check tray. Alabama chuckled. "Not bad, right," said the waitress, "I used to want to be a singer. The tips are better here." I lifted the bill. Alabama said, "Look," and jabbed my shin with her boot. In the tray was a playing card. Clean-edged. Colors bright. It could have just been slipped out of a pack. "Fuck," I said. "Fuck is about right," said Alabama. The queen of spades. Smiling her slight, sly, closemouthed, tyrant's smile.

31

Hey, ma, why you look so mad," said the snouty kid we were walk-running past. Alabama bodychecked him. He fell onto a pyramid of snow-dusted trash bags. His friends on the stoop all went, "Oohhhhh shit." More pigfaces. "You cunt," said the fallen kid. "That's the only thing it could mean," I said. "Nope," said Alabama, "you saw it. Him. You saw. No way." "Vincent could have done it, maybe," I said, "he did it with Irmgard. He said he couldn't but what do I know." "Does Vincent seem like he swings that big of a dick to you," said Alabama. "It's not taking out a bullet. It's not making a zombie owl. It's like a whole other level. So don't bring in your bullshit superstitions now." I wanted to tell her that my going to Catholic school did not mean I believed in resurrection. Except this was not, at bottom, true. You have to make concessions to the world and its methods of reasoning.

The at-ease quality gone from her shoulders. Switching as we walked under her jacket. A light snow was falling. The moon was high up. "Charthouse is not answering," she said, "so I'm in charge. Okay? I won't abuse it. It's just chain of command." "It's not the army," I said. A taxi whizzed by. Its roof light lit up. "Yeah, the army doesn't leave people behind," she said, "so maybe more things should be more like the army, did you ever think of that." Her boot heels hit the pavement hard. I had to struggle to keep pace. The queen of spades wrapped in a paper napkin in my pocket. Didn't want to damage it. We left a big tip.

Alabama and I didn't speak much on the walk to Karasarkissian's. The moon followed us. As it does. Snowflakes caught and melted in her eyelashes. Swelling with light as they melted. I watched. The stone-blue rats were sitting in front of the vacant lot next to the dark store. Lined up in a row. Not moving. Not minding, it seemed, the cold. They watched us. Followed our progress with their eyes and quick turns of their heads. "What is that all about," said Alabama. Her breath curling up. "Do we wait for him," I said. "It's freezing, let's wait in the basement. I left him a message. He'll come if he can." She had a point. What you don't know you don't know. It's just when you know you don't know it you suffer. Within, the headless mannequin loomed. Its antlers casting jagged, reaching shadows. I touched the globe in the window display. Spun it on its axis. "Stop fucking around," said Alabama. She was rolling back the carpet and opening the hatch. After we climbed down, it would unroll itself with a crackle of blue sparks. When I saw it do this the first time, I considered my final question to Charthouse the night of the salto answered. But now I wanted, for some reason, to know more. "You guys never told me how it ends up rolled flat on the ground," I said, "what the exact process is, I mean." "Charthouse will explain it," she said, "he set it up. Static electricity. I think." Her boots struck the ladder rungs. Each blow a cracked bell tolling. I followed her. Above me, in the store, I thought I saw a quick shadow cross a panel of light from the street. I paused. I watched. "Are you coming," said Alabama. I climbed down.

Green couch. Whiskey carboys. The sea snakes within them floating lazily, sleepily. They began to perk up as we approached, aiming their pointed blue heads at us. "They come from the other side, right," I said. Couldn't think of how else to express it. "Would not surprise me," said Alabama. "You mean he never told you," I said. "I don't need to know," she said, "so I don't." I dipped up a glassful. Handed it to her. Served myself. "Oh man," she said, "you forget what it's like." I had. My gullet warm, my stomach warm, my pain gone, my vision clear, my heart light. "I never got how anyone could be a drunk until I started drinking this," she said. The eels writhed. In pleasure from the praise. I assumed.

"Do you hear that," we both said at the same time. A crackle of static. Or the moment just before a peal of thunder. Or: the world itself had taken a breath. Then the music started. I'd never heard it before. Wild and piping. Strings and flutes. Alabama drew. Aimed at the hatch. The herbarium door. She backed against the wall perpendicular to the one the ladder rungs were screwed into. I followed her. Whoever came down we'd have the drop on. Nothing could get behind us. The music continued, growing wilder and wilder. A circus, held in a nameless forest by the banks of a river, I thought, glimmering with light. Alabama adjusted her grip on the gun. A door banged open. We heard it under the strange music. She checked the hatch. Nothing. It was the door to Vincent's herbarium. A voice entered the music. Human. "Ladies and gentlemen," it said, "allow me to introduce without further delay a world-renowned master of the art, Hobart the Magnificent!" It sounded the way Erzmund's voice sounded in my head, in my private mental auditorium, when I read the *Calendar*. Nasal and mighty. As though it issued from a mouth above which glistened an obsolete and untrustworthy mustache. The last syllable stretched and stretched. Unbearably. The fifes and fiddles sang and sawed away. A steel, wheeled table shot out of the open herbarium door. Eight feet long. A coroner's table. The herbarium far too small, I knew, to contain anything of that length. A white sheet covered the top. Through which you could pick out the contours of a human form: tip of nose,

THE ASSHOLES

ends of feet. "This isn't funny," Alabama said. I got ready. For what? Don't know. Violence. Speed. My own art, I suppose. The coroner's table skidded to a halt. The music reached a crescendo. The voice released the syllable it had been torturing. Silence. We approached the table. The form beneath the sheet unmoving. "We will find you, and we will kill you," said Alabama, "whoever thinks this is a joke." Her gun drawn. Her voice echoing.

The form beneath the sheet jerked. Leaped to its feet. A Halloween ghost. With no eyes or mouth. I heard Alabama's finger tighten on the trigger. The sheet seemed to whip itself into sudden life, darkening, reddening as it whirled, guided by a pair of small, well-formed human hands at the ends of thin, delicate arms. Beneath the sheet stood a boy in a tuxedo. Pristine black and white.

It was Hob. Throat whole. Eyes merry. A barely suppressed grin distorting his face. He finished whirling the white sheet through the air. Now black. A velvet cloak with a red satin lining. Clasped closed with a golden chain bearing a symbol. Lapels gleaming. Shirtfront blazing white. He looked like a fucking magician. "Abracadabra, bitches," he shouted, and jumped down from the table. Flubbed the landing. Ended up on one knee. "Still need to work on the dismount," he said, "but otherwise: sterling, though I say it myself." Alabama rushed up to him and grabbed him. "You asshole, I almost fucking," she said. Panting in fury. Her cheeks and neck bright red. She looked terrifying. Hob lifted two placating hands. "I deserve that. To be called that." "Hey, man," I said. Because I could think of nothing to say. "That's all? I return from the dead, and I get a 'Hey, man'? I was expecting a little more shock and awe," he said. He was grinning nakedly now. "What the fuck, Hob," said Alabama, "what the fuck." Still pissed. No longer crimson faced. "Did Charthouse know," she said. "Don't worry about him right now," said Hob, "I come bearing gifts." "First of all, are you actually alive," I said. "Ghosts don't trip over their own feet," said Hob. He had me there.

"Listen though. We won. It's over. Or it's as good as over. We won."
The next thing he said. This half-sick, half-ultrahealthy lambency
filled his face as he said it. "What do you mean we won," I said. Hob
gestured with two fingers. The steel table shot back into the herbarium. Wheels shrilling. The door slammed closed. He made another
pass and the green couch shot out from its accustomed place against
the wall and curved through the air, hovering two inches above the
cement floor. Gliding to a precise stop. Its velour skin just touching
our calves. "Holy shit, Hob," I said. "Eloquent as always," he said.
"Have a seat." I sat. Alabama sat. Hob crooked a finger and a stool
trotted over, its legs thumping irregularly. "Did you guys like hook
up while I was gone," he said, "you have that postcoital glow about
you." "Shut your mouth," said Alabama. "Doesn't matter, anyway,"
said Hob. "You can do whatever you want now. We won. We are
victorious. I mean there's still going to be some shooting but it's over.
They're finished. We're going to rip everything open. They're done."
He wasn't shouting. He wasn't gesticulating. His lapels gleamed in
the amber light. The eels in the carboys were circling furiously. "Hob,
who are you talking about," said Alabama. "Whom do you think,"
he said.

He pushed back his sleeves. Showed two empty hands. Clasped
them together. Whipped them apart. A deck of cards lay on his right
palm. Perfectly squared. He fanned it. We saw the full panoply. "This
deck, sir and madam, despite its appearance, requires the presence of
yet one more royal to be complete. Sir, I believe she is in your possession?" I checked my pocket. The queen of spades was still there.
Napkin-sheathed. "Lift it above your head and show the room, please,"
he said, "and then replace it in the napkin, in your pocket." I knew
what he was going to do. Another sleight I'd failed to master. He
snapped the deck shut. Passed his hand over it. Fanned it open again.
Fifty-two queens of spades. Their gazes blank and bloody-minded.
I didn't even bother checking my pocket. It would be empty. THE

CROWS COME HOME. That's the name Erzmund gave the sleight. I didn't understand until then why.

"The thing is," said Hob, "I'm sorry about it. About all the lying. But if he'd known it wouldn't have worked. He's too smart. Too sensitive. Was, anyway. You had to go in there blind." Alabama was covering her eyes and rocking lightly on the couch. "Are you kidding me," she said, "are you kidding me, Hob." Hob shifted on his stool. That weird glow still in his face. It made his cheeks look drawn and his eyes look shadowed. He looked, in fact, extremely tired. "You need to think rationally about this," said Hob. "Rationally," said Alabama. "I understand you're upset," said Hob. "Upset," said Alabama. "I was upset when I thought you were dead. I was upset after. Fuck, Hob, what the fuck is the matter with you." He fingered his golden chain. I saw what shape its clasp was in, now: the open eye. "Where's Vincent," I said. "He tried to give me a stroke. I saw him on the street." "Overdoing it," Hob muttered, "I told him none of you were to be touched."

To be touched: that sounded hollow. "It's done now, though. So you guys don't have to worry," said Hob. "I'll make it clear to Vincent that you're off-limits. And your families. I mean I can't promise anything about your second cousins." *Off-limits. You don't have to worry.* People only use those words when they're planning to knife you. I wondered if we could take him. The way he'd moved that couch suggested no. "Was Mr. Stone off-limits, too," said Alabama. Hob massaged his jawbone. The gesture of a man several decades older. "Look," said Hob, "you can't get everything you want. Terms of the deal. She goes AWOL when you guys show up. Stone gets the hook. He'd been living on grace anyway. Statistically I mean. So you can't even say it's unfair." *She.* I knew who he meant. Alabama did, too. "With her. A deal. With the Pale Scourge." "That's just offensive, Alabama. Their propaganda," said Hob. "And what do you mean done," I said. "That's the beauty part. Potash is done. He's gone. Don't you guys get it? You should be happy," said Hob, "I did this for you. I mean I did it for me but for you too. For all of us." He looked deathly sick. He looked radiantly healthy. He looked like a king and he looked like a beggar. I can't explain it. That inner light. His drawn face. "And what if we hadn't made it back," said Alabama. "Everybody makes it back," said Hob. "You're saying that based on what," I said. "The evidence suggests that you should not doubt my expertise, Michael." He had me there. "Where's Charthouse, Hob," Alabama said. Again.

"We won. Why don't you guys understand that. We're going to rip everything wide open. Everything. You don't even know. Look." He flicked his hands. A tumorous iron bracelet appeared in each. Riven clean through its circumference. "Look at these." He tossed a bracelet into my lap. As soon as I picked it up a rolling, vertiginous, slimelike sense of illness overcame me. The metal burning cold. "You see? That? That's over. How can you tell me it's not worth it. It's all going to change. Just wait. Wait and see. I promise. You won't even believe what we're going to do." "It's over for Mr. Stone, too, Hob," said Alabama. She'd gone stiff. I could feel her muscles quivering in rage. Or antici- pation. "Don't you do anything stupid, please," he said. I remembered how Hob had looked before we went up to the party. Weak. Afraid. Forlorn. I remembered his interrupted flight. The thud his frail body made on the gym floor. How he'd tracked me to the park without my noticing, the day he'd given me the book. Alabama's shoulders were shaking. I thought it was tears. It was not. Just a spasm she was fight- ing against. "There's no need for hysterics," said Hob, "seriously. This is a good thing."

She moved faster than I'd ever seen her move. Her gun out. Six inches from Hob's forehead. "A good thing," she said. "Alabama," said Hob, "I understand why you're mad." "Where's Charthouse," said Alabama. "It's useless to do that," said Hob. "Where's Charthouse," said Alabama. She cocked the hammer. An amputated sound. "You don't," said Hob. She tightened her finger around the black trigger. The noise of the shot deafened me. My skull ringing. My eardrums ringing. No vast night, here, into which the sound could be released. Just the concrete ceiling. Stink of cordite filling my nose and throat.

I looked. Expecting to see Hob with a hole in his head. A wound in his arm. Nothing. He was untouched. Smiling. Unruffled. He had his hand up. Palm out. Fingers spread. The bullet had halted itself in its flight. Alabama's face stony. A ponderous, precise blink of her pinkish eyelids. The echo died. Slowly. My ears hummed and rang. A high neutral tone. Silvery. Alabama stayed poised to shoot. The bullet quivered in the air. Hovering and rotating. End over end. It would have hit him, had it not been stopped, dead in the middle of his forehead. "Where's Charthouse," said Alabama. "Alabama," said Hob. "Where is Charthouse," said Alabama. "We can keep playing games all night if you want," said Hob, "even though it's not fair to you guys." This was true. It's hard to admit when you're outgunned. "Wide open," said Hob, "and you guys can be a part of it. You made it happen. It's yours. Do you understand that." "I understand it fine," said Alabama. She was staring into Hob's face. Looking for a fact. One undeniable truth. Her eyes narrowed. Her lips lightly parted. "Where's Charthouse," she said, "where is he. Just tell me. Even if." Almost a whisper. The bullet glowed: molten orange. It flowed upward in thin, bright threading streams, blossoming outward, darkening. I couldn't take my eyes off it. Hob was barely exerting himself. When you're in the presence of genius, you have to be impressed. A metal flower. An iris. "Hob," said Alabama, "where is he."

He eyed the flower. "It takes a lot of work to accomplish anything," he said, "you both know that. And part of that work is compromise. Stone was nonnegotiable." "What," said Alabama. Her voice flattened. Quiet. "And really John is the only part I feel bad about. I mean that. So don't be sentimental," said Hob, "because it was unavoidable. Once my brother got on board. He was propping him up. Stone too. But fuck him, actually. He was old. Vincent was like those guys that used to give Kennedy his painkillers. Sworn to secrecy." Hob proffered the bloom. "They make me think of you," he said, "irises. They're lovely, the way you are." The metal iris gleamed. The eels circled in their carboys. I smelled ozone and sulfur. As though we were already in an antechamber of hell. Blame my education for that image. If you go to a Catholic school, you'll leave with a picture of hell in your head. Inculcating it is their specialty.

Hob would not shut up, after that. After our silence. As though we had admitted defeat. He told us everything. How Messaline had come to him, shortly before he'd given me his copy of the *Calendar*. In a dream, he said. One so real you could not distinguish it from waking life. She wore a black gown. She had her raven with her. She told him about the *mappa*. About Quinn. Everything after that, said Hob, had gone as planned. A rarity. "And what would have happened if it hadn't," said Alabama. Hob shrugged. "I have only faith in you. Come on. You know that. Even if I do think big." He grinned. His teeth as blazing white as his shirt. He spoke with perfect equanimity. Explaining that Potash deserved what he'd gotten. That Quinn deserved worse. Charthouse and Stone, he said, were moving too slowly. Their whole moral understanding of the situation was outdated. They couldn't be expected to cope under current conditions. The constant vigilance and attrition. The crows. There was no need for it. They exacerbated the need for it. Modern life, he said, had moved past them. With Potash gone, he explained, life would change even more. In ways we could not yet imagine. We'd see. It would take time. Not much. Not anything unendurable. He seemed drunk. I felt drunk. Either from the whiskey or his slippery speaking. Or the late hour. Or all of it. The iris rotating in his hands. The two black arrows of his lapels. I asked where she was now. "You know where she is," said Hob. "So you're her boss," said Alabama. He didn't speak. He smiled.

Alabama shoved her gun back into her waistband and stood up. Hob never lost his odd, small grin. "Guys, this is like outside the boundaries," he said, "okay? Just wait. Just be patient. You'll see." Alabama sighed. Weary blood. Weary flesh. My eyelids dropping. I don't make speeches. "I'm leaving," I said. "What," said Hob. "You heard me," I said, "and you can kill me if you want. Or have her kill me or whatever. It won't make you right." It was bizarre: he could have murdered us. With a wave of his hand. With a thought. Instead he sat there, smiling and spinning the stalk. I kept expecting a blow. Or pain. Or simple darkness. Hob's face still unhealthily radiant. He would not look me in the eye. He twiddled the metal flower instead. "I would never do anything to hurt you guys," he said. His voice cracked as he said the word *hurt*.

I knew he meant what he said. Insane as it sounded. He looked too exhausted to lie. He looked too much like a young king to lie. We stood there. It was really awkward. The awkwardness made me forget, for one heartbeat. All of my muscles were twitching. Singing. Begging me to go after him. I hated it. I hated being beaten by this schoolmate. So weak and frail. He'd outplayed us, though. When you've lost, you've lost. No amount of fury will change that. "Good-bye," said Alabama. "Later, skater," said Hob. "I'm not coming back to school," he said to me, "so don't worry about like running into me in the halls. I have a lot on my plate right now." His voice deepened. He hoped we'd ask. Everyone wants to give up their secrets. In the end, you do. And I wanted to know. Part of me did, at least. The sick, sad, thought-loving part of me really wanted to know what he and Messaline had planned. What happened after we left Mountjoy. That's another sucker's proposition. Wanting to know. For knowing's sake. Look what it had gotten us so far. I offered my hand for a shake. That's what you do at the end of a game. Even when you lose. As Hob reached for it, I said, "Hey man, what's the capital of New Zealand." "What," he said.

Or started to say. I didn't let him finish. Smashed my forehead into his face. It's easier when your target is shorter than you. You can aim down. When they're the same height it's a harder problem. You have

232

to be more precise. Hob got to the whistle that precedes a W. We're polite in America. We try to answer questions when asked. I hit him dead-on. I didn't even have to drop into slow time. It was a bullshit maneuver. It was borderline criminal. I didn't care. He clucked. He whimpered. His thin nose spread. Blood gushed from it. Staining his white shirt collar. His lips. His teeth. He staggered backward. One step. Two. He fell to the ground. When your gun fails you, you have to rely on good old human confusion. That and your stony skull. If you pull a gun, your opponent is expecting a bullet. He can stop a bullet. He can't stop shit if he's thinking about New Zealand. Stuff like that, by the way, asking for a country's capital or telling a fascinating story is called misdirection. Erzmund is a major proponent of it. You get your target thinking about unrelated and trivial matters. That's when you make your play.

Hob was unconscious. Mouth open. Blood still leaking. "Is he going to choke," Alabama said. "Not now," I said. I turned him onto his side with my shoe. So the blood would run to the floor. Not back into his throat. His breathing came easier at once. "What if you hadn't knocked him out," said Alabama. "We wouldn't be any worse off," I said. "You have a point," said Alabama. The metal iris gleamed, eyelike, near the toe of her boot.

32

Lectures on morality. You have to leave them behind. Hob lying on his side at the bottom of the ladder. Grayish detritus from the gunshot on his cheeks. His blood mustache. His pale, thin face. Exultant even in unconsciousness. His combed hair. One strand loose. He looked smaller. I almost felt bad. You have to mete out in what measure you are meted unto, though. That's from the Bible. Alabama kicked the hatch closed. The clang resounded. I watched the carpet. Charthouse's last stand. With an electric crackle, it unrolled itself over the hatch. The headless mannequin. The globe. Their looming, swaying shadows. Alabama walking among them to the door. Hob, the king, alone and asleep under the floor. Life is hard to understand. This is one of the first things you learn as you get older. The snow had increased. I followed Alabama out into it. She was smoking. One of Vincent's. "Is that the last," I said. "It's the last," she said. "Can I have a drag," I said. "Of course," she said. "What are we going to use now," I said. "Aspirin, like pretty much everybody," she said. I handed it back. We stood there, in front of Karasarkissian's

THE WAR AGAINST

with the stone-blue sentry rats, trading it back and forth. I was glad no cops were around to accuse us of smoking weed.

She didn't say anything about Charthouse. His fate beyond our control at this point. Not that anything else was under our control. Not that anything is, ever, if you think about it. When you go up against a greater talent, you have to be ready to get outplayed. I didn't mention him either. Though we were talking about him, by not talking about him. I didn't even know him that well, and I was praying for his survival. Silently saying Ave Marias. Hard to estimate his chances. We stood and smoked. Eventually I stopped praying. Childish. You have to, though. "So the whole thing was like a waste," said Alabama. I knew what she meant. "It's not a waste," I said. "Nothing's a waste." "You don't even know," said Alabama. Strictly speaking, true. "There's nothing anyone in the world can do about people being cowards," I said, "that I do know."

"It's like five o'clock in the morning," Alabama said, "feels like." She was dead-bang right. At least according to my phone. "That's uncanny," I said. "It's not that uncanny," she said. "I don't want to go home," I said, "not right now." "I know," said Alabama, "me neither. Like what if you had to talk to your parents." The stone-blue rats cried out in sequence. Alabama stood slumped against the glass front window of the store. Shoulders down. Body lightly bowed. Hands linked at her belt buckle. A stripe of streetlamp light touching the soft curve of her cheek. "I don't know what we're going to do," she said. What she meant by we unclear. "Well," I said. "What," she said. I leaned in and tilted up her chin. I pressed my mouth against hers. Her lips tasted like smoke. Her tongue. Her warm breath. When you have to act, you have to act.

To my surprise, she kissed me back. I had been expecting her to execute a quick head-turn, so I'd get her neck, up near her jaw hinge. Or knee me in the balls. I honestly would not have minded either. I was bone-cold. She covered my ears with her warm palms. I pressed my forehead against hers. "Mike," she said. "What," I said. "I don't know," she said. "Neither do I," I said. Didn't matter. I heard a car. I shut my eyes. I opened them. Taxi luck: it descends when you least expect it. A cab was cruising along Ninth. Past the dead garden. He slowed as he saw us. I was giving the Hitlerian salute modern Americans use to hail cabs. Nobody ever remarks on this fact. In the backseat, Alabama let her head rest on my shoulder. She had her eyes closed. She didn't speak. I couldn't tell if she was asleep or awake. The driver kept glancing at us in his mirror. I looked at him until he looked away.

When we got to her house, the stone wolfhounds stared at us, mouths open. Alabama let us in. The bluish light of dawn was starting to fill the rooms of the first floor. It reduced every painting to a half-black, half-luminous cloud. We climbed the stairs. Nothing. Her mother or her father was snoring. "My mother snores five times as loud as that," I said. Alabama grinned. Just for a second. She locked her room door behind us. We stood there. Still cold. Looking at each other. It was one of the moments that make you grateful you were born. At least for me. Not because of her. I wasn't happy. Just glad I existed. Life, as I said, is hard to understand. She removed the gun from her waistband and laid it on her desk. I took off my coat. "So this is what my room looks like at the ass end of the night," she said. "Pretty grim," I said. Her thin, soft arms around my neck: that's the next thing I remember. How I nearly bashed my forehead into the wall, struggling out of my pants. How her nipples looked black in the dawn light. How dark her pubic thatch was. How I could still hear the snores.

We stood there naked. Unreality. The first thing I'd thought when I met her: *I wonder what she looks like naked.* Not carnal. Or sort of carnal. Also philosophical. How often do you get your first wish granted? Not often enough. Otherwise fewer people would perish from broken spirits. The vine tattoo wound down from her neck and across her sternum. A blossom, dark blue or purple, covered her left breast. The

THE WAR AGAINST

vine snaked past her navel, next to which another flower bloomed, and twined around her right thigh and ended at her right instep. I followed its course with my eyes. Again and again. Alabama poked me in the cavity above my solar plexus. "I don't have any condoms," she said, "so if you give me anything I'll kill you." I took hold of her wrist. Her radial artery beat against my fingers. Slower than my own hammering pulse. "I won't," I said. The snores choked themselves into silence and then resumed. "Jesus," said Alabama, "that does not sound healthy." "Is that your mother or father," I said. "My mother," she said. "Would you have shot me," I said. Didn't mean to. "When," said Alabama. "You know," I said. "Don't be an idiot," said Alabama. "It's difficult for me not to be one," I said. My throat dry. My mouth dry. My heart kicking at my ribs. "That's all right," Alabama said, "get moving." She climbed onto her bed. Huge and white. She parted her thighs. I knelt between them. Going on instinct. Soft skin of her inner thighs against my ears. Her palm at rest on the crown of my head. Her strong, acid-clean scent in my nose. Taste of her in my mouth. I was even harder than I'd been the day Messaline had assaulted me. Alabama murmured. I couldn't understand what she said. So I climbed up next to her. She kissed my neck and told me to lie on my back. She climbed on top of me. She guided me. She knew what she was doing. It's good to find yourself in the hands of an expert. I gasped as she pushed herself down onto my cock. From the shock. From the difference in temperature. She grunted. Sounded slightly surprised. "Are you all right," I said. "Relax," she said. The muscles in her lower back tensed under my hands. We tried to be quiet. This was difficult for me. Difficult for her. She made sounds in the back of her throat. I echoed them. In syncopation. Our breath mingled. Her cropped hair lightly abrading my ear.

The massive light of the moon rushed in. I did not see her whole. I saw her in swift fragments. A shoulder, a shin, her soft temples, the bluish hollow under her right arm. In this way her marvelous, fluent body, instead of appearing as just another phenomenon, just another

THE ASSHOLES

entry in the catalog of visible life, instead of this, it moved me. As a mountain would. Though I'd never seen a mountain. Or an ocean, maybe. Seen for the first time late at night, at a towering height, across an insurmountable distance. Clear voice. Pliant curve of her neck. The bed sighed rapidly under us. The headboard paddling the wall. She had these sharp, scimitar-shaped hipbones. She kissed me. I thrust upward. The sun appeared. Just a slice of it. Enough to tint the light yellow. I'd heard the whole roster of premature-ejaculation horror stories. I don't know how I lasted so long. Probably exhaustion. Or my committed masturbation routine.

"Don't come inside me," she murmured. "Okay," I murmured back. She lifted herself off of me. Sat back on her haunches. Wrapped one hand around the base of my cock. The first sunlight made me squint. She stroked me until I came. She was fingering her clit with her free hand. I came all over my torso. I grunted a curt, meaningless monosyllable. Couldn't help it. Her breathing ragged. Her eyes intent. "Jesus Christ, Wood," she said, "have you like never had sex. There's a towel in my bathroom." When I got back she was grinning up at me. "What's so funny," I said. "You also made like a pretty intense face," she said, "to be honest." I climbed in next to her. Her abdomen lightly furrowed with muscle and sheened with sweat. She fell asleep then. A real champion of sleeping: awake, then asleep. Eyes black, hair black, open mouth black.

Sun in my eyes. Sun in my open mouth. That's what woke me. Alabama's snores also contributed. Yellow, rich sunlight filled her room. A framed poster of an old man with white hair on her wall. At first I thought it was Mr. Stone. Then I read the huge black letters at the bottom: JANACEK. That composer she liked. The black letters directly above the black gun on her desk. Our tangled clothes on the floor. She slept with her limbs splayed out, as though she'd been hurled to earth. I had no idea where I was at first. As my dream drained away. I'd been dreaming of the temple. Of the statue whose face I could not see.

THE WAR AGAINST

Music drifted in. Piano. I couldn't identify it. I did know, however, that I'd lost my opportunity to leave undetected. "If you want to put the dogs on it," mumbled Alabama. Out of her sleep. I had no idea what she meant.

I dressed as quietly as I could. Not quietly enough. "So you're just going to fuck me and leave," said Alabama. Her voice hard. Cold. Furious. I shot my gaze up. Pure panic. Filthy shoelaces draped across my fingers. She was grinning. "Man," she said, "that was too easy." She was propped on her forearms and elbows. "I'm a cheap date," I said. "I mean," she said, "you're like the size of a building but you get this caught-in-the-headlights look. It's kind of great." I tried to think of a refutation. Her description, however: accurate. You know your own face at that age. You spend a lot of time watching it in mirrors. "See, you're doing it right now," she said. She was sitting up. I kept checking her out. It was hard for me, as I said, to believe that I was seeing her naked. Again. Good fortune follows on the heels of mis-fortune. A classical teaching. "I would like," said Alabama, "to fuck you again, to be perfectly honest. I think logistically it might be difficult." "I have to get home," I said, "my parents have probably got an APB out on me." I didn't know what an APB was. They said it on TV. "Yeah," said Alabama, "plus if you stick around any longer Mark and Lena will make you eat breakfast with us, and I really wouldn't want that to happen to my worst enemy."

When she said *enemy*, it brought everything back. Crashing into the sunlit silence. Hob. Charthouse. Mr. Stone. We didn't speak. The not-speaking stretched. "Look," she said, "I'll do some digging. I'll let you know." "That sounds good," I said. The sound of our voices was, suddenly, hollow and lonely. Voices on a vast, dark, irremediable plain. I blinked. I cleared my throat. She was standing now, toga'd in a sheet. She locked her palms around the back of my neck. "Don't get all weird," she said. "I won't," I said. We stayed like that. I was listening to her breathe. Feeling her fine-built ribs expanding and contracting under my hands. Lungs, heart, brain, eyes, healthy blood. All of it. My pain was back. All of it. I didn't mind. "Good-bye," she said. "Good-bye," I said. She unlaced her hands. I started running. When you have to leave, you have to leave. Her parents saw me as I rushed down their stairs. They were sitting and eating. Lilies in a green glass vase on their breakfast table bowed. "Hello," said her father. Mr. Sturdivant held a plank of bacon aloft on a fork. Couldn't call him Mark. "Hello," said her mother. Mrs. Sturdivant was tipping a pitcher, a blue rooster. Water leaped from the lip. Couldn't call her Lena. I kept running. And that's how I lost my virginity.

_33_

C hief merit of running: you don't have any ideas. You just run. That's all there is. Your blood, your lungs, your feet. As a result, I don't remember when I first noticed the crows. I was almost home. I'd slowed to a jog. Figured I'd done about five miles. Enough to sweat off the smell of sex. In case I had to do any explaining to my parents. I began to construct a story that wasn't a lie. I spent the night at a friend's. Which friend, my father asked in my imagination. I didn't even like to lie hypothetically. So I said: you don't know them. It was downtown. Does this friend have a name, said my notional mother. That's when I saw the crows. A loose, whirling murder of them in the sky above Park. More than I'd ever seen in once place before. Crying and diving. Dipping to a roof. Seizing an eave. Launching up again. Other pedestrians noticed. A guy stopped near a proud blue mailbox to watch. Craned his head back. His grayish porkpie hat fell into the gutter. "Fucking crows," he said as he retrieved it. No purer illustration of human nature. The hat matched his suit, though. I would have been pissed too. More crows joined the mass. Broken, inky, linear

THE ASSHOLES

streams. Hurtling across the blue, blue sky to join the congregation. I sped up. Running as fast as I could. My lungs burning.

Human din and buzz. A male voice saying above the ground notes, "Get back, please." Hoarse cries of the crows. All sizes. Tiny daws. Huge deaconly ravens. A loose crowd around my building door. That's what I saw. An ambulance. That's what I saw. The crows circling overhead. Clatter of wings. Their repeated, delighted cries. The mottled, whirling shadow they cast. Two paramedics, both bald, were guiding two stretchers through the building doors. On each a body in a black bag. A garbage bag, I thought. "Can we get a little room, please," said the fatter paramedic. He was voluntarily bald: a shaved, shiny scalp, stubble just visible. His name tag read MARUCCI. "These marriage," said the thinner paramedic. He was involuntarily bald: a gray fringe encircled the top of his neck. His name tag said LEVINSON. They both saw me staring. "What you want, kid," said Levinson. He had an accent. Not French. Not Spanish. Couldn't place it. "What's your name," said Marucci, "what's your name." He had an accent. Brooklyn. "What do you mean," I said. "Is your name Mike Wood," said Marucci. "What," I said. "Kid, we talk to you," said Levinson. They took hold of one gurney. Levinson lifted it over the lip of the ambulance. Marucci shoved it the rest of the way in. Why do corpses need an ambulance, I thought. Levinson lifted the second gurney up over the lip of the ambulance. Marucci shoved it the rest of the way in. Its metal cried out against the metal of the first gurney. The crows cried out above. "Listen, Mike," said Marucci, "this isn't what you think. You're not in any trouble." "Trouble," I said. I couldn't get my breath. There's only one reason paramedics talk to you. When you're the next of kin. I was having trouble catching my breath. "No, I'm just late, I'm just late," I was saying. The faces in the crowd around the ambulance door: solemn. Secretly delighted. That's human nature. To love the tragedy of others.

The crows swooped and cried out. Also in delight. I recognized people from my building: the Changs, from eighteen B. Herman Brown, who was over ninety and still wore a sharp-creased sky-blue suit every day. He was literally about five feet tall. If that. None of them would look me in the face. "What happened," I kept saying, "what happened." Levinson took me by the shoulder. "Kid, we try to tell you." His blue sleeve rode up his arm. I saw a tattoo there: a rifle. An old rifle. "You have a gun tattooed on your arm," I said, "I just got a tattoo." He pulled his sleeve down. "Don't worry," said Marucci. "Everything is going to be fine." Levinson slipped through the crowd. I was starting to cry. I tried not to. Those two black bags. It's humiliating to cry in public. Even when you don't have any choice. I was taller and broader-shouldered than both the paramedics. Than most of the people in the crowd. Garbage bags. "They need to redesign those," I choked out. My molars locked. "Human beings are better than garbage." "Kid, what are you talking about," said Marucci.

Not to be touched. A lie. *Not to be touched.* If he'd hurt them, my mother or father, I thought, I would disembowel him. I'd buy a hunter's knife and disembowel him. "Like a deer," I said. *Like a deer,* said an agreeing inner voice. Weight of the haft in my palm. Weight of the blade in the air. My vision constricted. White fuzz at the edges. "Shit, you faint," I heard Levinson say. Then the crowd right in front of us opened and I saw my parents standing there. Flanking Marucci. The crows screaming and screaming away. My sight stopped failing. The white roar I'd heard ceased. Although I went on weeping. Out of relief. Maybe simple exhaustion. They wore the same clothes they had on when they'd left for the movies. The flesh beneath my mother's eyes inflated and torn looking. Though it was whole. Lack of sleep. Tears.

She walked up and slapped me across the face. "Where were you," she said. She's short. Not strong. Her slap did not hurt. I was grateful for it. It stopped the tears. "I'm sorry," I said. "I should have called." "You are royally screwed, mister," said my father. "Royally. Where were you," he said. *I saw someone come back from the dead. I found out that I'm an accessory to premeditated murder. I saw the end of one battle in a war and the start of another. I had sex for the first time.* "Was with a friend," I said. "Oh, a friend," said my mother, "isn't that nice, a friend. You didn't answer your phone. We were up all night. We called five hospitals. We called the cops." My father was covering his mouth with his hand. "What happened," I said. "It's Nathan and Dunya Lorbeerbaum," said my mother. "Other than that we don't know." Levinson slammed the ambulance hatch doors closed. "Ready for rolling," he said. Marucci said, "Sir. Ma'am." The ambulance left. Sirens on. Lights on. Everybody makes way for the dead.

The crowd dispersing. Their coagulate shadow coming apart. Their cries getting softer and weaker in the hard, blue distance. My parents and I stood there. "If you need to spill, then spill," said my father, "we know you. We know it can't be anything that bad." I saw Potash fall. Wounds in his palms. Heard him sigh after the bullets had shattered his skull and pierced his brain. His blood hit my pants cuffs. The tremendous night above. The berries. The river. The temple. The roar. All of it. "It's just," I said. "What," said my father. "I can't," I said. "Can't what," said my mother. "I get all worried and knotted up about school. Because I don't do as well as you want me to. I can tell I don't." I hate lying. To my parents more than anyone else. I am good at it despite that. You have to be. If you want to succeed in any art. The best lies also aren't full-on, full-blown lies. They're just irrelevant truths. "We know you work hard, Mike," said my father. "I'm sorry," my mother said. "No, I deserved it," I said. True. Beyond any possible doubt. The fake poinsettia trembled in Henry's breath as we passed through the lobby door. "For this we pay maintenance," said my father.

A long shower. I lost track of minutes. My hands pink and pruned. The ache from my run. From my sleepless night. From the art. They all mingled under the water. Hot as I could stand it. I leaned my forehead against the tiles. Smelled bleach. Shampoo. I let it all drain away. You learn to do that. If you play football. When you lose. When you get mauled and hurt. You leave it in the showers. You have to. Otherwise you can't go on. This was part of Coach Madigan's homiletic cycle. He was dead right. So it drained and dripped away. Except for the pain. I was used to that. I hadn't had a nosebleed in weeks. Which I took to be a sign. Not of improvement. Simple adaptation, maybe. I wondered why the crows had been watching. A sick surveillance effort. An attempt to send a message. I didn't care. I was home. I had no idea what to do about Alabama. Call her. Not call her. I assumed the latter. You don't necessarily want, I thought, to talk to the person you just slept with. Given everything else. I turned off the water. Inhaled the steam. My parents used this one brand of soap, Waterman's. It smelled like almonds. I toweled off. I wrapped my lower half.

My father was waiting for me in my room. His hands behind his back. "Hey," he said when I came in. "Hey, Dad," I said. "This friend of yours. That you were with last night. Have we met," said my father. "I don't think you've met them," I said. I knew *them* was ungrammatical. I didn't want to say anything about Alabama if I didn't have to. Didn't want to be indiscreet. "Does this person have a name, or, perhaps, a gender," said my father. Water dripped from my chin. "Alabama," I said. "Lovely name," said my father. He whipped his hands out from behind his back. He was holding an azure box of condoms. SPARTAN. A guy with a crested helm on the outside. "I am too young to be a grandfather, as I said," said my father, "I am in the prime of my fucking life, in fact. And don't tell your mother I gave you these. Because she might slay us both." I took the box. My father shook my hand. I heard him humming that song—about the sadder but wiser girl—as he trundled down the hallway to the kitchen.

I read the box copy. Powerful stuff. Pleasure and safety. Spermicidal lubricant. All sounded good and necessary. I hid it in my sock drawer. I turned off the light. I lay down on my bed. I shut my eyes. A cold draft leaked in through the window next to my head. I hadn't drawn the curtain. Because it was only late morning. I almost fell asleep. The cold wind stroking my cheek. I stood at the edge of the great abyss. Sleep heals us. I used to be a sound sleeper. So I know. I remember standing at the edge of the great abyss, friendly as an ocean. Then I opened my eyes.

To my credit, I didn't say anything. I just looked. On my fire escape, still clad in her dark suit and white shirt, was Messaline. Leaning against the rail. Her raven perched next to her. Opening and closing its beak. She showed me her wrists. Free of the iron bracelets. She had her hair bound up. To reveal the full shining scar on her throat. A wound, now, to be proud of. I stood to face her. "What do you want," I said. As quietly as I could. She looked me up and down. She smiled. Licked her lips. Good thing Hob was gay, I thought. Otherwise he'd have had no chance. My cock was stone-hard, yet again. Completely against my will. "What do you want," I repeated. She pressed palm to window. I knew what I was supposed to do. I pressed mine to the corresponding spot. An image flooded into my head. Acidic. Blood-stinking. She stood in a living room, filled with pear-colored light. A picture on the wall, of an old man and an old woman standing on a beach. At one edge the pink eave of a hotel. At the other a potbellied stranger walking the surf line. The Lorbeerbaums. Who now kneeled coughing and gasping, grabbing their fat throats, at Messaline's feet. In front of a couch covered in rose-patterned cloth and one of those flesh-grabbing transparent covers old people use. The Lorbeerbaums flopped and thrashed. Their faces crimson. Their faces purple. Their tongues black. They stopped their struggle. They slumped at her feet. She lifted a boot and placed it on Mrs. Lorbeerbaum's neck. The show ended. I drew my hand back. I was freezing. As dead cold as if I'd been out there with her.

Messaline grinned. Rather, she showed me her teeth. White. Flawless. *Open the window*, I thought, *why not. Two in one day. You'd be a champ.* I heard my sick giggling. Her naked form. On the page of the book Mr. Stone had shown me. Her scar. Her fists. Her cold breath. I gave her the finger. She just kept smiling. Climbed onto the railing. Spread her arms. Shut her eyes. Bent her knees and dove backward. Arms stretched above her head. As though in victory. A black and pale flash. The raven took off. My breath was condensing in the air of my room. "The golden lion tamarin is a small New World monkey of the family Callitrichidae," I heard a British voice say on our TV.

34

The most difficult maneuver in *The Calendar of Sleights* is, in Erzmund's opinion, also the simplest. It is the last one he mentions, and he explains quite bluntly that most experts fail even to approach mastering it. *Only those who have truly understood my meaning*, he writes, *those who have cast off all doubt and hesitation, all posturing, will attain to this height of heights, this nonpareil. All things perfect are as excellent as they are rare.*

It's called THE TRIUMPH OF THE FOOL. It requires two props, other than an unopened deck of cards. One is a wooden table, *as long as a vigorous man is tall and twice as wide*, in Erzmund's words. One is a sharp knife. The sleight is simplicity itself. You open the deck, having gotten an audience member to vouchsafe that it is, in fact, new and untampered with. You flex it in your nondominant hand, reverse-bowing until the cards fountain into the air. Once they are all aloft, your bring the knife, in a long, swooping arc, down onto the table. The point enters the wood. Speared in the middle of the blade will be the Joker. The Fool. Erzmund provides no instructions on the mechanics of this sleight. He describes it more or less as I have. And it has baffled many accomplished magicians. There are numerous methods to achieve the effect. Retaining a joker with a palm or a reverse palm. Picking it from the air instead of piercing it with a blade. Purpose-built knives. Purpose-built tables. Or—and this is a common expedient—making a hash of it merely as a prelude to another sleight. Missing the Fool deliberately because you have arranged a duplicate to be drawn from a target's pocket or shoe.

None of these methods are sanctioned. None of them are, in fact, permitted. How do we know this? Erzmund does not name them in his account of the sleight; in every other sleight described in the *Calendar* he provides at least two sets of instructions on effecting it, through preparing the deck or through legerdemain. THE TRIUMPH OF THE FOOL he merely describes more or less as I have. Open the deck. Release the cards. Strike with the knife. Strike the Fool. The sleight itself is of course a joke. An assault on the idea, on the structure of the book. It can only be done properly through the unmediated use of the art. No hold-outs. No stock shuffles. No palms. No other impediment. I release the cards. I breathe deeply. I watch as the world slows down. I see the Fool fluttering his foolish flutter. I wait until he comes within the compass of my arm. I strike. *Harder than you dare*, says Erzmund. Always.

Mr. Stone. Potash. Vincent and Hob. John Charthouse and god knows who else. You carry things with you. They accompany you. Will you or nill you. It's human fate. The dead live alongside their killers. I woke up. I went to school. I studied the daylight arts. That's another term from Erzmund, who implies that he left school as early as he could and took to the roads. I came home. I studied other arts. I slept. The wind and the rain. Who said that? It's in Shakespeare. Sister Faith Hope sang it aloud when we came to the song in *Twelfth Night*. A sweet, simple, piping melody. She was heavyset and heavy jawed, with a fringe of mustache across her fleshy upper lip. Her voice:

pure. Bodiless. Like light. "When that I was and a little tiny boy," she sang, "with a hey, ho the wind and the rain / A foolish thing was but a toy / For the rain it raineth every day." We all shut up. We all would have preferred her singing to be mockable. It was not. I had learned, after a long delay and totally by chance, the name of the song Charthouse had whistled in his moments of distraction or doubt. The rain it raineth every day. Especially that spring.

Thunderstorms, more or less constant. Slashing rain. They filled Saint Cyprian's with a gray light. Which I found almost as unendurable as Hob's absence. Or the way everyone accepted it. As though he'd never existed. As though he'd erased himself completely from memory. I tried, once, out of that perverse impulse to toss a brick through a window that has dogged me my entire adult life, and began, I think, in that stormlit, tumultuous spring, asking Sister Immaculata when he would be back. In world history. She was explaining Pol Pot and his massacres. He killed people because they wore glasses. In his opinion this made them intellectuals. Little has changed since then, except we have fewer massacres. Sister Immaculata looked at me. Her eyebrows cocked. "Mr. Wood, please keep your attention to the topic at hand. I've never taught a student by that name," she said. Greg Gilder snorted. I swung my head to stare at him. He shut his wide, weak mouth. I never tried again. No point in kicking. What's past is past and doesn't matter. You could call that, too, THE TRIUMPH OF THE FOOL. Futility. Whatever you like.

Or consider those marks on Mr. Stone's wall. Casualties. Their only monument gone now, I imagined. I hadn't counted them. Hadn't had time. Now I will never know, I thought, even the number of our cause's dead. You can't waste time on the unanswerable, however. The living will live. Even though the dead remain at their heels. Football continued. The postseason. Workouts and scrums. Coach Madigan shuttled us up to his mother's house twice a month, that spring, and set us to work cleaning her gutters of leaves and other filth. I found

THE WAR AGAINST

cans of beer. I found a bird's torn-off wing, a white knuckle of bone protruding. The feathers stiff and black. All the other kids on the team, except Dalmacio Zingales, complained. I didn't mind. If my grandmother had gutters, I would have wanted help cleaning them. She lived in a project. An old-people project. She barely had windows. She refused to move out to Long Island. My father had tried and tried to sell her on the idea. You'd think what with her dislike of blacks and Hispanics she'd want to be in a majority-white town. No dice. You can't predict how people will act. Although she did get completely wasted at Easter dinner and launch into a new tirade. This time about Albanians. "I'm telling you it's a nation of psychopaths, Tommy," said my grandmother. A pink scrap of lamb dangling from her fork. The color of the Lorbeerbaums' faces before they died. That much I remembered. "Ma, we're celebrating the resurrection of the savior here," said my father. "God wants us to be honest," said my grandmother.

Spring. I hate it. I'm a summer, fall, and winter man. Rain, mud, the raw hurry of sticky leaves opening: not for me. The slick face of the season. Why does spring become the metaphor for freshness and love in this world? It's nothing of the kind. It has a dreadful and improvisational smile, and a vegetal reek. That's not love. Love is unequivocal. On the first day of April, some prick from the park service located and captured Irmgard. No one believed the reports at first. They all thought it was a prank. WELL, OWL BE! So ran a front-page *Post* headline. The picture showed the aforementioned prick from the park service—ID'd in the caption as Dr. Henry Garbauskas, fifty-one—holding Irmgard. She looked the same as she did the night we had released her. He held her upside down, by her legs. Her feathers violet. Her eyes dull yellow. Garbauskas wore green shorts. Shit-brown socks up to his white, fistlike patellae. A mustache, badger-colored. He had no head-neck differential. By which I mean his head was the same width as his gawky, knobbed neck. "What won't they think of next," said my father, "a purple owl." I wanted to explain. That once Garbauskas ran his tests he'd be in for a tremendous deflation. You could tell from the photo that finding Irmgard represented the high point of Garbauskas's life so far. The set of his socks said so. The messy mustache. I couldn't think of a way to say all this that wouldn't make me sound like a schizophrenic. So I kept my mouth shut. If you're a reanimated piece of taxidermy, your appetites probably no longer torture you. Survival comes easy. "They caught her near Belvedere Castle," he said, "a classy dame." He stopped reading. Waved at me with his tennis racket. He'd finally had to break down and buy new sneakers. Bright orange. Yellow trim. He still went over them with a toothbrush. They looked sharp. They chirped stiffly at every step. The cry of the new. My mother was in Hong Kong. She missed the owl story.

People can explain anything to themselves. Without too much effort. Even Dr. Garbauskas, when he found out there was nothing in Irmgard other than bones and horsehair, would regard it as a queer neurological phenomenon. Improper taxidermy. Reflex action. No more. Alabama said, "That guy looks like a child molester" first thing when I showed her the paper. She was correct. "Well, owl be," she said, "that's actually kind of great." Also correct. "Mark and Lena hate this paper," she went on. "They make a big deal out of how terrible it is. Fascistic. Mark says that. He calls a lot of things fascistic. You can't take him seriously." I enjoy the *Post*. It tells good stories. That's what we seek out, in this unpredictable life. It's how, in fact, I had ended up in the impossible position I occupied that spring. Alabama and I walked along in silence. "So she's immortal now," I said. "Until they cut her up for science," said Alabama. "Vincent didn't think this through," I said.

She was waiting for me outside my building, smoking and watching the silvery threads of the rain. I had not expected her. The day after she took my virginity, I worked up the nerve to call her. Managed to stop myself. Didn't seem right. I could imagine her face when she heard me, blank, serene. I think that's what stopped me. Or her gun. Hard to say. I admit that when I wasn't practicing, when I was alone, before sleep, listening to the thunder or the wind, watching the spastic white the lightning cast on the walls—of course I was thinking of her. When I jerked off. When I ran. But every day that passed without seeing her made me proud. I'd overcome a stupid, childish need. To hold on, maybe.

I thought I saw her once. I was running my usual route through the park. North toward the Meer, then back south through the Pinetum. It was almost dark. I had my hood drawn tight against the air. On an upthrust keel of schist, as I panted through its shadow, I saw a slim figure. Male or female: could not say. Definitely wearing a leather jacket. When I spun to look (without stopping; I love to run backward because of its intense stupidity) I saw nothing and no one, just a wavering leaf of light from a security lamp. Yes, I wanted to fuck her again. Or just to be with her. But more than that, I wanted to talk. The chief need. A knot in my throat. Hob. Vincent. Potash. Charthouse. When I slipped into sleep, I dreamed about him and about Hob. The same dream for each. Charthouse appeared in a painting, an ornate oil painting. Hung on the wall of a room that stretched infinitely away from me in every direction. His eyes shut and his lips pressed together. He wore a coat that buttoned high over the chest and swept away in two long tails. Green. The color of the *Calendar*. I learned later that this kind of coat is called a frock coat. Hob I never saw. Only heard: I was sitting in a damp forest, on the wet ground, with huge grayish trees looming overhead. From the impenetrable thicket came the choked, trilling sound of a child sobbing and crying out. I knew it was his voice. Though I had no basis for knowing so.

The rain hit my hood. Alabama didn't offer me space under her umbrella. She did offer me a cigarette. Just a Camel. Nothing salvatory there. "So," I said. Alabama just started walking. She didn't answer when I asked where we were going. She kept scanning the air. Hob used to do that. Three drenched crows sat on a branch above us. Definitely watching. "Still at it," I said. We plodded on. I saw no point in asking any more questions. I finished my smoke. She offered me another, without speaking. THE TRIUMPH OF THE FOOL. Literal-sounding. Actually a paradox. The Fool gets knifed. How can he triumph? Maybe by being wounded or dying. That's one theory. Maybe the man or woman with the knife is the fool. That's another theory. Maybe the Fool, in this case, is Erzmund, and his triumph consists in nothing more than completing your education in the art. As far as anyone can be educated in it. No one knows. No one will know.

We walked to the park. We didn't speak. We climbed a hill. To a shelf of rock. When we reached the crest I saw that it overlooked my running route. "Have you been following me," I said. "I had to make sure," she said, "like double sure." Kicking a rhomboid of free stone. On the lawn below us, the rain glistened. I wasn't insulted. She had a valid point. "I passed muster with Charthouse," I said. I remembered: the subway car full of rain. I remembered: the tunnel full of lightning. I wanted to go on record. "Yeah, well," she said, "he's seen better days." She picked up the stone. "We've all seen better days," I said. "How much," she said, "you wanna bet I can hit that guy in the purple hat with this rock." Her target had jogged into view as she spoke. The rain had emptied the park otherwise. She hefted the dirty chunk of quartz in her palm. She hurled it. "No bet," I said. We waited. The quartz flew through the air. Out across the fields. In a huge, high arc. We lost sight of it in the gray rain. We lost sight of it against the blank sky. "Come on," Alabama said under her breath. The guy in the purple hat started freaking out. Stopped. Looked around. Jabbed his head back and forth. It was clear she'd scored a hit. "You owe me like a billion dollars," she said, "that was a sterling throw." The hat man ran on. When he neared us he didn't even spare a glance. A red trickle crept down his face, next

THE WAR AGAINST

to his left eye. "Just tell me what you want," I said. Mostly because I was wet and cold. "We need to go see a man about a dog," she said. And I'd been standing there worried that she was, in fact, going to shoot me. For an inscrutable betrayal. Not of her. Of a principle I didn't even know had been put in place.

35

Nothing ever turns out the way you imagine it will. You think there's going to be someone telling you the great and painful secrets of this world. And that's exactly what happens. But it doesn't help. It only harms. You. Those around you. The world itself. You stand in the light of revelation. All occurrence seems as pointless and endless as it did before. That's the trouble with revelations. What they reveal isn't hidden. It's so obvious we refuse to see it.

I assumed Charthouse had kids. Possibly my age. His voice had that well-marinated quality you find among family men. At least my own father's voice. From coaxing and yelling. So maybe I expected his son to greet us. No son. No wife. At least not present. I saw them in pictures. His wife was nice looking. She had thick-framed glasses and a bright smile. His daughter looked exactly like him and his son looked exactly like his mother. The photos covered the foyer wall and spread out over the wall above the steel- and glass-clad appliances of the open kitchen and the two living room walls that were not made of windows. Through the glass I saw the city. The ornate points of the buildings piercing low cloud. The public trees gleaming, wet and dark. Traffic lights, headlights, cop lights all pulsing, all flowing. I guess you could call it harmony. Runoff dripped from Alabama's umbrella. Runoff wormed its way down my back. "It's going to be hard," said Alabama. I saw, then, that her eyes, their whites, were red, the lids bruised. Even before I saw the bed, a hospital bed with its upper section canted toward the windows, I heard him. Heard his clotted, ragged breathing. Wet newspaper being torn.

Simple chaos. Division and disintegration. End of the world. That's another meaning of the Fool. He represents all that stands outside the governable. He plays no role in the deck. Yet he is an integral part of the deck. He has no value, yet he persists and persists. When he appears, you may consider it a sign of suspension. Improvisation. Pure art. Charthouse lay in the white bed. His hands and arms lay inert on the white blanket. Wasted. Arms of a starving man. In one hand a handkerchief, white also with red dots. He wore a loose blue tee shirt with the words ALTGELD'S HARDWARE printed on it. It was loose because his torso and thorax were as wasted as his arms. His collarbones thrust against his skin. His cheeks concave, his cheekbones jutting. He gestured at us as we approached the bed. And bent, contracted, as a spasm of coughing seized him. Before he could get the handkerchief to his mouth, I saw the blood spray from his lips. His skin was gray. Literally gray, as gray as the rain. The whites of his eyes blue. "I see you're staring," he rasped. Another blood-slick cough. He started again. "I see you're staring at my eyes. It's called cyanosis." Coughed again. This time he got the cloth up in time to block the blood spray.

Vincent had propped him up: Hob's words. I understood now. "Charthouse," Alabama said, "we're here." "Can you help me," he said. Alabama didn't answer. The rain beat the windows. "So, Big Mike," he said. His lips glowed with pink spittle. Crimson, vivid, open sores decorated his cheeks, his neck, his arms. "I'm not contagious," he said.

Alabama was rattling through a series of orange pill jars on the table next to him. "In the big bottle," he said. Alabama shook two into his palm. "Where are your glasses," I said. I knew how this went. Just a more severe version of our trips to see Mrs. Madigan. "Above the sink," said Charthouse. I trotted to the hard-glinting kitchen. As the faucet hissed, Charthouse hissed too. "The ideal of service. I see your education was not wasted on you." His hand trembled as he raised the glass to his cracked lips. Also beset with sores. Water slopped over. "Sans eyes sans teeth," he said. I steadied the glass. Helped it to his mouth. He still smelled like ozone. Also like rotting meat. His breath and his sweat. He was covered in sweat. It had darkened his whole shirt to navy, except for a small patch on his right shoulder. Still sky blue. A victorious and futile flag. "He did a number on us," said Charthouse. "We did a number on ourselves," said Alabama. "That's the run of the play," said Charthouse. Another spasm racked him. His arm smashed into a steel stand holding an IV bag. The tube fed into the flailing arm. I caught the stand before it fell. Before even Alabama got to it. The ideal of service. A fresh cut open now on his forearm where it had struck the metal. Not a serious blow. Alabama slapped a gauze pad on it and Charthouse let out a noise I could not decipher at first. Empty. Rattling. A laugh. He was laughing. "Gilding the lily at this point," he said. "That's right," said Alabama. She finished twisting a beige bandage. "There's no what's it called," she said, "none of those metal clips." Charthouse laughed his empty laugh again.

He didn't lecture. He didn't even talk much. We sat with him. His wife and children stared at us. The rain worsened. Thunder grinding. Lightning forking and touching the building spires. I wanted to ask: *Are you doing this?* I kept my mouth shut. I got him another glass of water when he dropped the first one. He slept for five minutes. I couldn't look at Alabama. She didn't look at me. Sitting side by side. Watching his ruined chest rise and fall. When he woke up, he said: "You're still here? You are gluttons for punishment." He sounded exactly like my father. That's what I thought at the time. Later on I was less sure. It might have been despair. Or the simple unreality of the room, the rain, the woman I'd lost my virginity to, the dying man, the bed, the pill bottles, the photographs, the voided light. "I need," he said. Couldn't finish. Alabama was nodding. From a drawer in the medicine table, she took out a pair of blue latex gloves. Put them on. Then removed an ampoule of clear liquid and a syringe wrapped in green-and-white paper and plastic. "You know how to do this," said Charthouse. "You explained," said Alabama. She drew up a syringe full of the clear liquid. Charthouse said: "I wish there was better news. They're going to come after you. You know that." "Hob got what he wanted," I said, "why would he come after us." "I said they," said Charthouse. "They," I said. "You think Potash was the man on top," said Charthouse, "he has masters. Had them. Chain of command."

Alabama was flicking the syringe with her finger. They did that in hospital shows. "And you know there isn't anything else," he said, "anything else at all." He gestured, faintly, briefly, with his handkerchief. Took in his body. His medical apparatus. All of it. "There isn't anything else," he repeated, and then his breathing changed. Faster, higher. His feet kicked under the white sheet. Not enough to move it much. "Oh, fuck, oh, fuck," he said, "Alabama, oh, fuck, oh, fuck." She stuck the needle into this Y-junction thing in the IV tube, just under the bag, and hit the plunger. Her face stony. "I don't like to use profanities," said Charthouse. I could barely hear it. His head fell forward. His breathing slowed. I couldn't look away. I heard nothing other than his breathing as it faded. I saw nothing other than his sore-riddled arms. Life had contracted itself to this single, infinite instant. When the artery in his emaciated neck stopped jumping, the rest of my senses came back. I heard Alabama say: "Please help." And then the tinny sound of an operator speaking through an open line. "We need to leave," she said to me. "Ma'am? What is your emergency? Ma'am? What is your emergency?" the operator buzzed as the phone swung on its pristine cord. *He still has a landline*: That's what ran through my head. Again and again.

THE TRIUMPH OF THE FOOL could also be read as the triumph of the innocent. No one is more innocent than the Fool. By definition. Since guilt is perfectly coextensive with knowledge. A sea and its shore. Which meant: I was not guilty of Potash's death. Which meant: neither was Alabama. Which meant: nothing, nothing, nothing, nothing, nothing. It never turns out how you expect. Worlds and lives end in a single instant. That's the worst. There's no respite. No mercy. No time. One moment you stand on this side of the line, in the sunlight. The next you stand on that side of the line, in perpetual night. We said good-bye on the street in front of Charthouse's building. When I say we said good-bye, what I mean is this. We stood in the rain. Alabama under her umbrella. I was under an eave. Not deep enough to keep me dry. Alabama pulled off the gloves. Tossed them in a corner trashcan. She was shaking. Her whole body now, not just her hand. She started to cry. Not loudly. I doubt if anyone walking past would have noticed. I did. I put a palm on her shoulder. She let it rest there for one breath. Two. Her skin hot. I felt it through the jacket, through her indigo sweater. Then she said, "Don't touch me. No offense, but don't." I stepped away. I'm no idiot. "So what happens now," I said. "I don't know. And why would you even ask me." The tears clotted her voice. Two strands of mucus hung from her nose. "We're in danger," I said. "I'm not running," she said. The strands lengthened and broke. "Don't look at me. Don't look at me right now," she said. "Not much point to fleeing," I said, "even if you planned on it." "This is such fucking bullshit," she said. "I know," I said. She stopped crying. Wiped her nose with her sleeve. She would not look at me. "What are we going to do," I said.

She spun. Jabbed her forefinger into my chest. "Are you retarded? There's no we." "It's just," I said. Tried to say. She shouted me down. The finger-blow caused an instant ache. She had hit a cluster of nerves.

Without trying. "There's no we anymore. Not now. Not anymore. Were you not paying any attention up there? Were you just sitting there like a piece-of-shit jock dickhead, you dumb fuck?" She was screaming. I saw her uvula. Rain beads in her eyelashes. "I didn't mean," I said. "You didn't mean? That's great. That solves everything," she said. Silence. Rain noise. The hawking wind off the river. "We," she said. Her voice dense with scorn. I had no response. No counterargument. She was right. *We* as a concept no longer applied. The Fool, remember, only exists in the singular. That's his privilege and his damnation. Alabama started walking. Without another word. Her boots scraped the sidewalk. Precise and rhythmic. I saw her. In her quiet room. In that blue light. Poised above me. Half-smiling. I almost called out to her. I swear I almost did. Before she turned onto Hubert, the vision vanished. She was gone too. I couldn't hear the sound of her boots.

It didn't hurt. It didn't feel like anything. Whatever else you can say about the Fool, he's free. I started to run. The ambulance came as I hit Laight. Threw gray crowns of water from a rut in the cobbles. Siren lights stained the pavement. Building walls. My hands and my sleeves. The colorless air. When the last echoes died, I realized I was whistling. I knew the tune. I knew the words.

A NOTE TO THE READER

The Calendar of Sleights is fictional, but the concepts and techniques outlined in it—as the initiated have no doubt already discerned—are not. The *Calendar* is directly inspired by (and takes its name from a phrase within) S. W. Erdnase's instructional treatise on legerdemain *The Expert at the Card Table*. The true identity of the pseudonymous Erdnase remains a point of controversy among historians of magic, and I will not presume to offer any theories about it. But I must thank here the Conjuring Arts Research Center in Manhattan for generously allowing a neophyte like me to delve into the mystery via their archives.